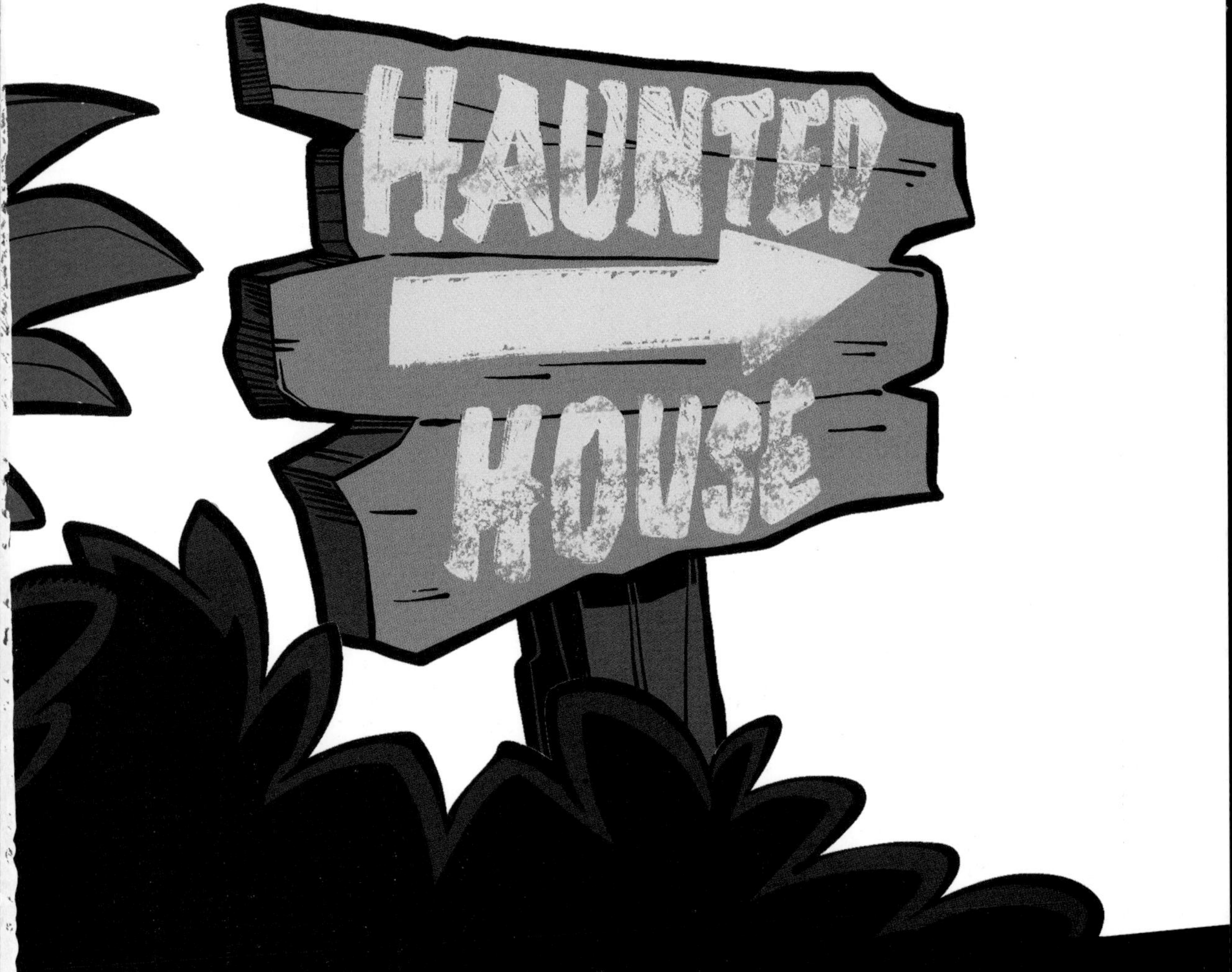
HAUNTED
HOUSE

PRESTONPLAYZ

THE MYSTERY OF THE SUPER SPOOKY SECRET HOUSE

HarperAlley is an imprint of HarperCollins Publishers.

PrestonPlayz: The Mystery of the Super Spooky Secret House
Copyright © 2023 by Preston Arsement
All rights reserved. Printed in the United States of America.
No part of this book may be used or reproduced in any manner whatsoever
without written permission except in the case of brief quotations embodied in critical
articles and reviews. For information address HarperCollins Children's Books,
a division of HarperCollins Publishers, 195 Broadway, New York, NY 10007.
www.harperalley.com

Library of Congress Control Number: 2022930817
ISBN 978-0-06-306514-7 — ISBN 978-0-06-332199-1 (special edition)

Typography by Joe Merkel
23 24 25 26 27 LBC 5 4 3 2 1

First Edition

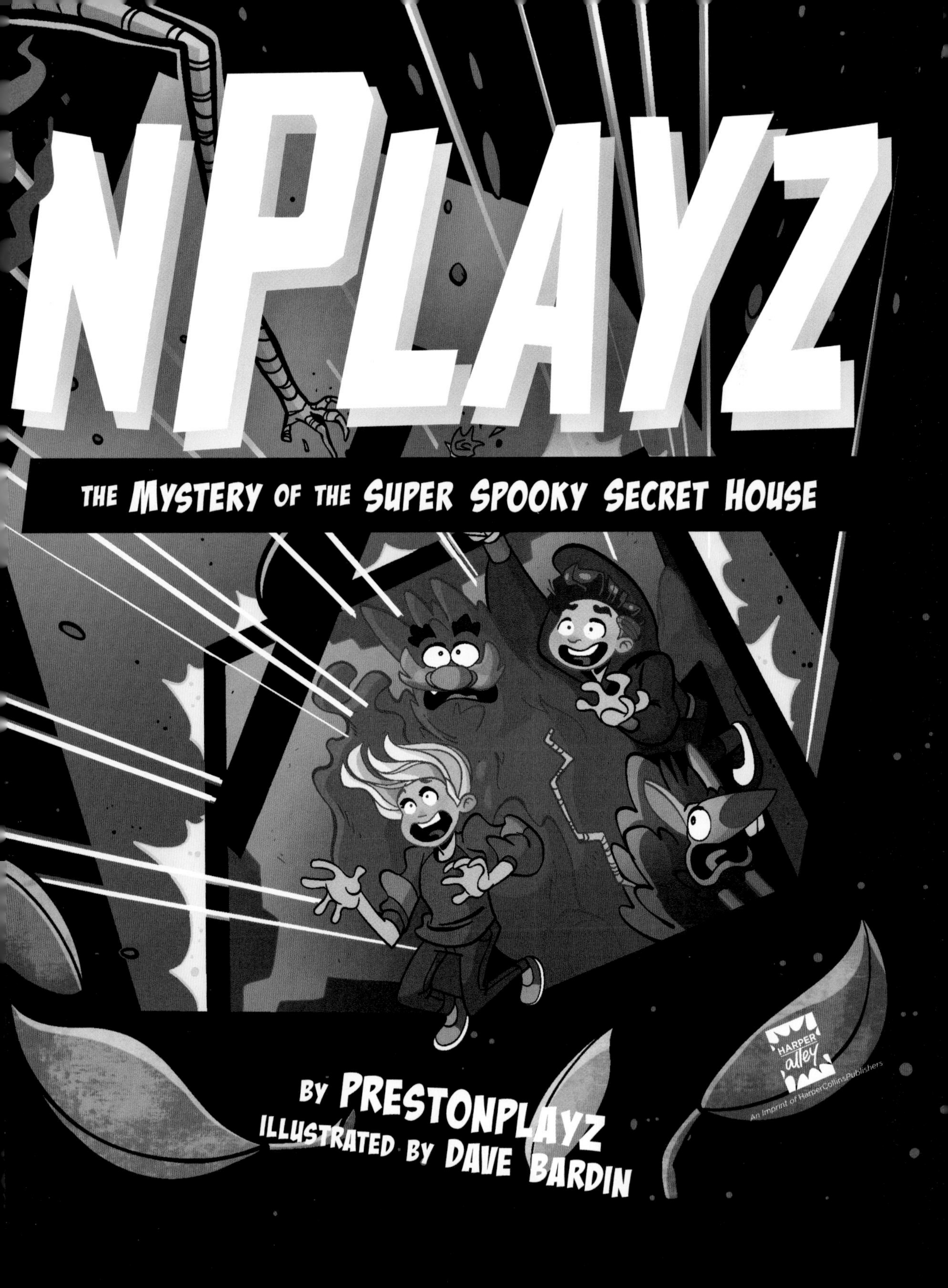
NPLAYZ
THE MYSTERY OF THE SUPER SPOOKY SECRET HOUSE
BY PRESTONPLAYZ
ILLUSTRATED BY DAVE BARDIN
HARPER alley
An Imprint of HarperCollinsPublishers

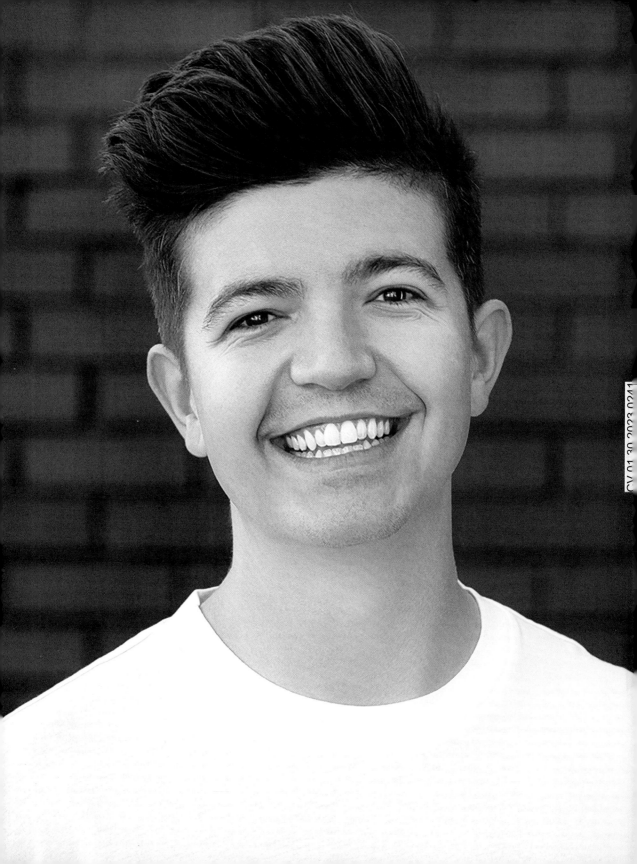

This is amazing!

It's Preston here, and I'm so thrilled to have written my first-ever graphic novel! Crazy, right? This story is so cool. I think you're really going to like it. It's got me and Bri and Grumpus and Shivers, and a lot of your other favorite characters. It's also a super spooky mystery-adventure that scared me when I read it— and I wrote it!

Anyway, it means the world to me that you've decided to read this book. I worked really hard to make it fun and zany and full of twists and turns. It's got riddles that are fun to solve and bad guys who have a lot of heart. It's a story about trying new things and facing your fears— and also about friendship.

Anyway, have fun! Read on! I think you'll be surprised when you read what happens next.

And as always, thanks for being a fan.

Love!
Preston

CHARACTERS

PRESTON

Preston is a fun-loving creator who is always looking for a new challenge for his viral online videos—and sometimes that challenge is to spend the night in a spooky house of secrets!

BRIANNA

Brianna is always willing to see the bright side of every situation. She's compassionate and caring, but she can be fierce when someone messes with her friends.

SHIVERS

Shivers is a neurotic mess who is looking for love in all the wrong places. But there's more to this rat than nerves. He has lived quite a life of adventure . . . if you believe him.

GRUMPUS

Grumpus is a monster and Shivers's best friend. Grumpus doesn't really believe the crazy stories Shivers tells, and he doesn't believe in haunted houses—until now!

E. WALLY WADSWORTH

E. Wally Wadsworth has been keeping his family carnival tradition alive for many years, but that time may be coming to an end. Does he have one more trick up his sleeve to save his amusement park from going out of business?

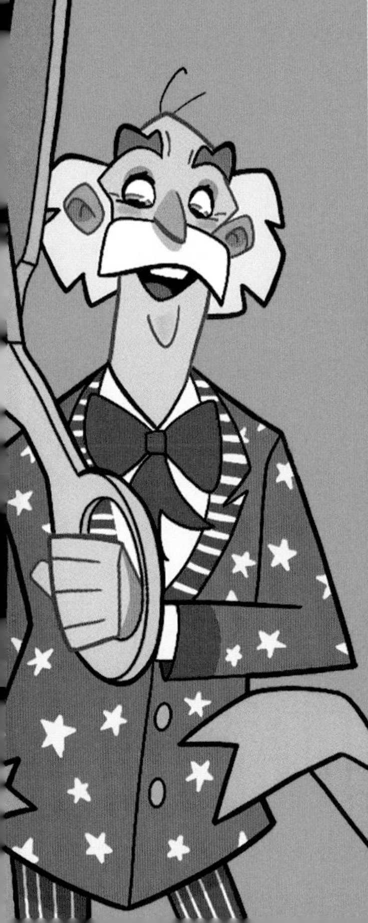

KAT LAVENDER

Preston's sassy neighbor who hates rats, which is bad news for Shivers. Kat loves making trouble almost as much as she loves fashion!

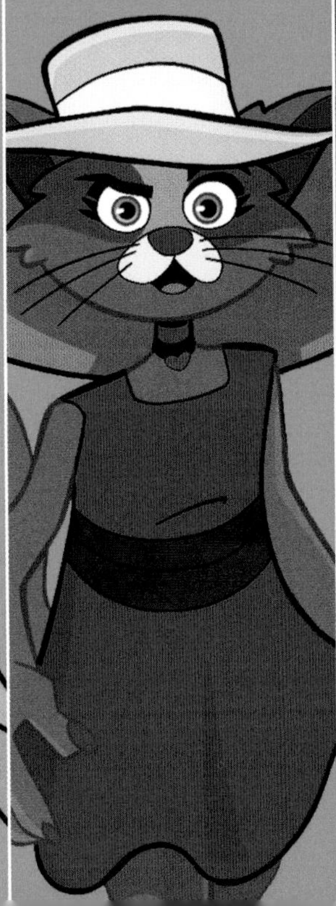

GERALD

Gerald is a preppy cat lover who worships the ground Kat walks on.

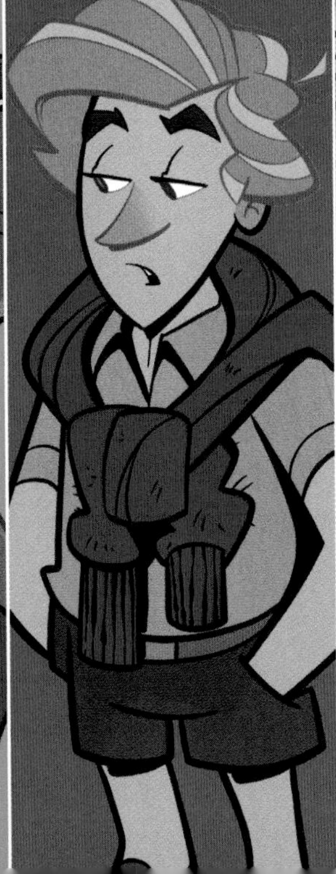

ELIJAH

Elijah is the ghostly eternal caretaker of the Super Spooky Secret House. How he got there is a mystery, and how he'll get out is another one. Eternity is a long time!

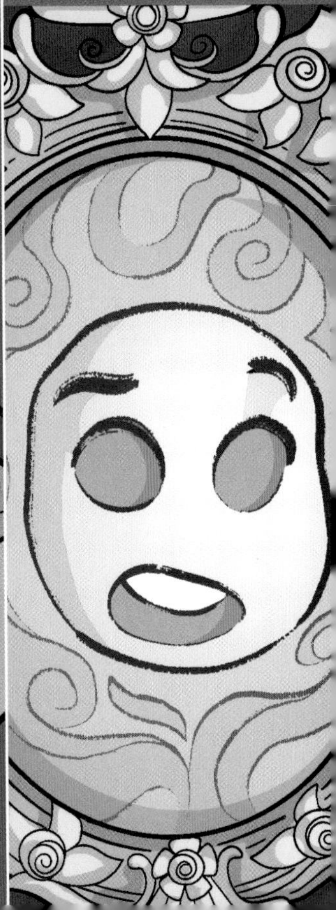

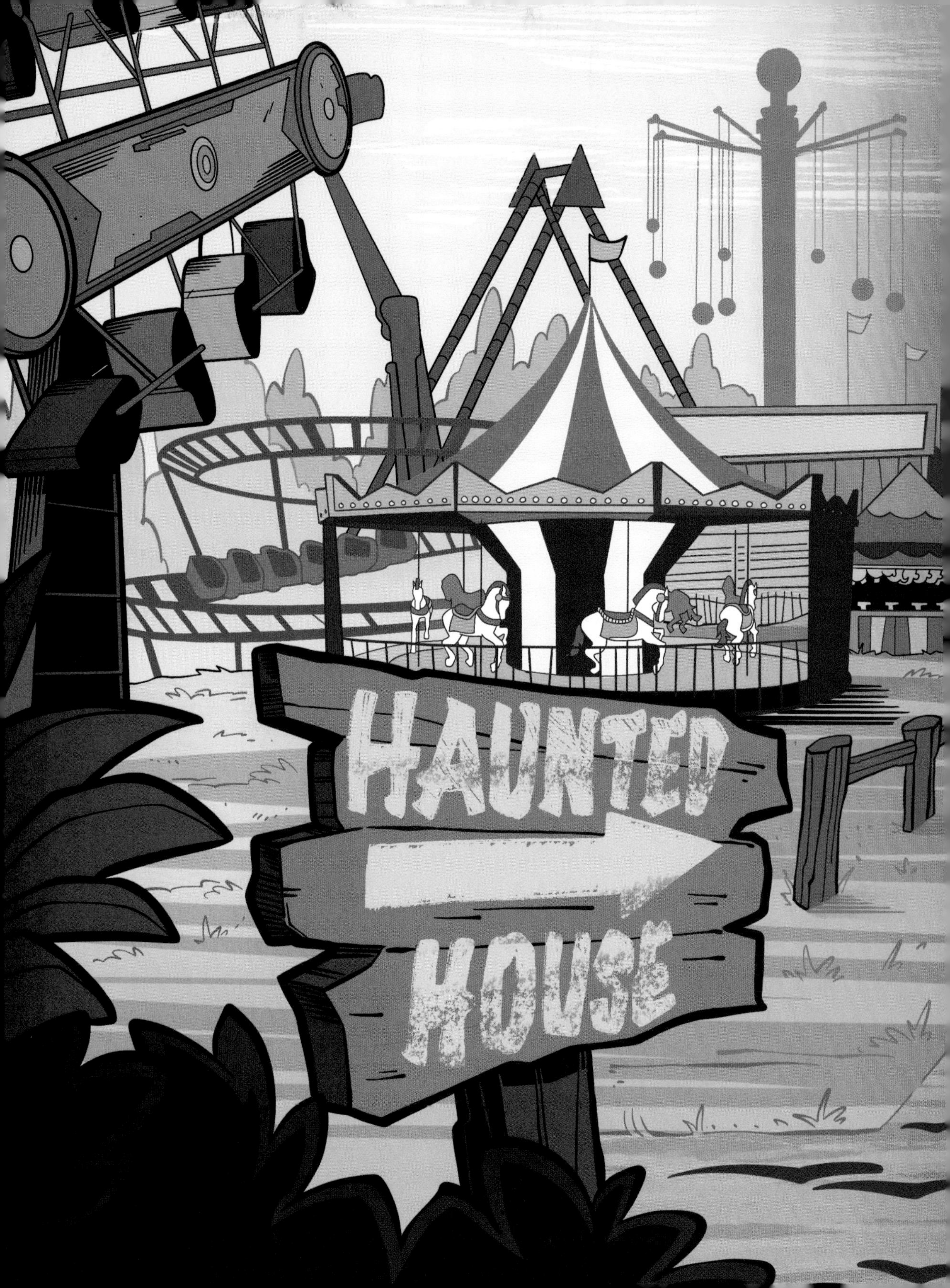
HAUNTED
HOUSE

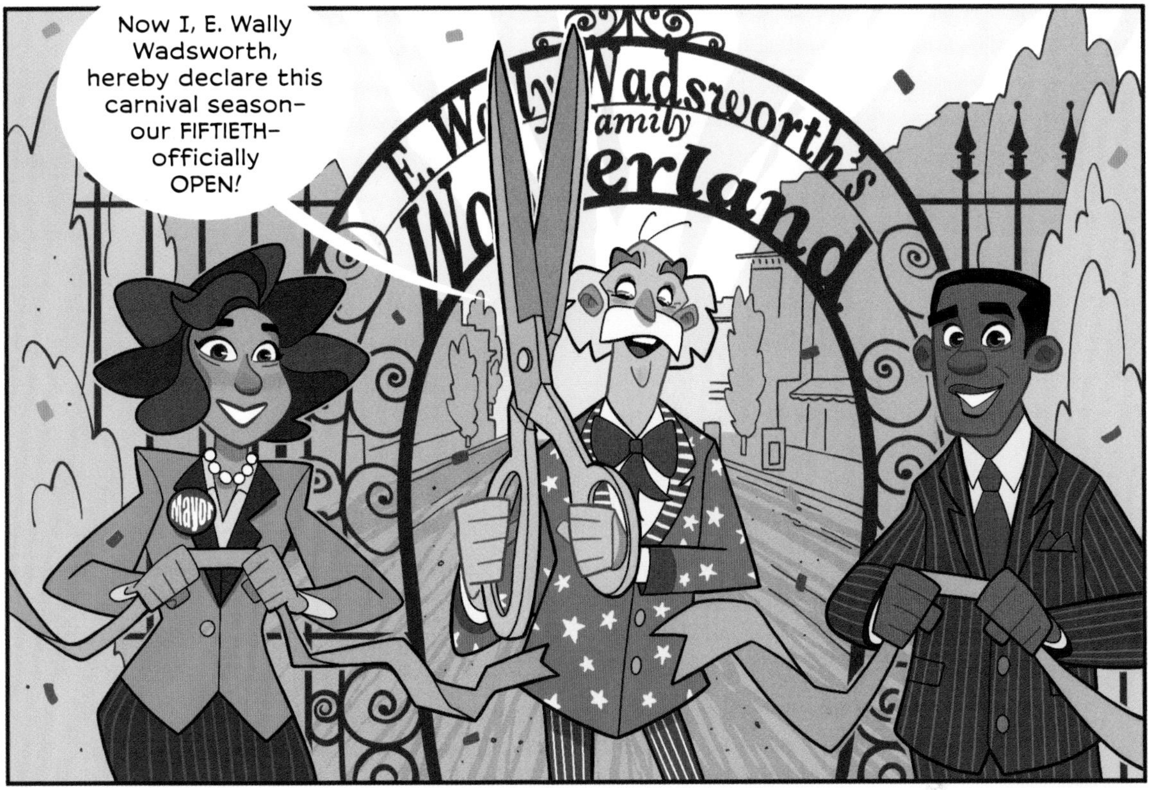
Now I, E. Wally Wadsworth, hereby declare this carnival season–our FIFTIETH–officially OPEN!
E. Wally Wadsworth's Family Wonderland
Mayor

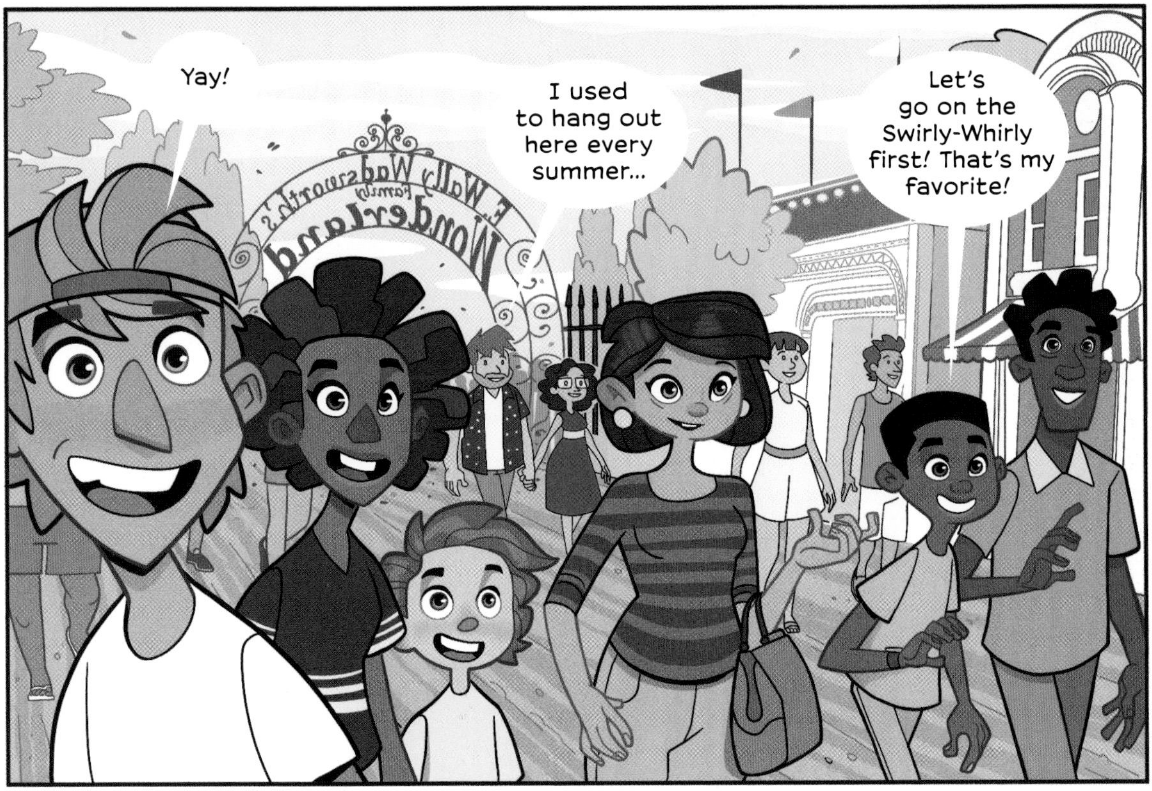
Yay!
I used to hang out here every summer...
Let's go on the Swirly-Whirly first! That's my favorite!
E. Wally Wadsworth's Family Wonderland

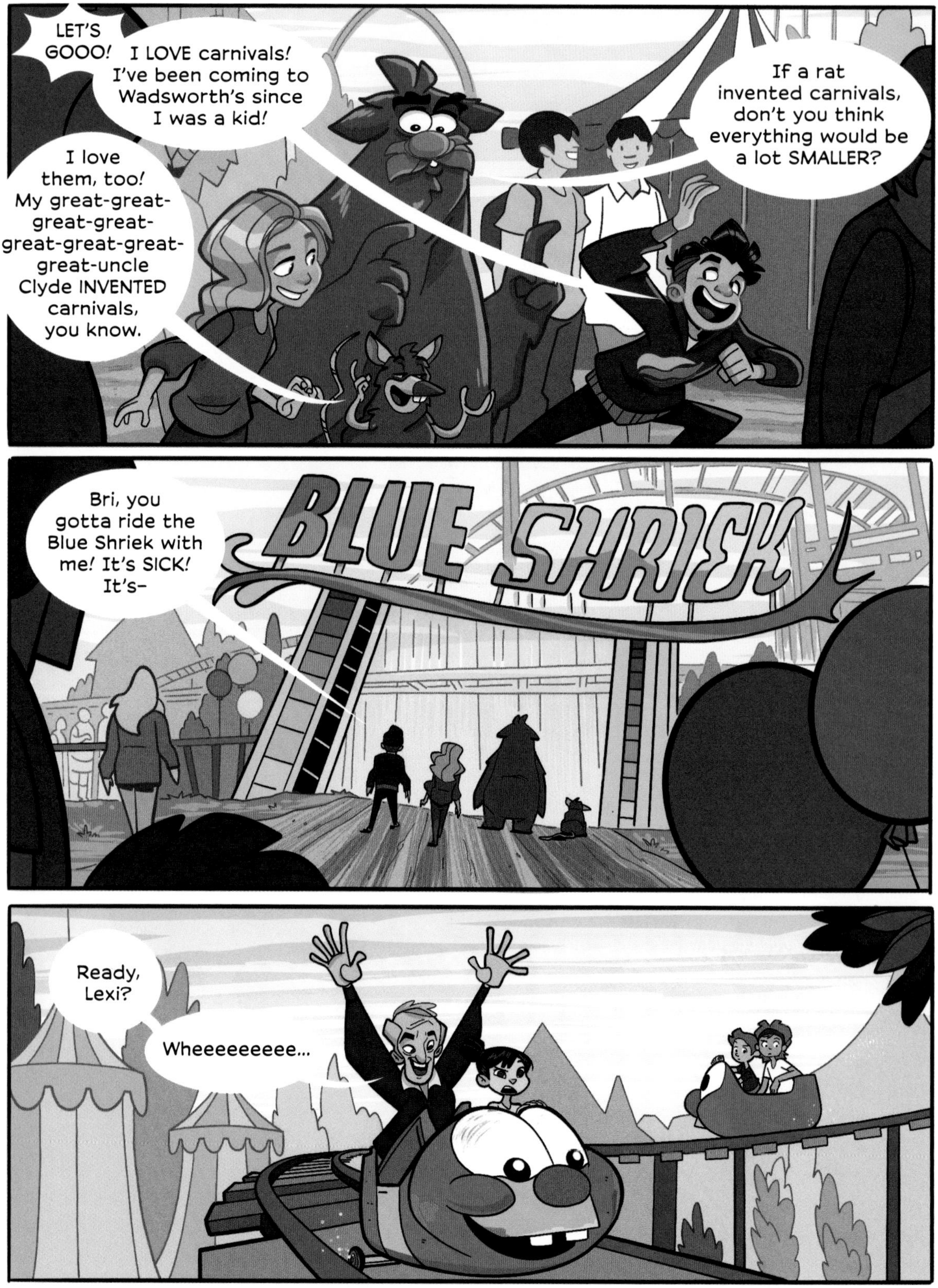
LET'S GOOO!
I LOVE carnivals! I've been coming to Wadsworth's since I was a kid!
If a rat invented carnivals, don't you think everything would be a lot SMALLER?
I love them, too! My great-great-great-great-great-great-great-great-uncle Clyde INVENTED carnivals, you know.
BLUE SHRIEK
Bri, you gotta ride the Blue Shriek with me! It's SICK! It's–
Ready, Lexi?
Wheeeeeeeee...

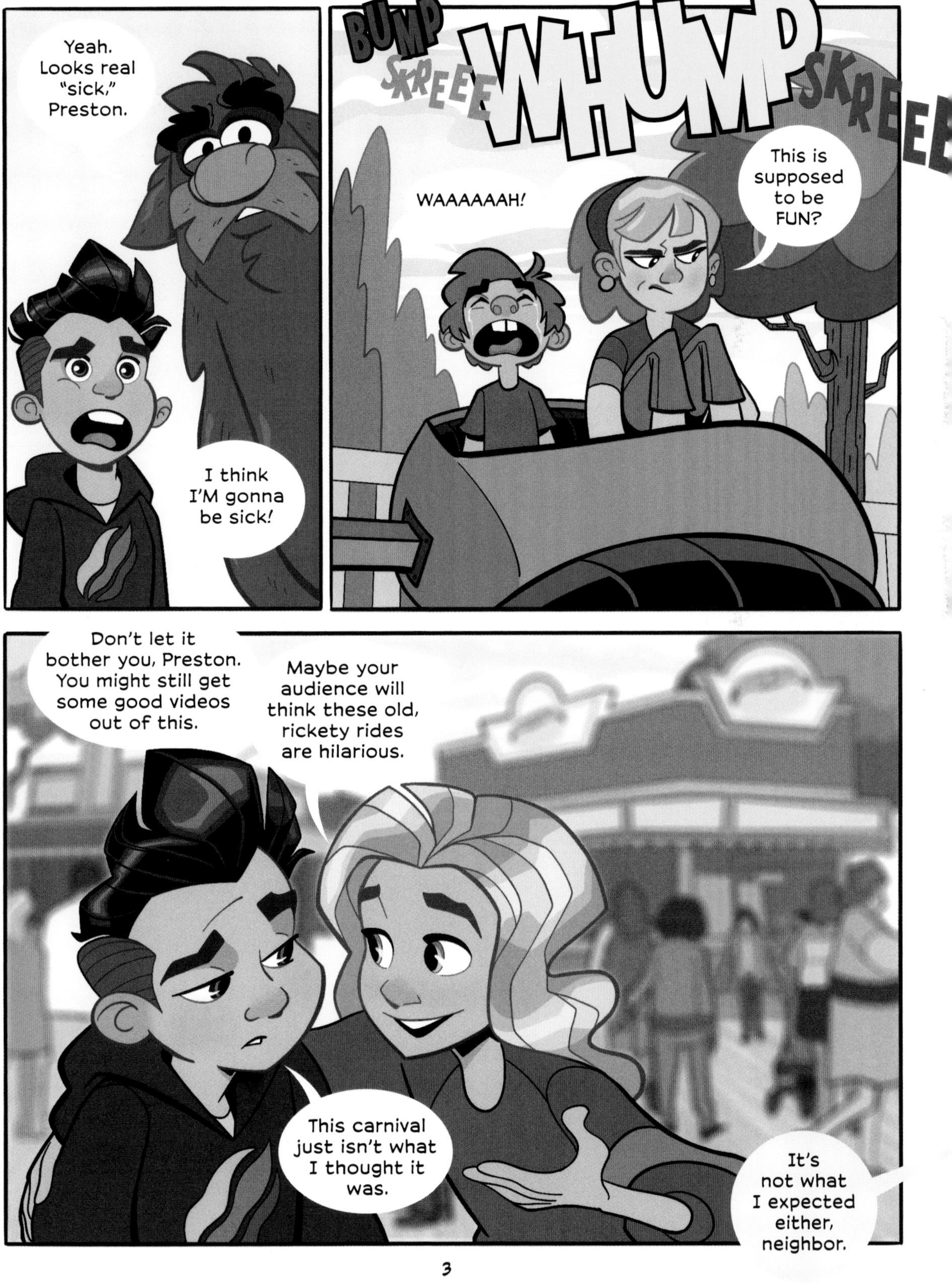
Yeah. Looks real "sick," Preston.
I think I'M gonna be sick!
BUMP
SKREEE
WHUMP
SKREEE
WAAAAAAH!
This is supposed to be FUN?
Don't let it bother you, Preston. You might still get some good videos out of this.
Maybe your audience will think these old, rickety rides are hilarious.
This carnival just isn't what I thought it was.
It's not what I expected either, neighbor.

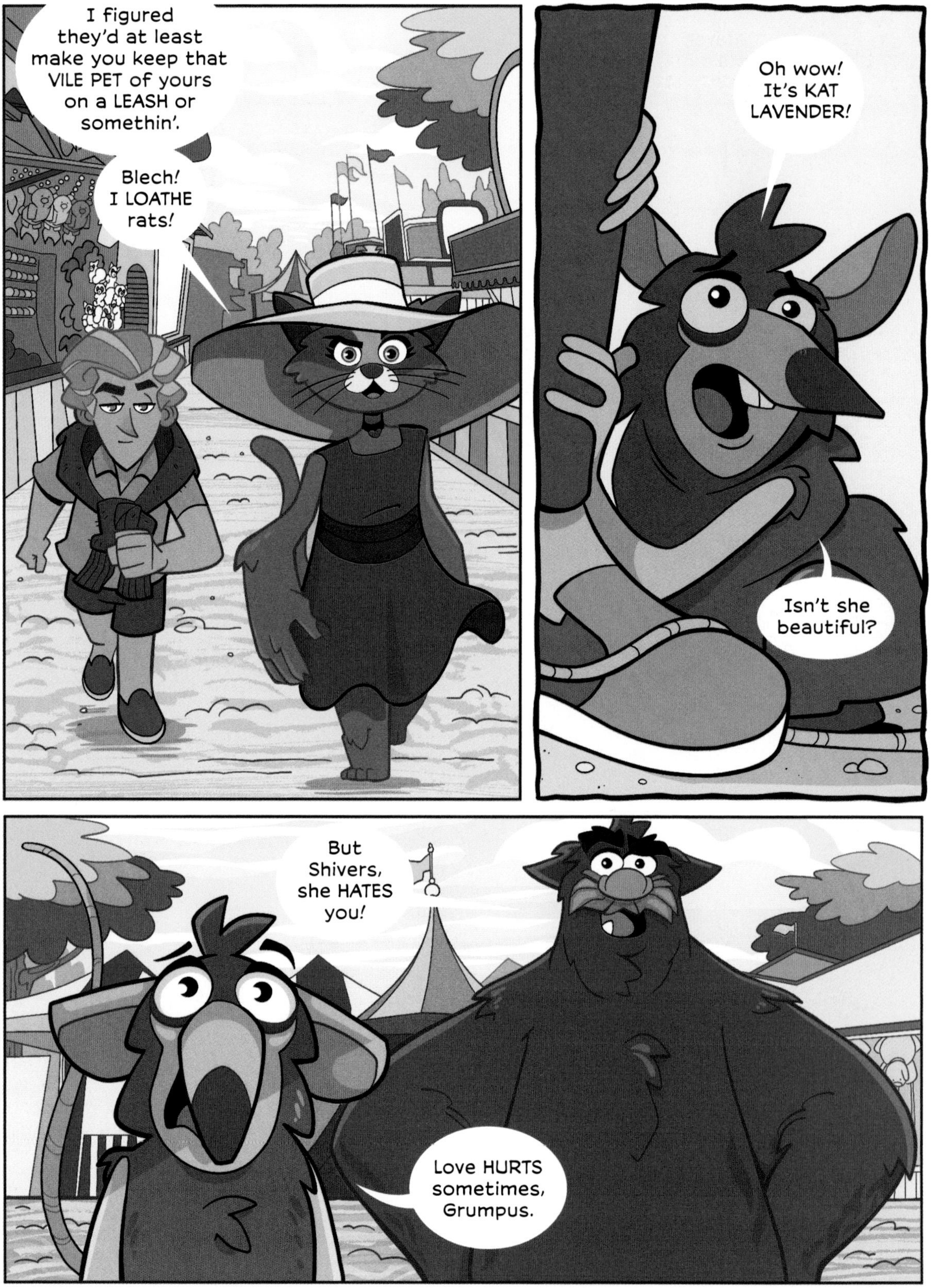
I figured they'd at least make you keep that VILE PET of yours on a LEASH or somethin'.
Blech! I LOATHE rats!
Oh wow! It's KAT LAVENDER!
Isn't she beautiful?
But Shivers, she HATES you!
Love HURTS sometimes, Grumpus.

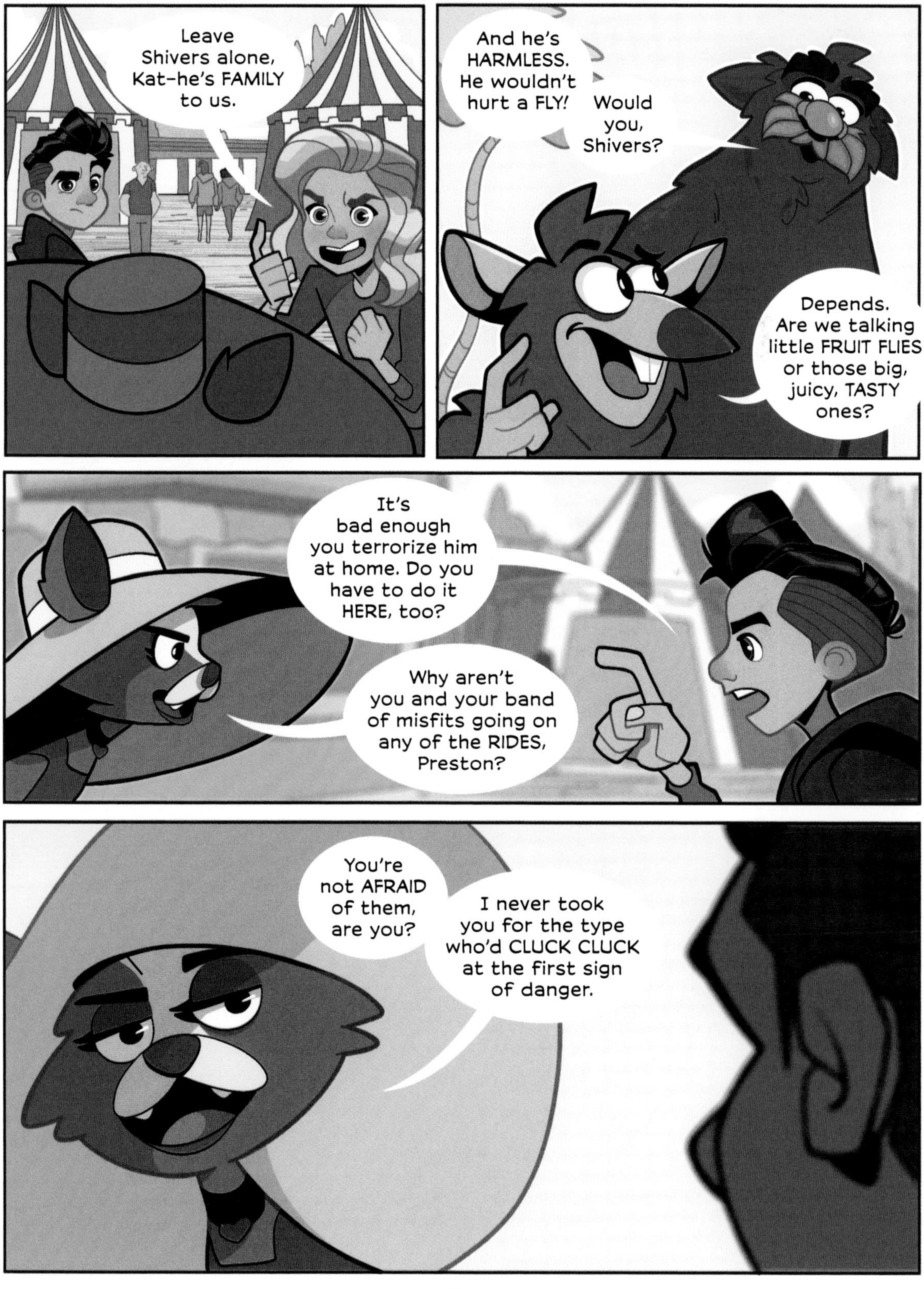
Leave Shivers alone, Kat–he's FAMILY to us.
And he's HARMLESS. He wouldn't hurt a FLY!
Would you, Shivers?
Depends. Are we talking little FRUIT FLIES or those big, juicy, TASTY ones?
It's bad enough you terrorize him at home. Do you have to do it HERE, too?
Why aren't you and your band of misfits going on any of the RIDES, Preston?
You're not AFRAID of them, are you?
I never took you for the type who'd CLUCK CLUCK at the first sign of danger.

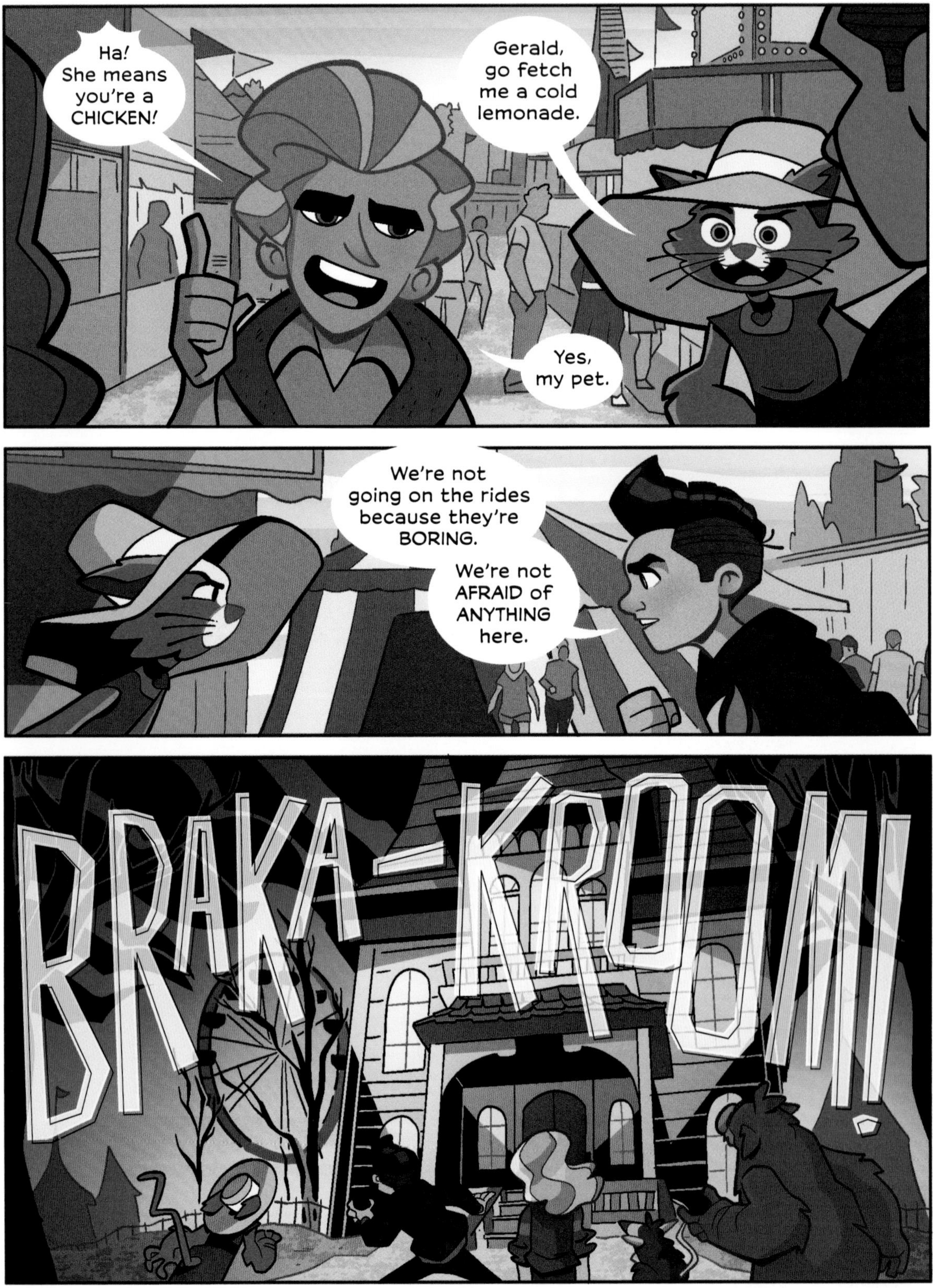
Ha! She means you're a CHICKEN!
Gerald, go fetch me a cold lemonade.
Yes, my pet.
We're not going on the rides because they're BORING.
We're not AFRAID of ANYTHING here.
BRAKA-KROOM!

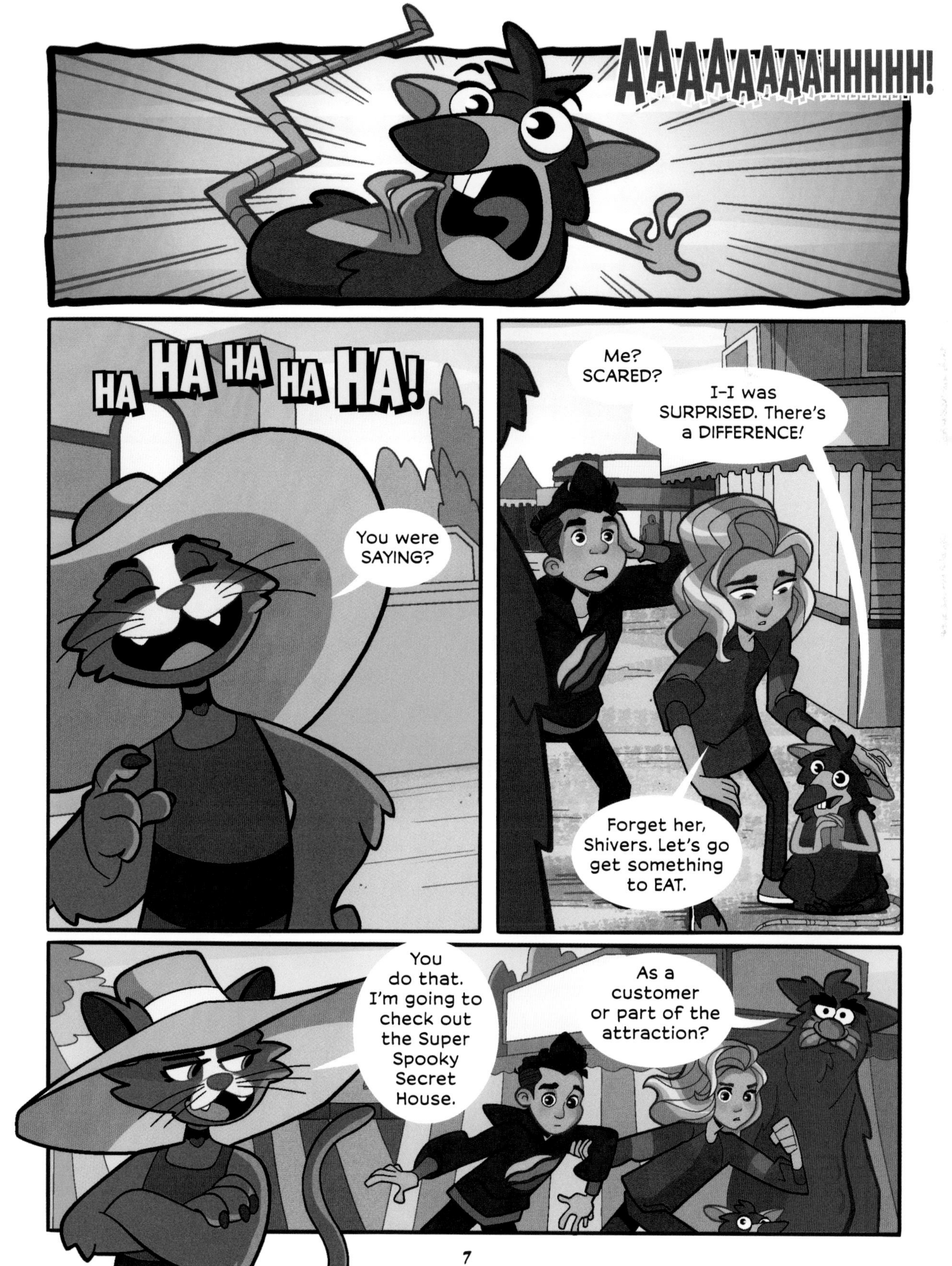
AAAAAAAAHHHHH!
HA HA HA HA HA!
You were SAYING?
Me? SCARED?
I-I was SURPRISED. There's a DIFFERENCE!
Forget her, Shivers. Let's go get something to EAT.
You do that. I'm going to check out the Super Spooky Secret House.
As a customer or part of the attraction?

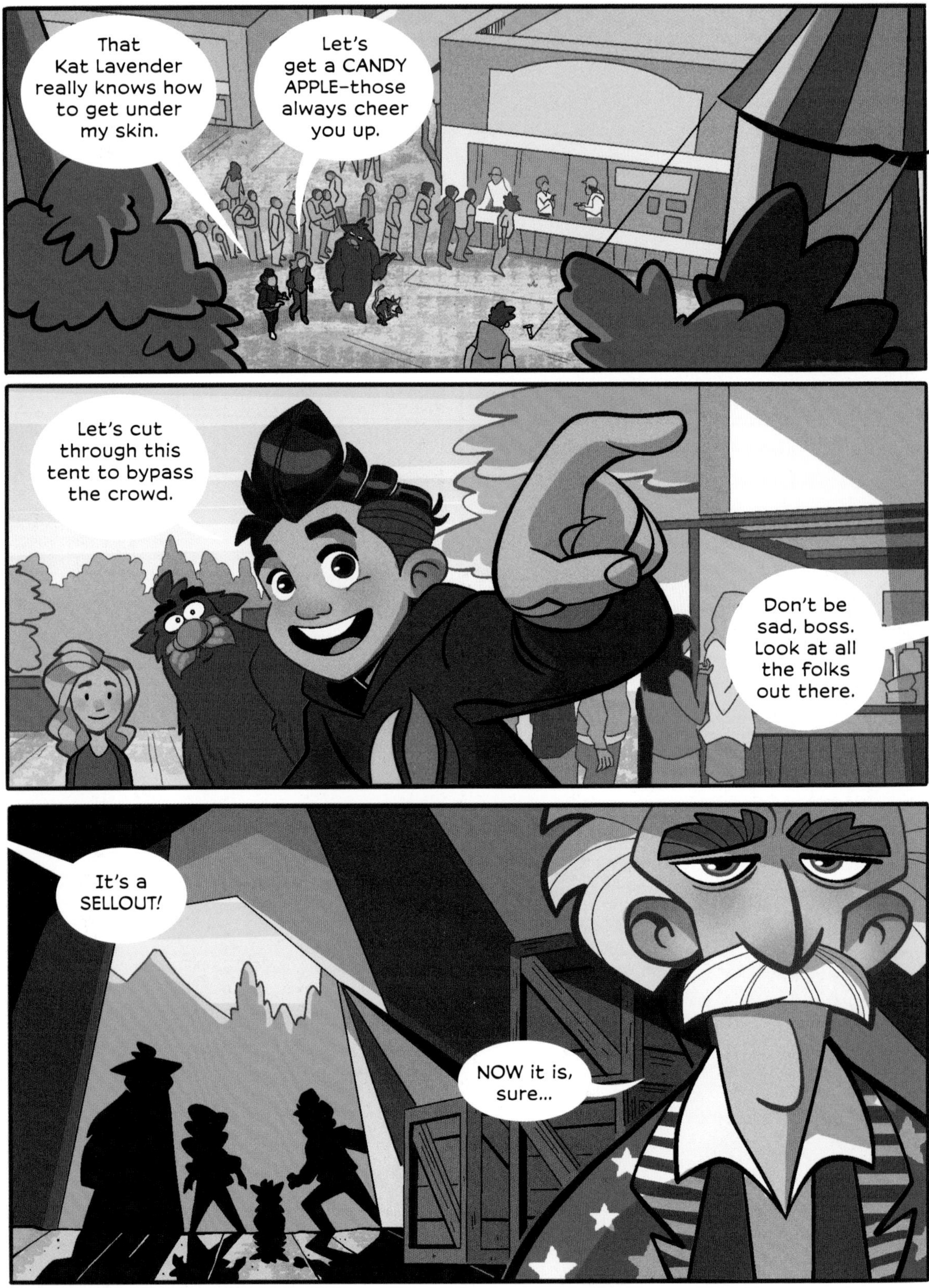
That Kat Lavender really knows how to get under my skin.
Let's get a CANDY APPLE–those always cheer you up.
Let's cut through this tent to bypass the crowd.
Don't be sad, boss. Look at all the folks out there.
It's a SELLOUT!
NOW it is, sure...

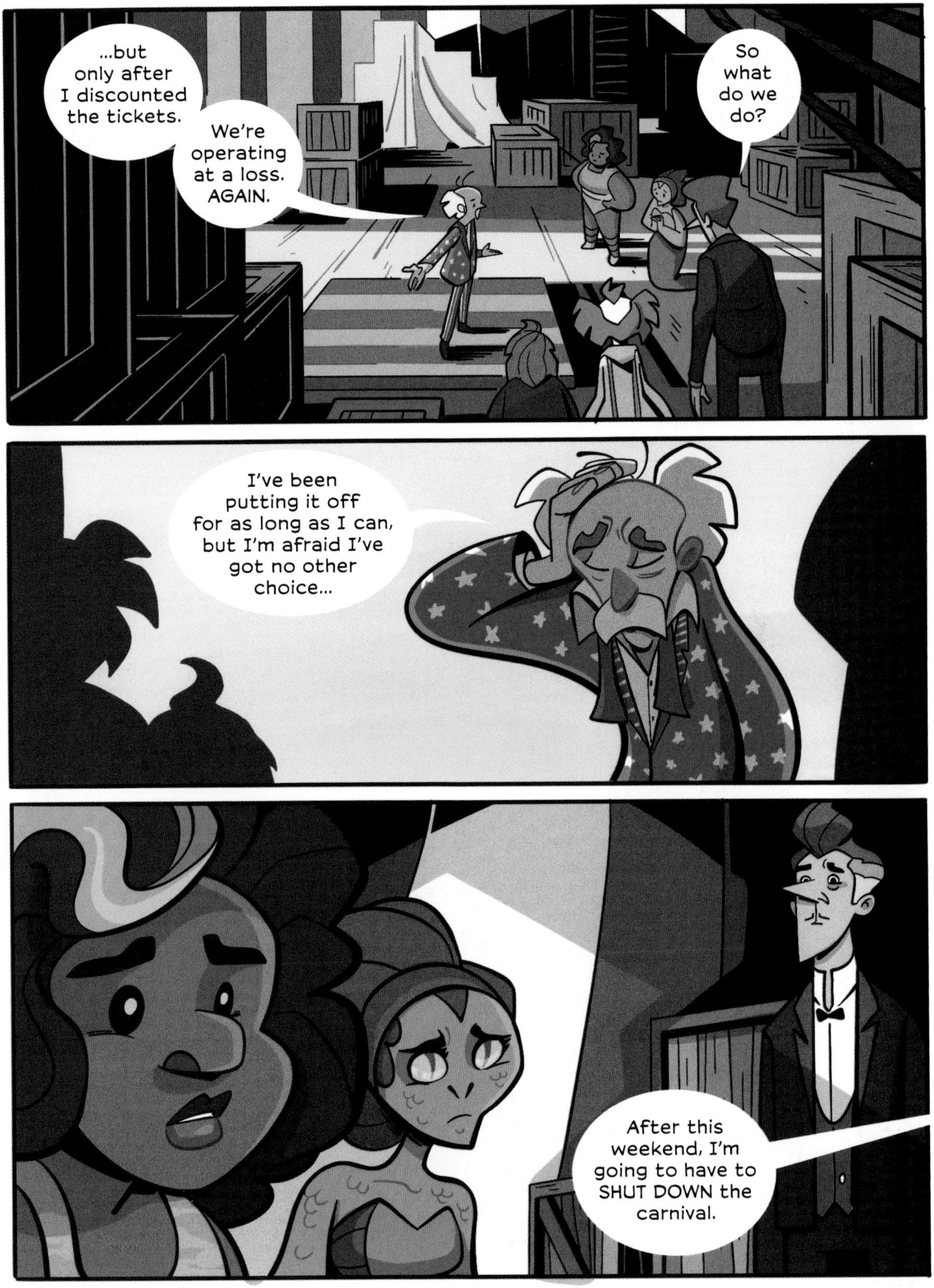
...but only after I discounted the tickets.
We're operating at a loss. AGAIN.
So what do we do?
I've been putting it off for as long as I can, but I'm afraid I've got no other choice...
After this weekend, I'm going to have to SHUT DOWN the carnival.

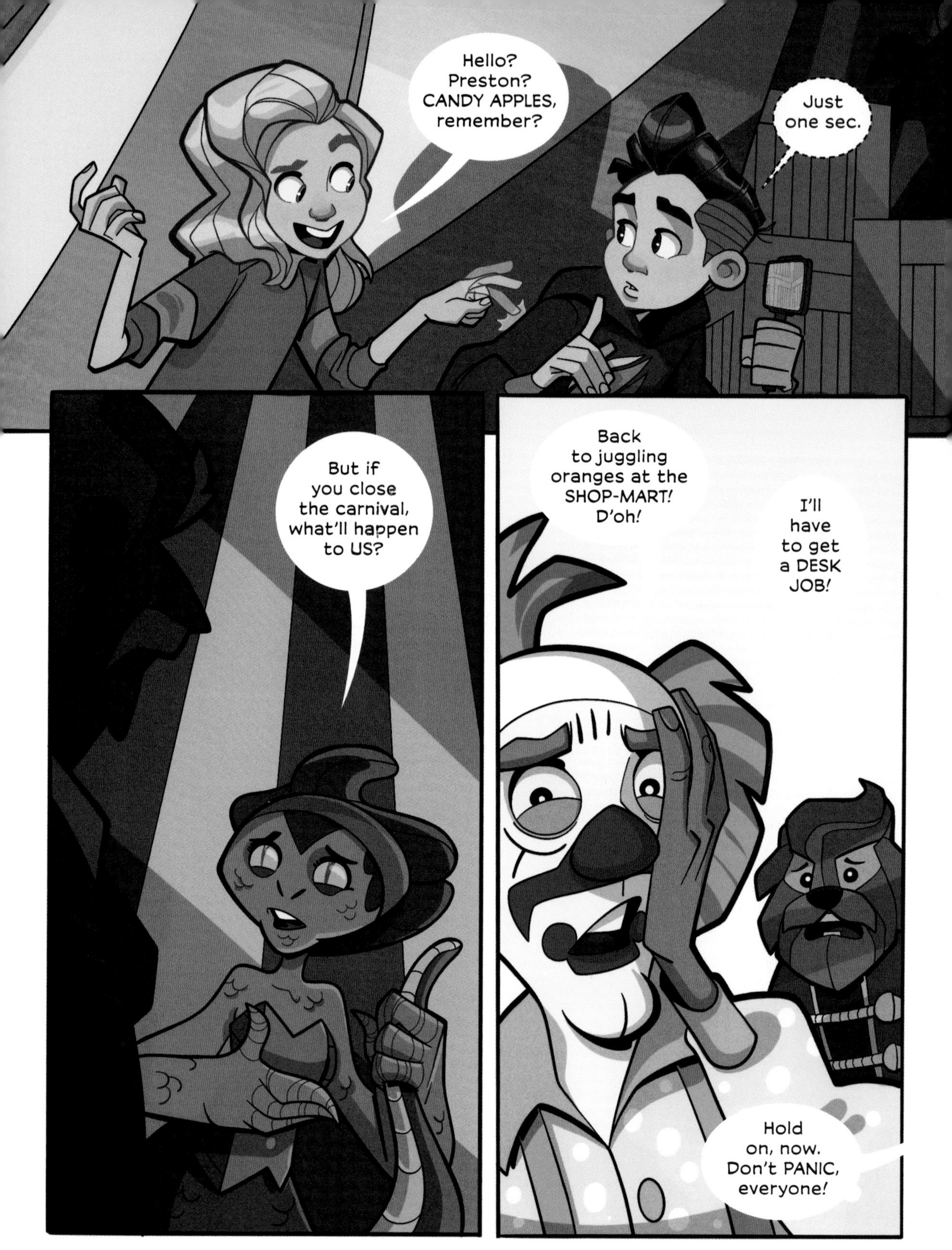
Hello? Preston? CANDY APPLES, remember?
Just one sec.
But if you close the carnival, what'll happen to US?
Back to juggling oranges at the SHOP-MART! D'oh!
I'll have to get a DESK JOB!
Hold on, now. Don't PANIC, everyone!

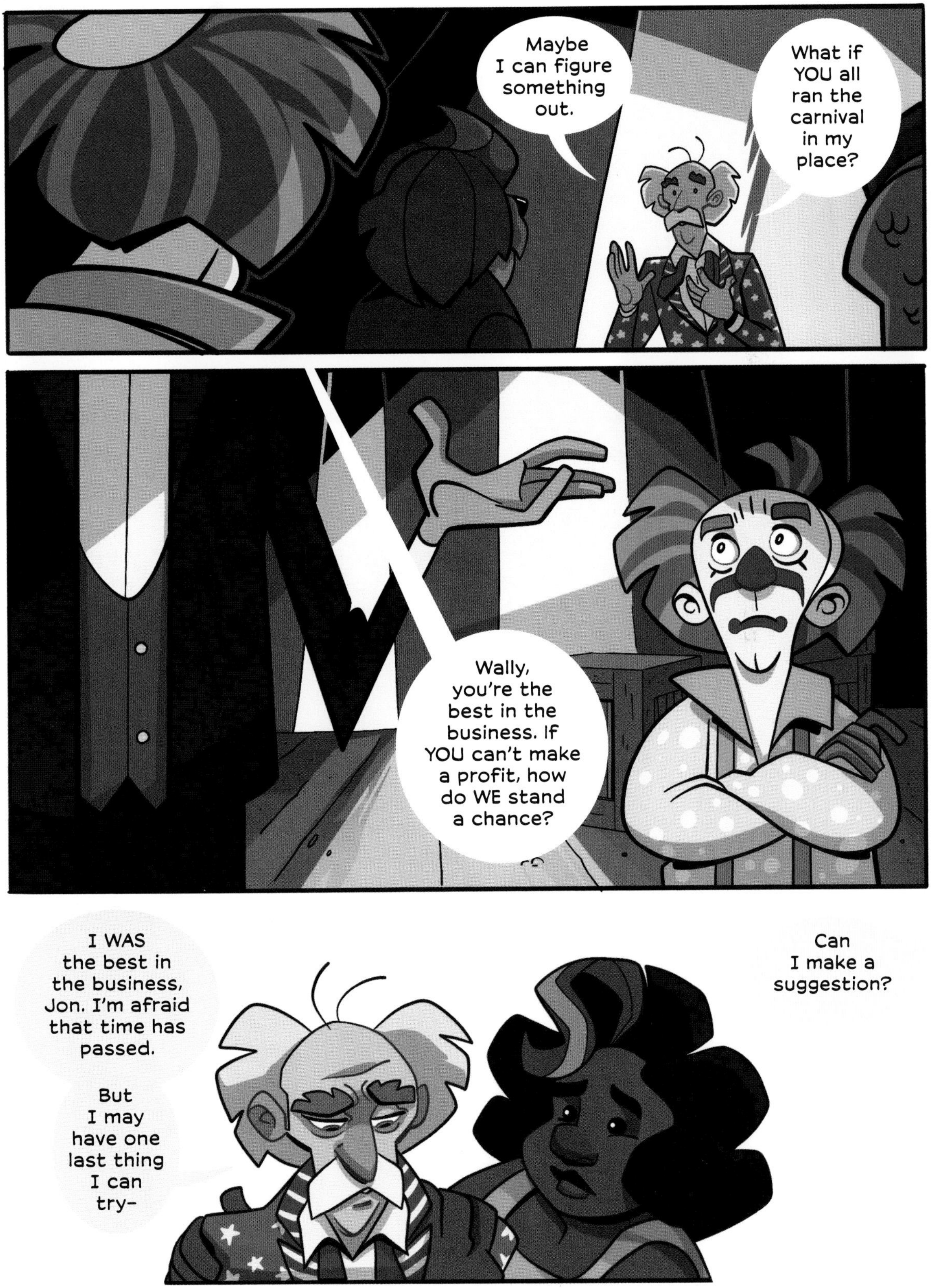
Maybe I can figure something out.
What if YOU all ran the carnival in my place?
Wally, you're the best in the business. If YOU can't make a profit, how do WE stand a chance?
I WAS the best in the business, Jon. I'm afraid that time has passed.
But I may have one last thing I can try-
Can I make a suggestion?

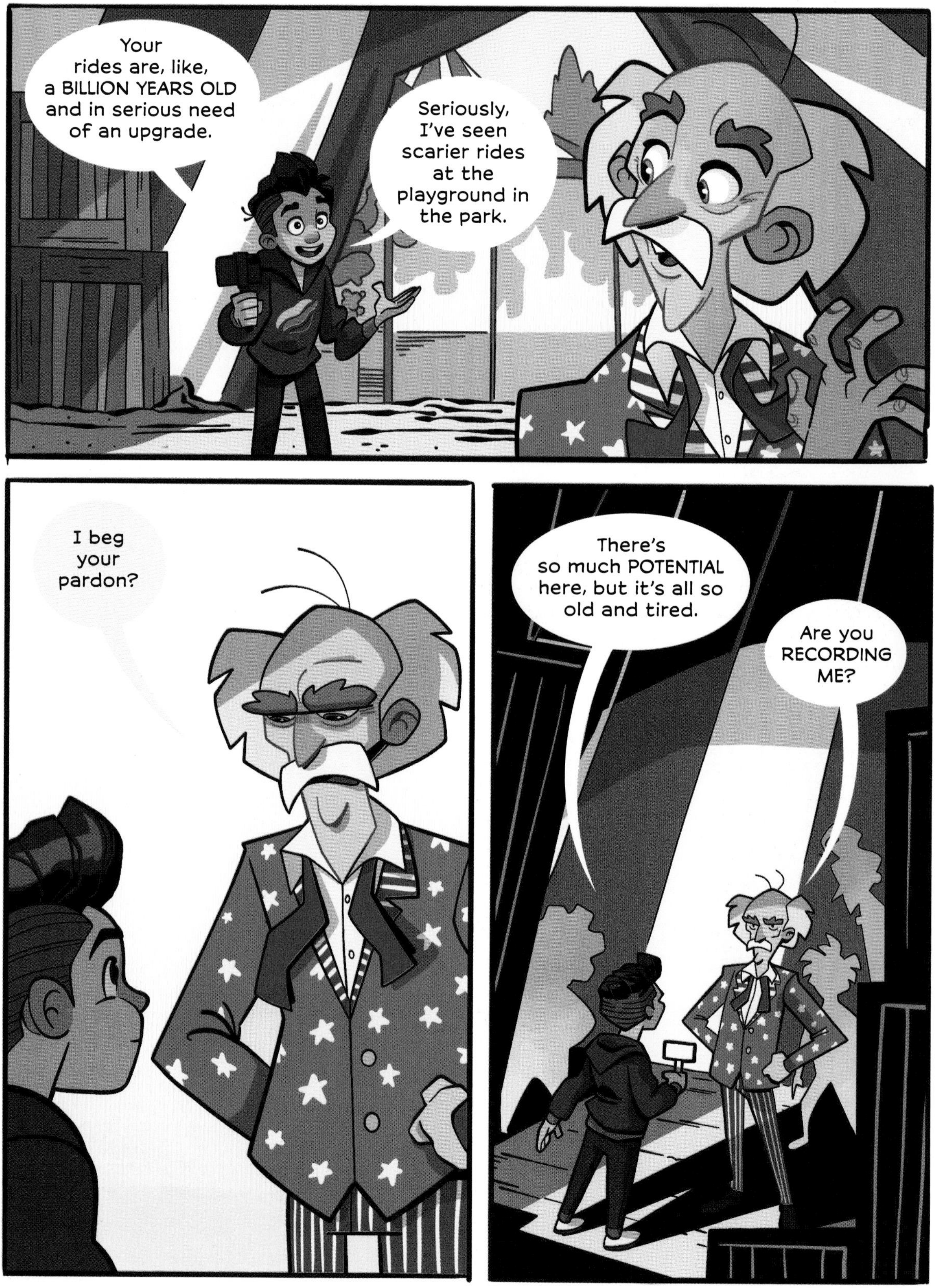
Your rides are, like, a BILLION YEARS OLD and in serious need of an upgrade.
Seriously, I've seen scarier rides at the playground in the park.
I beg your pardon?
There's so much POTENTIAL here, but it's all so old and tired.
Are you RECORDING ME?

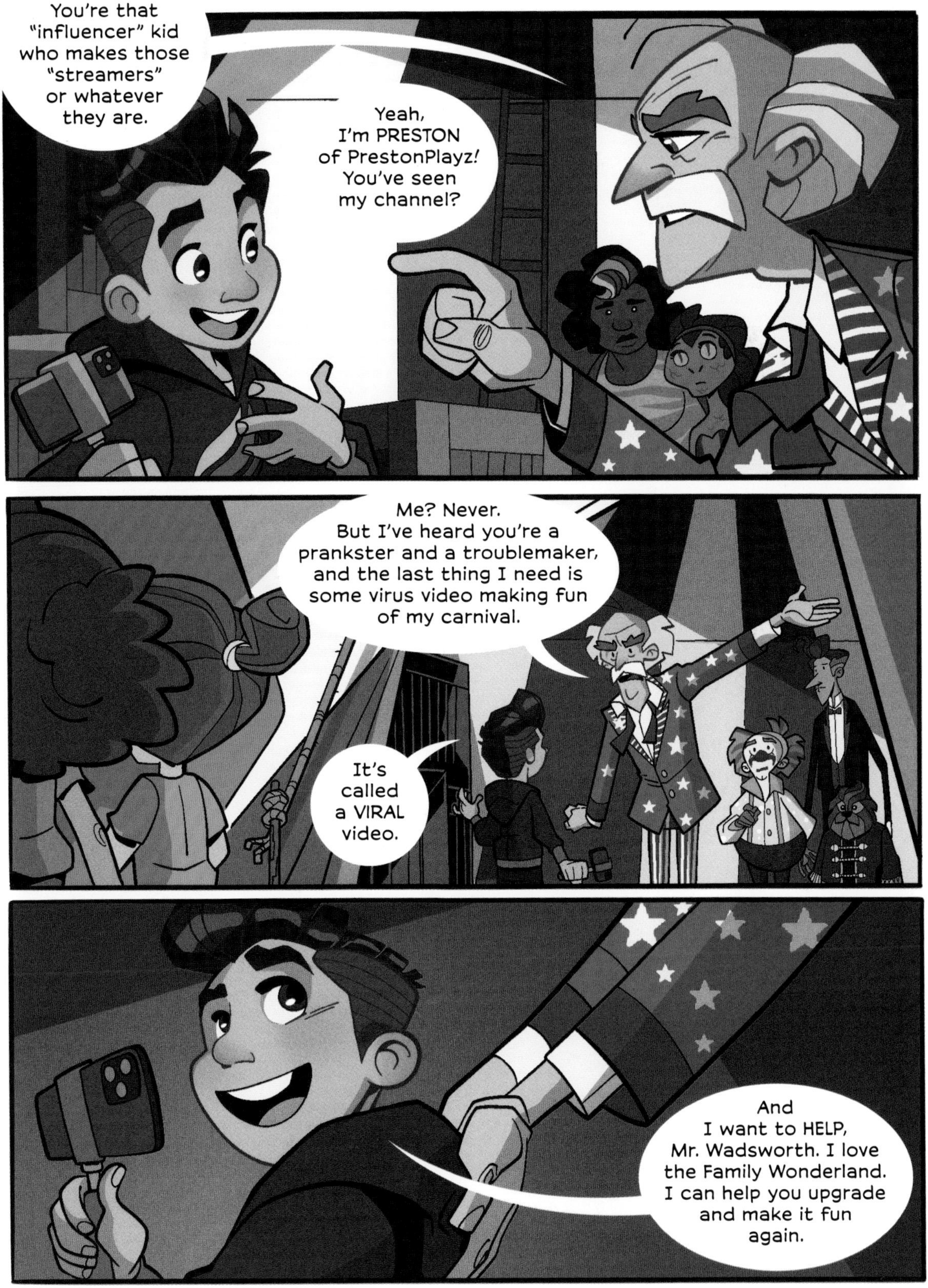
You're that "influencer" kid who makes those "streamers" or whatever they are.
Yeah, I'm PRESTON of PrestonPlayz! You've seen my channel?
Me? Never. But I've heard you're a prankster and a troublemaker, and the last thing I need is some virus video making fun of my carnival.
It's called a VIRAL video.
And I want to HELP, Mr. Wadsworth. I love the Family Wonderland. I can help you upgrade and make it fun again.

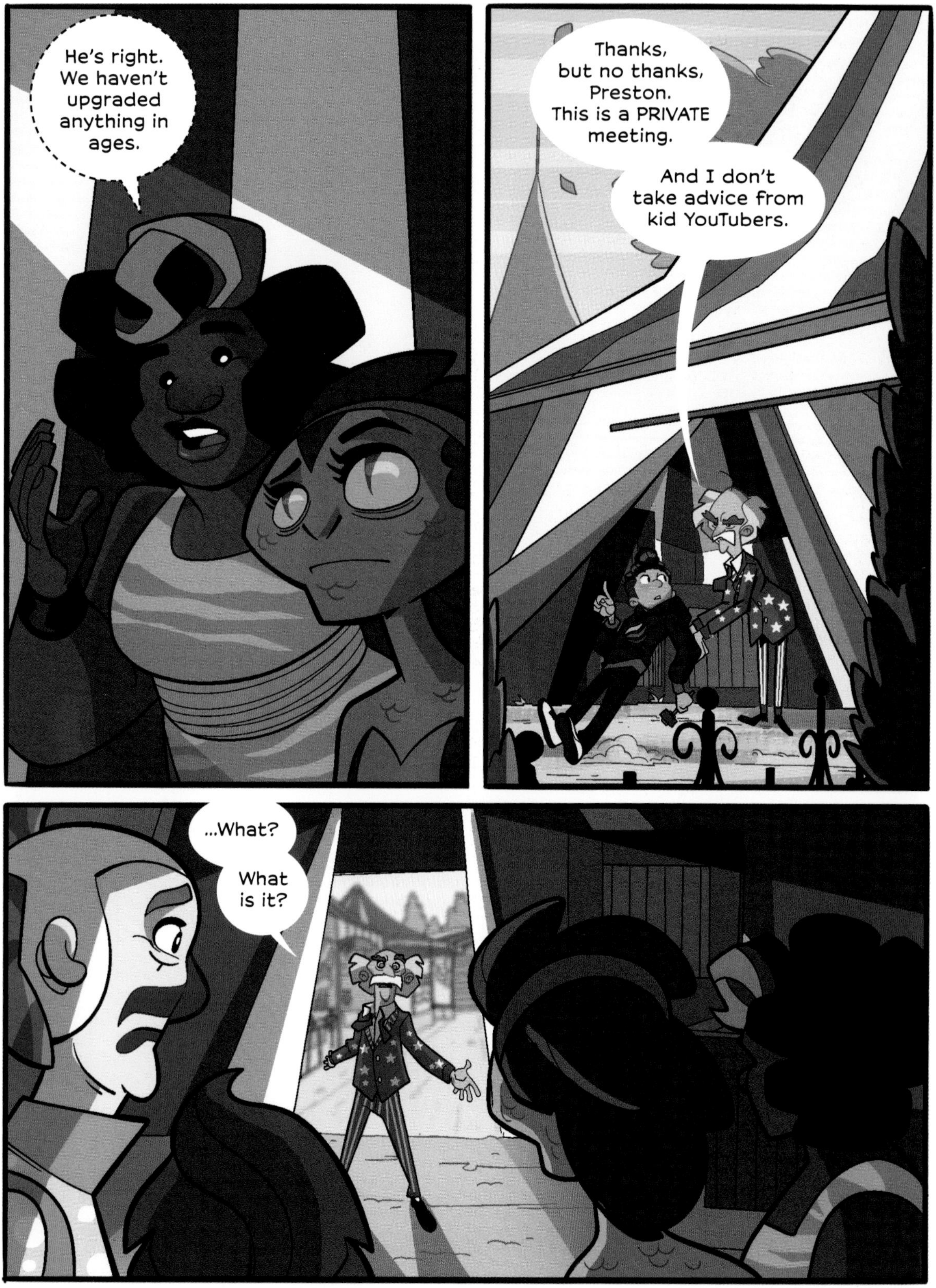
He's right. We haven't upgraded anything in ages.
Thanks, but no thanks, Preston. This is a PRIVATE meeting.
And I don't take advice from kid YouTubers.
...What?
What is it?

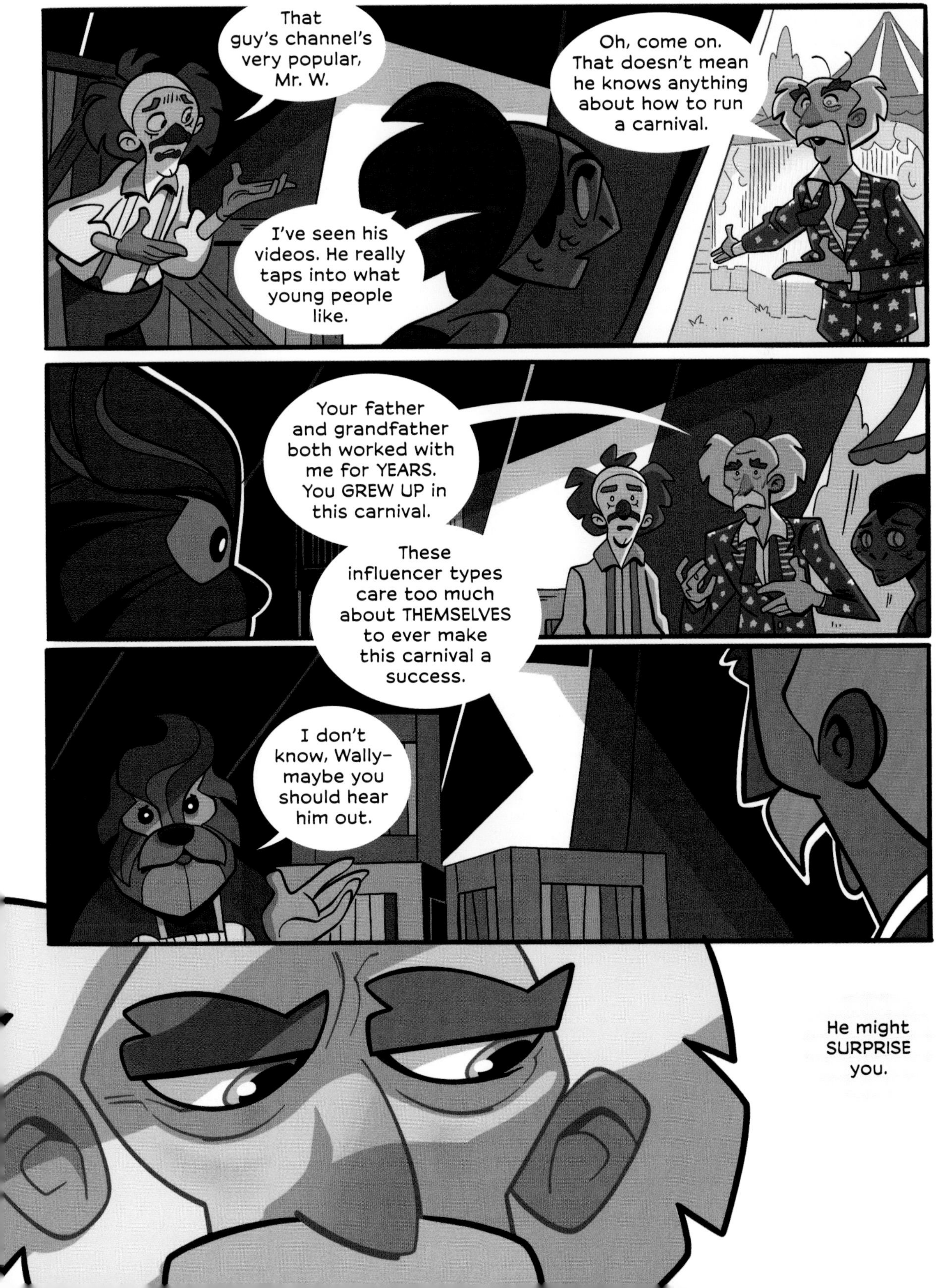
That guy's channel's very popular, Mr. W.
I've seen his videos. He really taps into what young people like.
Oh, come on. That doesn't mean he knows anything about how to run a carnival.
Your father and grandfather both worked with me for YEARS. You GREW UP in this carnival.
These influencer types care too much about THEMSELVES to ever make this carnival a success.
I don't know, Wally– maybe you should hear him out.
He might SURPRISE you.

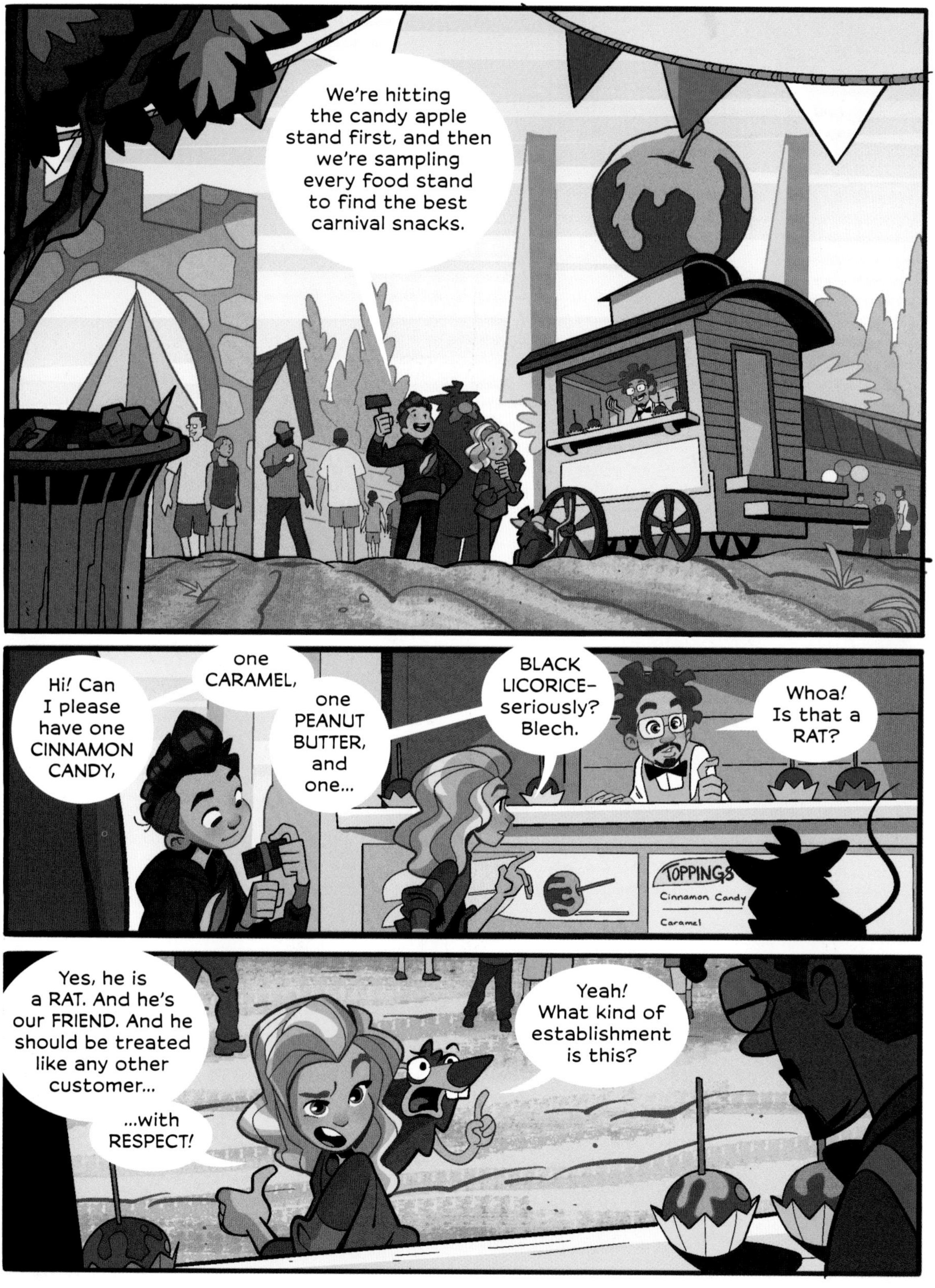
We're hitting the candy apple stand first, and then we're sampling every food stand to find the best carnival snacks.
Hi! Can I please have one CINNAMON CANDY,
one CARAMEL,
one PEANUT BUTTER, and one...
BLACK LICORICE– seriously? Blech.
Whoa! Is that a RAT?
TOPPINGS
Cinnamon Candy
Caramel
Yes, he is a RAT. And he's our FRIEND. And he should be treated like any other customer...
...with RESPECT!
Yeah! What kind of establishment is this?

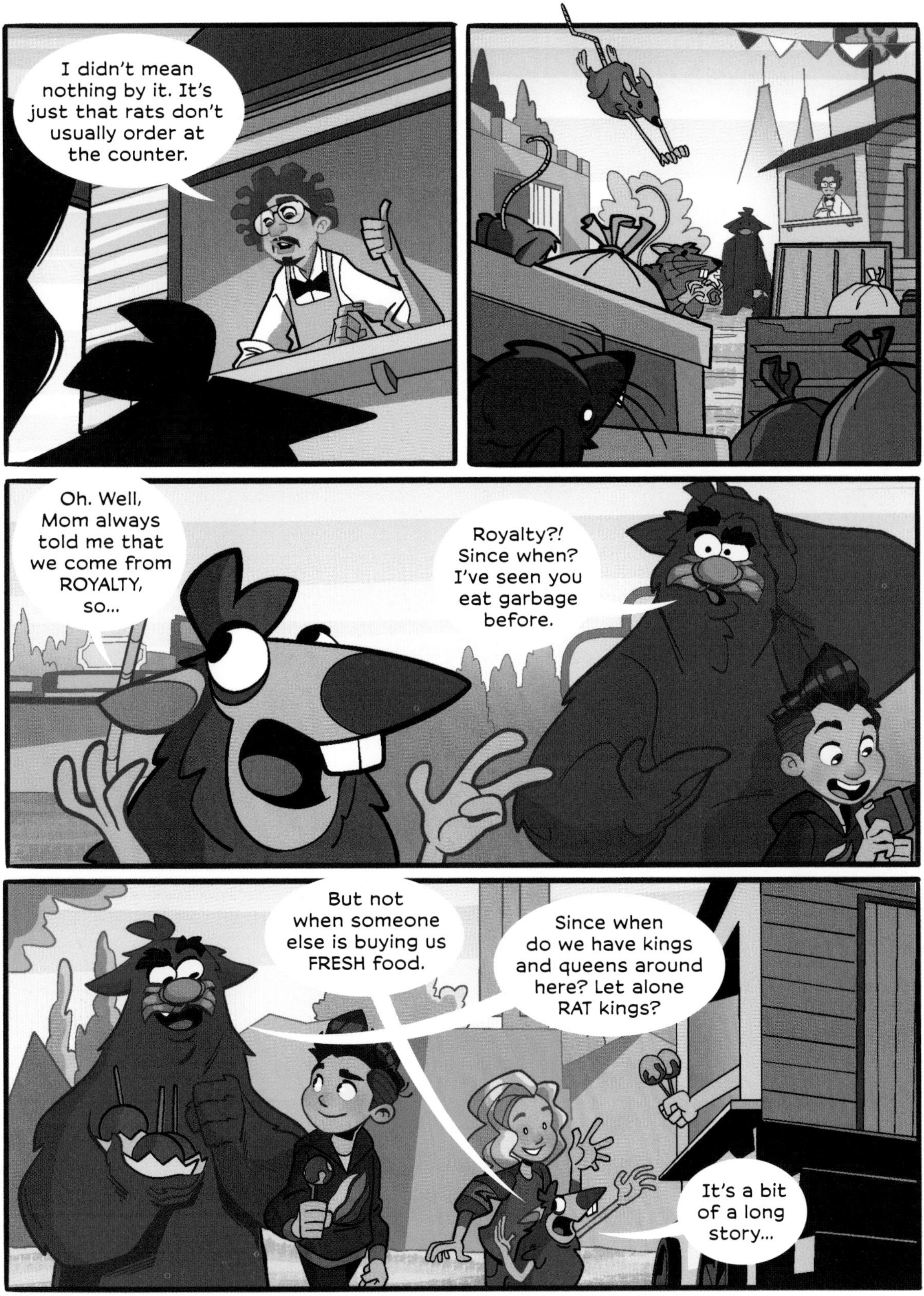
I didn't mean nothing by it. It's just that rats don't usually order at the counter.
Oh. Well, Mom always told me that we come from ROYALTY, so...
Royalty?! Since when? I've seen you eat garbage before.
But not when someone else is buying us FRESH food.
Since when do we have kings and queens around here? Let alone RAT kings?
It's a bit of a long story...

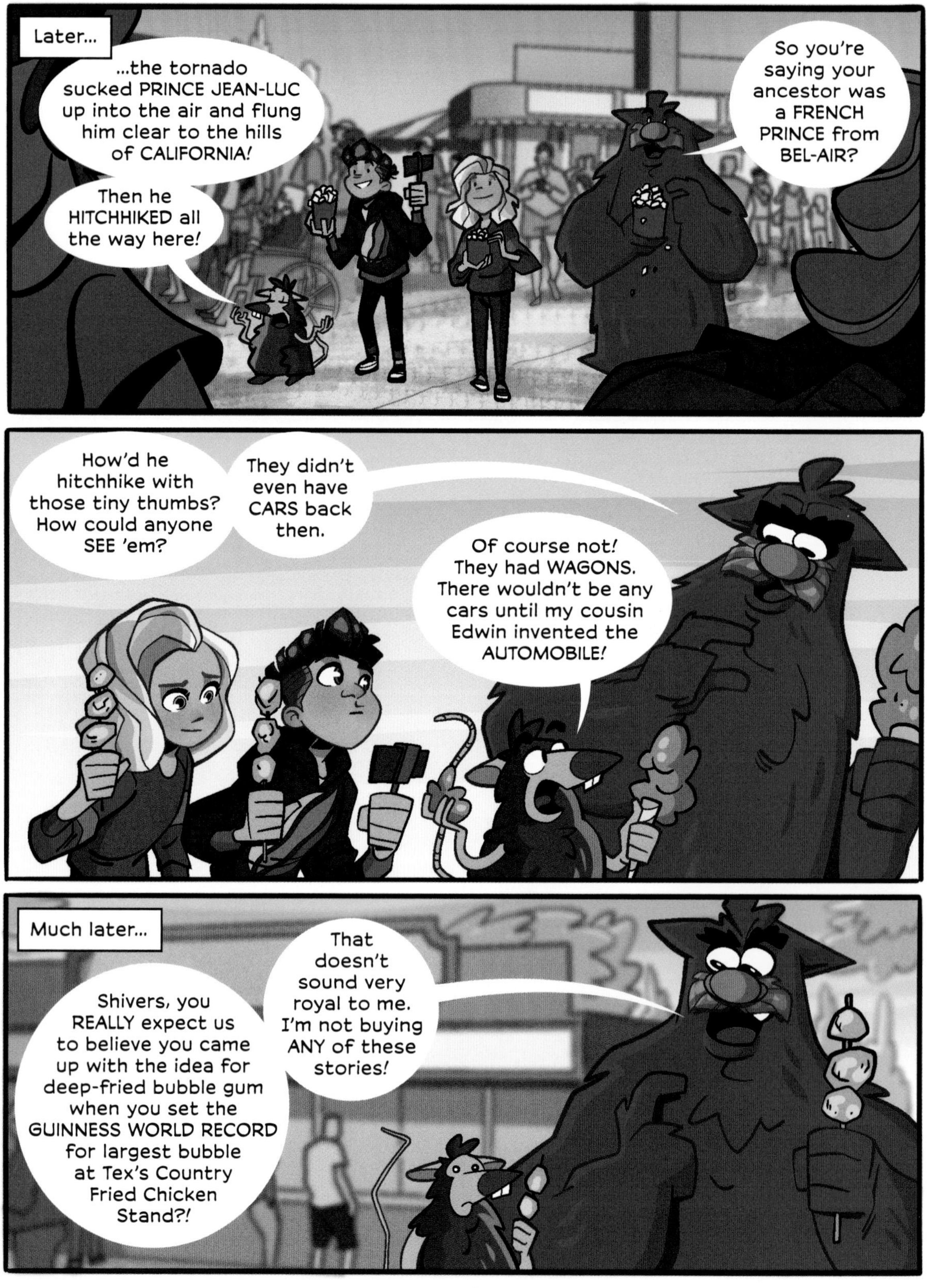
Later...
...the tornado sucked PRINCE JEAN-LUC up into the air and flung him clear to the hills of CALIFORNIA!
Then he HITCHHIKED all the way here!
So you're saying your ancestor was a FRENCH PRINCE from BEL-AIR?
How'd he hitchhike with those tiny thumbs? How could anyone SEE 'em?
They didn't even have CARS back then.
Of course not! They had WAGONS. There wouldn't be any cars until my cousin Edwin invented the AUTOMOBILE!
Much later...
Shivers, you REALLY expect us to believe you came up with the idea for deep-fried bubble gum when you set the GUINNESS WORLD RECORD for largest bubble at Tex's Country Fried Chicken Stand?!
That doesn't sound very royal to me. I'm not buying ANY of these stories!

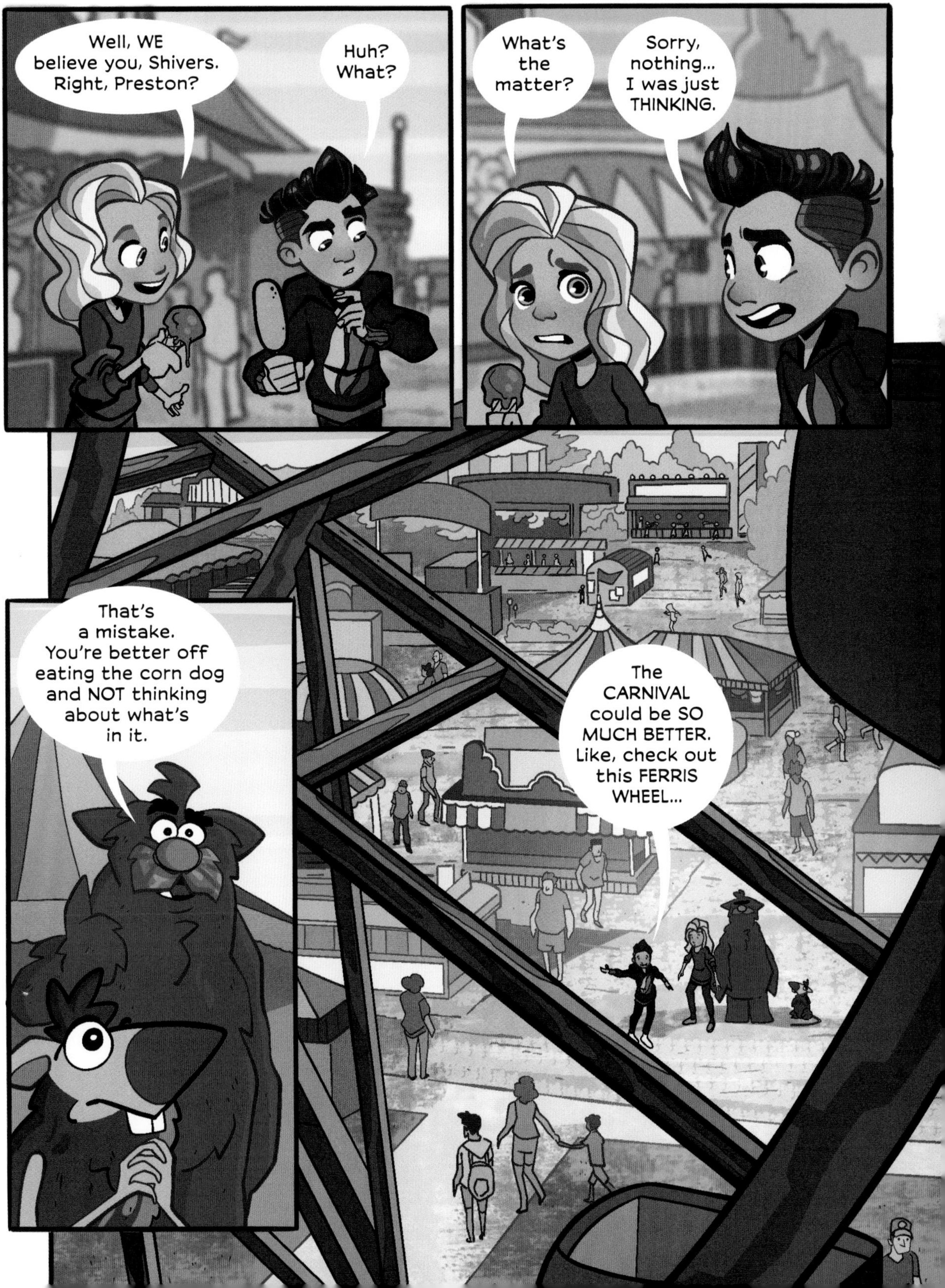
Well, WE believe you, Shivers. Right, Preston?
Huh? What?
What's the matter?
Sorry, nothing... I was just THINKING.
That's a mistake. You're better off eating the corn dog and NOT thinking about what's in it.
The CARNIVAL could be SO MUCH BETTER. Like, check out this FERRIS WHEEL...

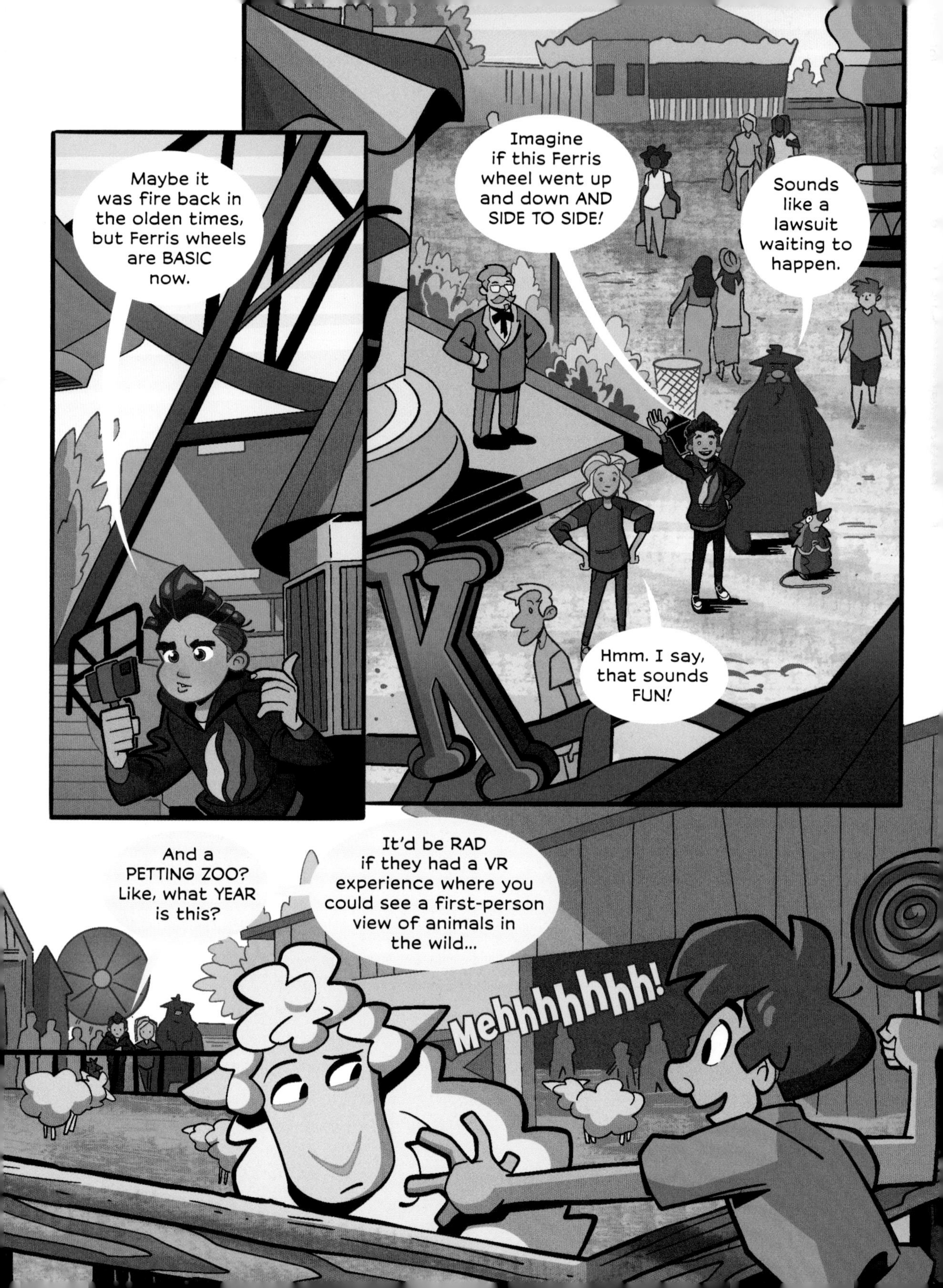

Maybe it was fire back in the olden times, but Ferris wheels are BASIC now.
Imagine if this Ferris wheel went up and down AND SIDE TO SIDE!
Sounds like a lawsuit waiting to happen.
Hmm. I say, that sounds FUN!
And a PETTING ZOO? Like, what YEAR is this?
It'd be RAD if they had a VR experience where you could see a first-person view of animals in the wild...
Mehhhhhhhh!

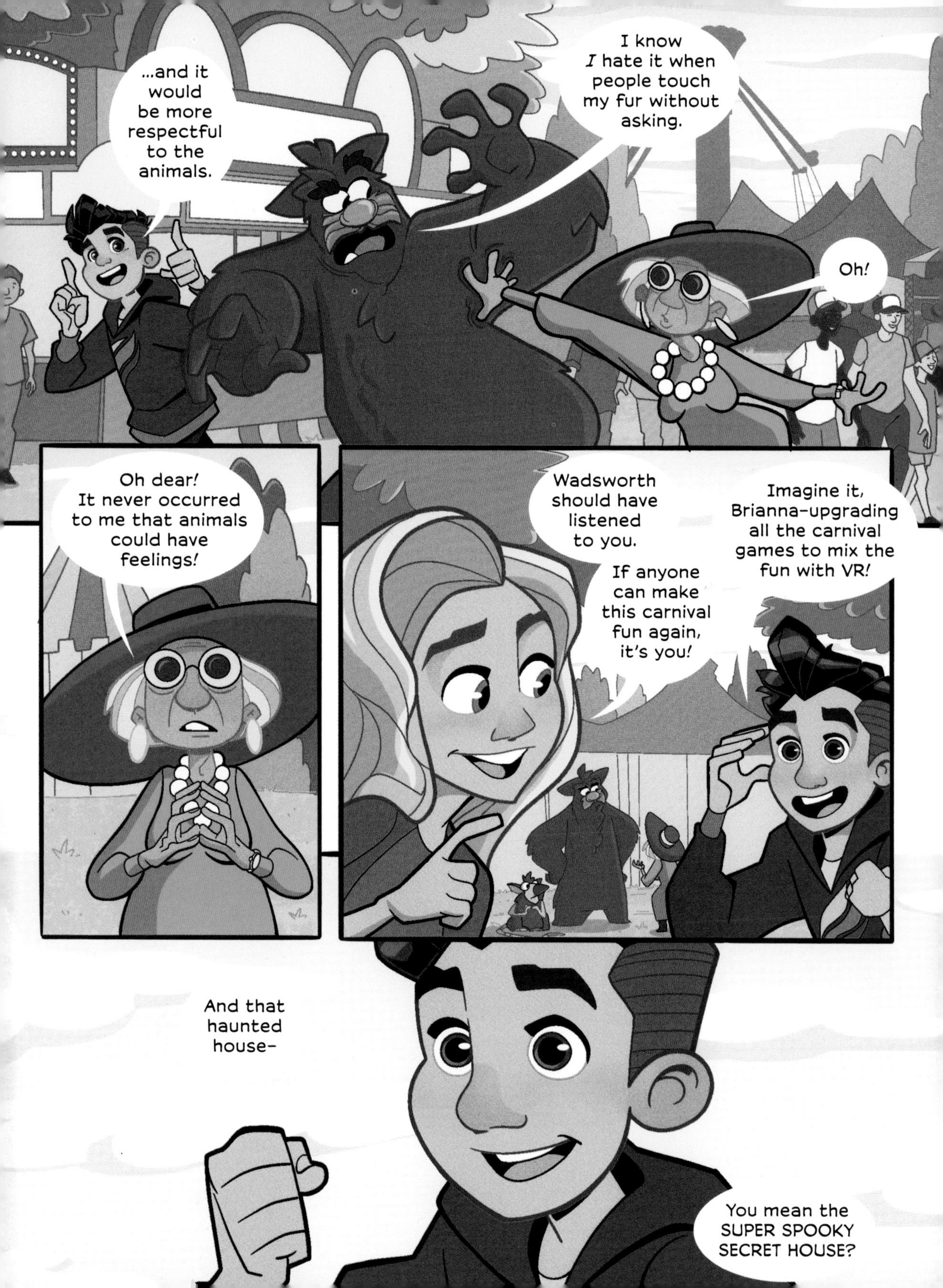
...and it would be more respectful to the animals.
I know *I* hate it when people touch my fur without asking.
Oh!
Oh dear! It never occurred to me that animals could have feelings!
Wadsworth should have listened to you.
If anyone can make this carnival fun again, it's you!
Imagine it, Brianna–upgrading all the carnival games to mix the fun with VR!
And that haunted house–
You mean the SUPER SPOOKY SECRET HOUSE?

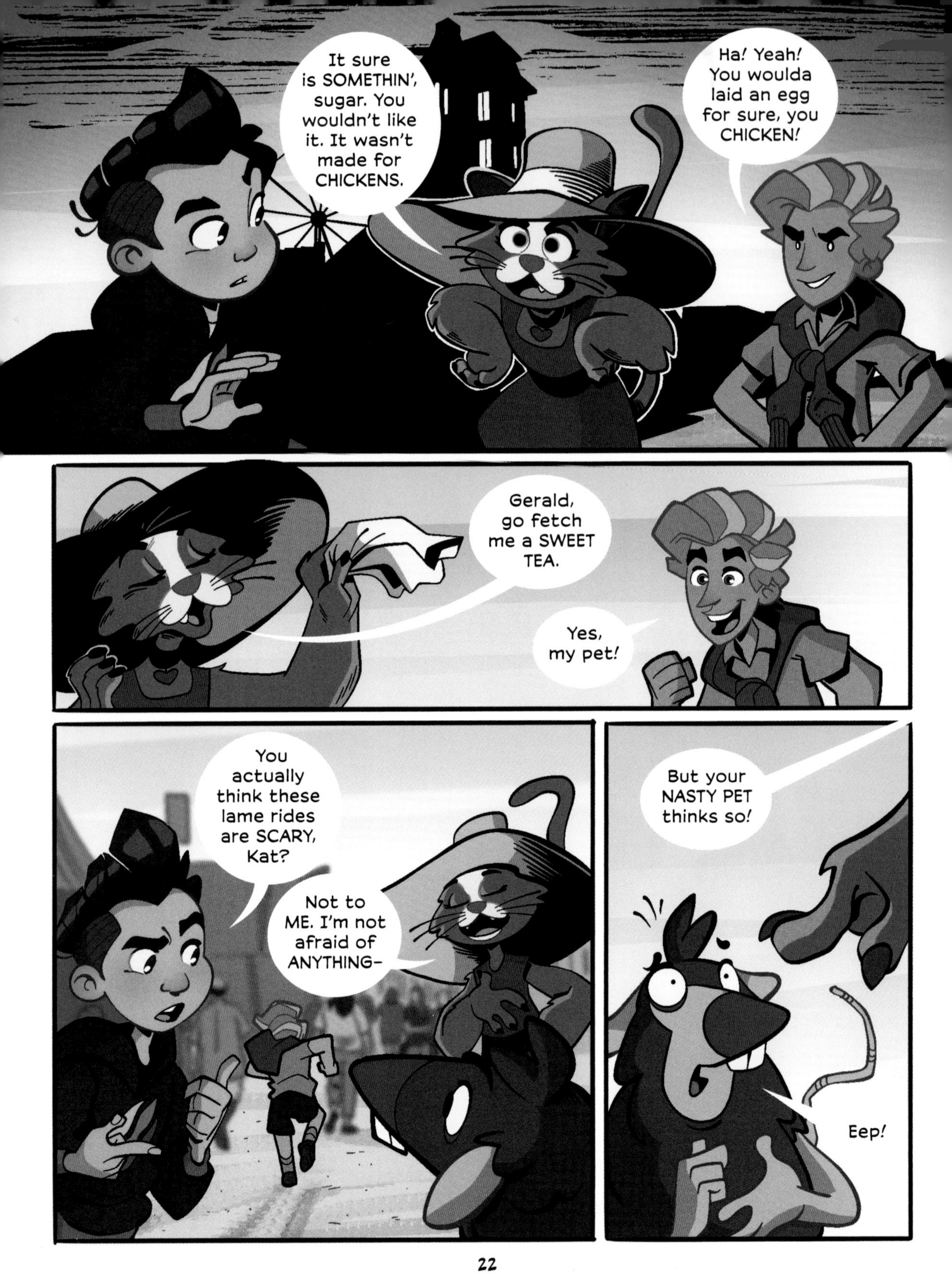
It sure is SOMETHIN', sugar. You wouldn't like it. It wasn't made for CHICKENS.
Ha! Yeah! You woulda laid an egg for sure, you CHICKEN!
Gerald, go fetch me a SWEET TEA.
Yes, my pet!
You actually think these lame rides are SCARY, Kat?
Not to ME. I'm not afraid of ANYTHING–
But your NASTY PET thinks so!
Eep!

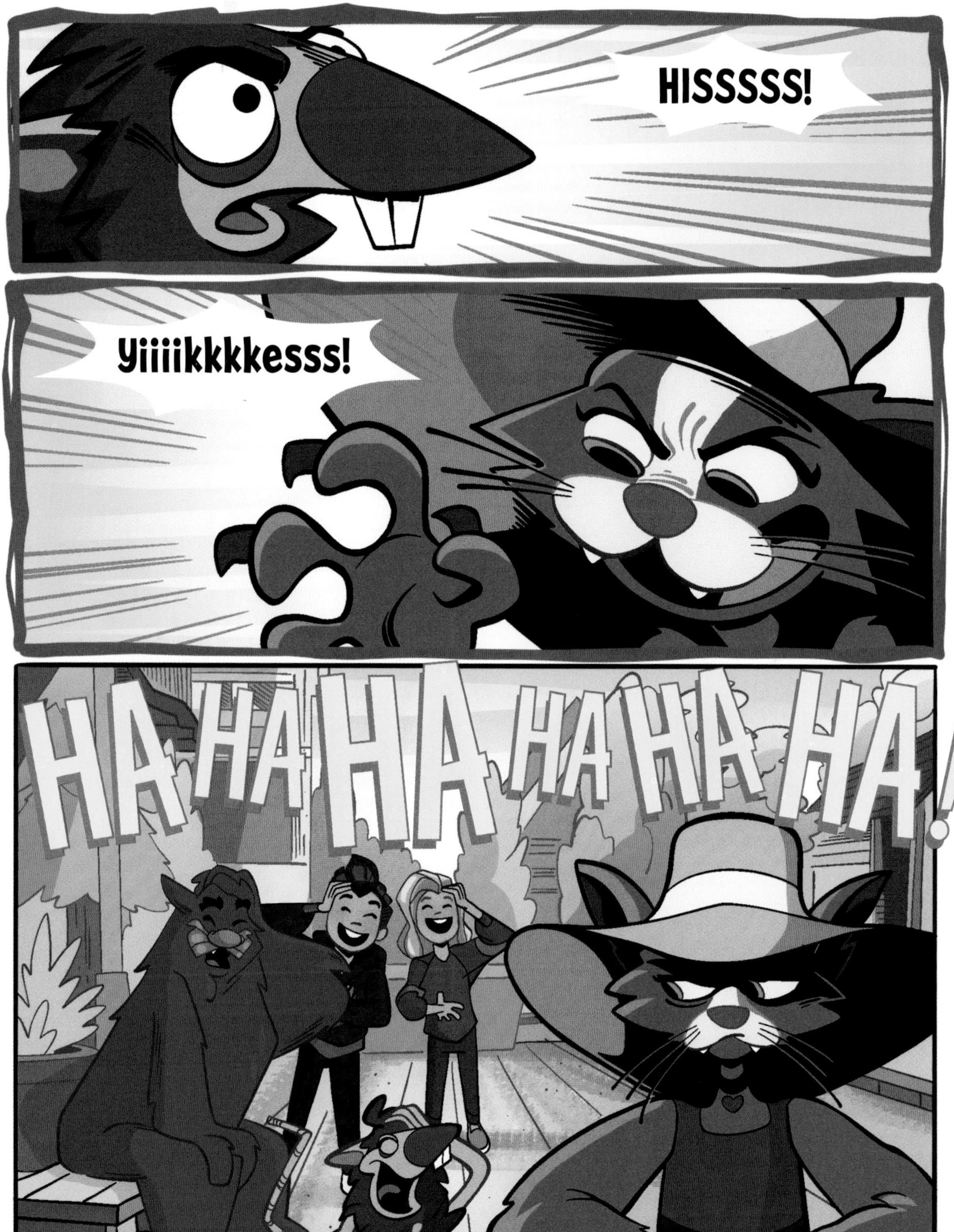
HISSSSS!
Yiiiikkkkesss!
HA HA HA HA HA HA HA HA!

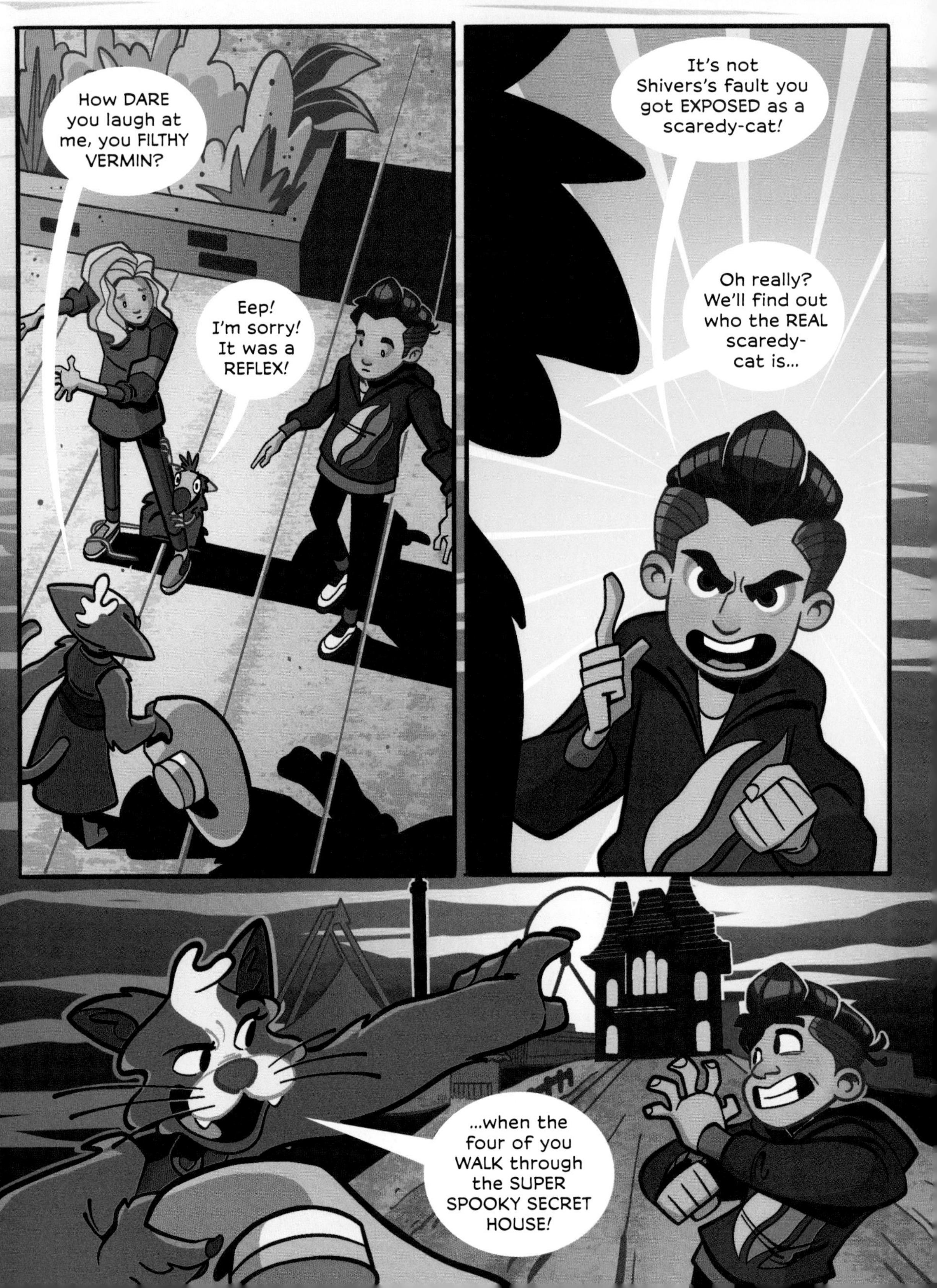
How DARE you laugh at me, you FILTHY VERMIN?
Eep! I'm sorry! It was a REFLEX!
It's not Shivers's fault you got EXPOSED as a scaredy-cat!
Oh really? We'll find out who the REAL scaredy-cat is...
...when the four of you WALK through the SUPER SPOOKY SECRET HOUSE!

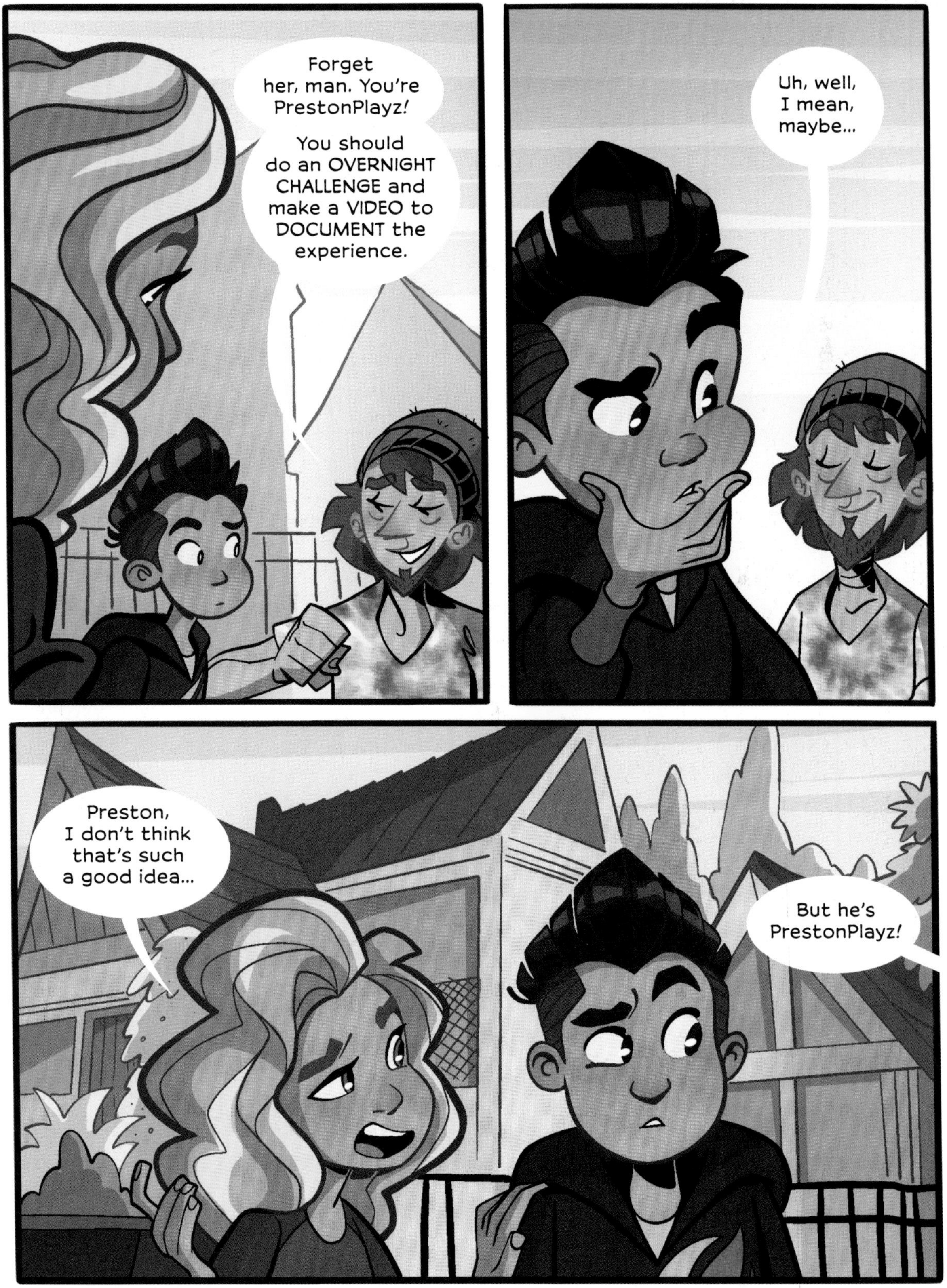
Forget her, man. You're PrestonPlayz!
You should do an OVERNIGHT CHALLENGE and make a VIDEO to DOCUMENT the experience.
Uh, well, I mean, maybe...
Preston, I don't think that's such a good idea...
But he's PrestonPlayz!

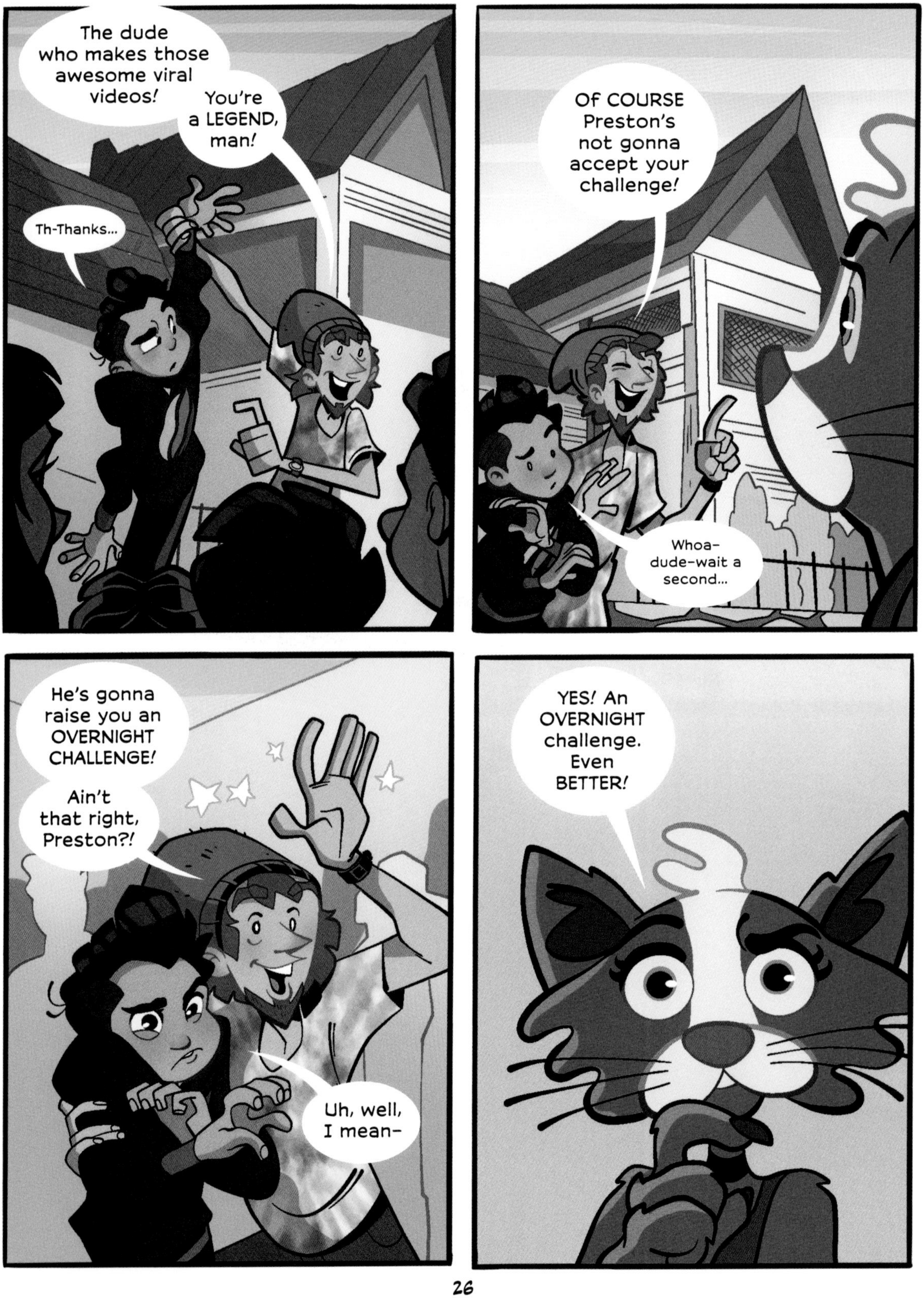
The dude who makes those awesome viral videos!
You're a LEGEND, man!
Th-Thanks...
Of COURSE Preston's not gonna accept your challenge!
Whoa-dude-wait a second...
He's gonna raise you an OVERNIGHT CHALLENGE!
Ain't that right, Preston?!
Uh, well, I mean-
YES! An OVERNIGHT challenge. Even BETTER!

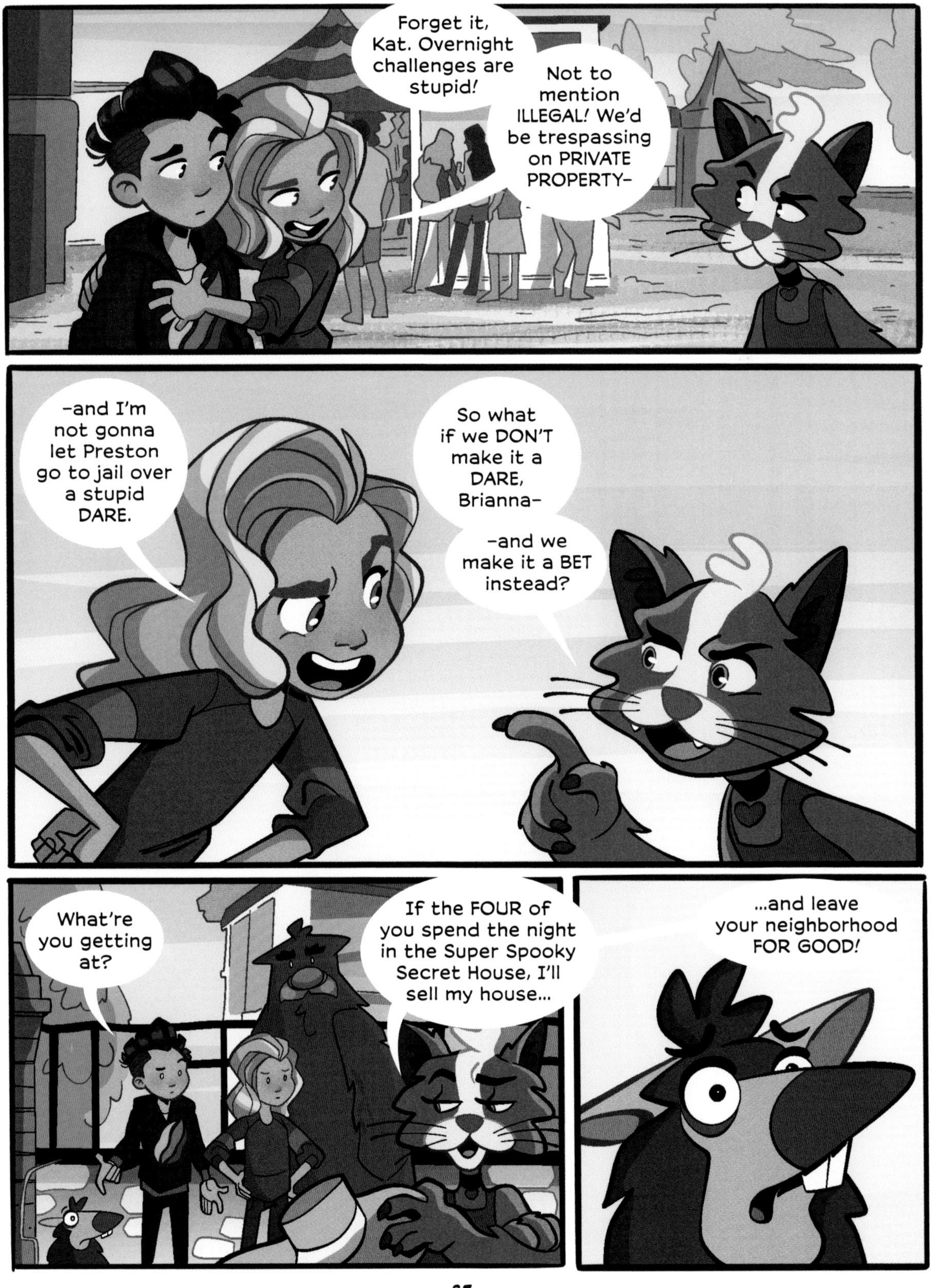
Forget it, Kat. Overnight challenges are stupid!
Not to mention ILLEGAL! We'd be trespassing on PRIVATE PROPERTY–
–and I'm not gonna let Preston go to jail over a stupid DARE.
So what if we DON'T make it a DARE, Brianna–
–and we make it a BET instead?
What're you getting at?
If the FOUR of you spend the night in the Super Spooky Secret House, I'll sell my house...
...and leave your neighborhood FOR GOOD!

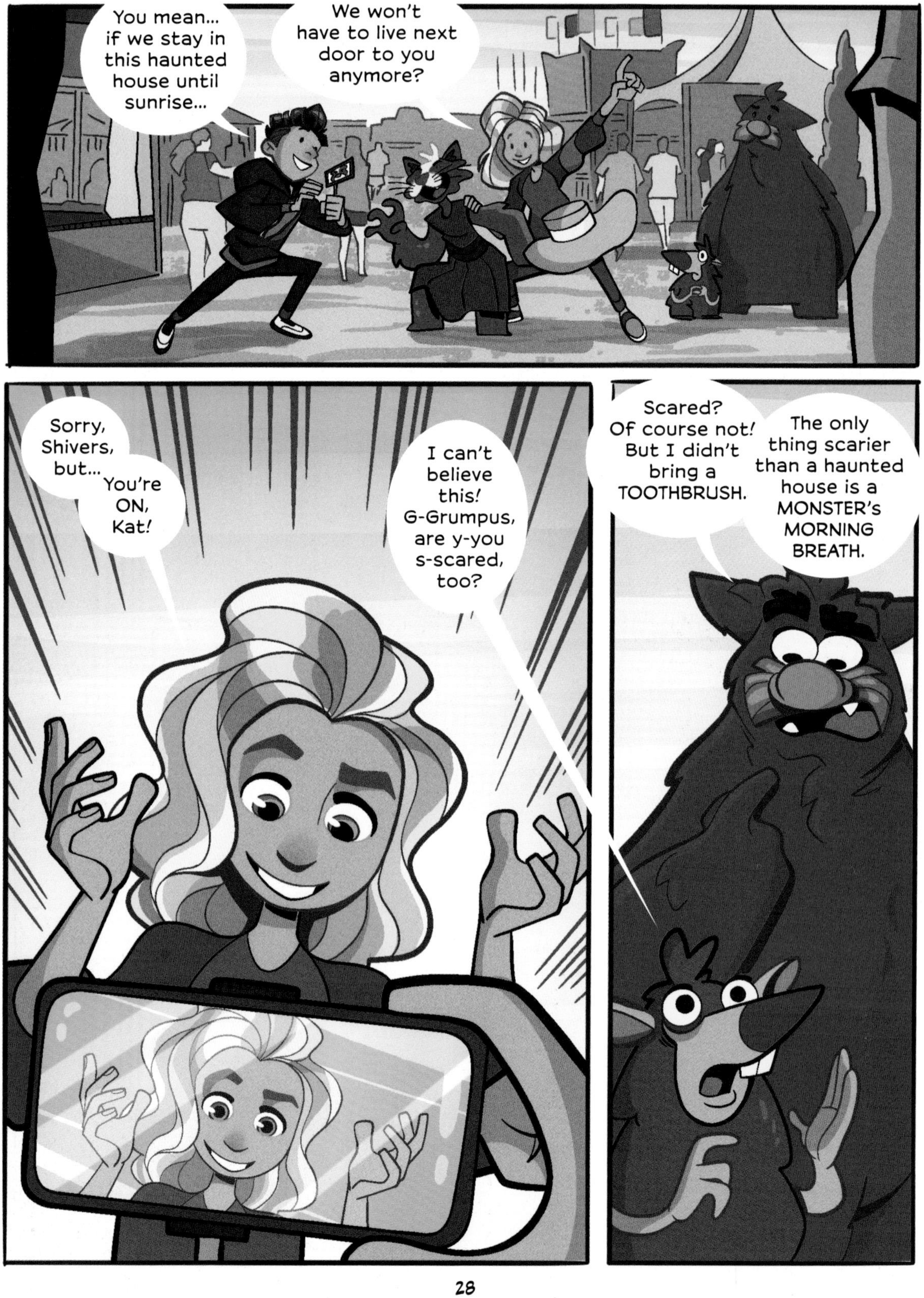
You mean... if we stay in this haunted house until sunrise...
We won't have to live next door to you anymore?
Sorry, Shivers, but...
You're ON, Kat!
I can't believe this! G-Grumpus, are y-you s-scared, too?
Scared? Of course not! But I didn't bring a TOOTHBRUSH.
The only thing scarier than a haunted house is a MONSTER's MORNING BREATH.

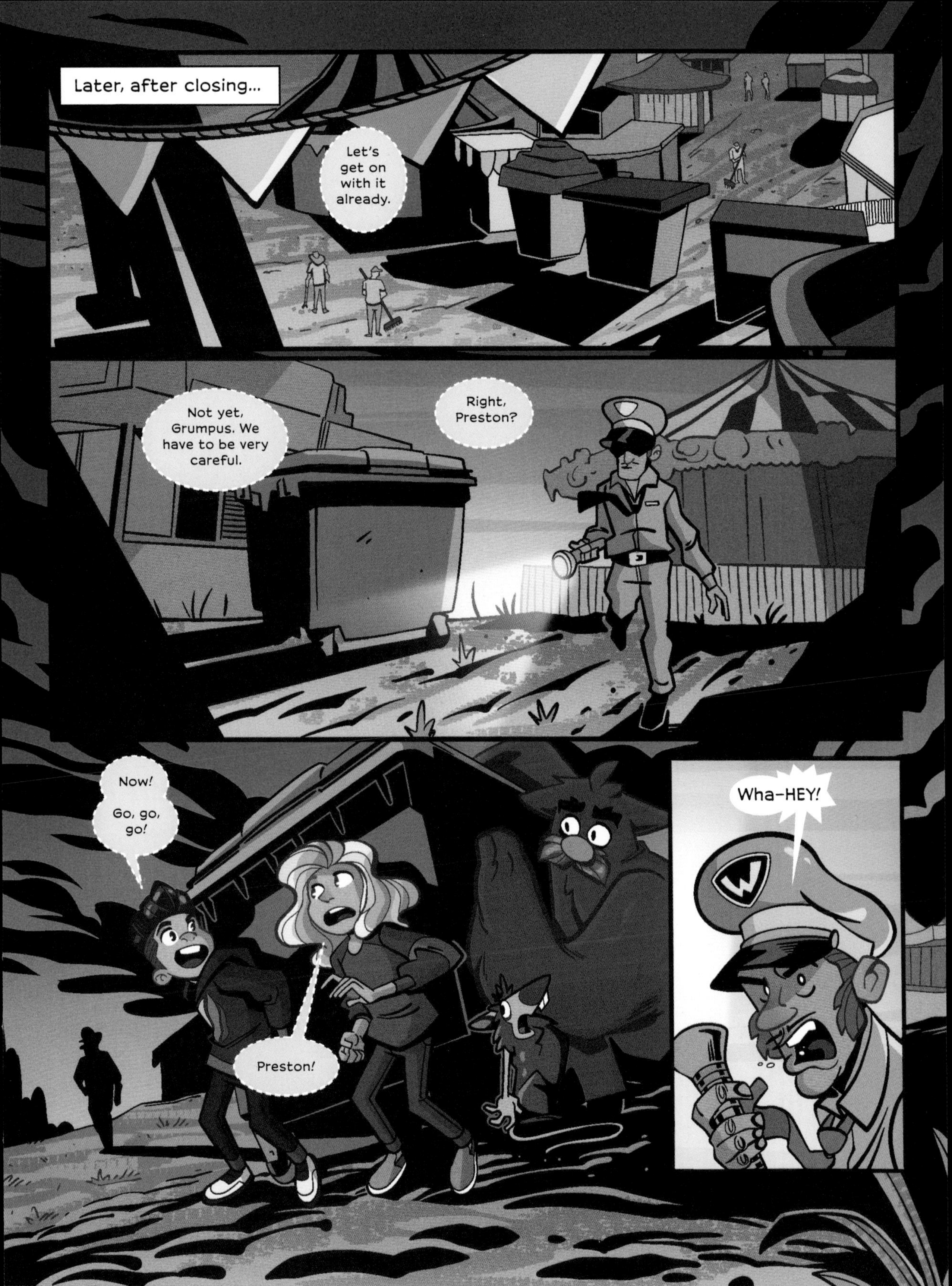
Later, after closing...
Let's get on with it already.
Not yet, Grumpus. We have to be very careful.
Right, Preston?
Now!
Go, go, go!
Preston!
Wha-HEY!

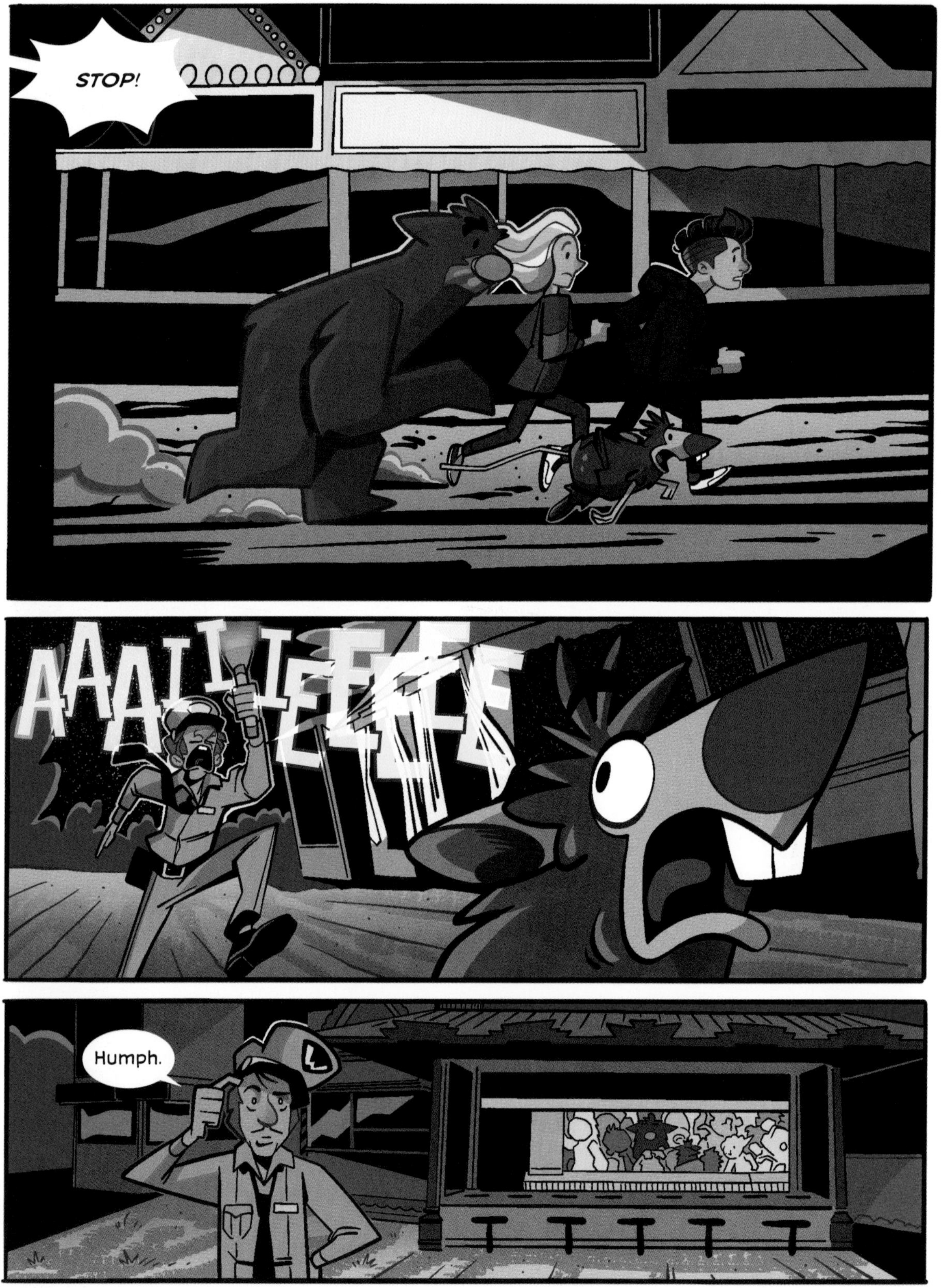
STOP!
AAAIIIEEEEE
Humph.

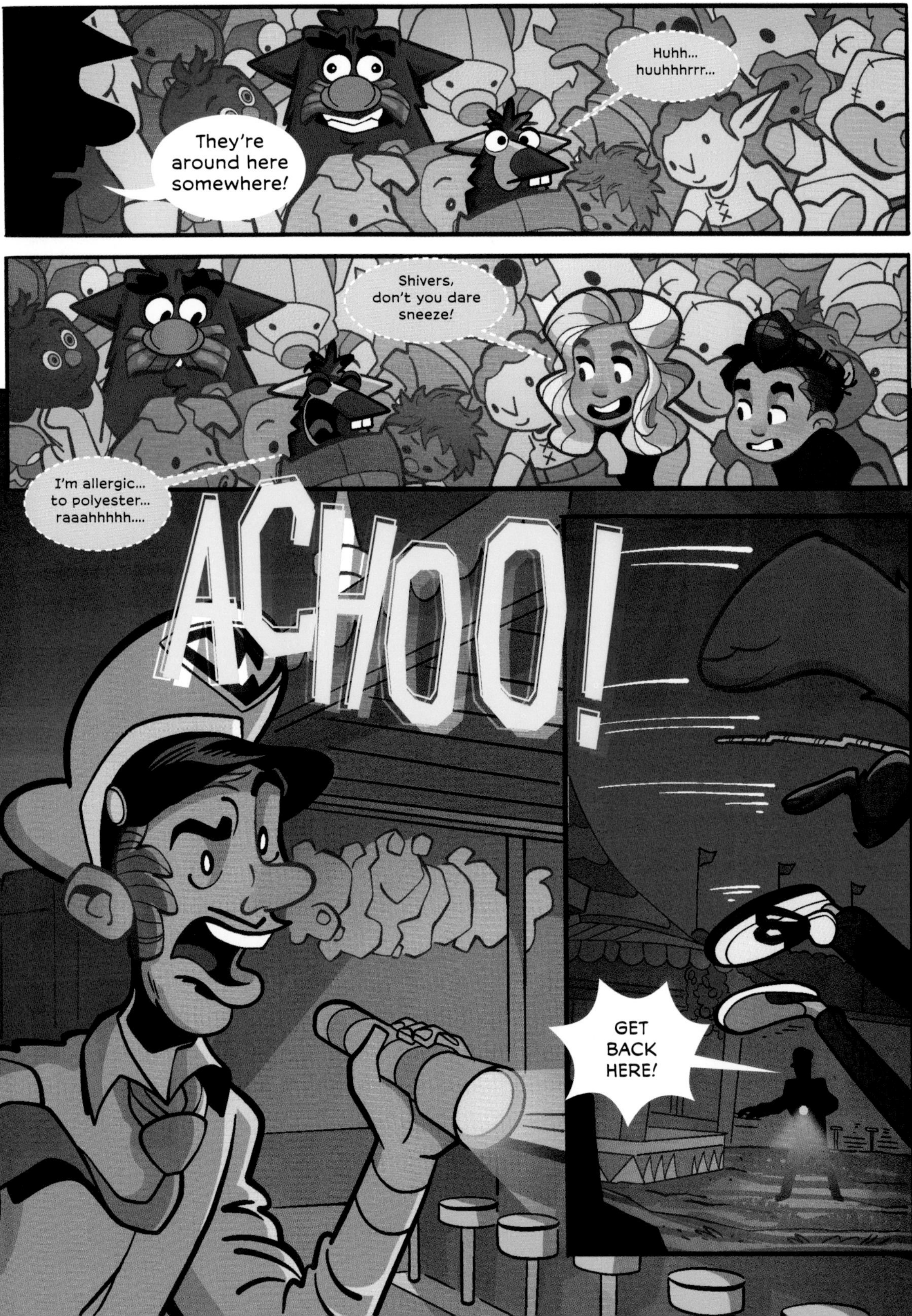

They're around here somewhere!
Huhh... huuhhhrrr...
Shivers, don't you dare sneeze!
I'm allergic... to polyester... raaahhhhh....
ACHOO!
GET BACK HERE!

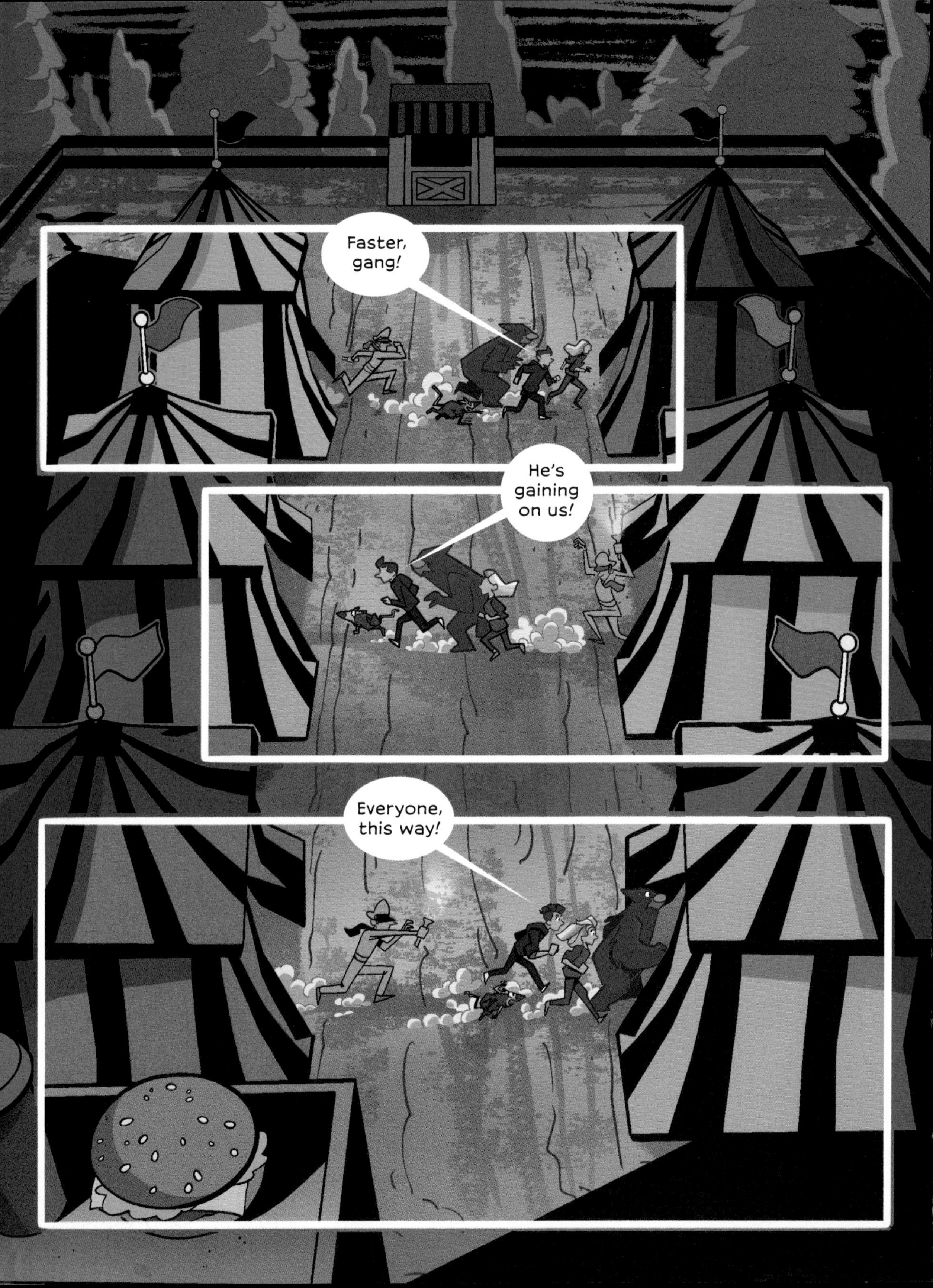
Faster, gang!
He's gaining on us!
Everyone, this way!

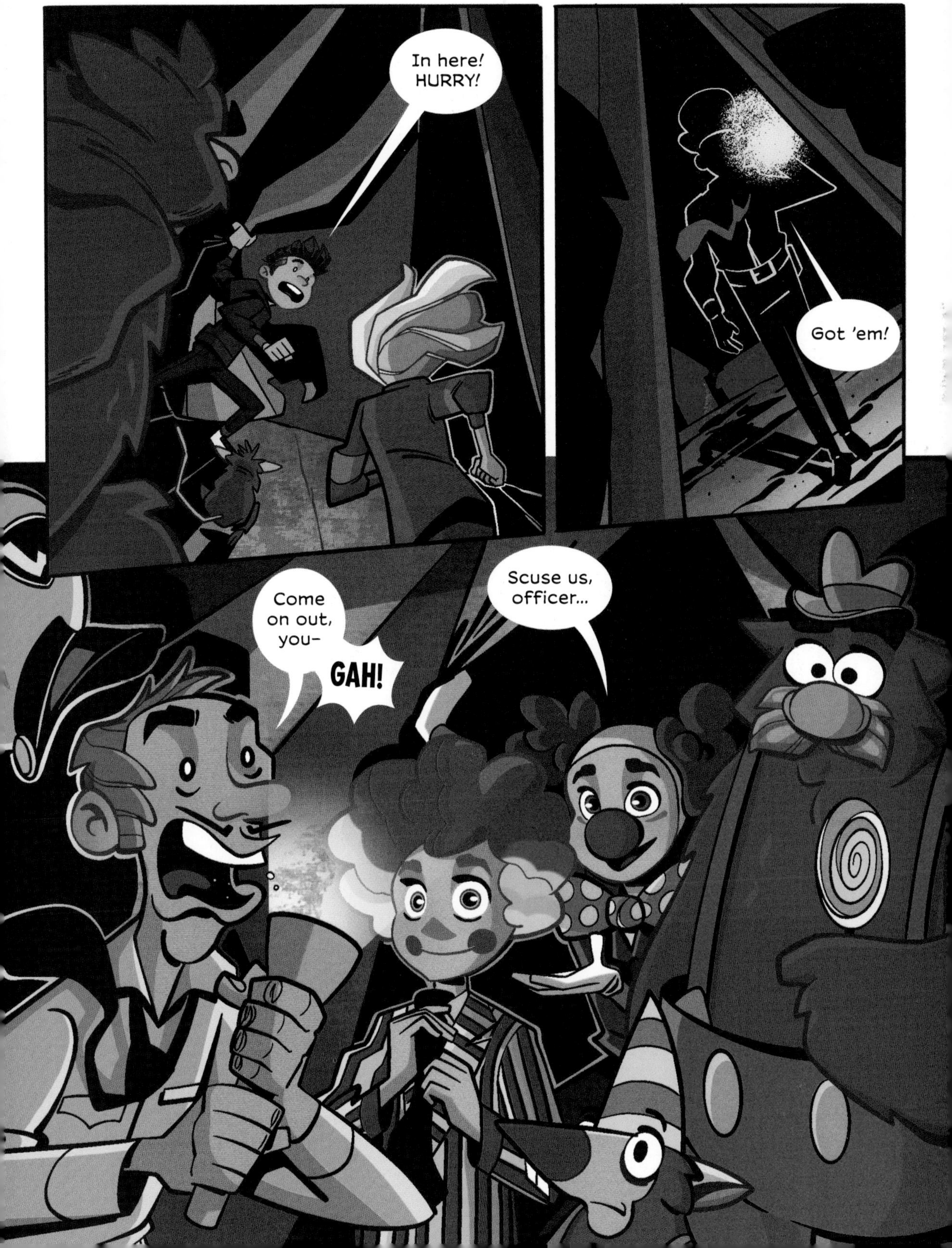
In here! HURRY!
Got 'em!
Come on out, you-
GAH!
Scuse us, officer...

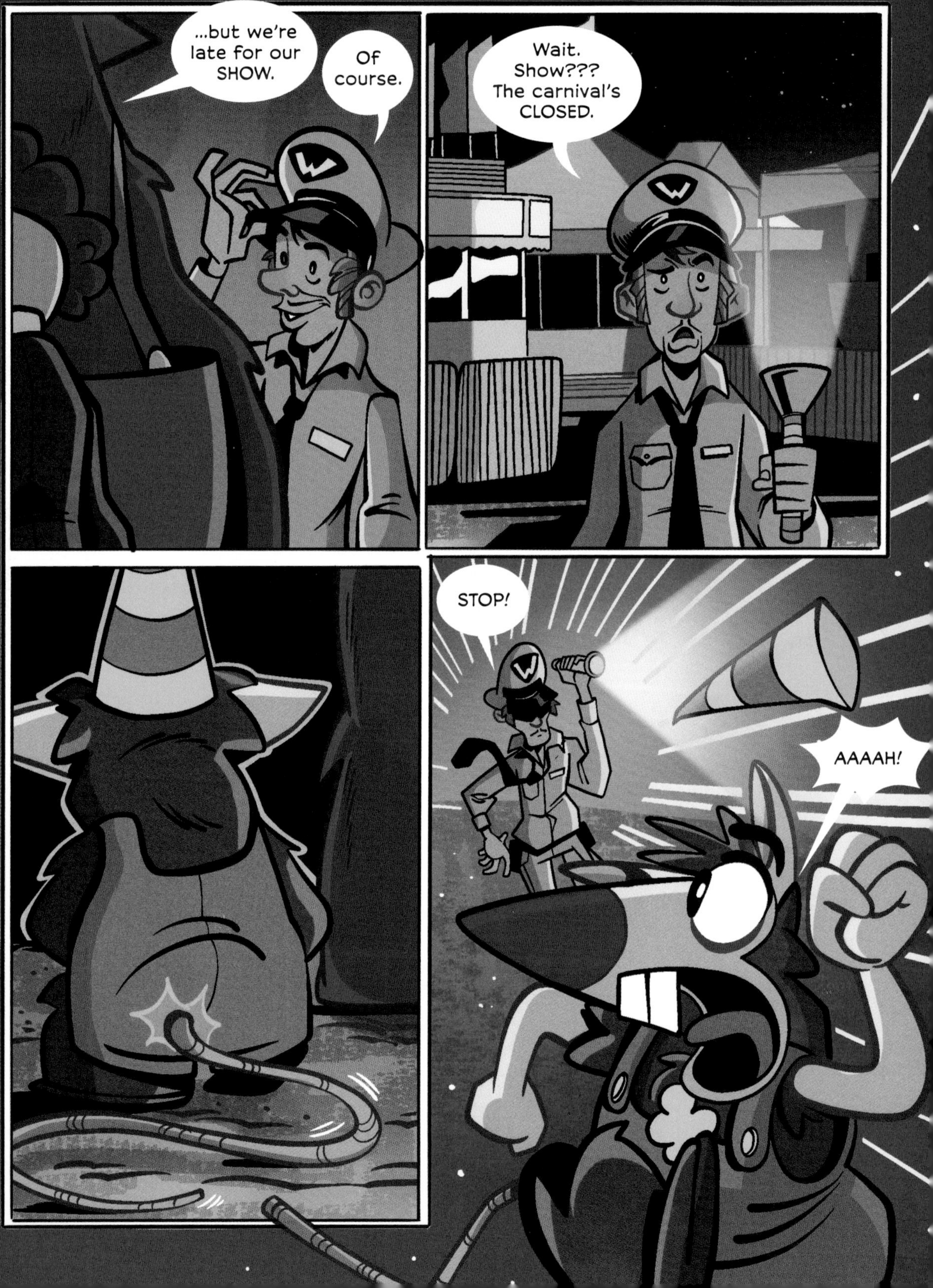
...but we're late for our SHOW.
Of course.
Wait. Show??? The carnival's CLOSED.
STOP!
AAAAH!

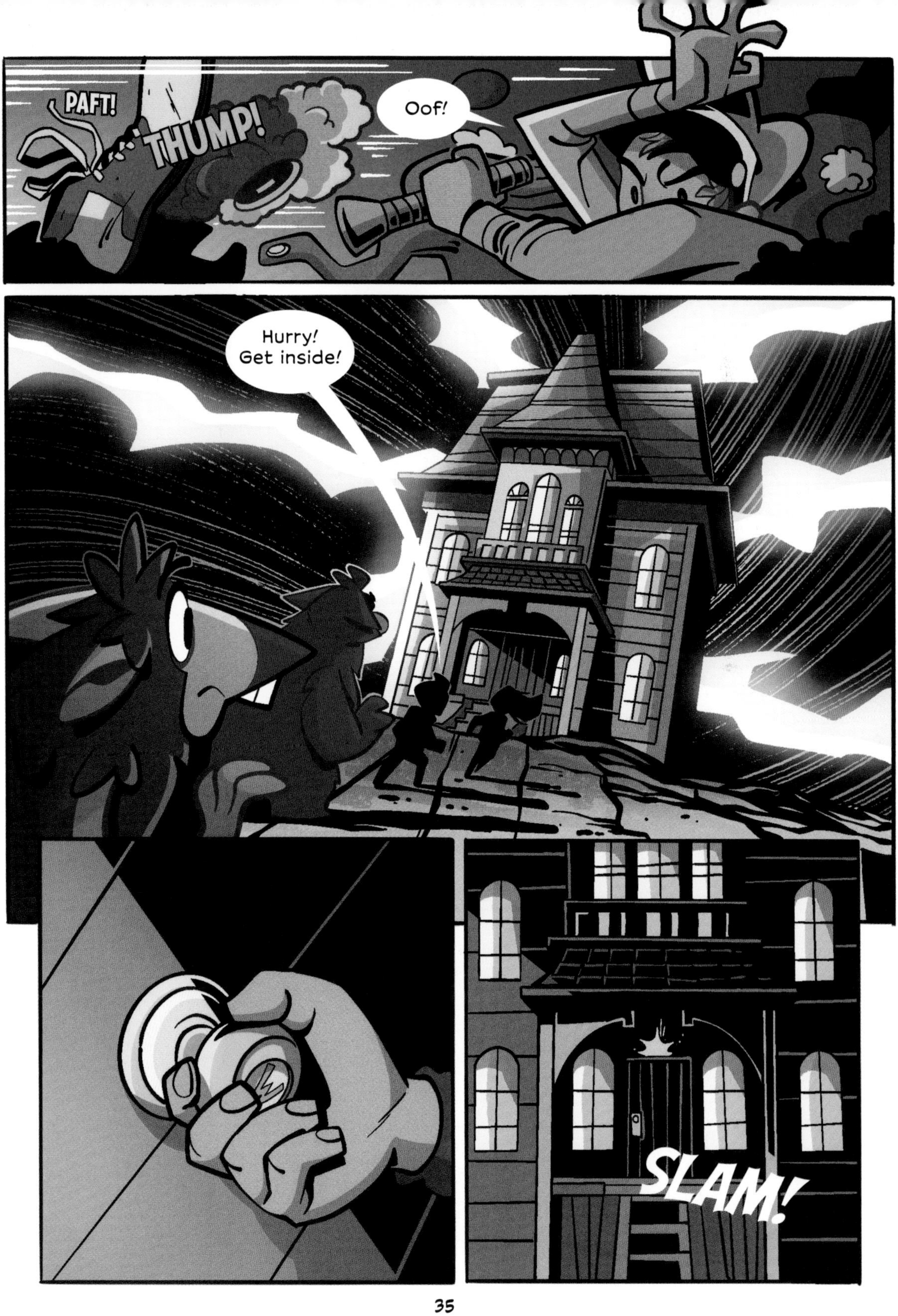
PAFT!
THUMP!
Oof!
Hurry!
Get inside!
SLAM!

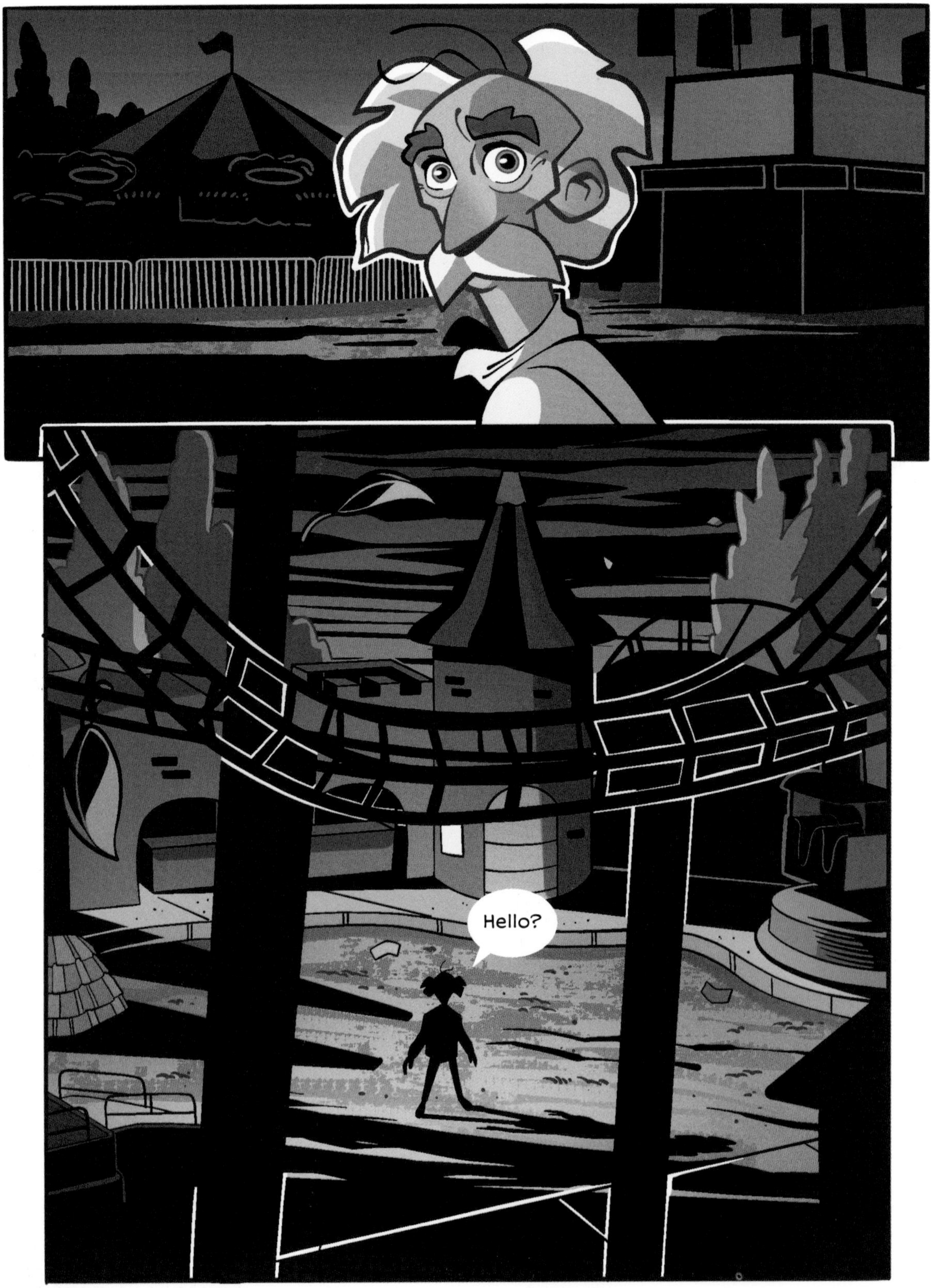
Hello?

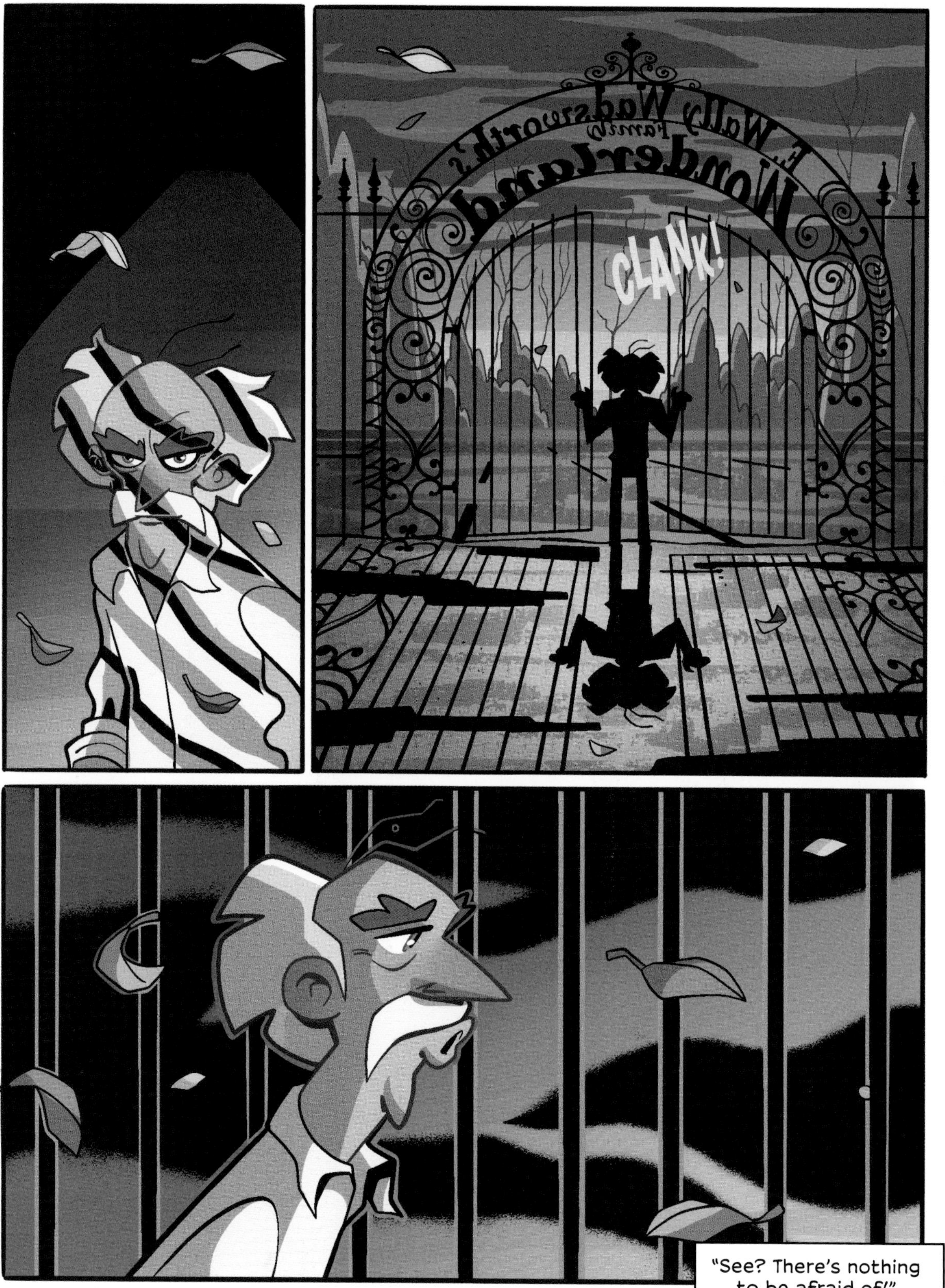
CLANK!
"See? There's nothing to be afraid of!"

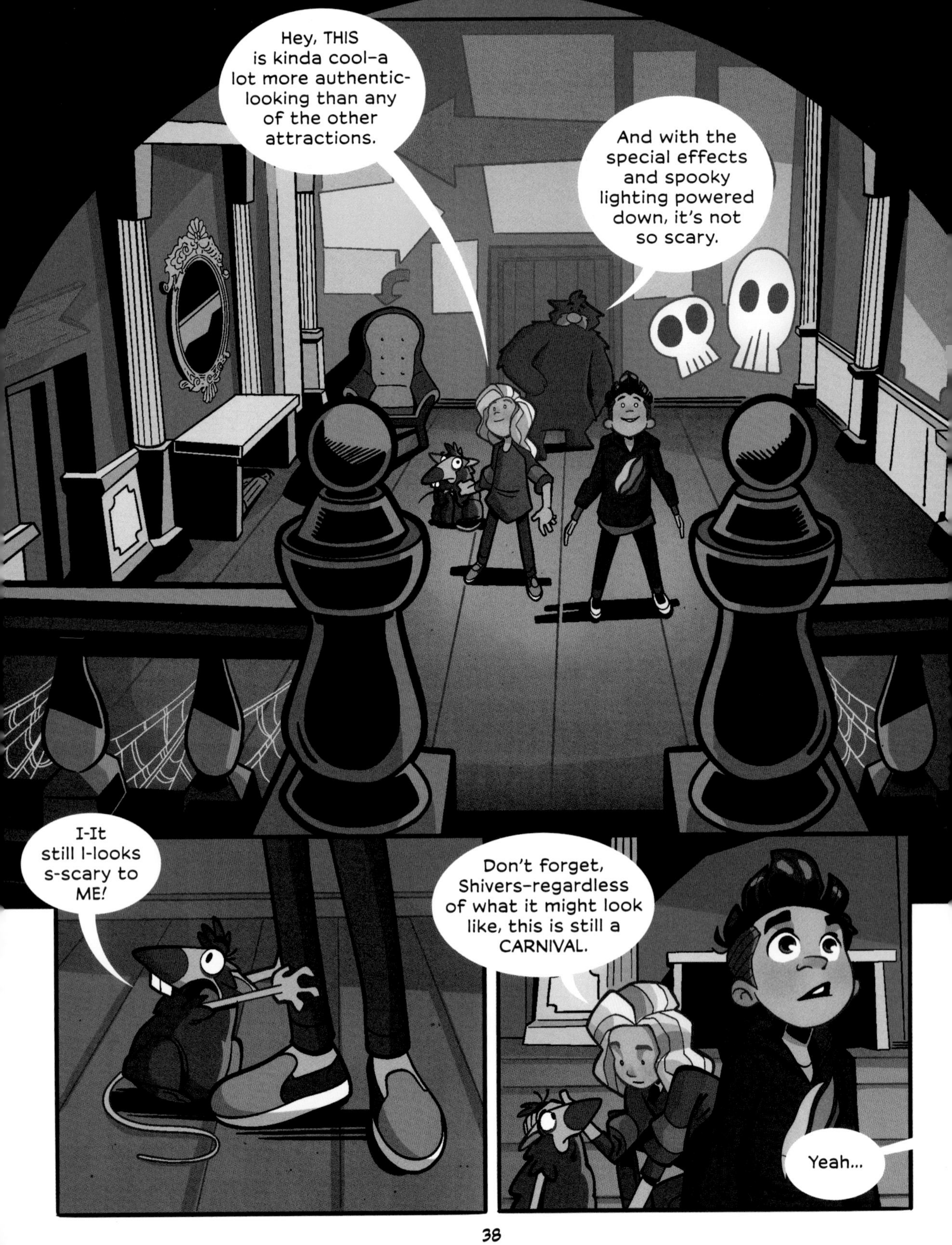
Hey, THIS is kinda cool–a lot more authentic-looking than any of the other attractions.
And with the special effects and spooky lighting powered down, it's not so scary.
I-It still l-looks s-scary to ME!
Don't forget, Shivers–regardless of what it might look like, this is still a CARNIVAL.
Yeah...

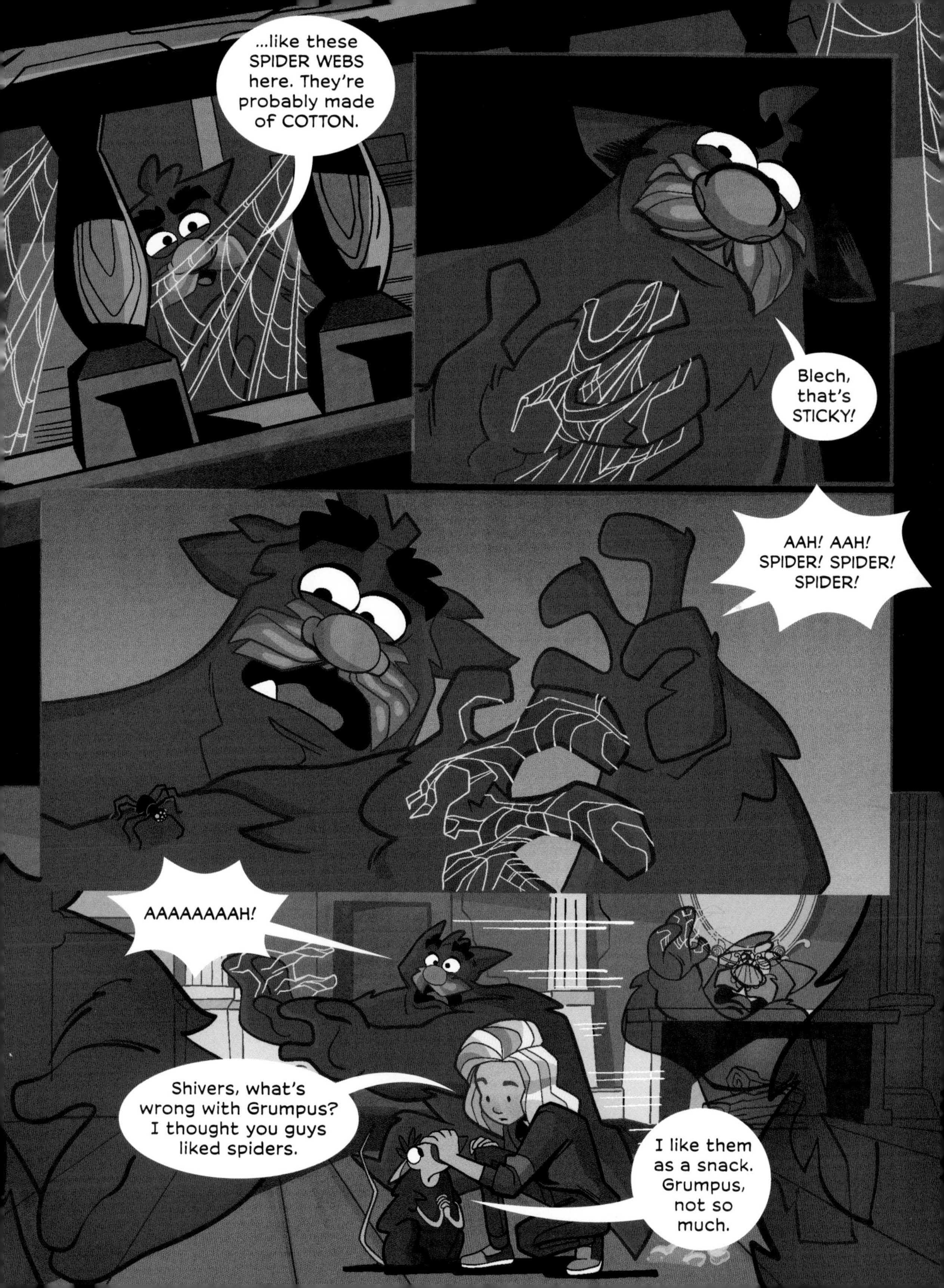
...like these SPIDER WEBS here. They're probably made of COTTON.
Blech, that's STICKY!
AAH! AAH! SPIDER! SPIDER! SPIDER!
AAAAAAAAH!
Shivers, what's wrong with Grumpus? I thought you guys liked spiders.
I like them as a snack. Grumpus, not so much.

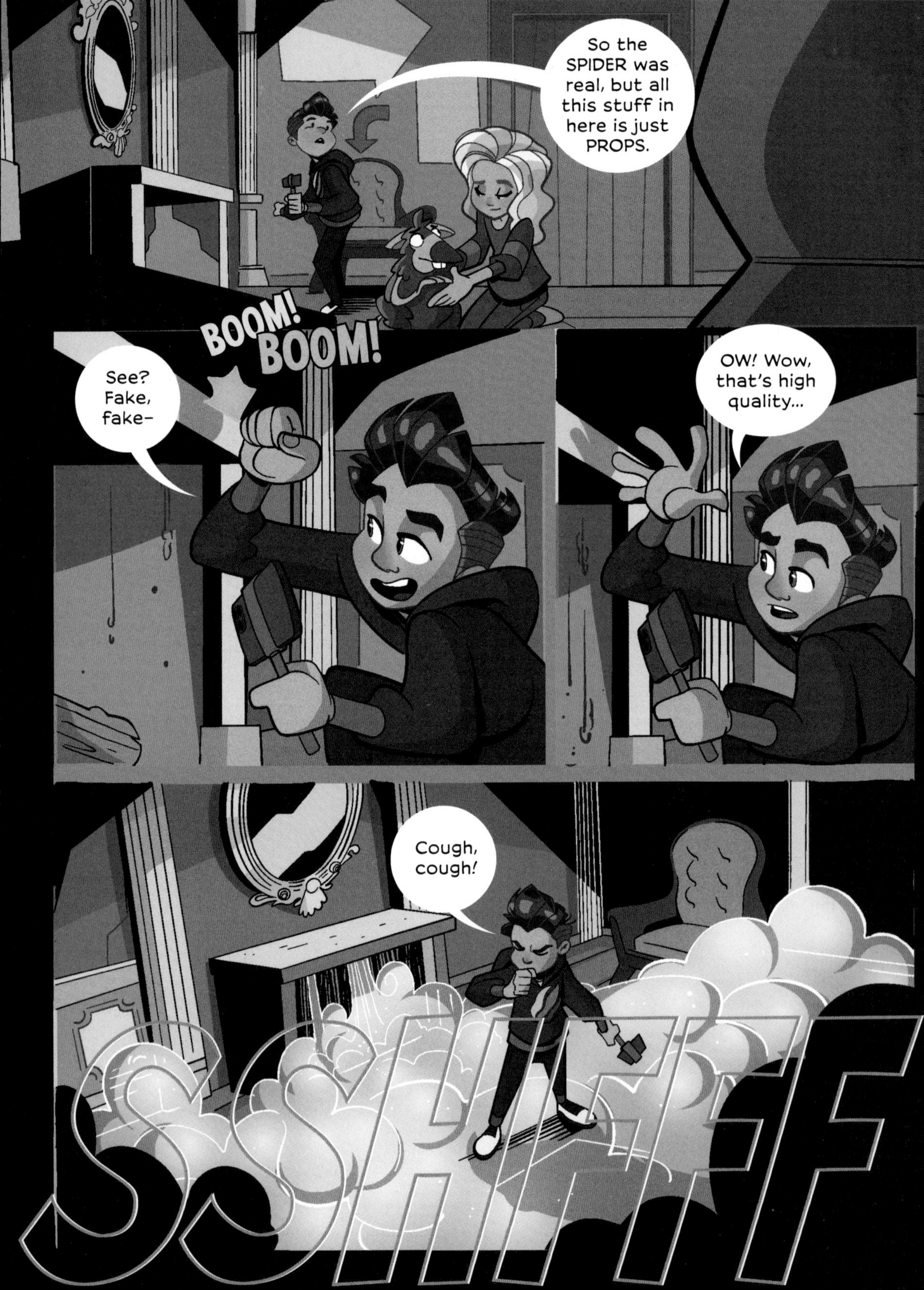
So the SPIDER was real, but all this stuff in here is just PROPS.
BOOM! BOOM!
See? Fake, fake-
OW! Wow, that's high quality...
Cough, cough!
SCHFFF

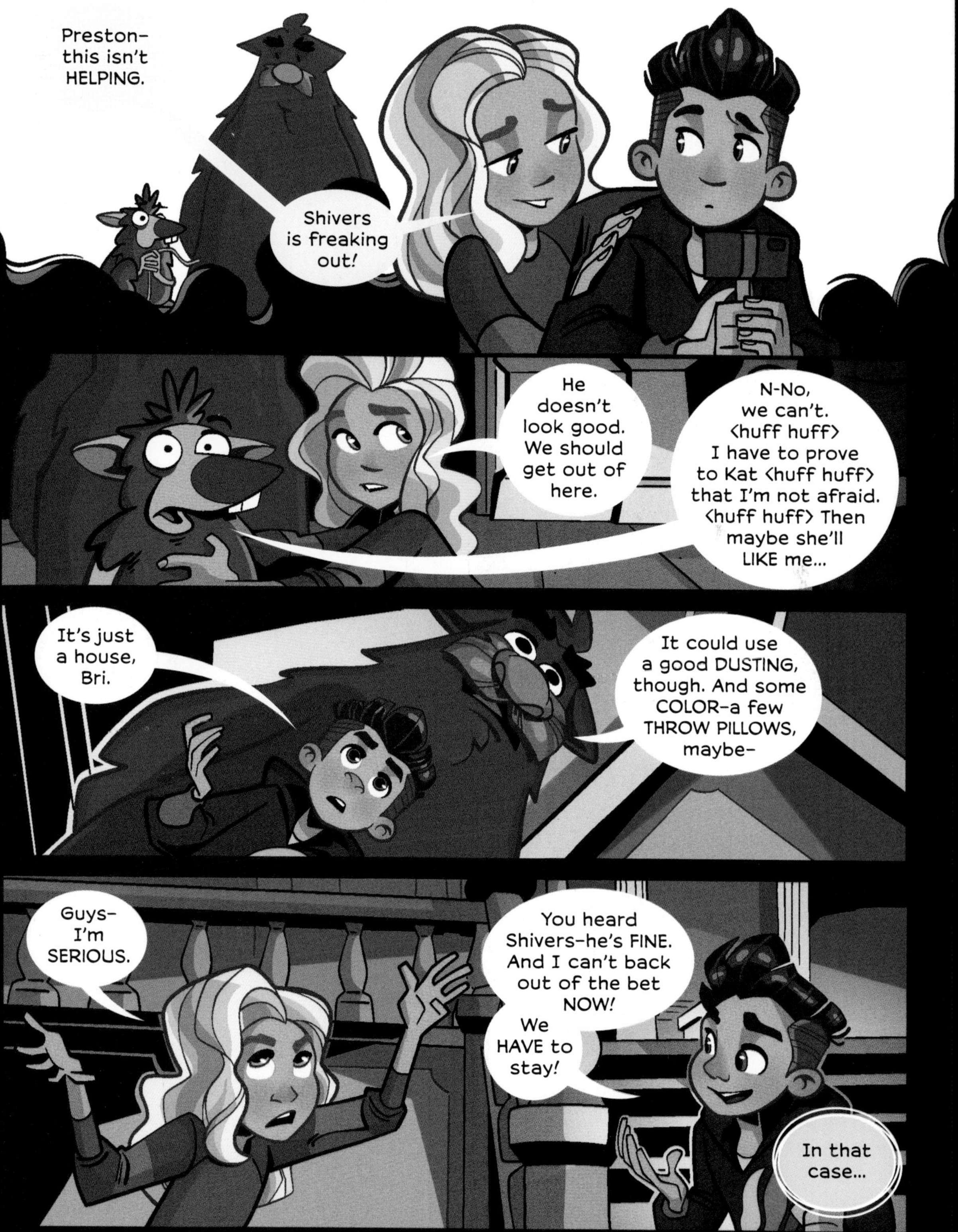
Preston–
this isn't
HELPING.
Shivers is freaking out!
He doesn't look good. We should get out of here.
N-No, we can't. <huff huff> I have to prove to Kat <huff huff> that I'm not afraid. <huff huff> Then maybe she'll LIKE me...
It's just a house, Bri.
It could use a good DUSTING, though. And some COLOR–a few THROW PILLOWS, maybe–
Guys– I'm SERIOUS.
You heard Shivers–he's FINE. And I can't back out of the bet NOW!
We HAVE to stay!
In that case...

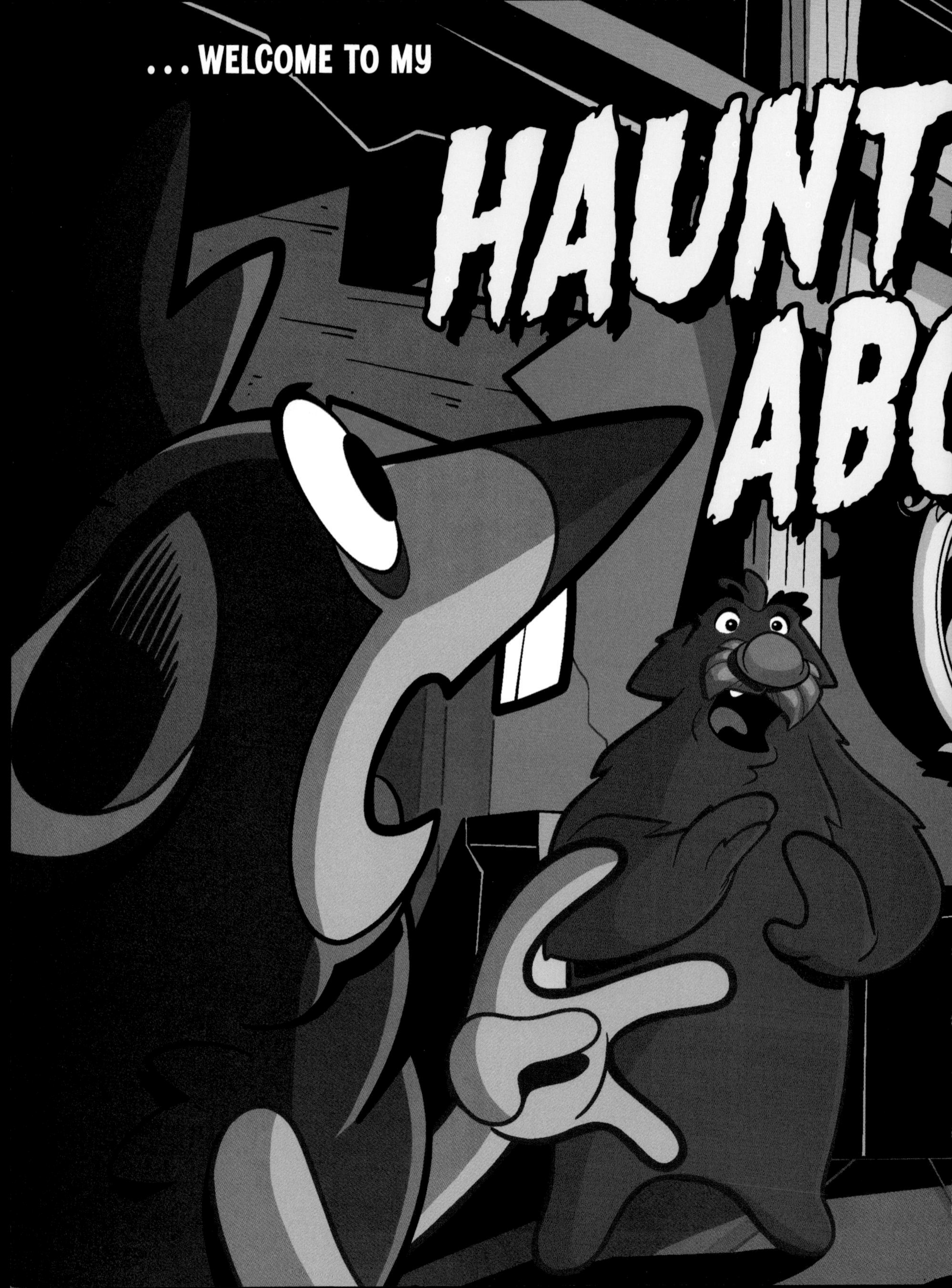
. . . WELCOME TO MY

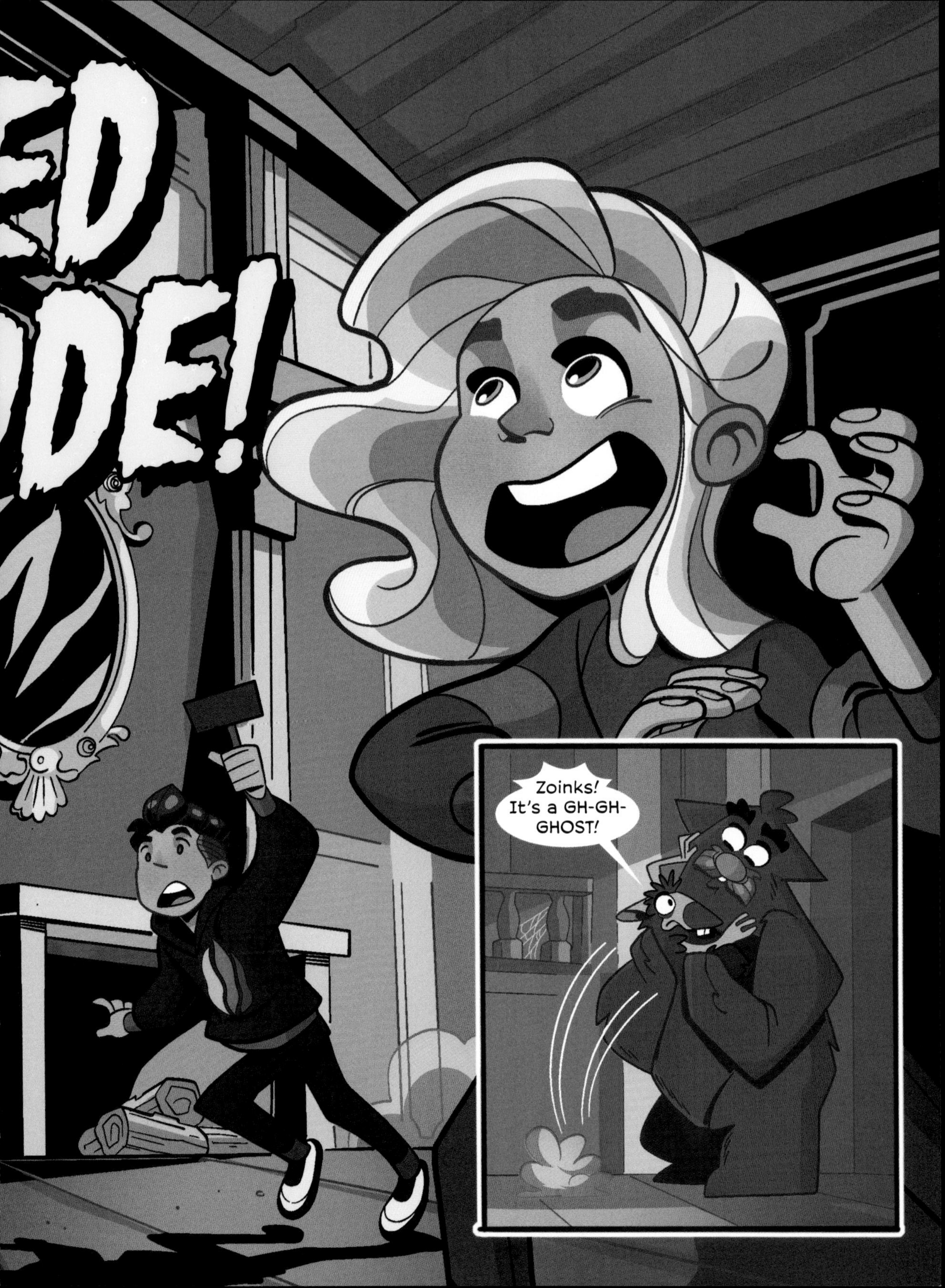
ED
DE!
Zoinks! It's a GH-GH-GHOST!

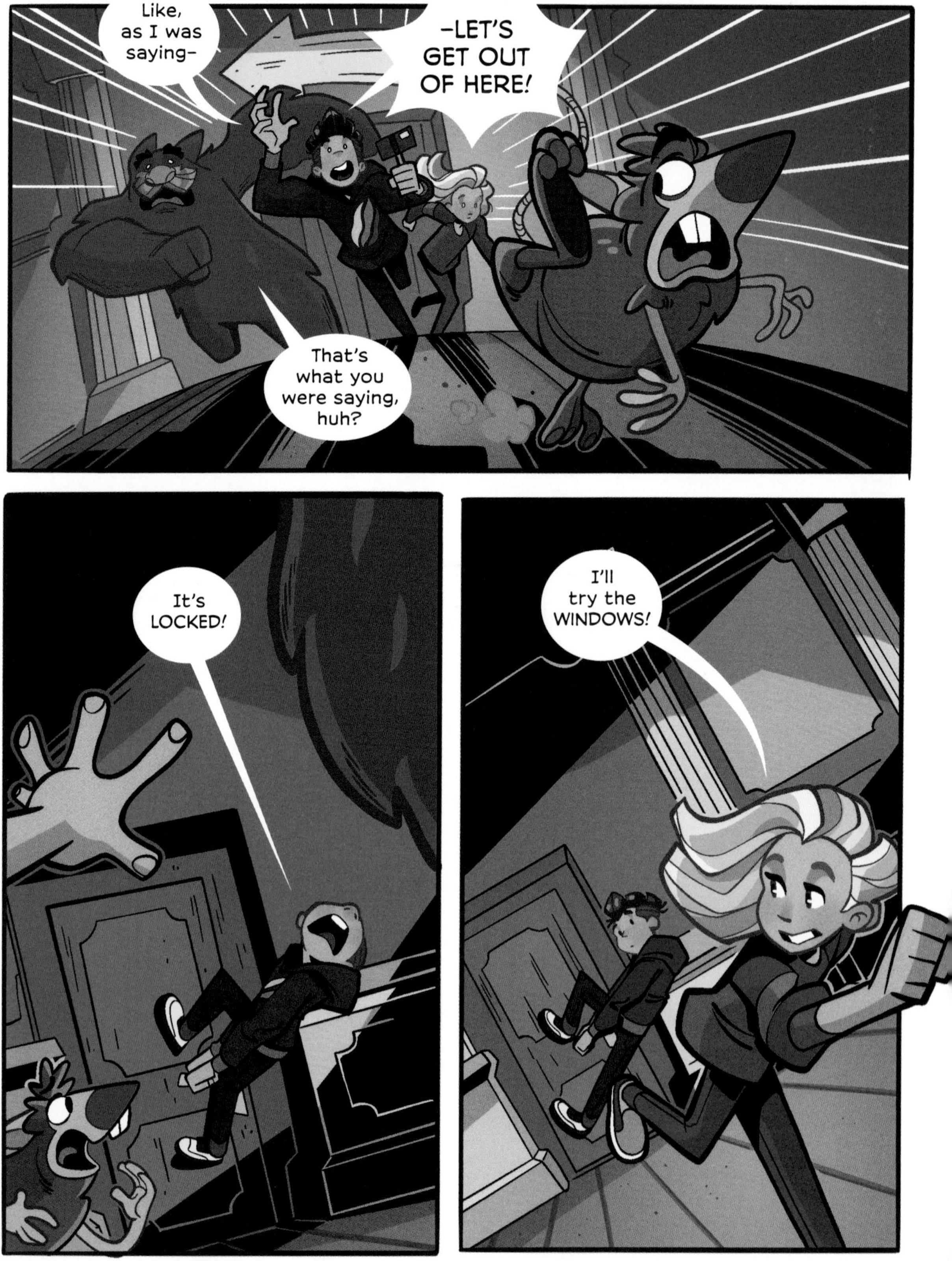
Like, as I was saying-
-LET'S GET OUT OF HERE!
That's what you were saying, huh?
It's LOCKED!
I'll try the WINDOWS!

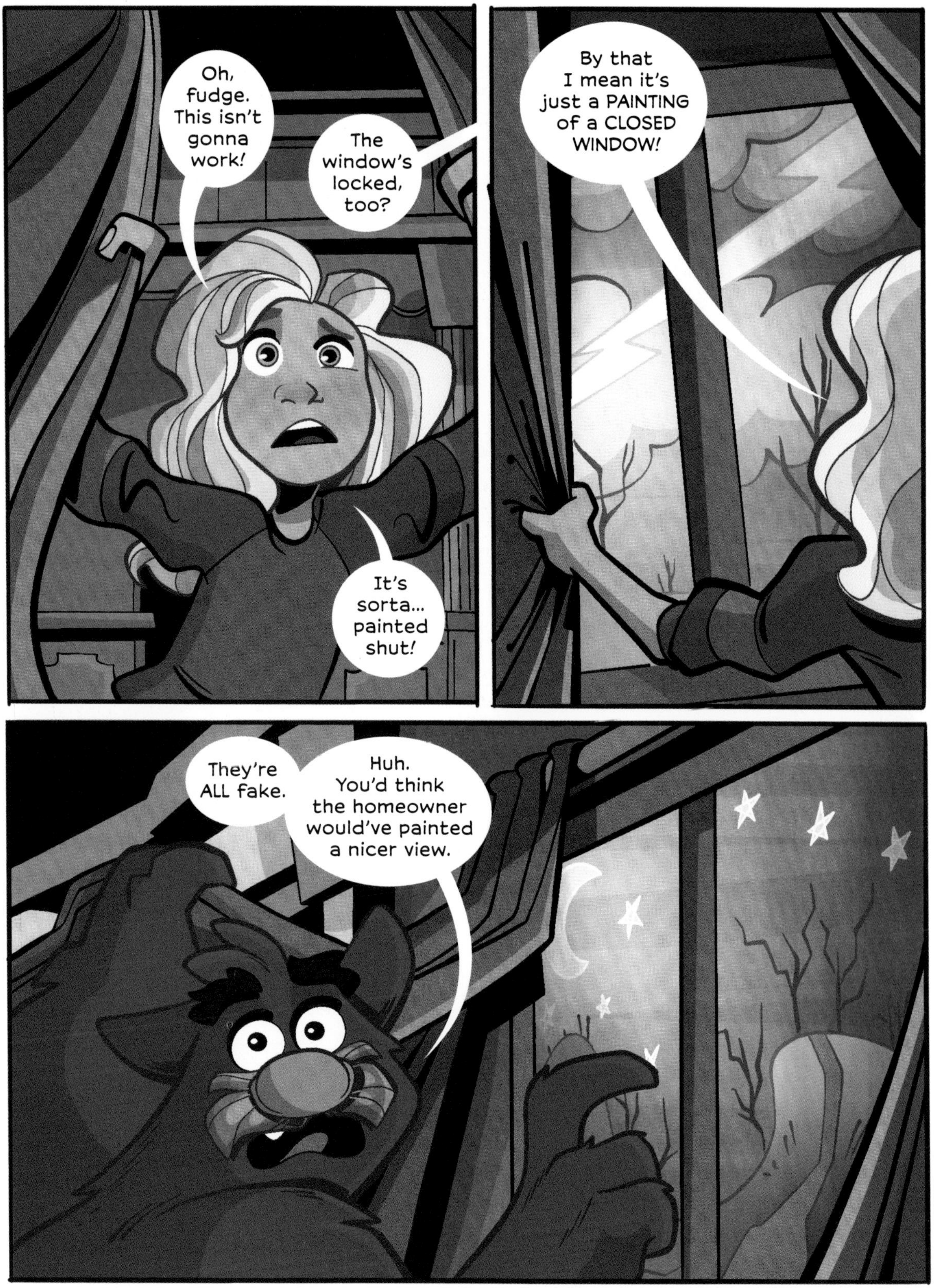
Oh, fudge. This isn't gonna work!
The window's locked, too?
It's sorta... painted shut!
By that I mean it's just a PAINTING of a CLOSED WINDOW!
They're ALL fake.
Huh. You'd think the homeowner would've painted a nicer view.

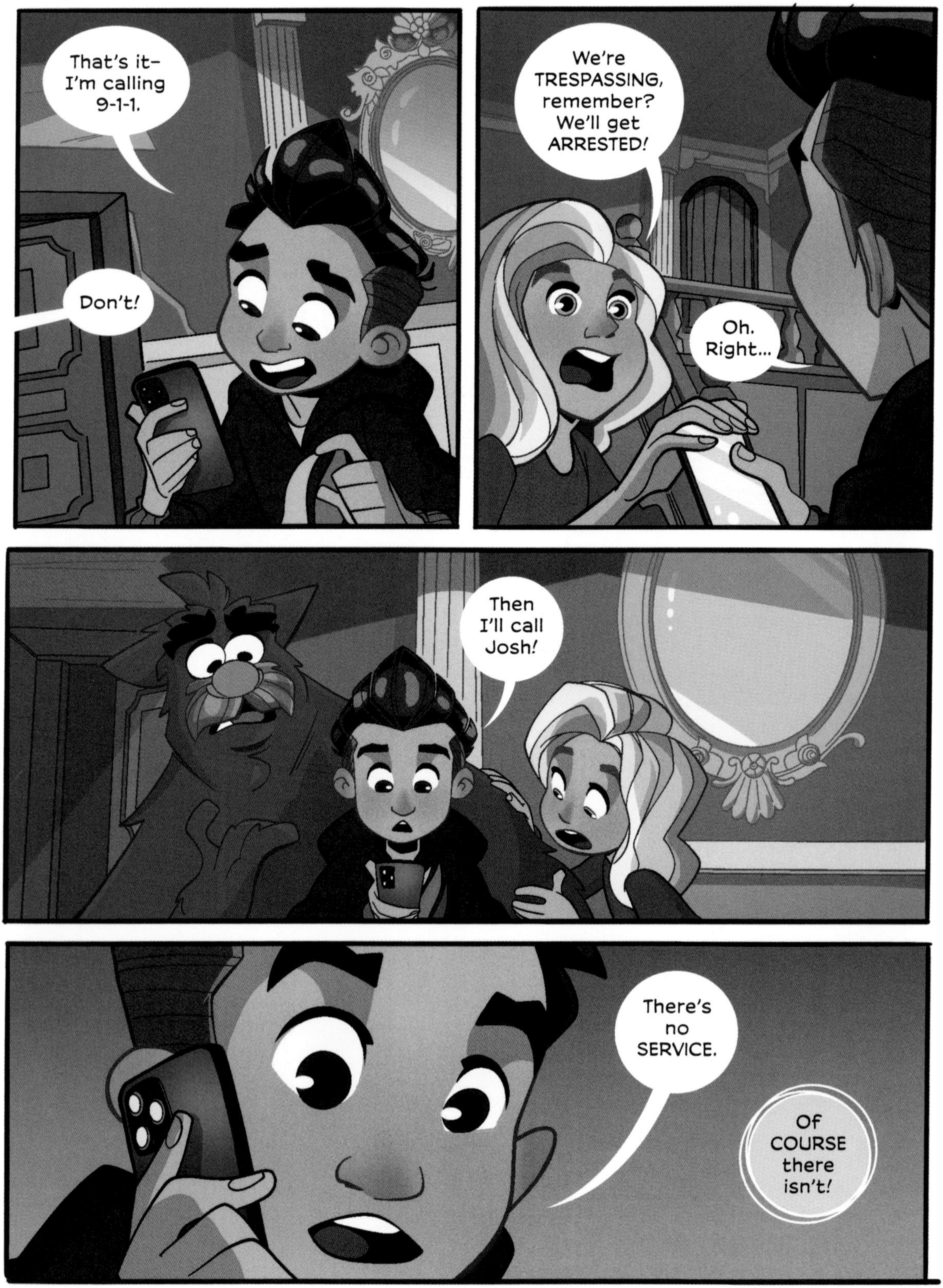
That's it–
I'm calling
9-1-1.
Don't!
We're
TRESPASSING,
remember?
We'll get
ARRESTED!
Oh.
Right...
Then
I'll call
Josh!
There's
no
SERVICE.
Of
COURSE
there
isn't!

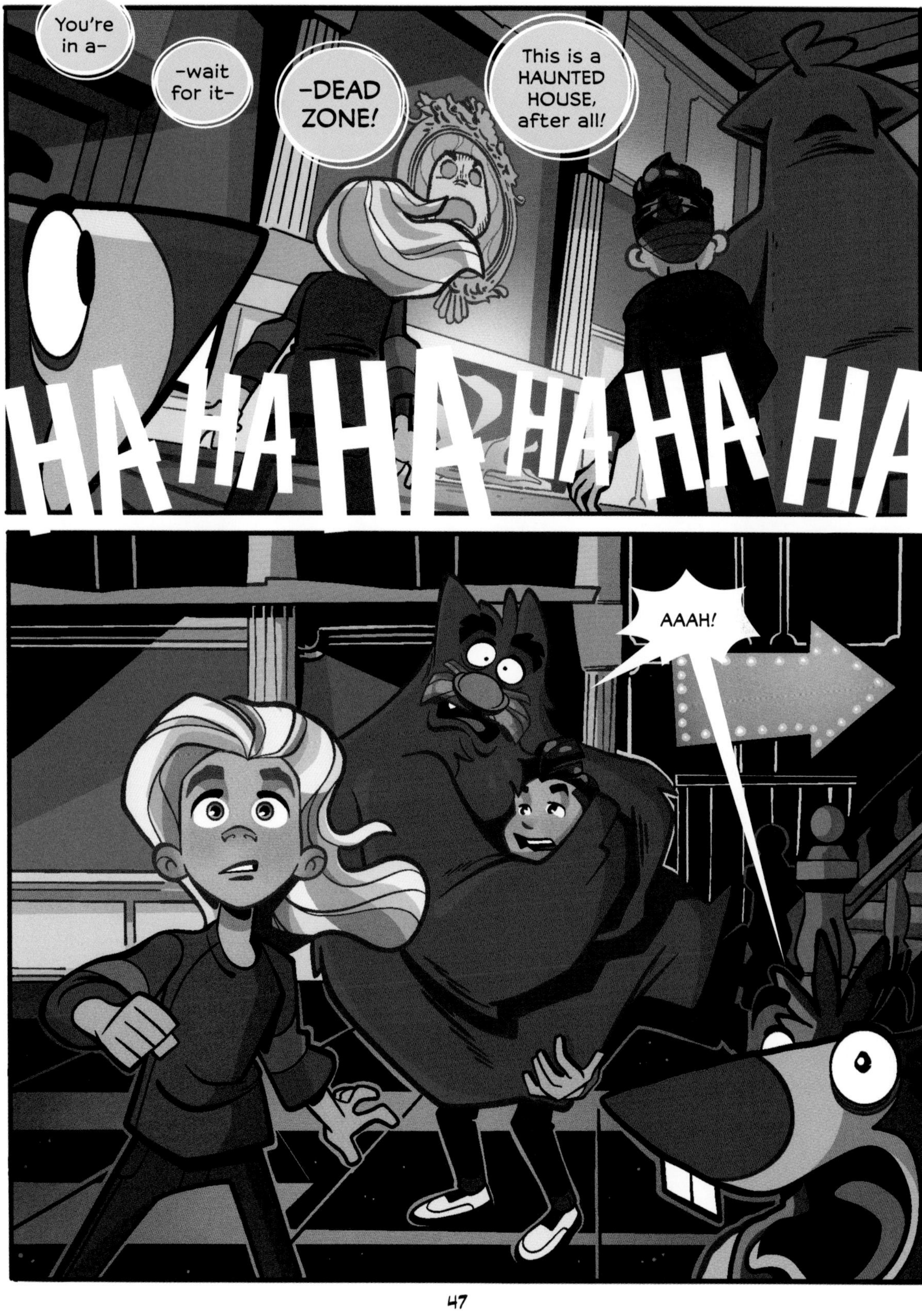
You're in a-
-wait for it-
-DEAD ZONE!
This is a HAUNTED HOUSE, after all!
HA HA HA HA HA HA HA HA
AAAH!

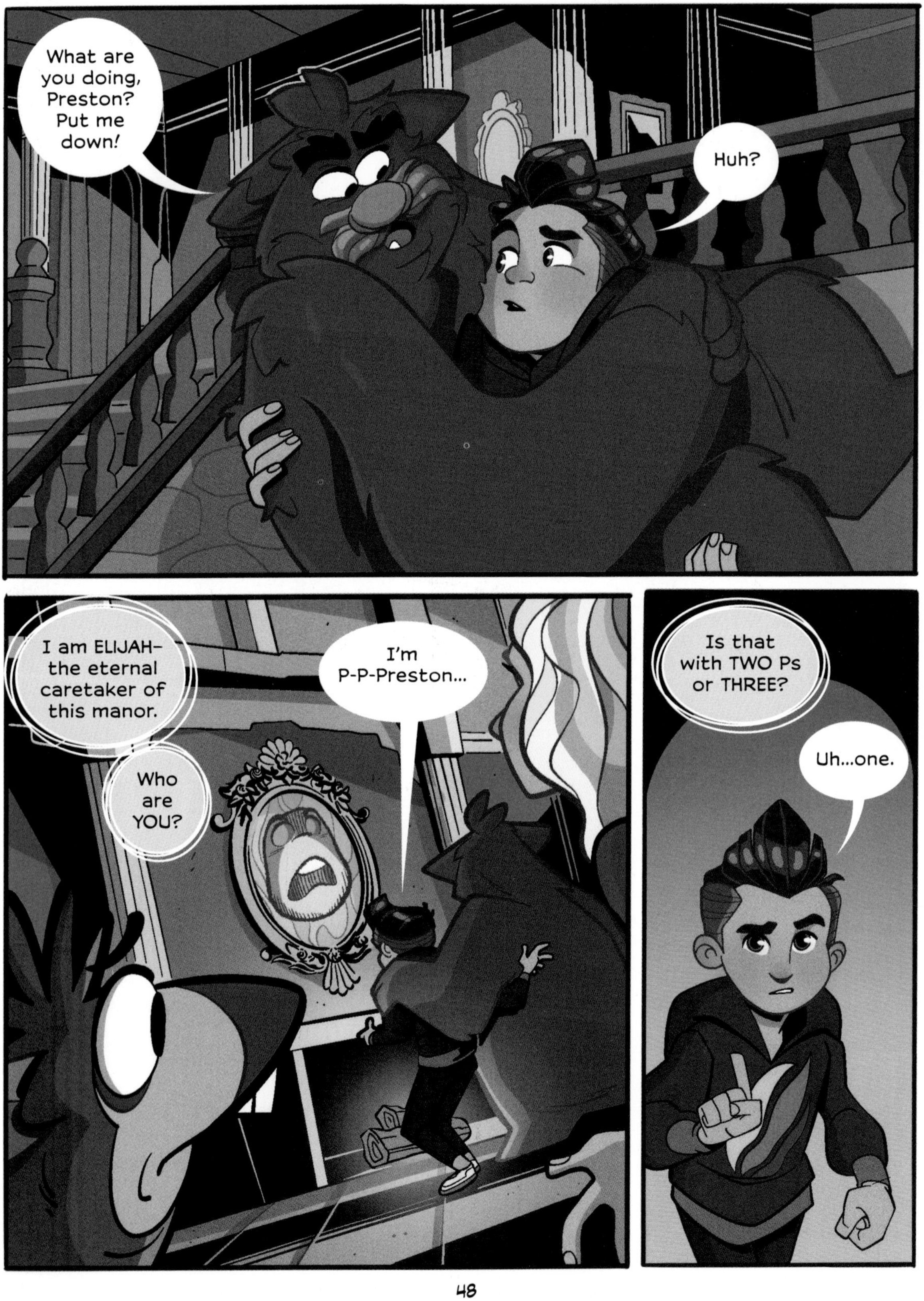
What are you doing, Preston? Put me down!
Huh?
I am ELIJAH–the eternal caretaker of this manor.
Who are YOU?
I'm P-P-Preston...
Is that with TWO Ps or THREE?
Uh...one.

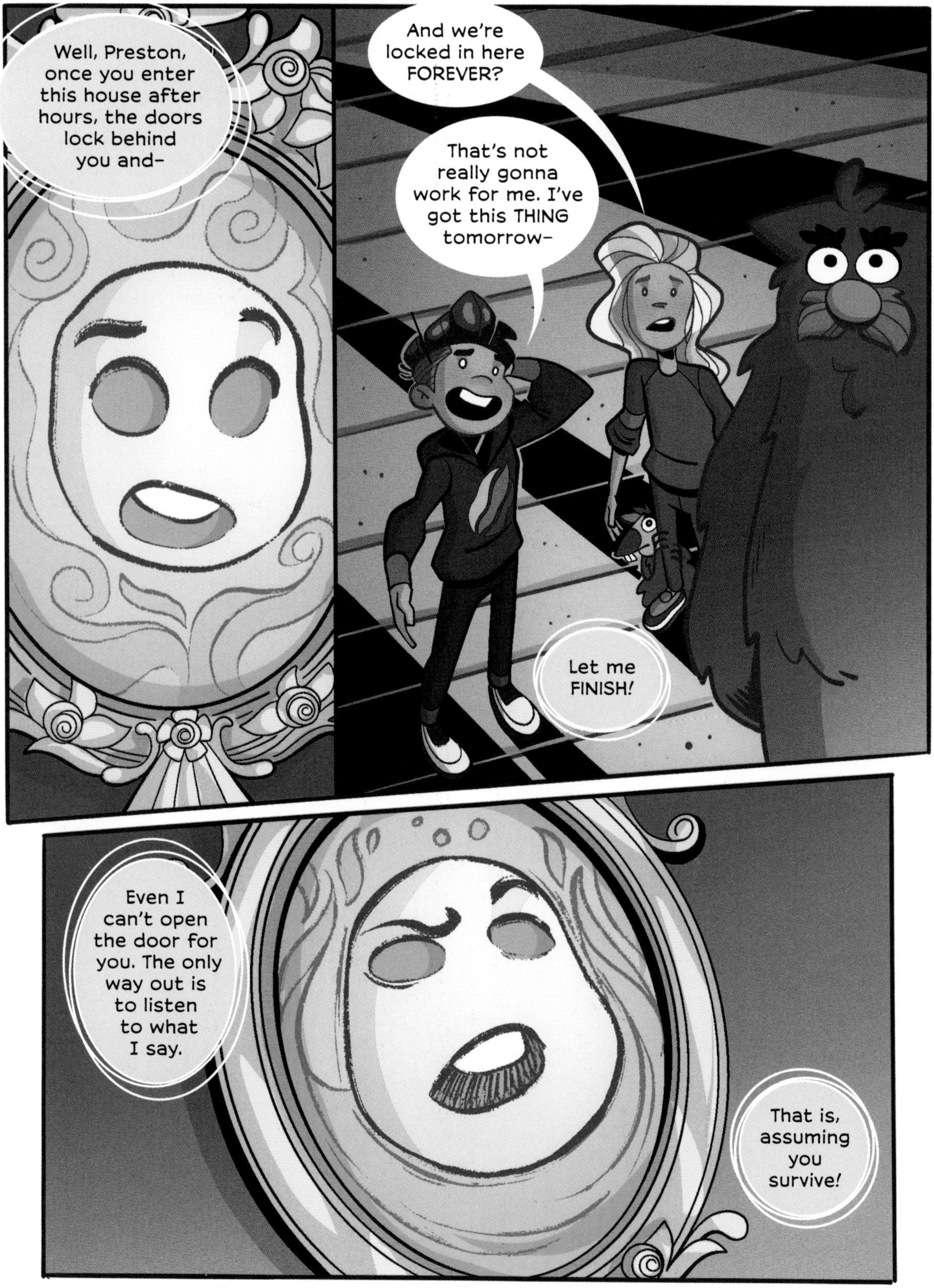
Well, Preston, once you enter this house after hours, the doors lock behind you and–
And we're locked in here FOREVER?
That's not really gonna work for me. I've got this THING tomorrow–
Let me FINISH!
Even I can't open the door for you. The only way out is to listen to what I say.
That is, assuming you survive!

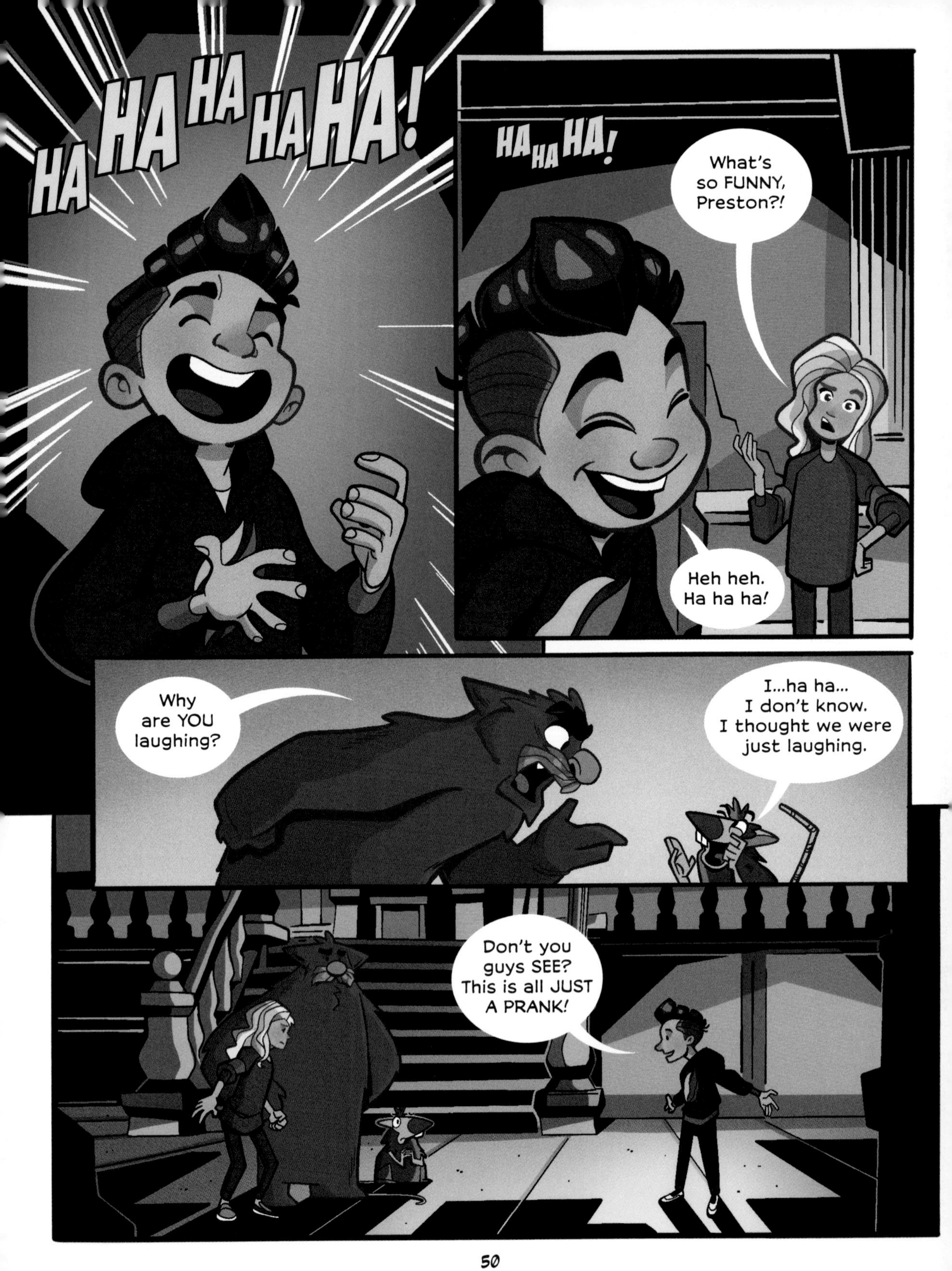
HA HA HA HA HA!
HA HA HA!
What's so FUNNY, Preston?!
Heh heh. Ha ha ha!
Why are YOU laughing?
I...ha ha... I don't know. I thought we were just laughing.
Don't you guys SEE? This is all JUST A PRANK!

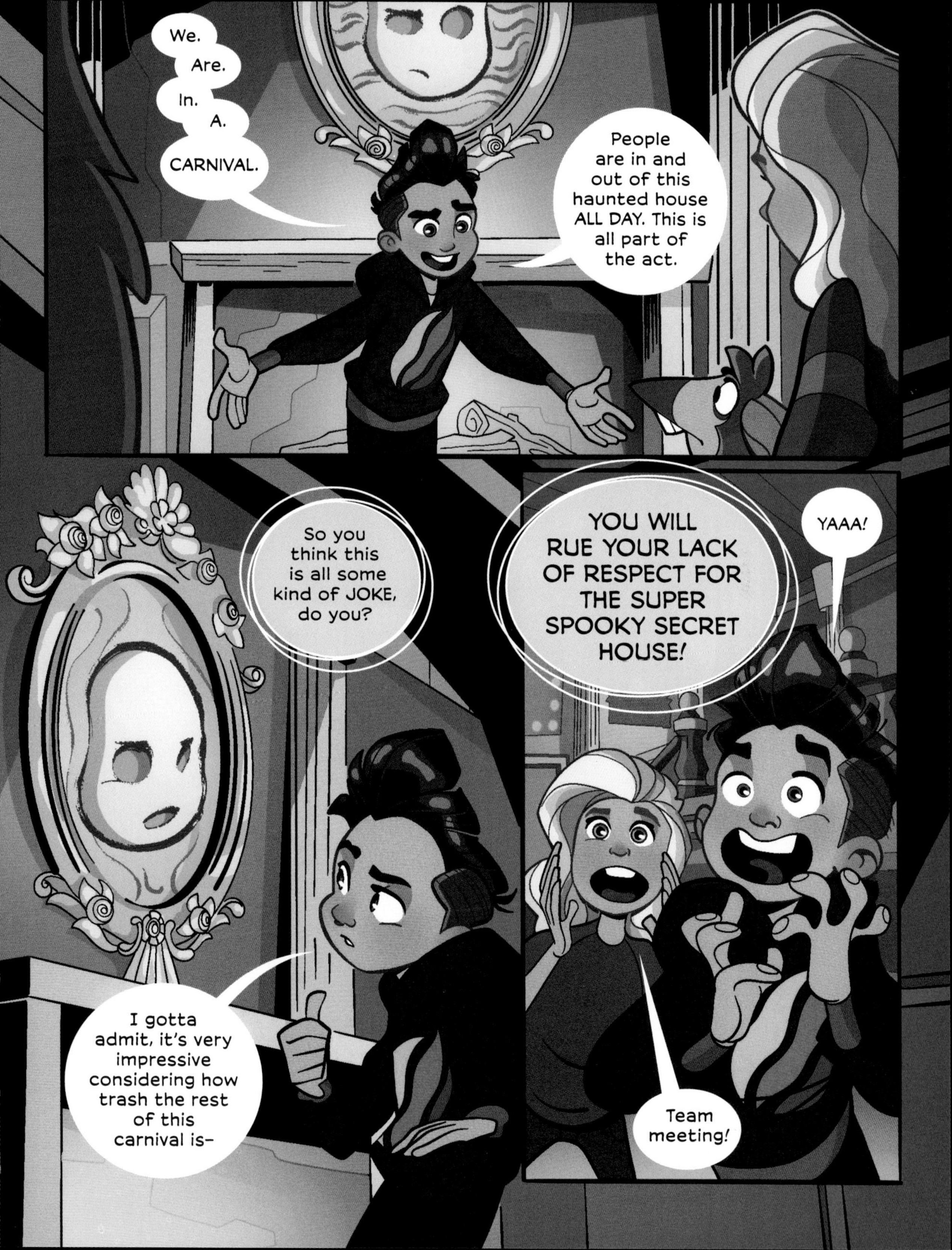
We.
Are.
In.
A.
CARNIVAL.
People are in and out of this haunted house ALL DAY. This is all part of the act.
So you think this is all some kind of JOKE, do you?
I gotta admit, it's very impressive considering how trash the rest of this carnival is–
YOU WILL RUE YOUR LACK OF RESPECT FOR THE SUPER SPOOKY SECRET HOUSE!
YAAA!
Team meeting!

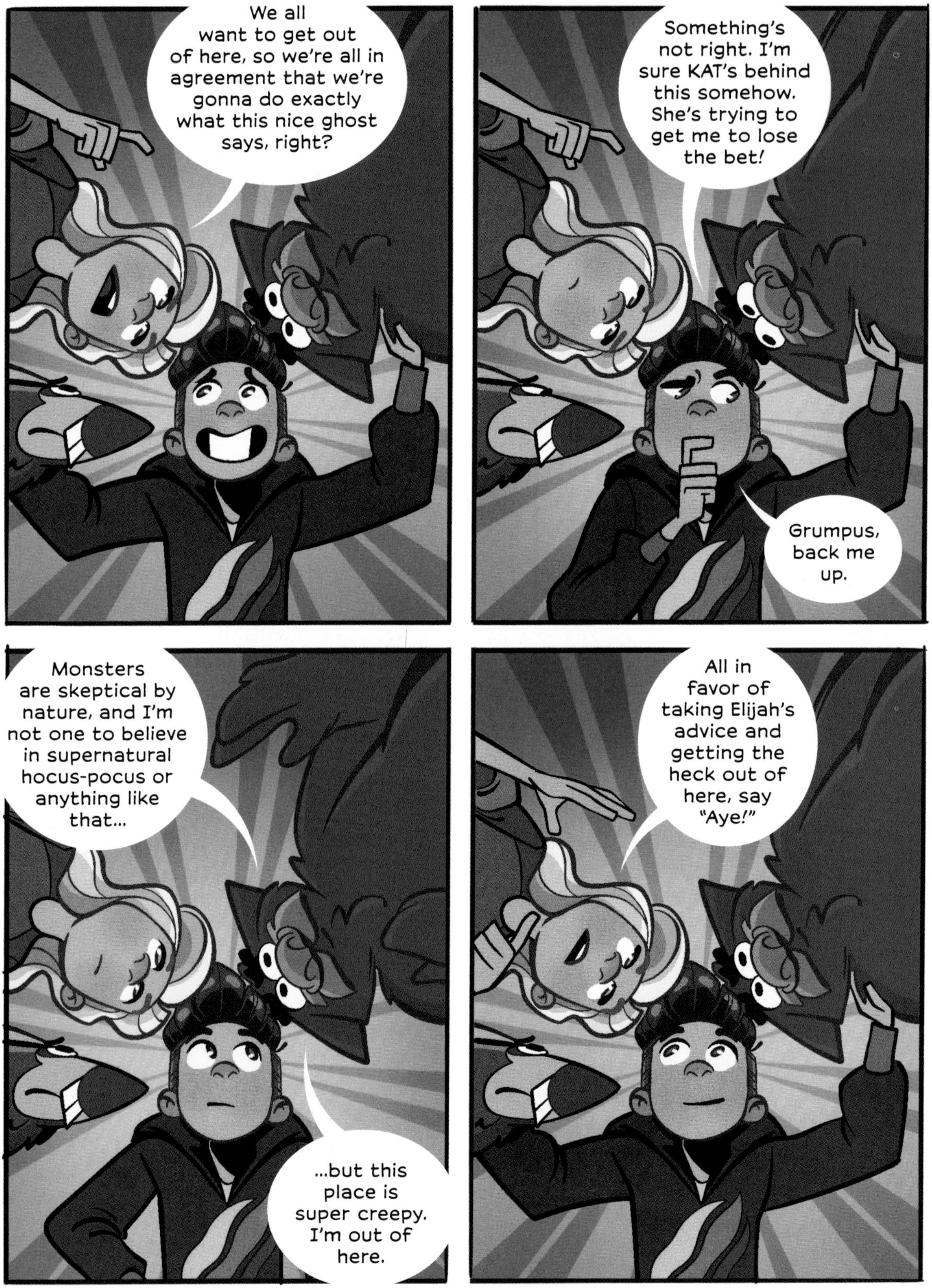
We all want to get out of here, so we're all in agreement that we're gonna do exactly what this nice ghost says, right?
Something's not right. I'm sure KAT's behind this somehow. She's trying to get me to lose the bet!
Grumpus, back me up.
Monsters are skeptical by nature, and I'm not one to believe in supernatural hocus-pocus or anything like that...
...but this place is super creepy. I'm out of here.
All in favor of taking Elijah's advice and getting the heck out of here, say "Aye!"

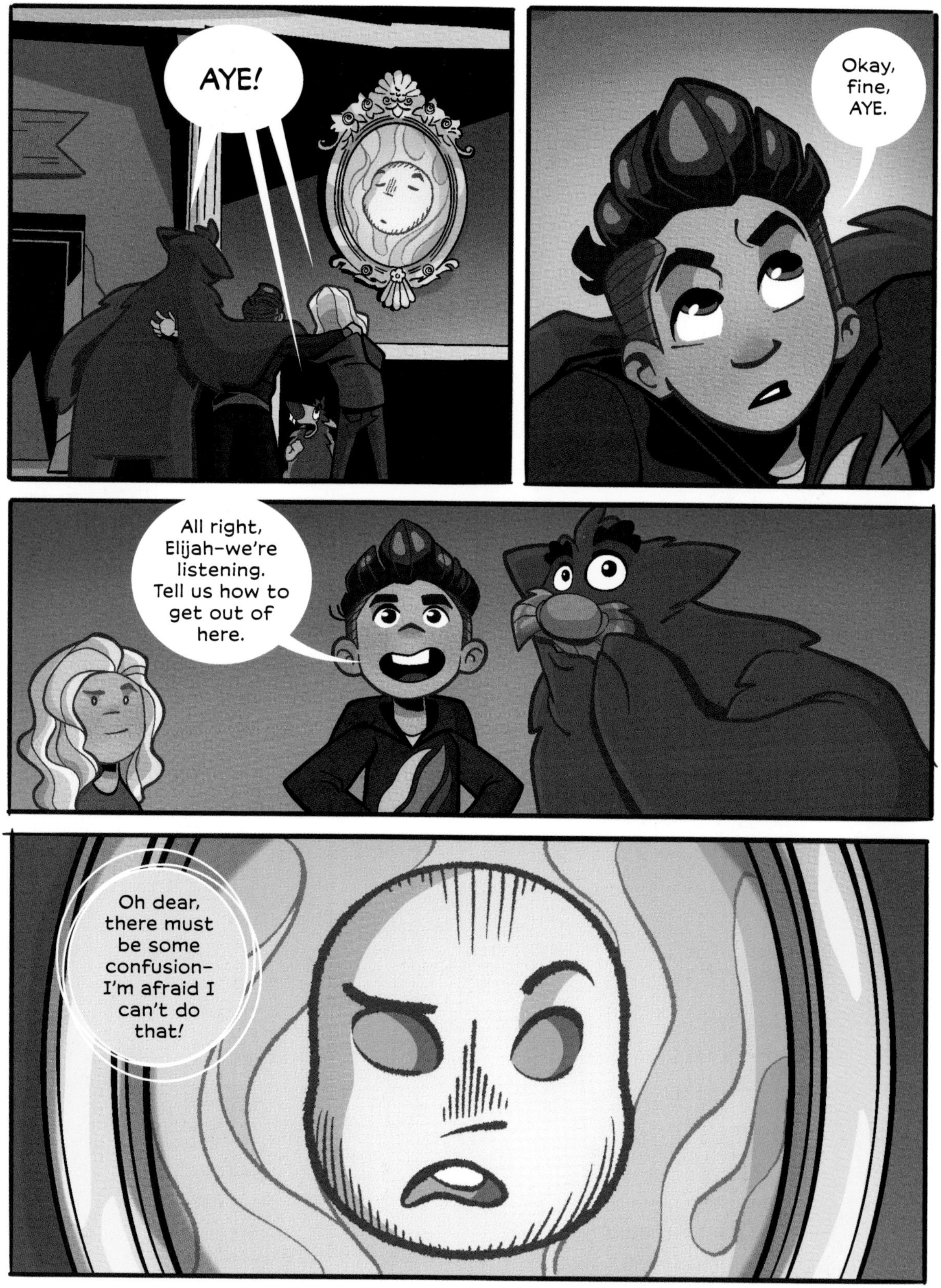

AYE!
Okay, fine, AYE.
All right, Elijah–we're listening. Tell us how to get out of here.
Oh dear, there must be some confusion– I'm afraid I can't do that!

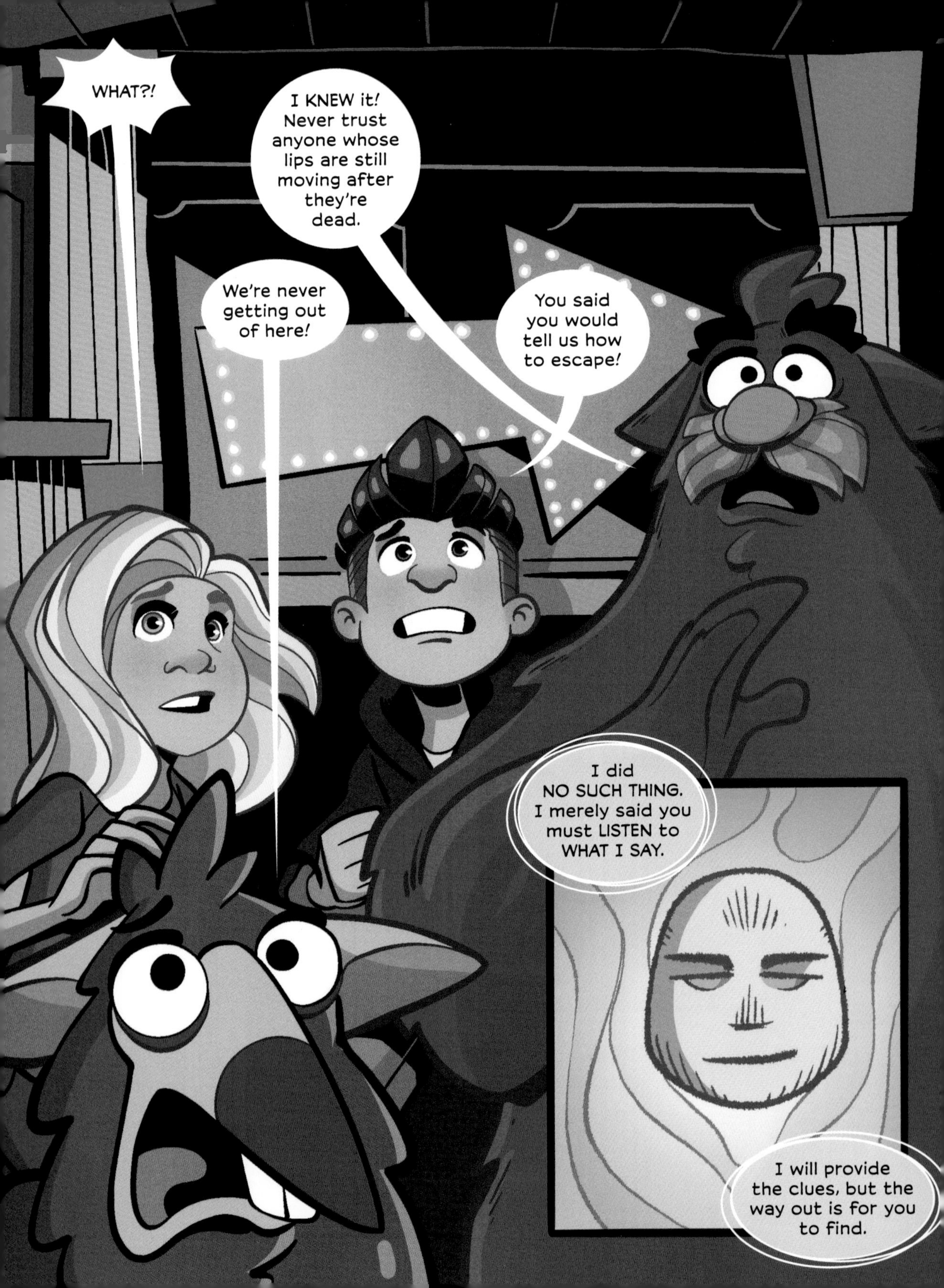
WHAT?!
I KNEW it! Never trust anyone whose lips are still moving after they're dead.
We're never getting out of here!
You said you would tell us how to escape!
I did NO SUCH THING. I merely said you must LISTEN to WHAT I SAY.
I will provide the clues, but the way out is for you to find.

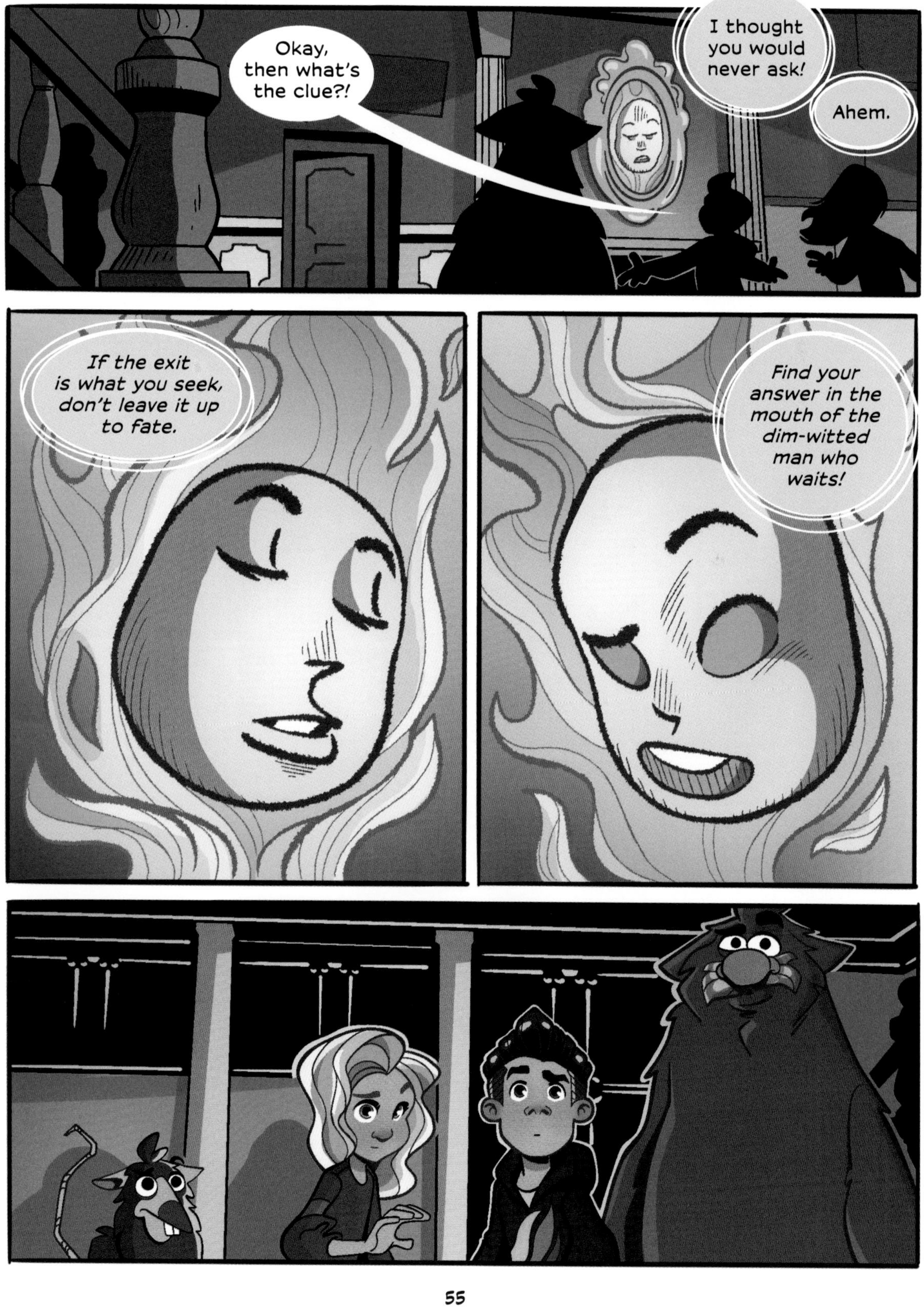
Okay, then what's the clue?!
I thought you would never ask!
Ahem.
If the exit is what you seek, don't leave it up to fate.
Find your answer in the mouth of the dim-witted man who waits!

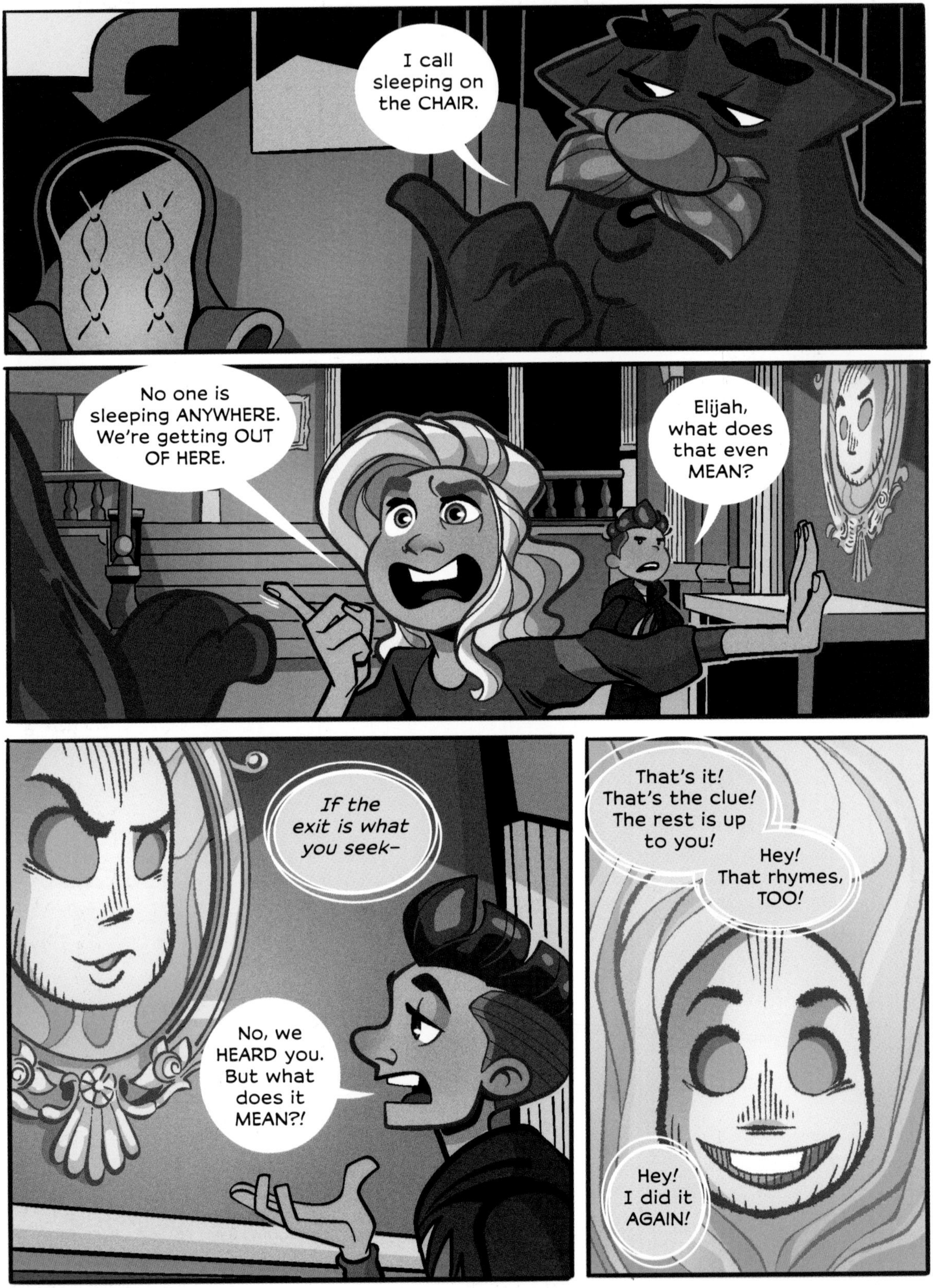

I call sleeping on the CHAIR.
No one is sleeping ANYWHERE. We're getting OUT OF HERE.
Elijah, what does that even MEAN?
If the exit is what you seek–
No, we HEARD you. But what does it MEAN?!
That's it! That's the clue! The rest is up to you!
Hey! That rhymes, TOO!
Hey! I did it AGAIN!

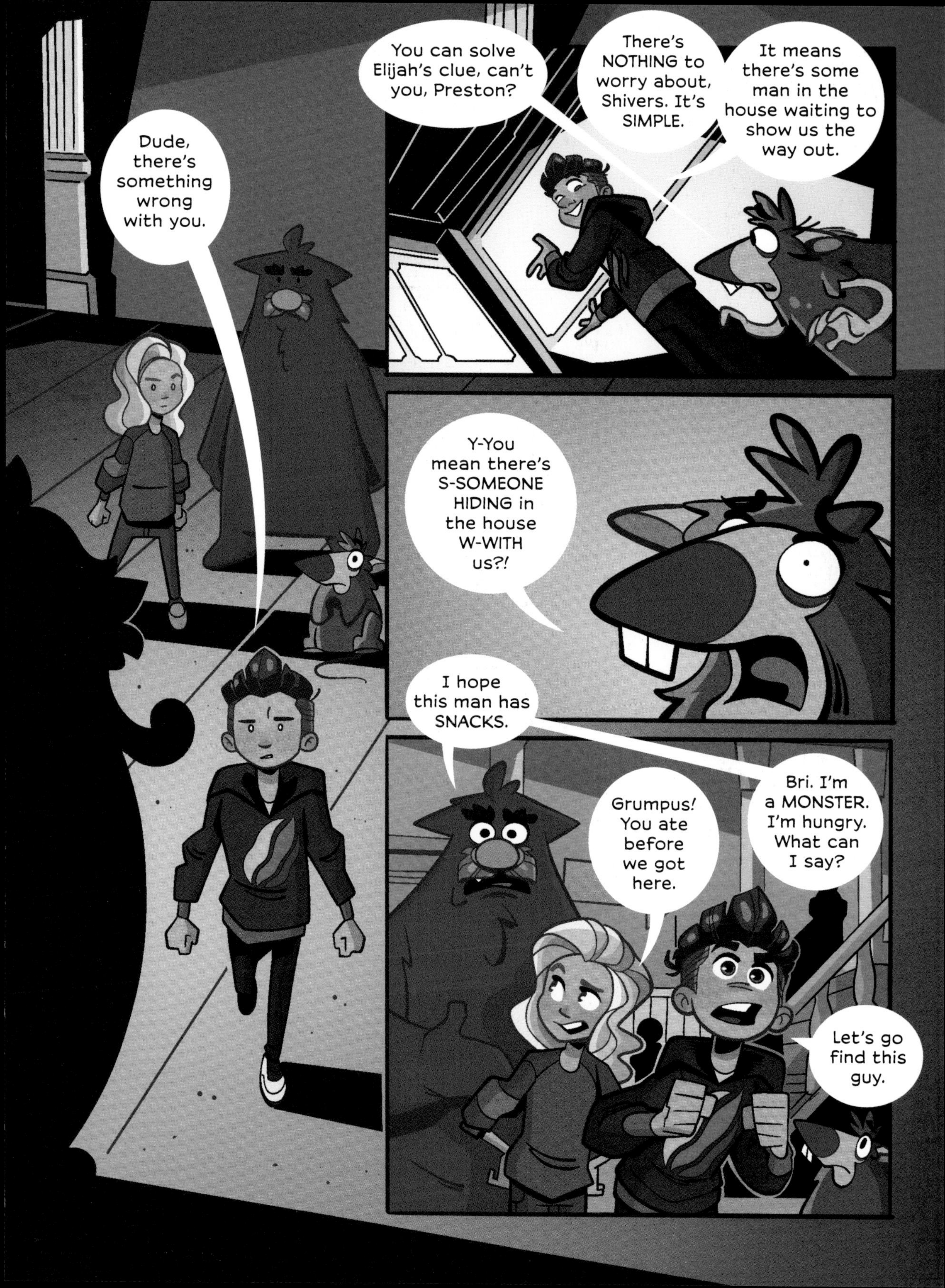
Dude, there's something wrong with you.
You can solve Elijah's clue, can't you, Preston?
There's NOTHING to worry about, Shivers. It's SIMPLE.
It means there's some man in the house waiting to show us the way out.
Y-You mean there's S-SOMEONE HIDING in the house W-WITH us?!
I hope this man has SNACKS.
Grumpus! You ate before we got here.
Bri. I'm a MONSTER. I'm hungry. What can I say?
Let's go find this guy.

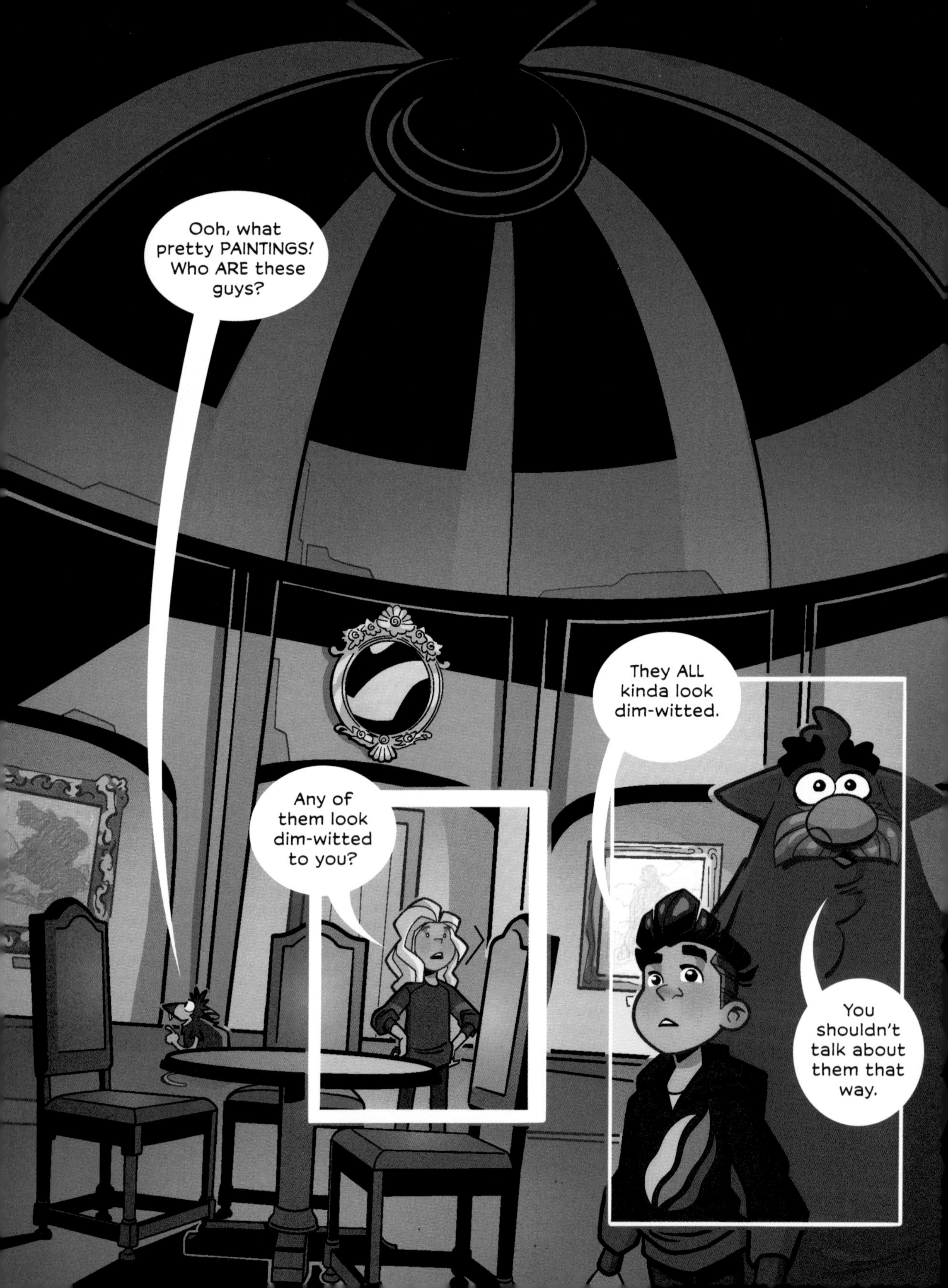
Ooh, what pretty PAINTINGS! Who ARE these guys?
Any of them look dim-witted to you?
They ALL kinda look dim-witted.
You shouldn't talk about them that way.

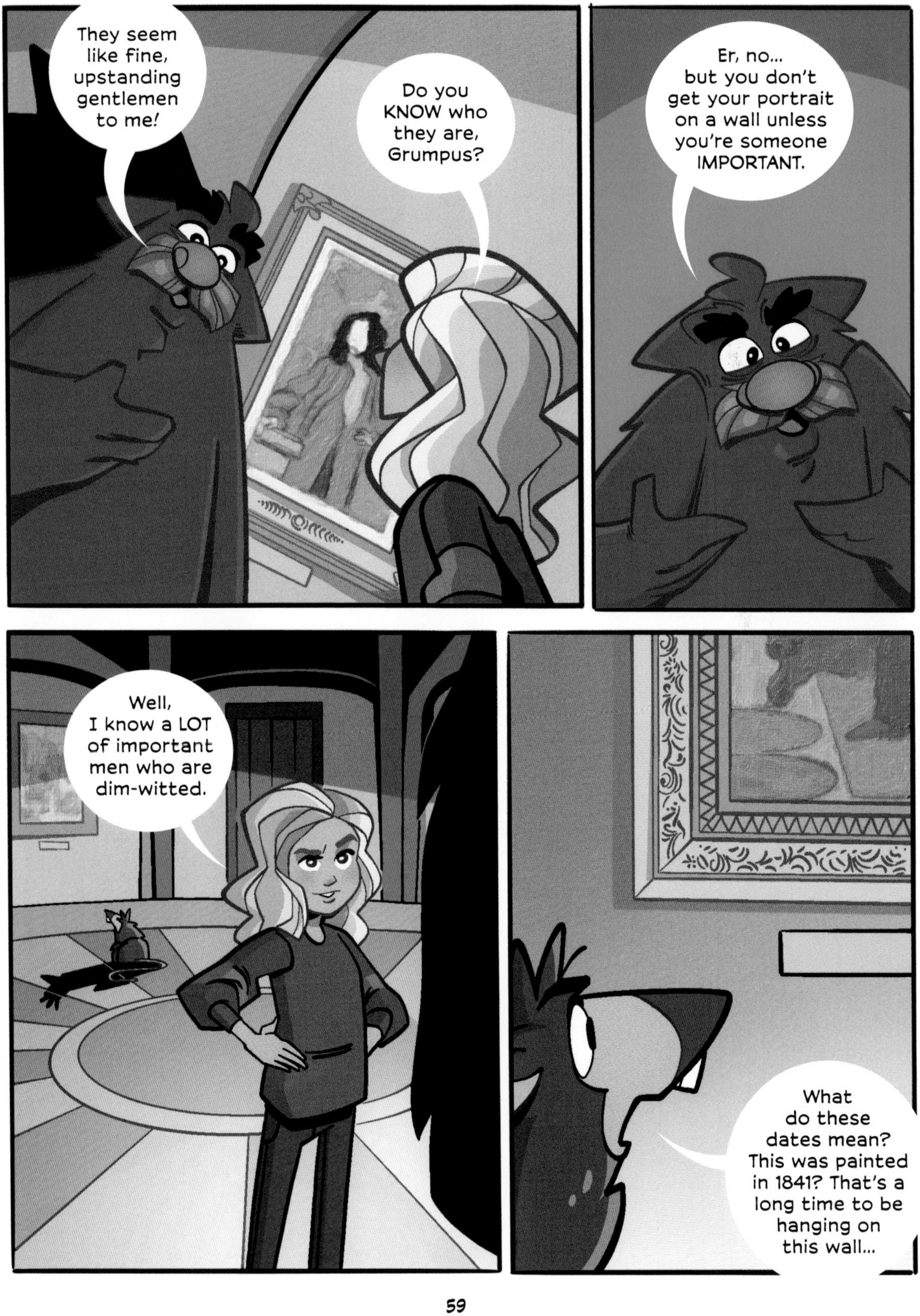
They seem like fine, upstanding gentlemen to me!
Do you KNOW who they are, Grumpus?
Er, no... but you don't get your portrait on a wall unless you're someone IMPORTANT.
Well, I know a LOT of important men who are dim-witted.
What do these dates mean? This was painted in 1841? That's a long time to be hanging on this wall...

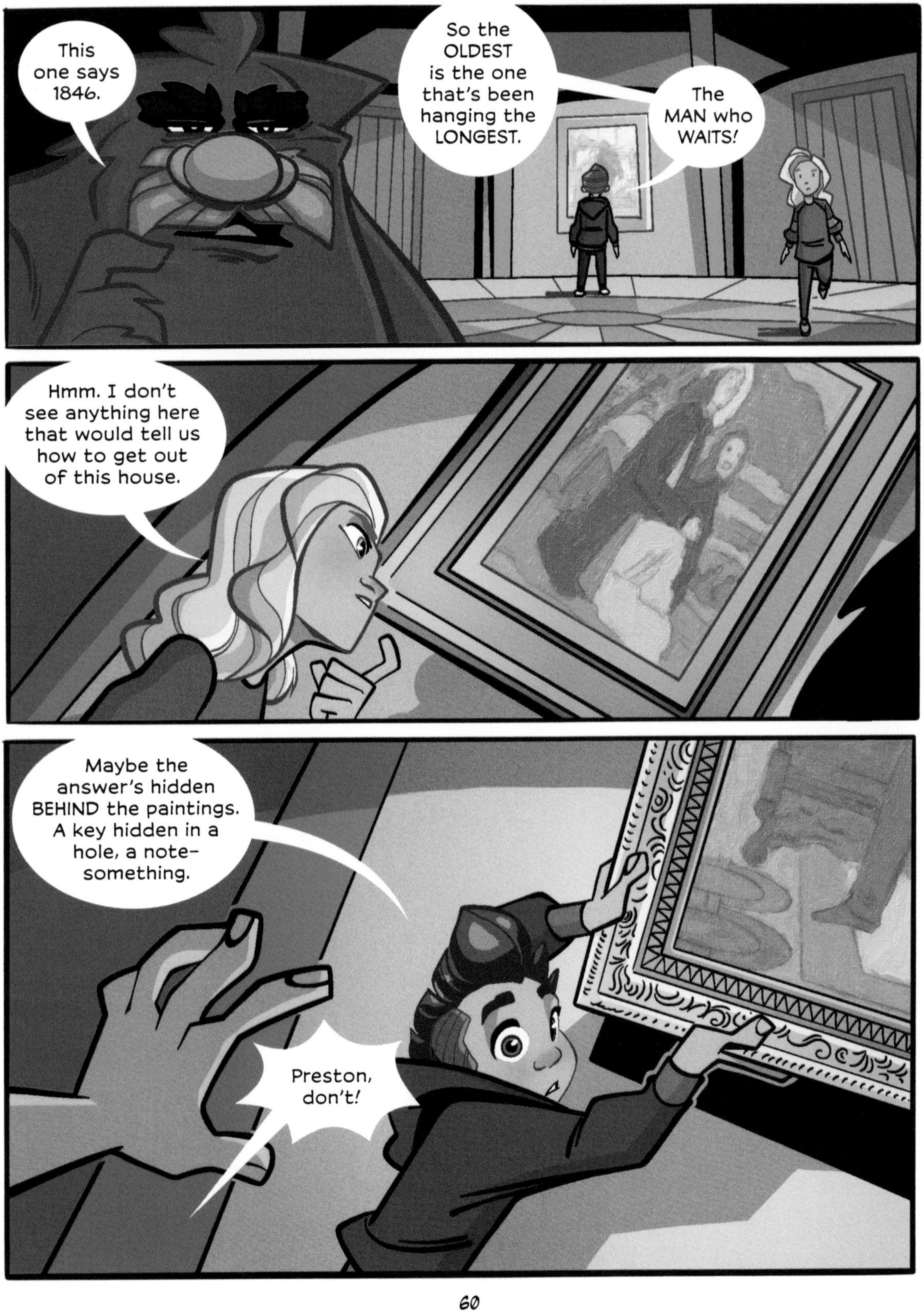
This one says 1846.
So the OLDEST is the one that's been hanging the LONGEST.
The MAN who WAITS!
Hmm. I don't see anything here that would tell us how to get out of this house.
Maybe the answer's hidden BEHIND the paintings. A key hidden in a hole, a note-something.
Preston, don't!

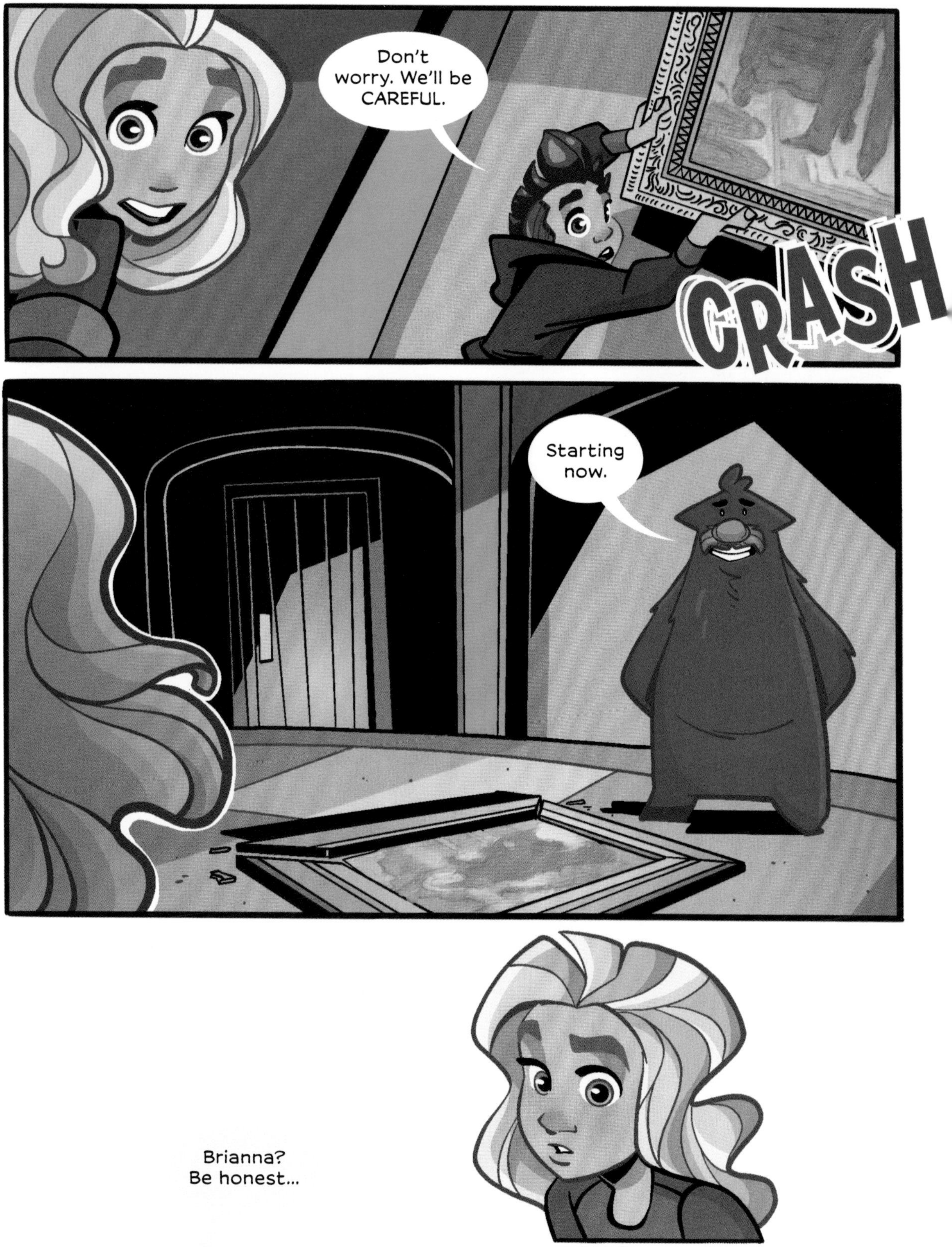
Don't worry. We'll be CAREFUL.
CRASH
Starting now.
Brianna? Be honest...

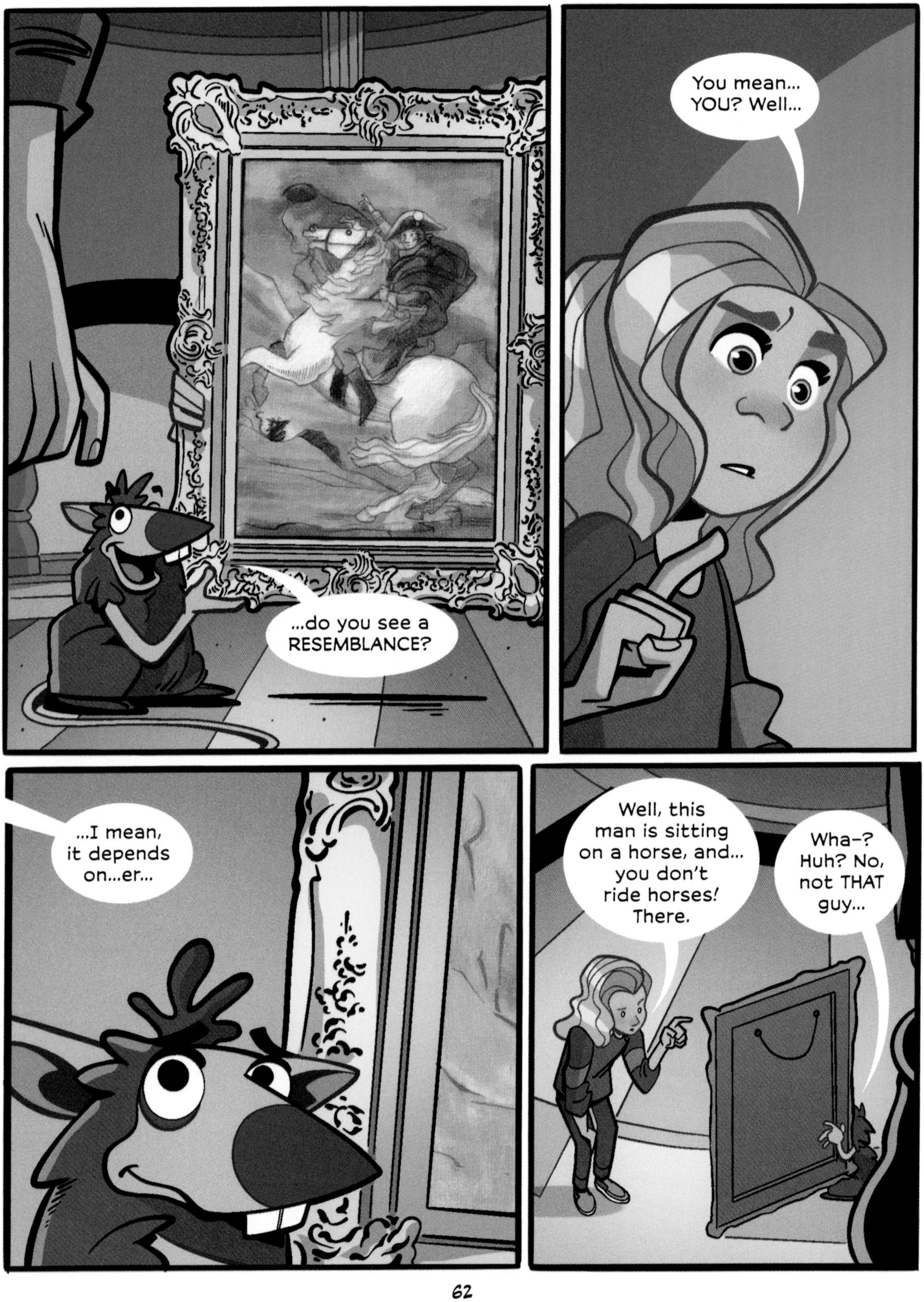
...do you see a RESEMBLANCE?
You mean... YOU? Well...
...I mean, it depends on...er...
Well, this man is sitting on a horse, and... you don't ride horses! There.
Wha-? Huh? No, not THAT guy...

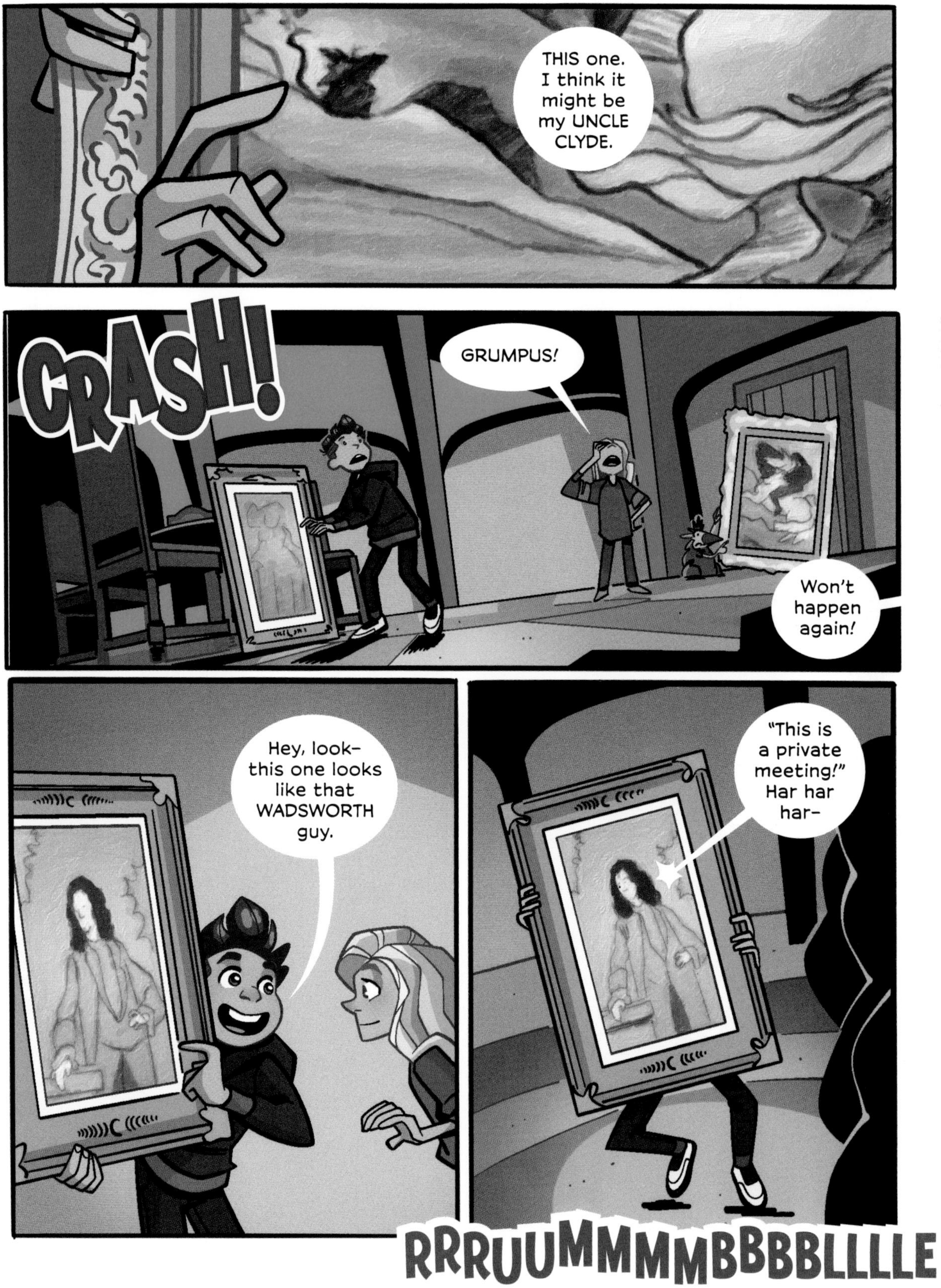
THIS one. I think it might be my UNCLE CLYDE.
CRASH!
GRUMPUS!
Won't happen again!
Hey, look–this one looks like that WADSWORTH guy.
"This is a private meeting!" Har har har–
RRRUUMMMMMBBBBLLLLE

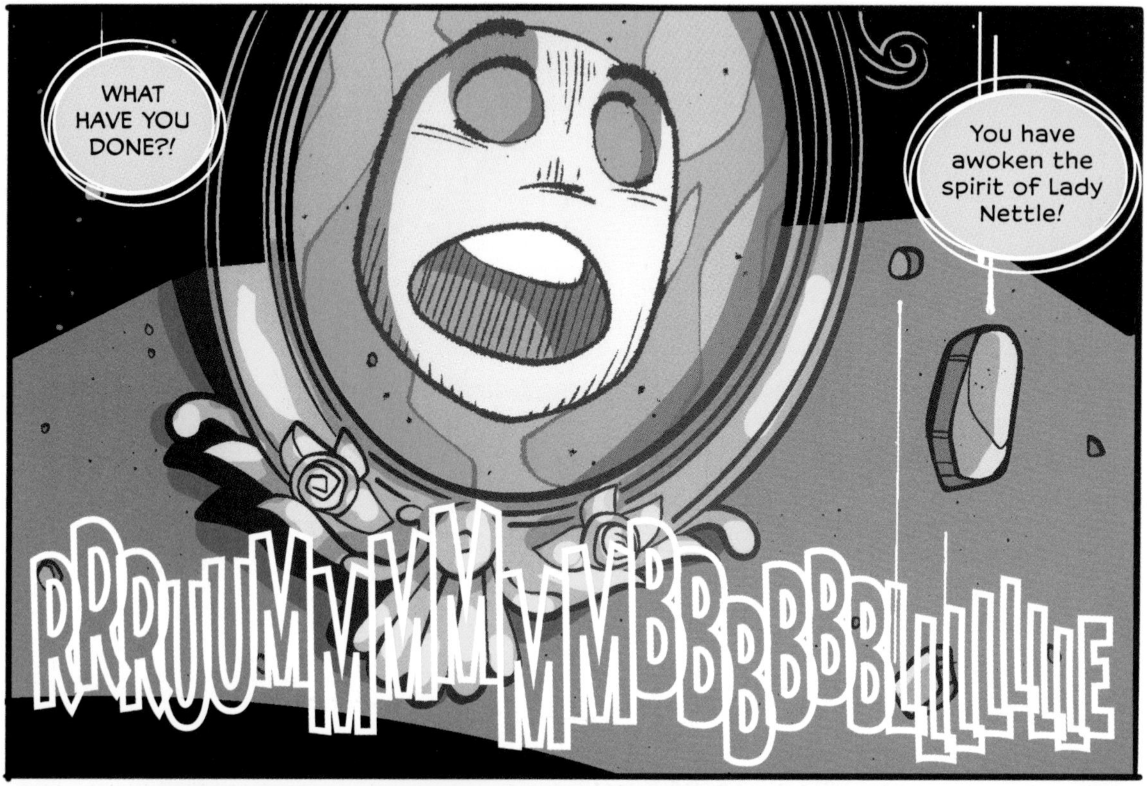
WHAT HAVE YOU DONE?!
You have awoken the spirit of Lady Nettle!
RRRUUMMMMMMMBBBBBLLLLLE

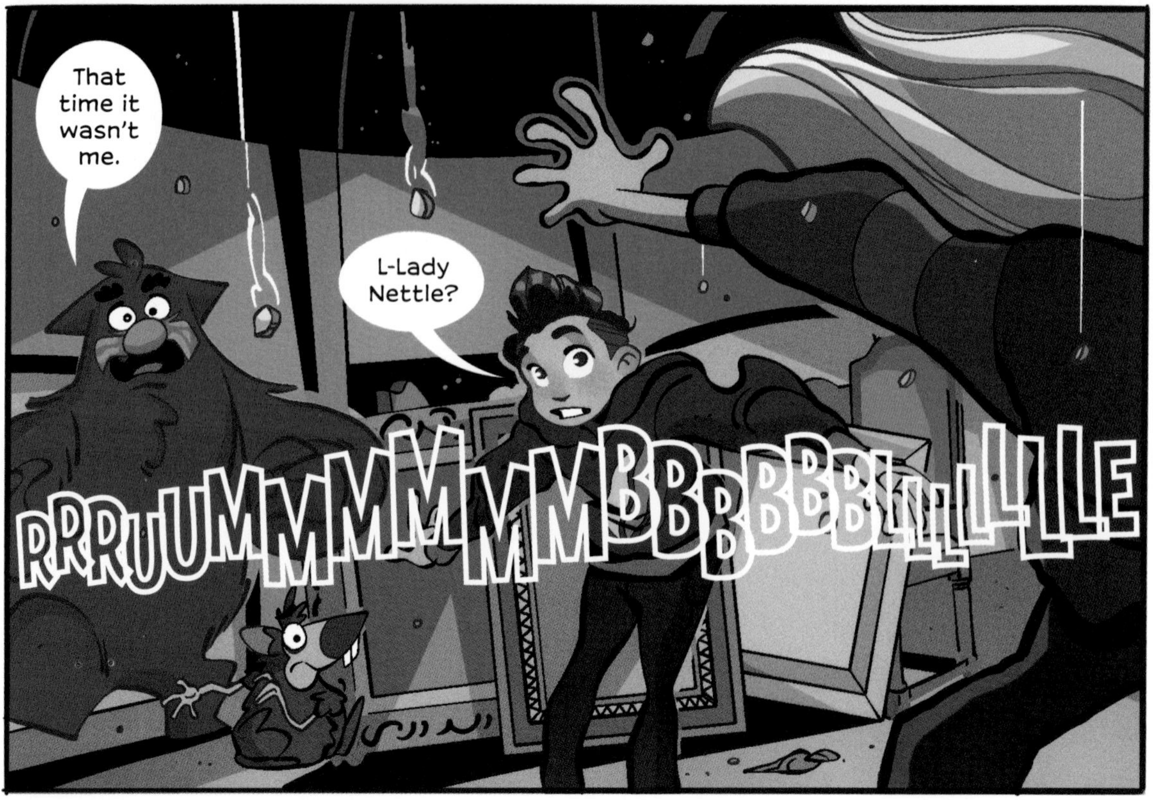
That time it wasn't me.
L-Lady Nettle?
RRRUUMMMMMMMBBBBBLLLLLE

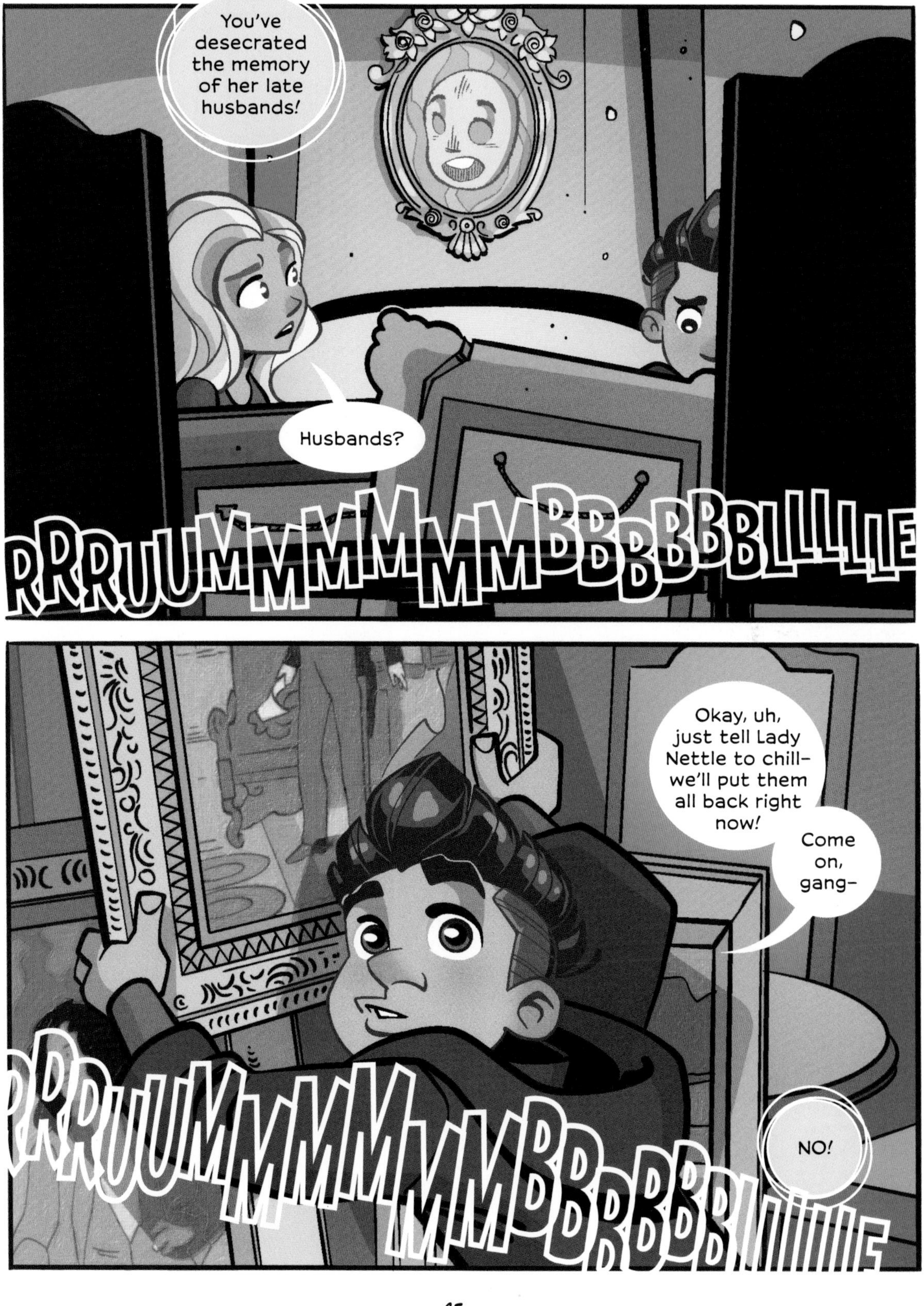

You've desecrated the memory of her late husbands!
Husbands?
RRRUUMMMMMMMMBBBBBBLLLLLIE
Okay, uh, just tell Lady Nettle to chill– we'll put them all back right now!
Come on, gang–
RRRUUMMMMMMMMBBBBBBBLLLLLLE
NO!

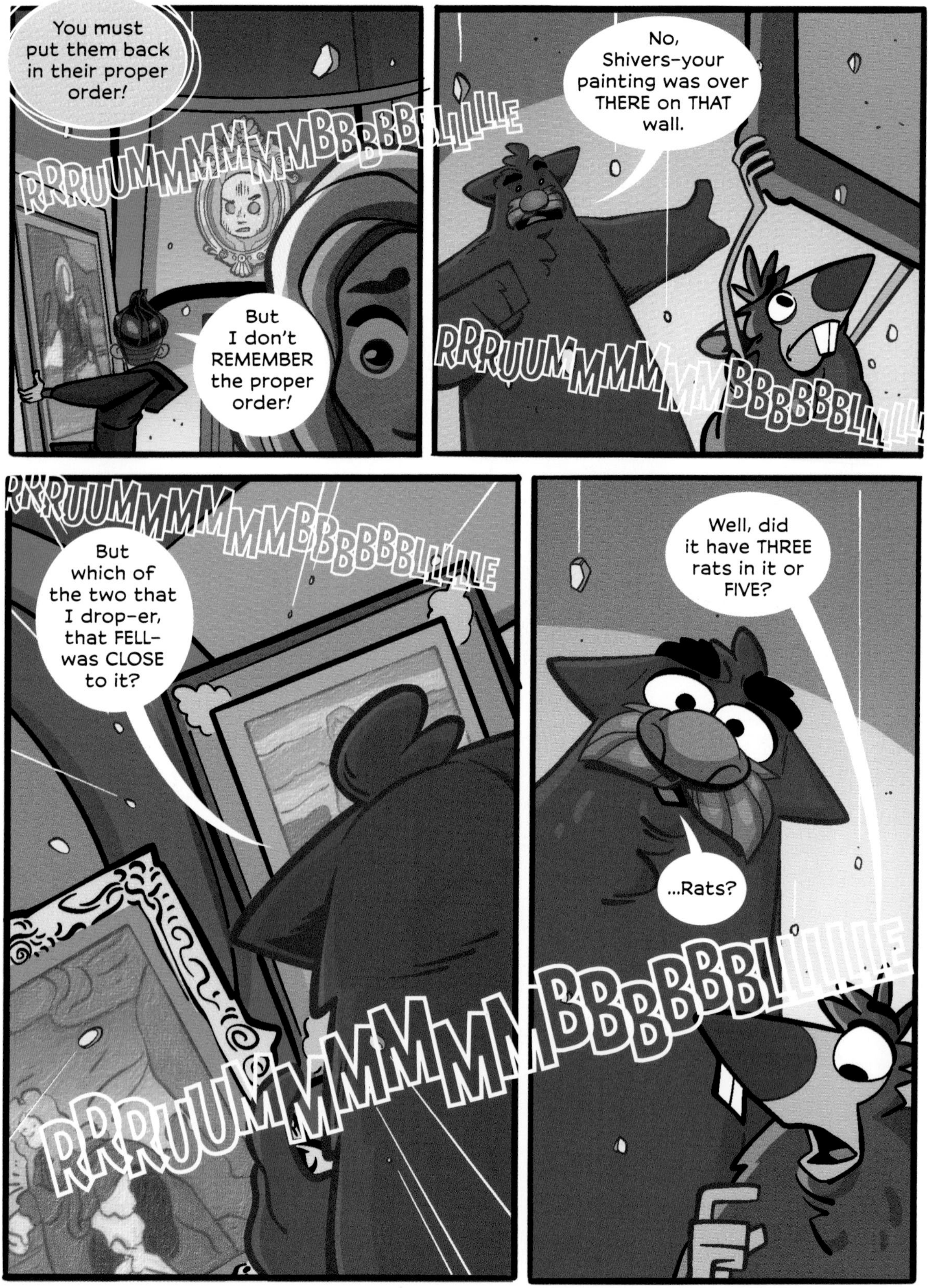
You must put them back in their proper order!
RRRUUMMMMMMMBBBBBLLLLE
But I don't REMEMBER the proper order!
No, Shivers—your painting was over THERE on THAT wall.
RRRUUMMMMMMBBBBBBLLLLL
RRRUUMMMMMMMBBBBBLLLLE
But which of the two that I drop—er, that FELL—was CLOSE to it?
Well, did it have THREE rats in it or FIVE?
...Rats?
RRRUUMMMMMMMBBBBBBBLLLLE

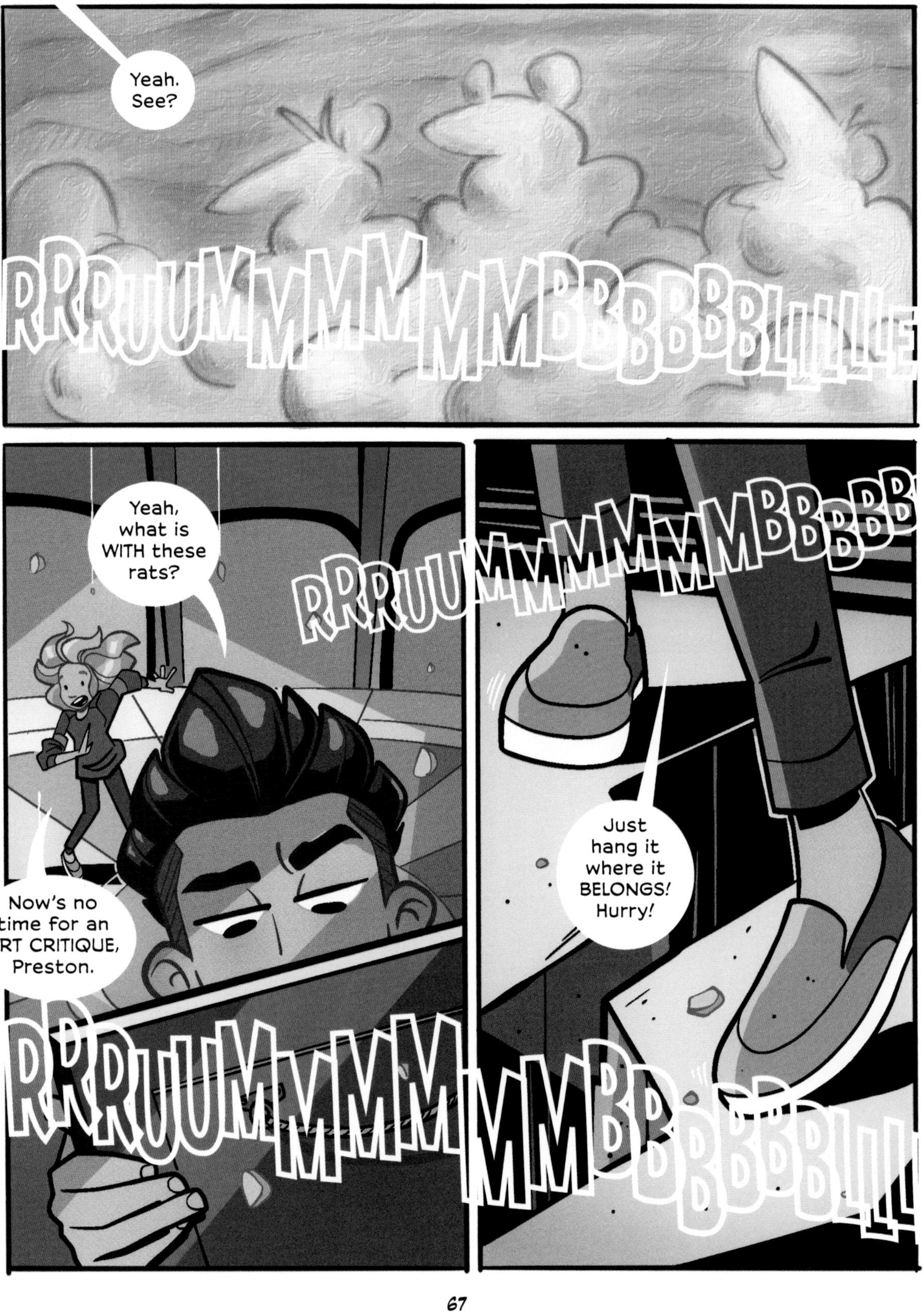

Yeah. See?
RRRUUMMMMMMMBBBBBLLLLLE
Yeah, what is WITH these rats?
Now's no time for an ART CRITIQUE, Preston.
RRRUUMMMMMMMMMBBBBBLLL
RRRUUMMMMMMMMBBBB
Just hang it where it BELONGS! Hurry!

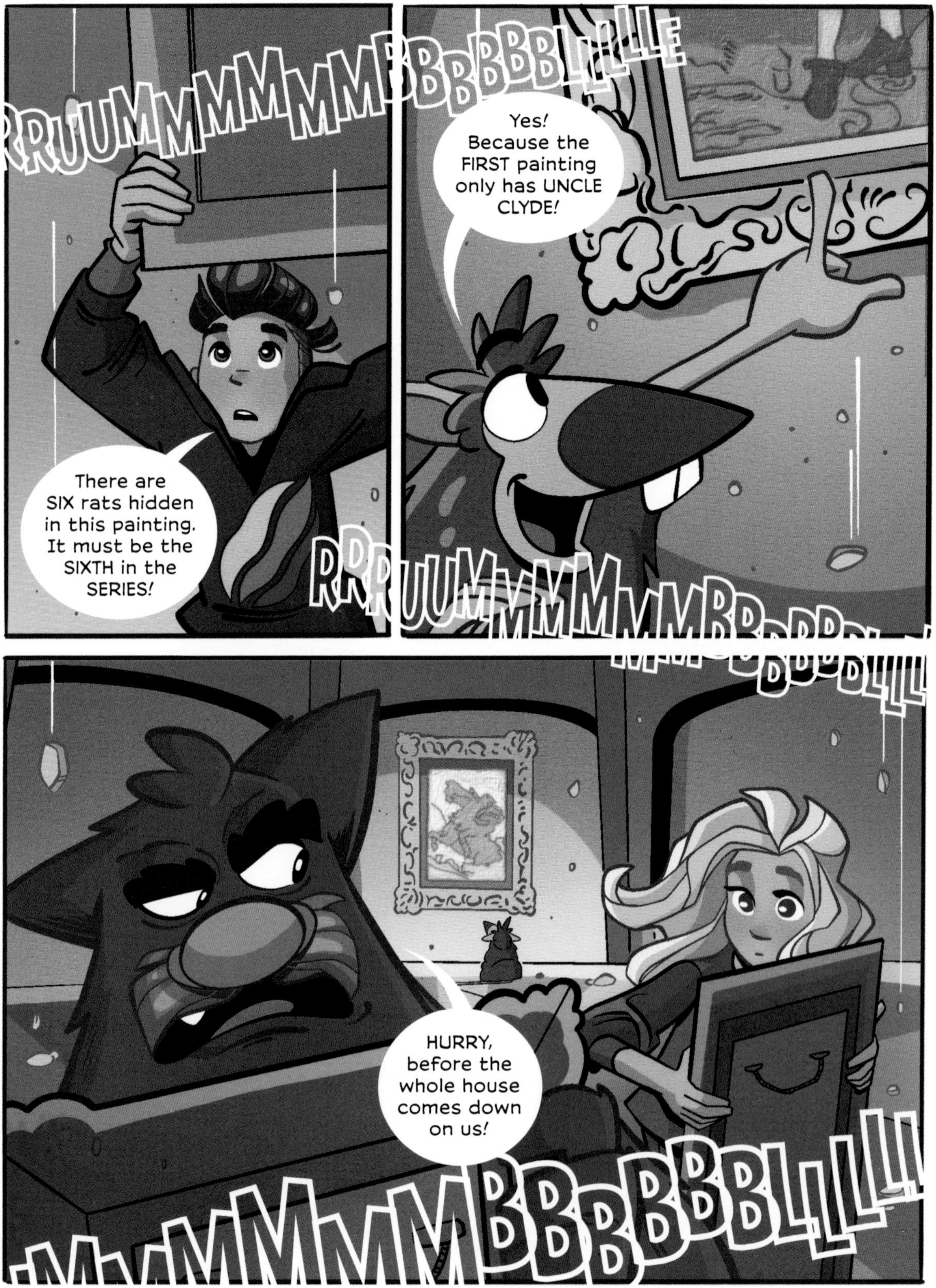
RRUUMMMMMMMBBBBBBLLLLE
There are SIX rats hidden in this painting. It must be the SIXTH in the SERIES!
Yes! Because the FIRST painting only has UNCLE CLYDE!
RRRUUMMMMMMMBBBBBLLL
HURRY, before the whole house comes down on us!
MMMMMMMBBBBBBBBLLLL

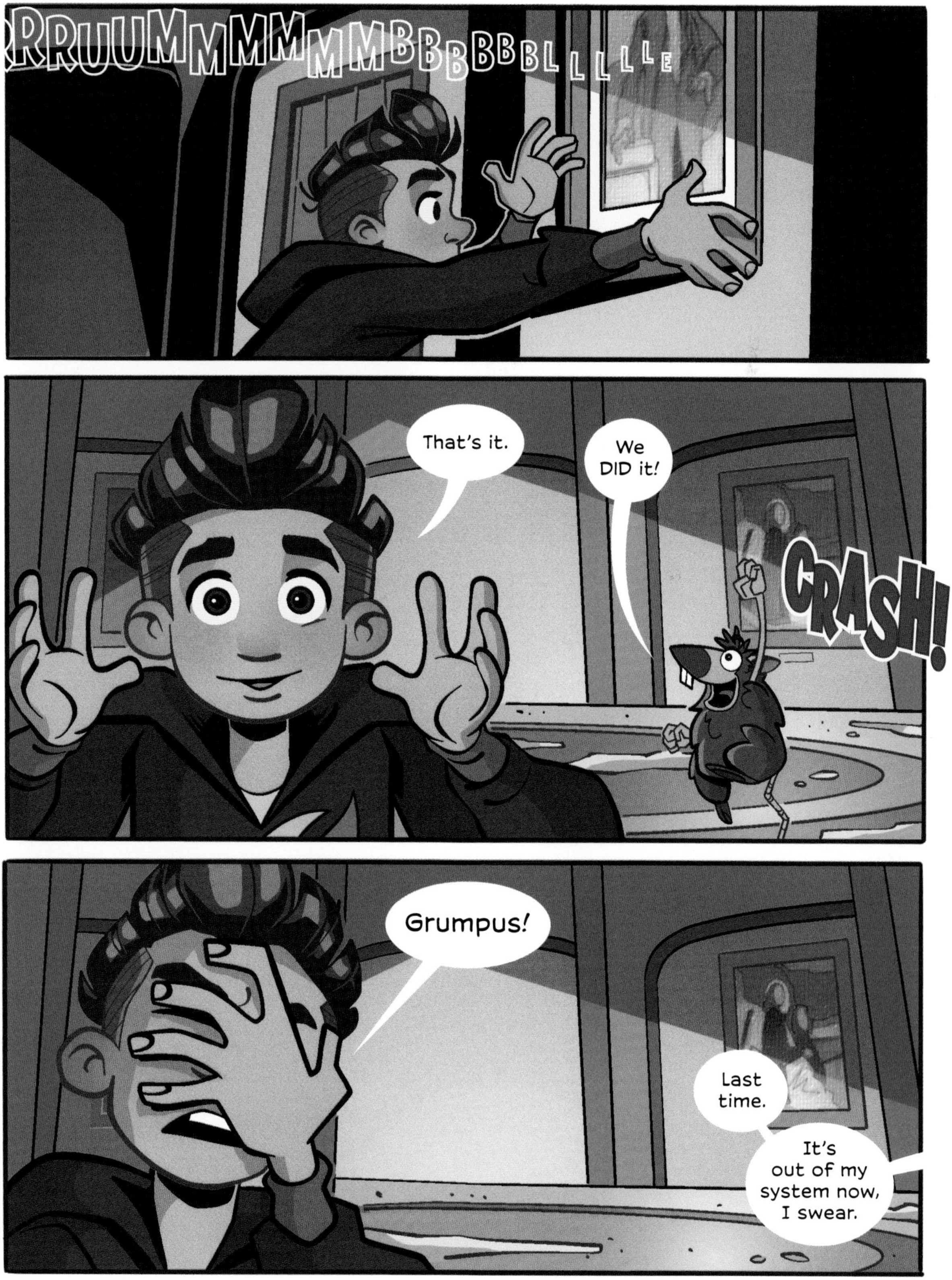
RRRUUUMMMMMMMMBBBBBLLLLLE
That's it.
We DID it!
CRASH!
Grumpus!
Last time.
It's out of my system now, I swear.

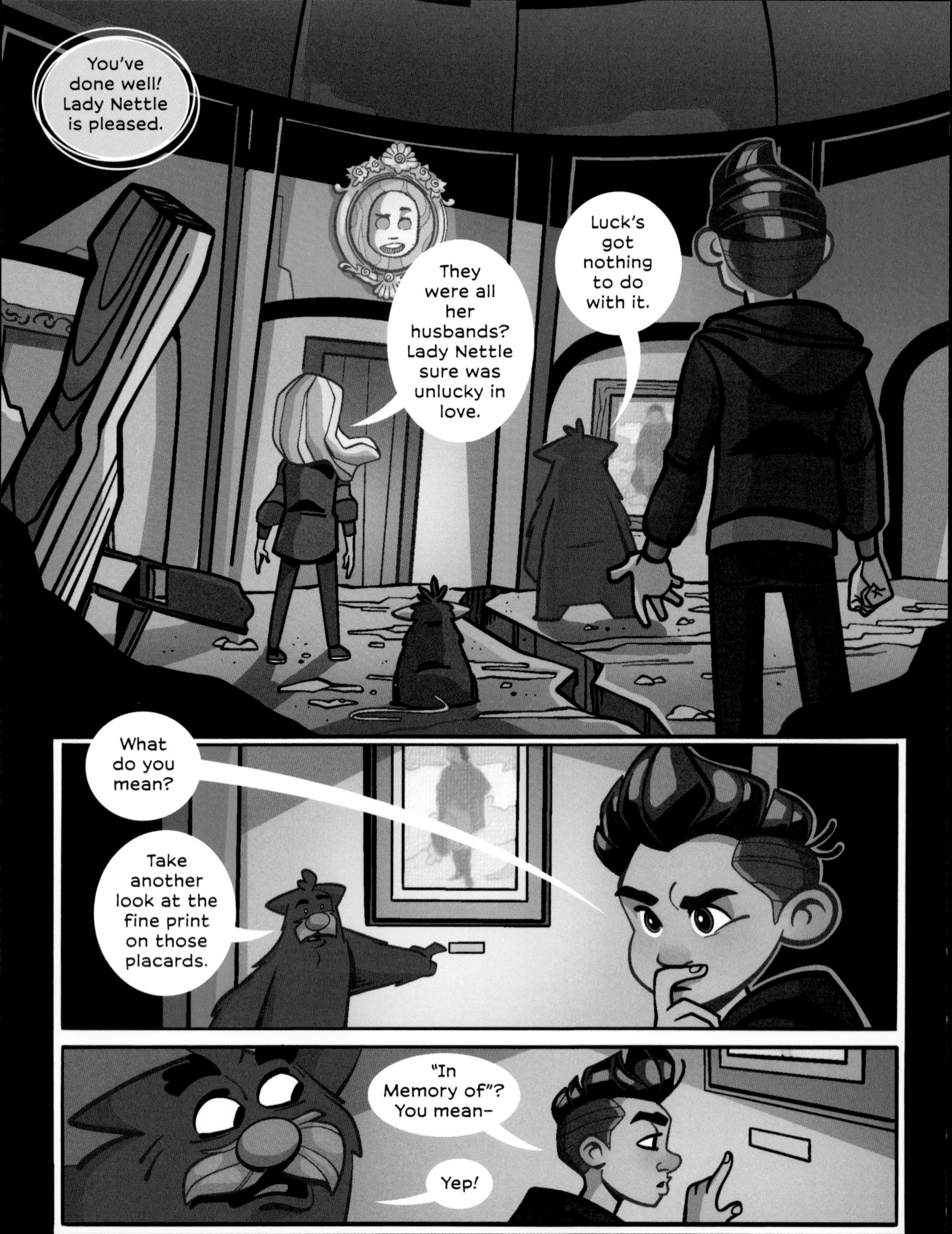
You've done well! Lady Nettle is pleased.
They were all her husbands? Lady Nettle sure was unlucky in love.
Luck's got nothing to do with it.
What do you mean?
Take another look at the fine print on those placards.
"In Memory of"? You mean–
Yep!

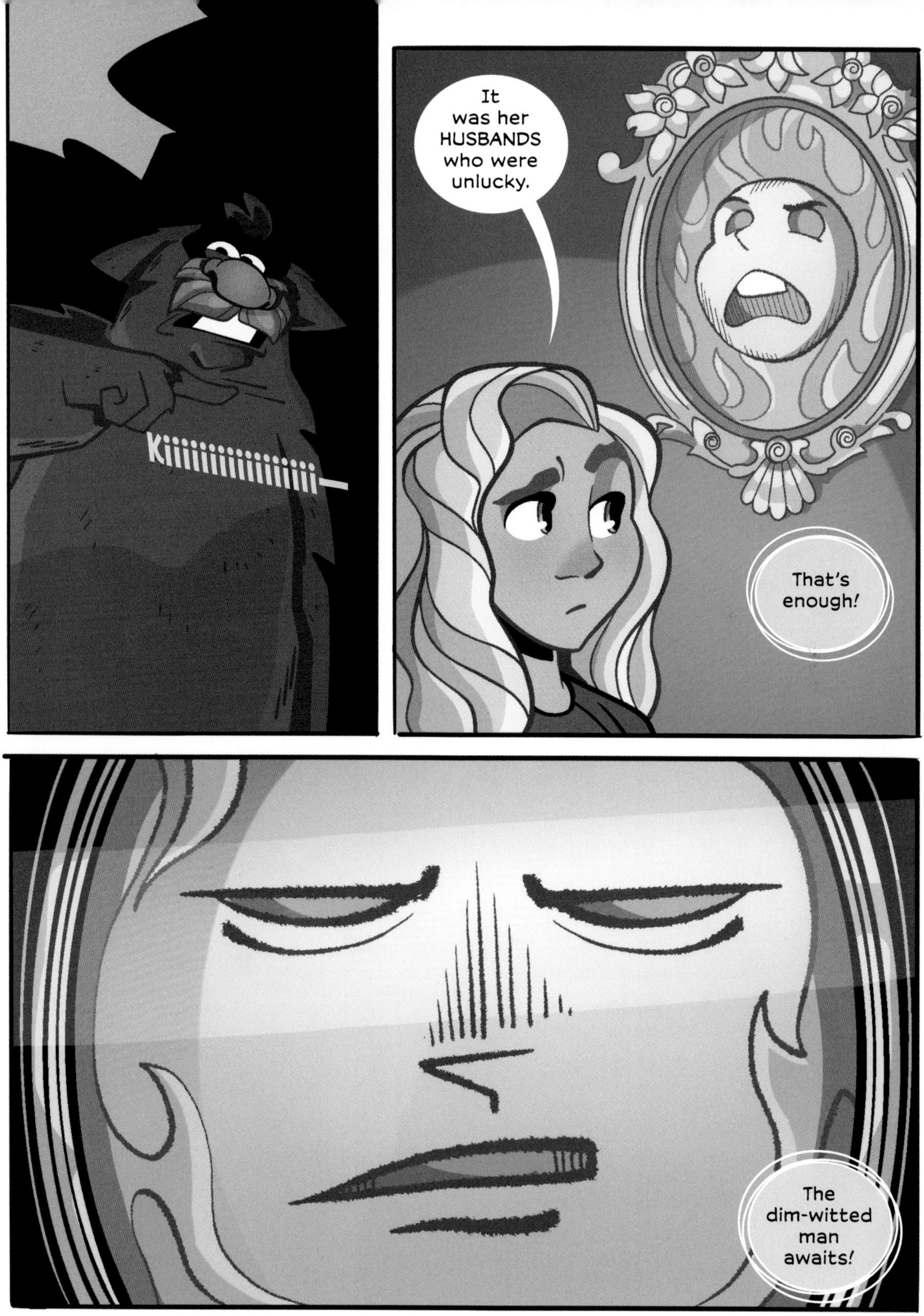
Kiiiiiiiiiiiiiiiii
It was her HUSBANDS who were unlucky.
That's enough!
The dim-witted man awaits!

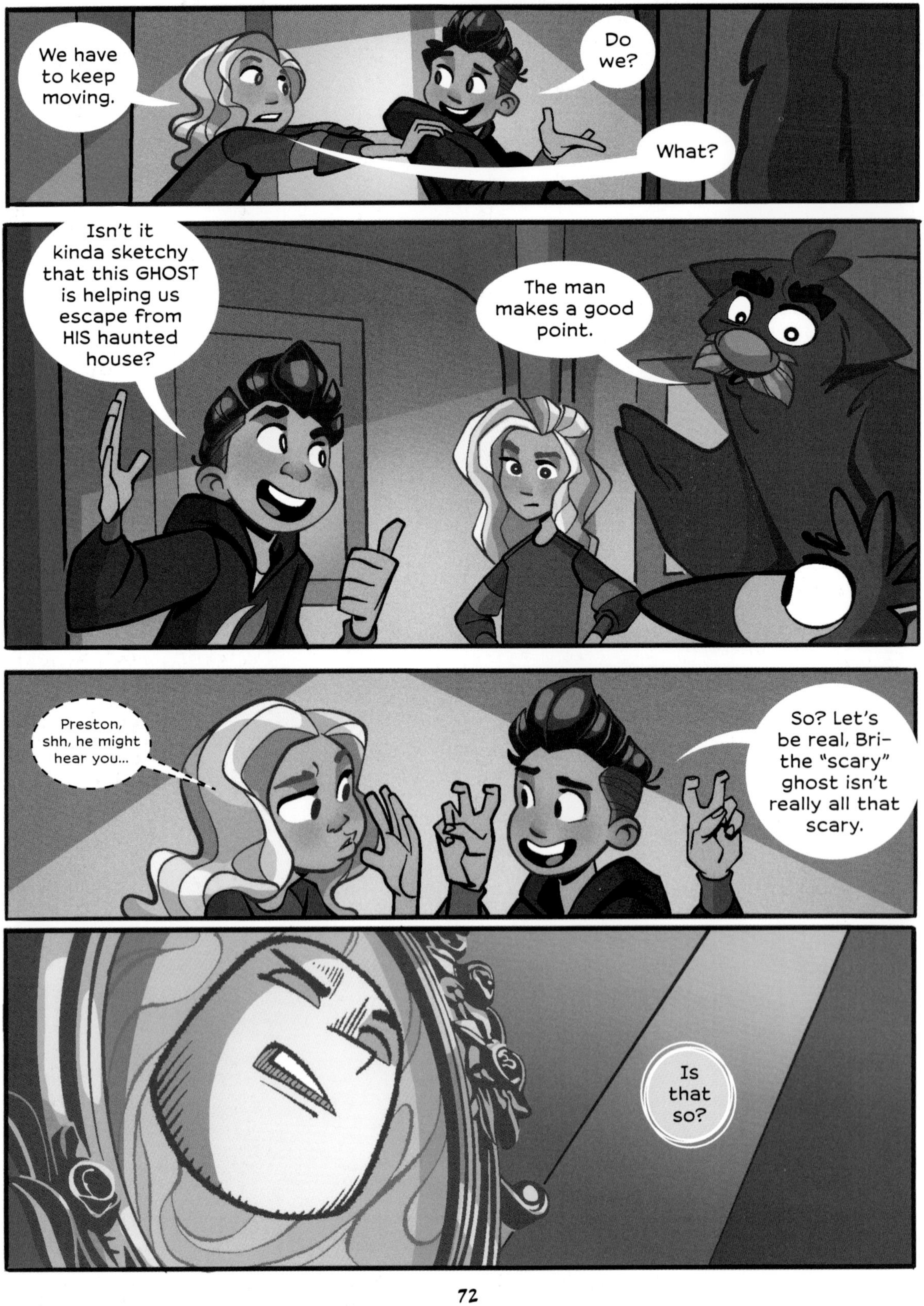

We have to keep moving.
Do we?
What?
Isn't it kinda sketchy that this GHOST is helping us escape from HIS haunted house?
The man makes a good point.
Preston, shh, he might hear you...
So? Let's be real, Bri– the "scary" ghost isn't really all that scary.
Is that so?

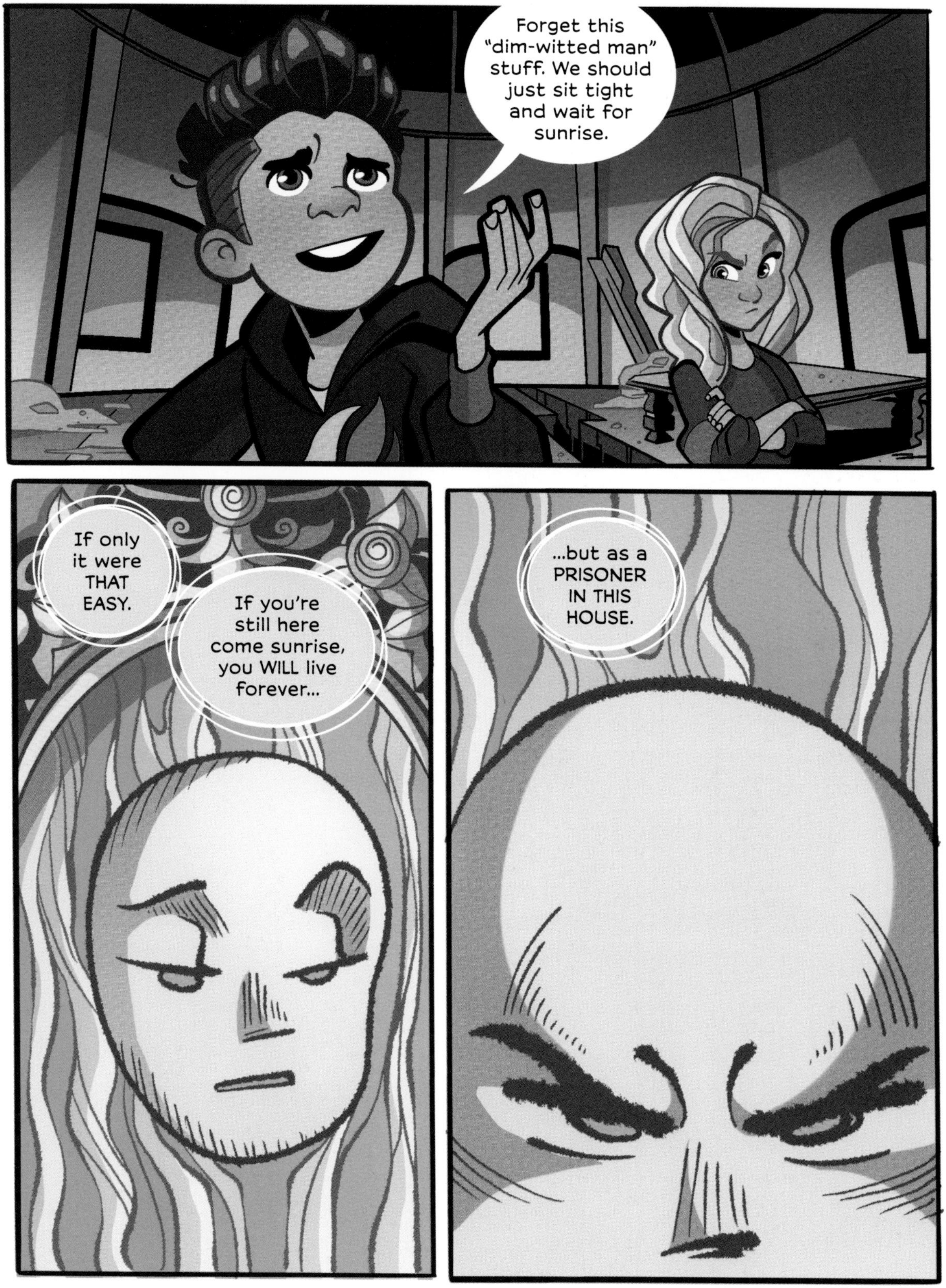
Forget this "dim-witted man" stuff. We should just sit tight and wait for sunrise.
If only it were THAT EASY.
If you're still here come sunrise, you WILL live forever...
...but as a PRISONER IN THIS HOUSE.

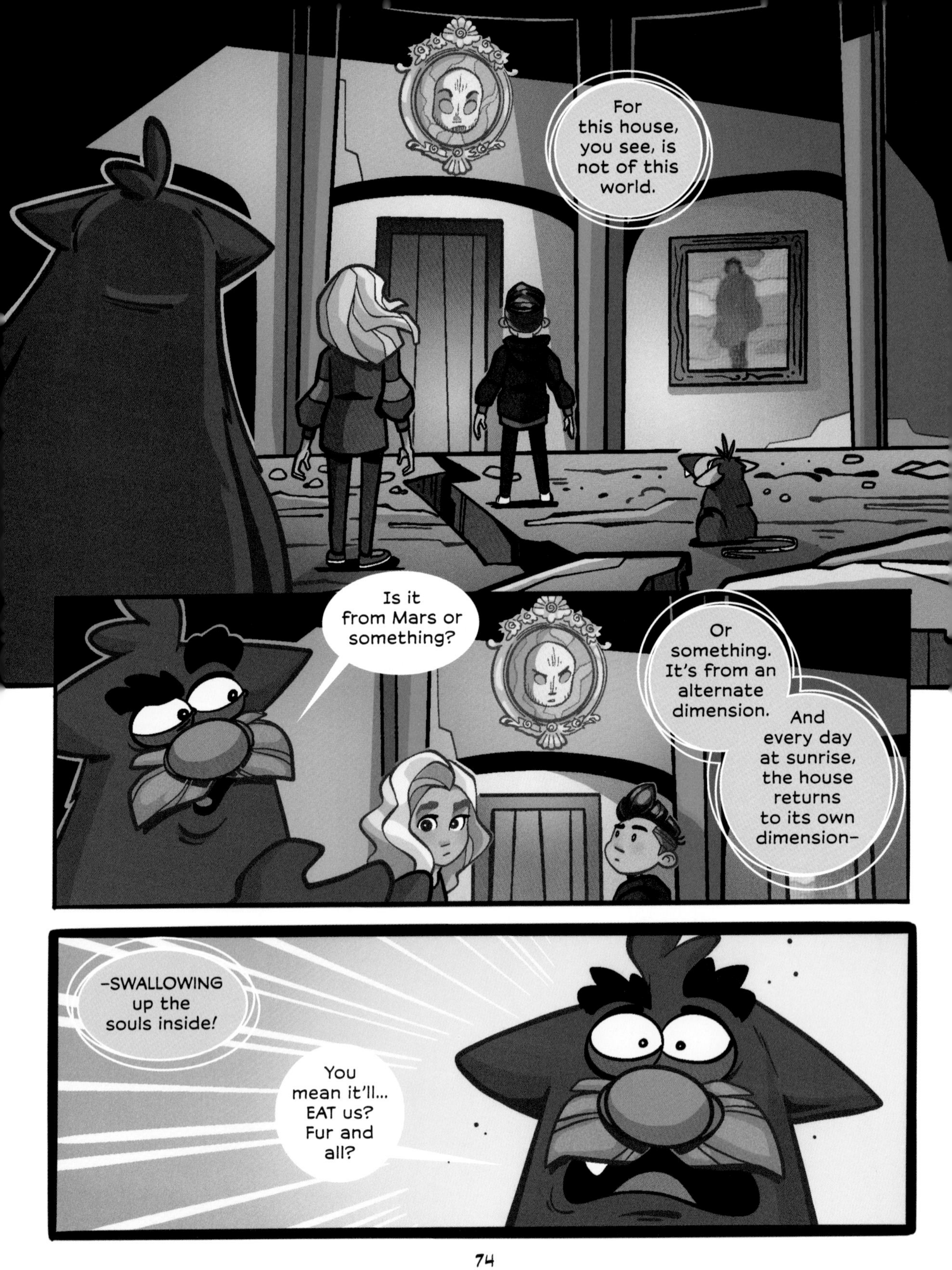
For this house, you see, is not of this world.
Is it from Mars or something?
Or something. It's from an alternate dimension.
And every day at sunrise, the house returns to its own dimension–
–SWALLOWING up the souls inside!
You mean it'll... EAT us? Fur and all?

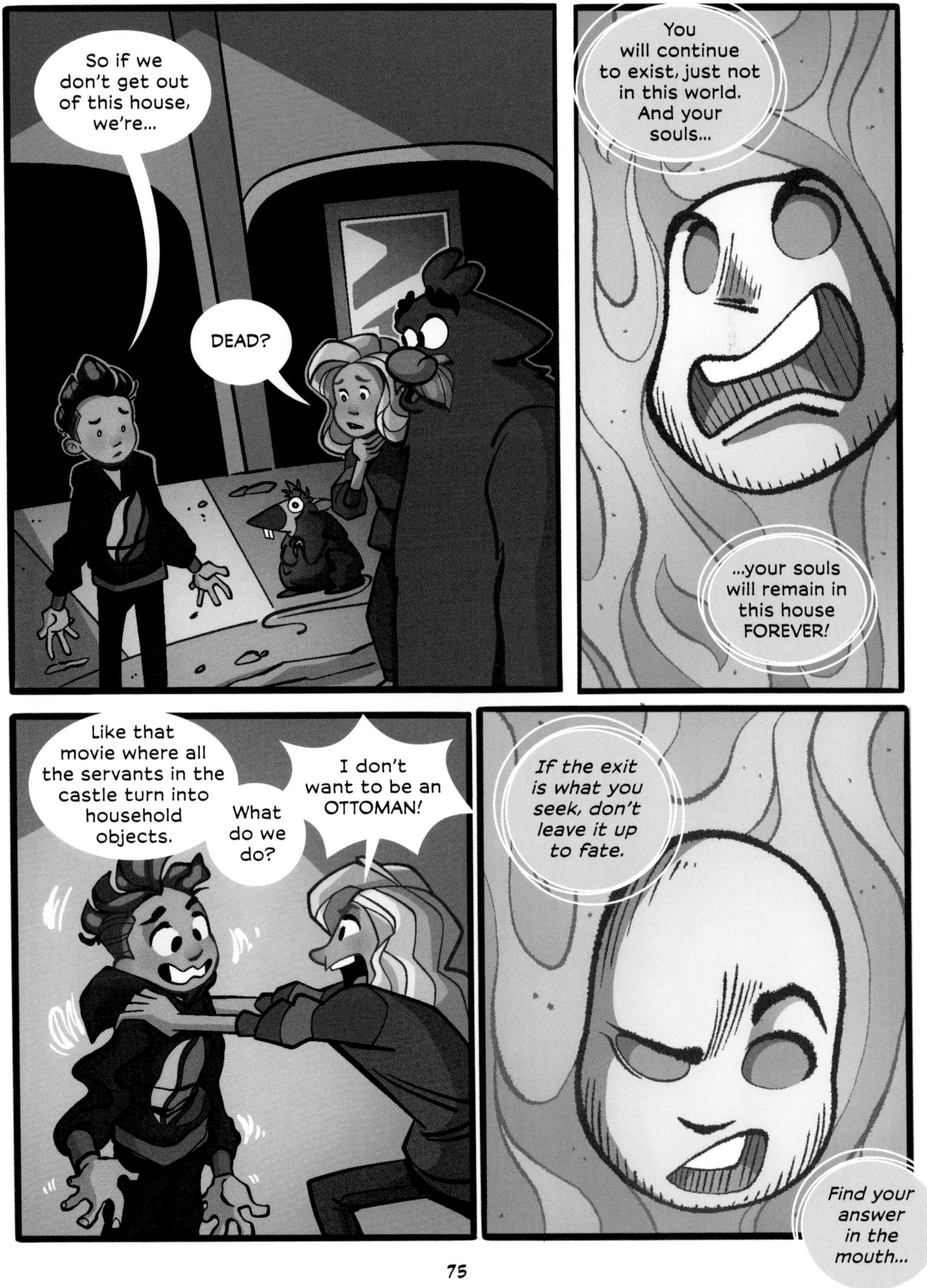
So if we don't get out of this house, we're...
DEAD?
You will continue to exist, just not in this world. And your souls...
...your souls will remain in this house FOREVER!
Like that movie where all the servants in the castle turn into household objects.
What do we do?
I don't want to be an OTTOMAN!
If the exit is what you seek, don't leave it up to fate.
Find your answer in the mouth...

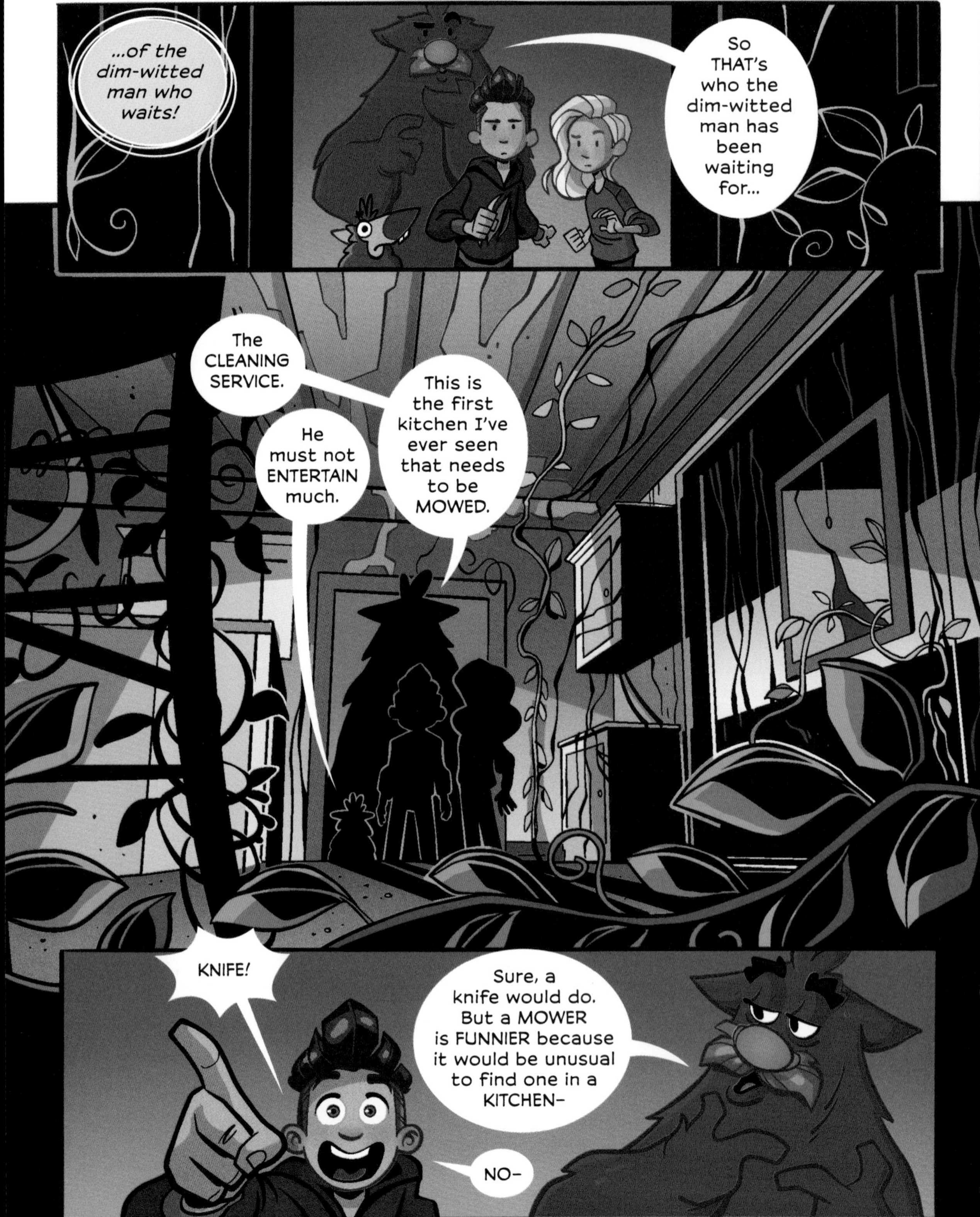
...of the dim-witted man who waits!
So THAT's who the dim-witted man has been waiting for...
The CLEANING SERVICE.
This is the first kitchen I've ever seen that needs to be MOWED.
He must not ENTERTAIN much.
KNIFE!
Sure, a knife would do. But a MOWER is FUNNIER because it would be unusual to find one in a KITCHEN–
NO–

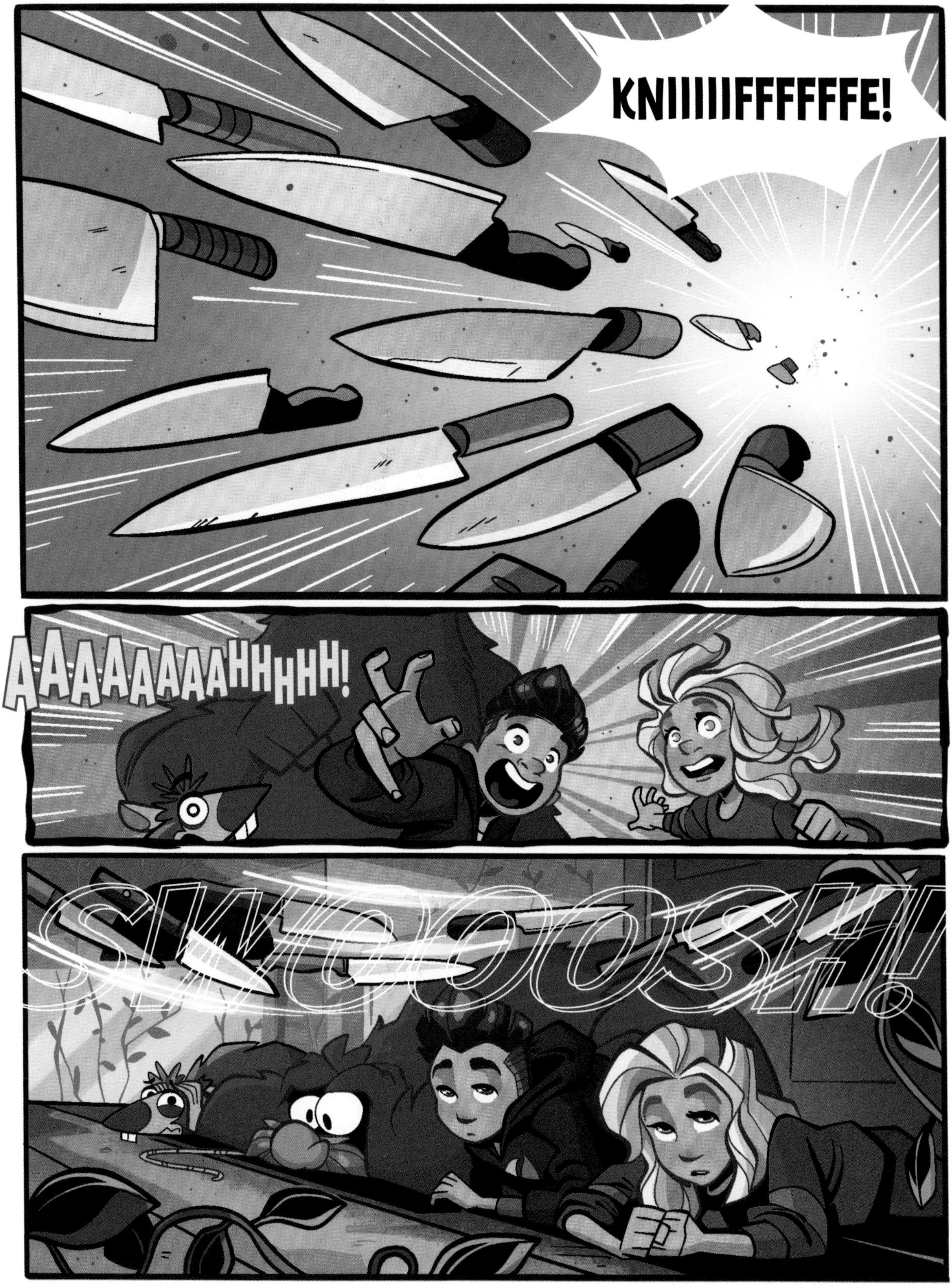
KNIIIIIIFFFFFFE!
AAAAAAAAHHHHH!
SWOOOSH!

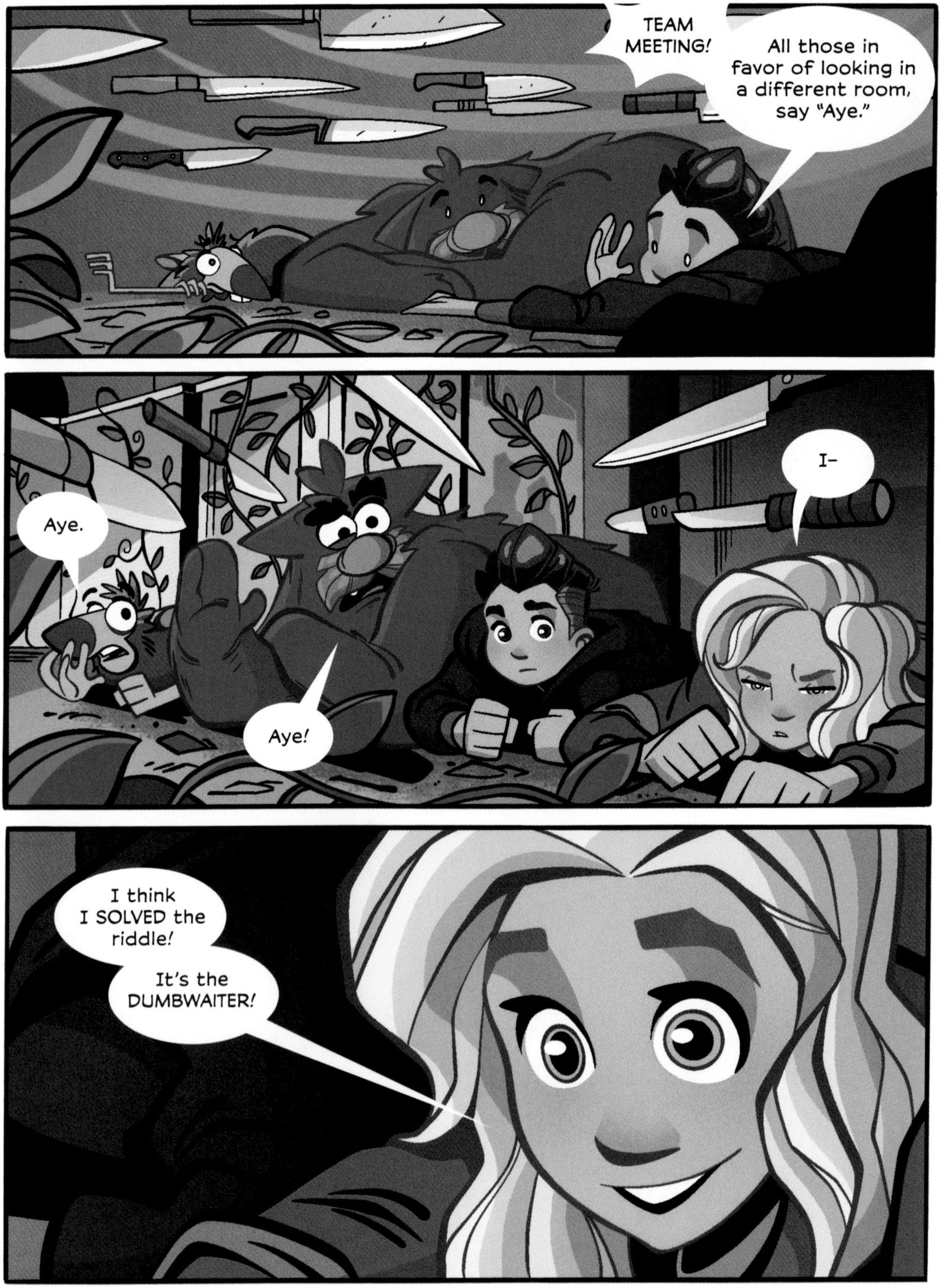
TEAM MEETING!
All those in favor of looking in a different room, say "Aye."
Aye.
Aye!
I–
I think I SOLVED the riddle!
It's the DUMBWAITER!

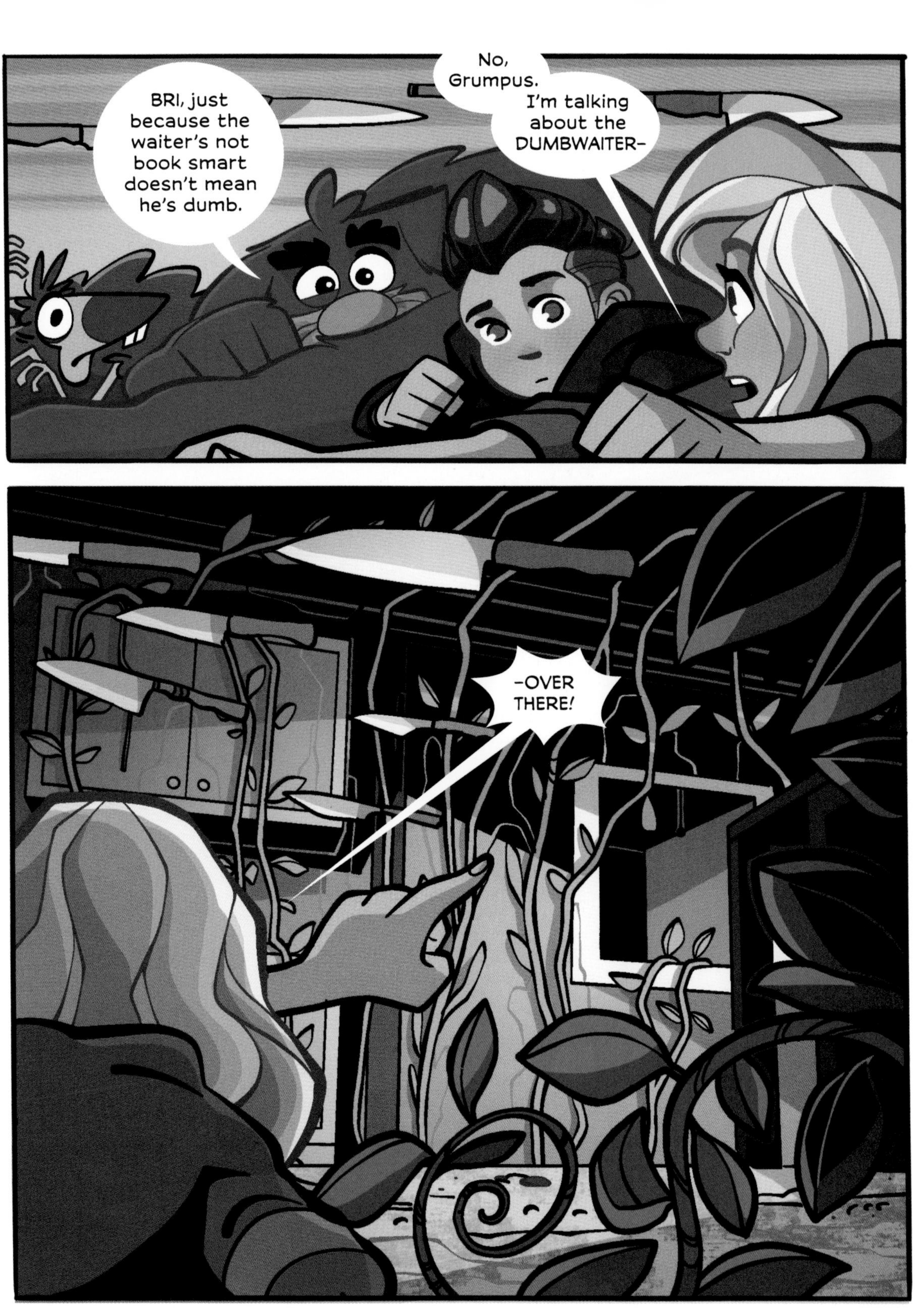
BRI, just because the waiter's not book smart doesn't mean he's dumb.
No, Grumpus. I'm talking about the DUMBWAITER–
–OVER THERE!

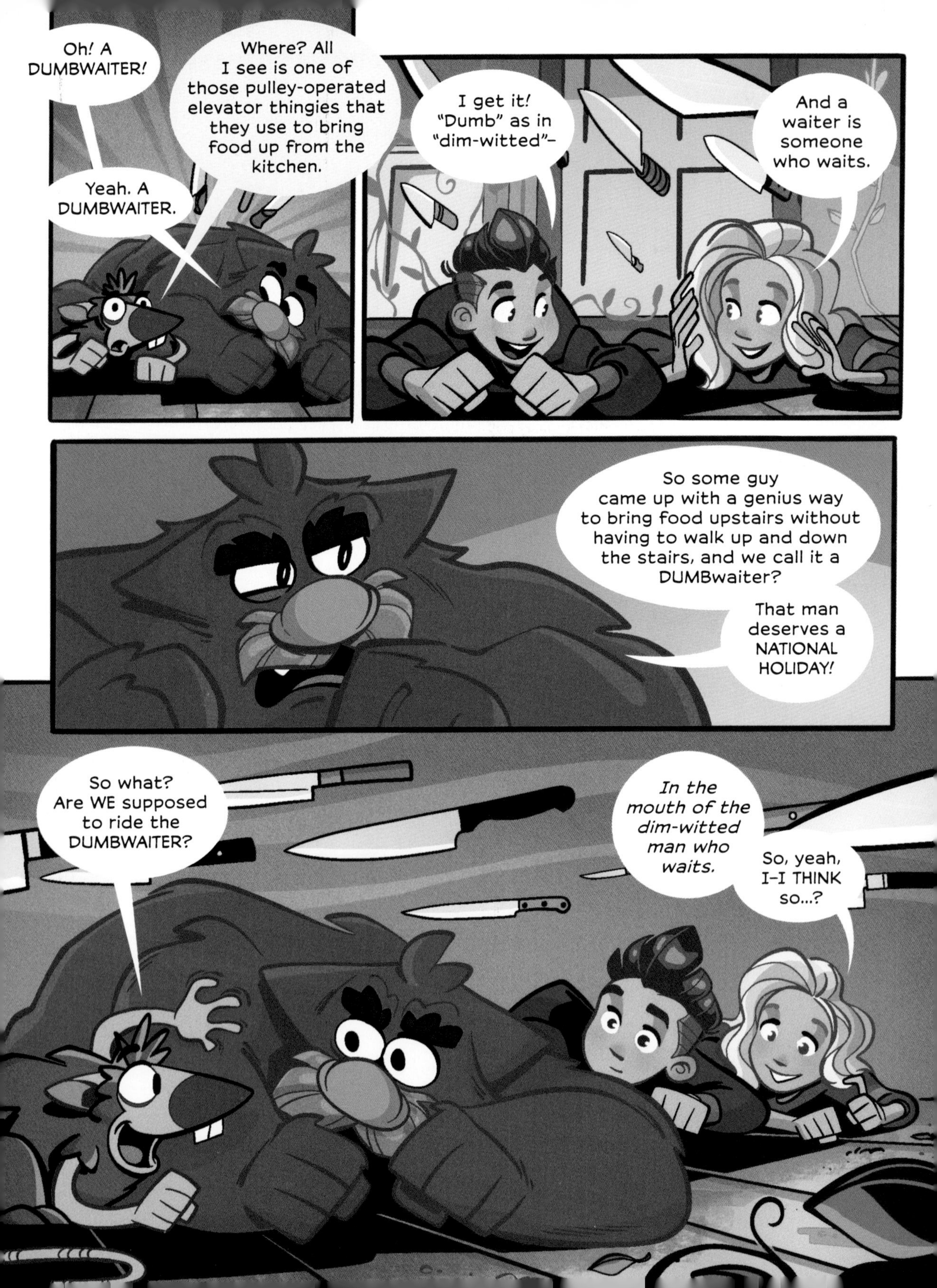
Oh! A DUMBWAITER!
Where? All I see is one of those pulley-operated elevator thingies that they use to bring food up from the kitchen.
Yeah. A DUMBWAITER.
I get it! "Dumb" as in "dim-witted"–
And a waiter is someone who waits.
So some guy came up with a genius way to bring food upstairs without having to walk up and down the stairs, and we call it a DUMBwaiter?
That man deserves a NATIONAL HOLIDAY!
So what? Are WE supposed to ride the DUMBWAITER?
In the mouth of the dim-witted man who waits.
So, yeah, I–I THINK so...?

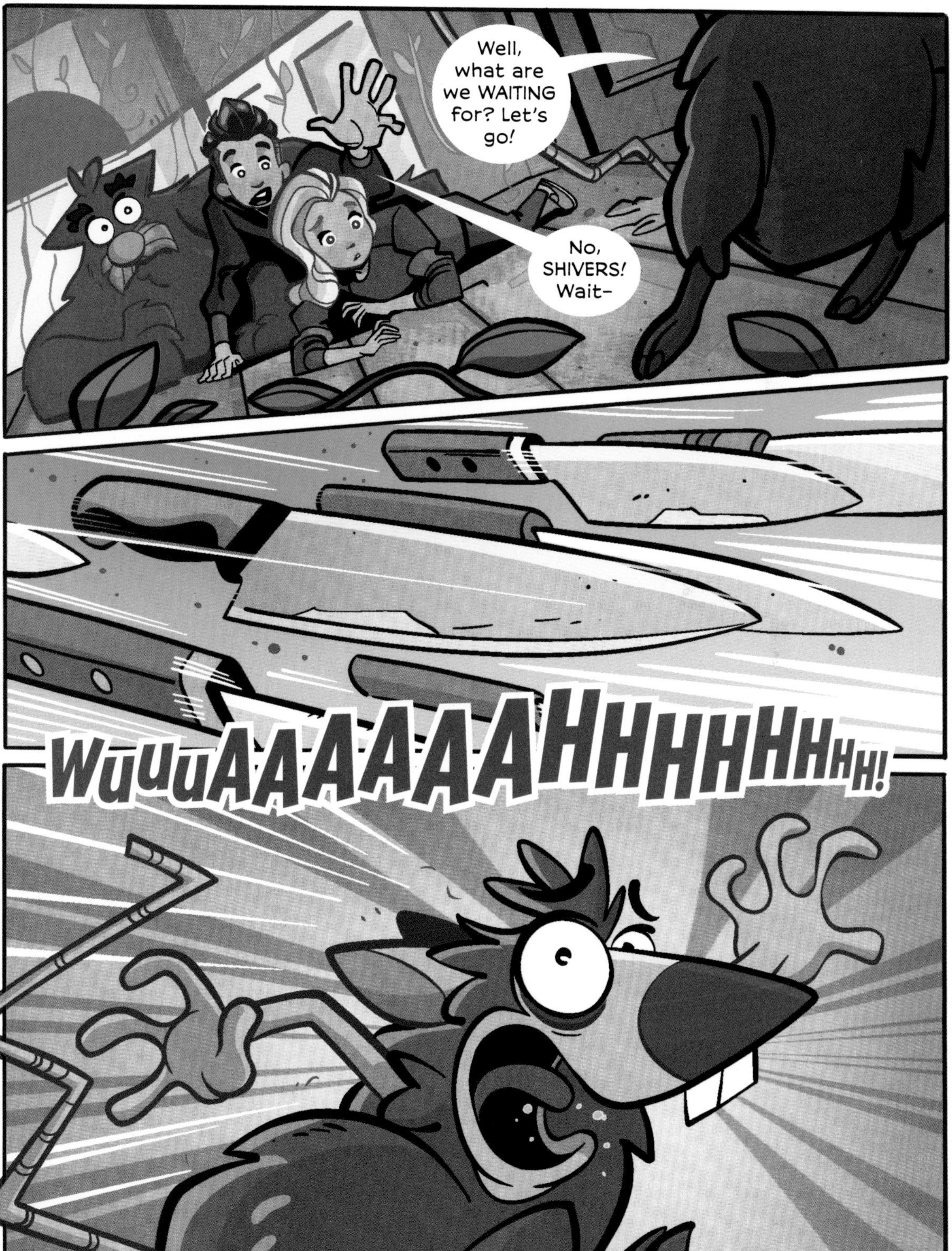
Well, what are we WAITING for? Let's go!
No, SHIVERS! Wait-
WuuuAAAAAAAHHHHHHHHH!

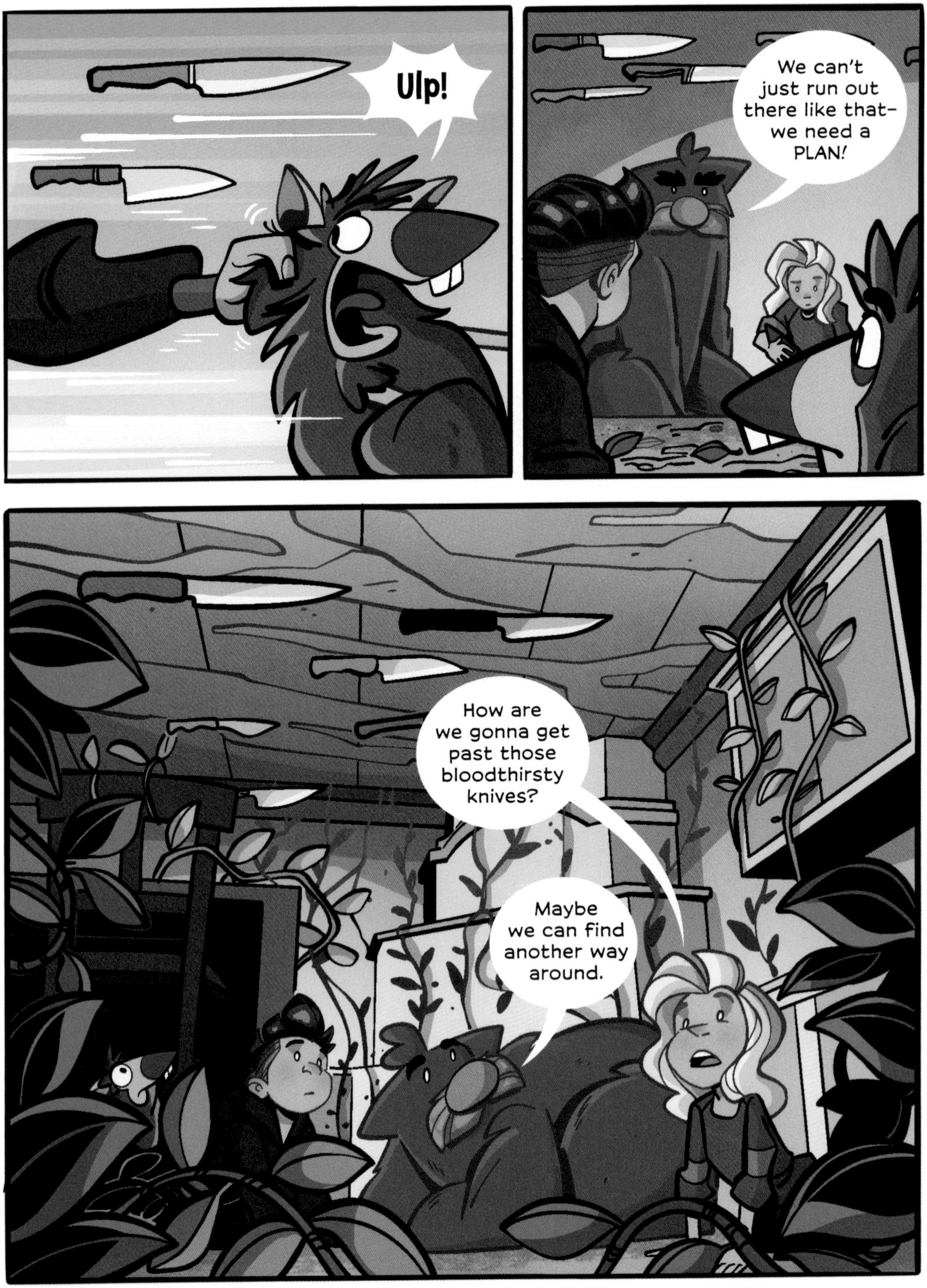
Ulp!
We can't just run out there like that– we need a PLAN!
How are we gonna get past those bloodthirsty knives?
Maybe we can find another way around.

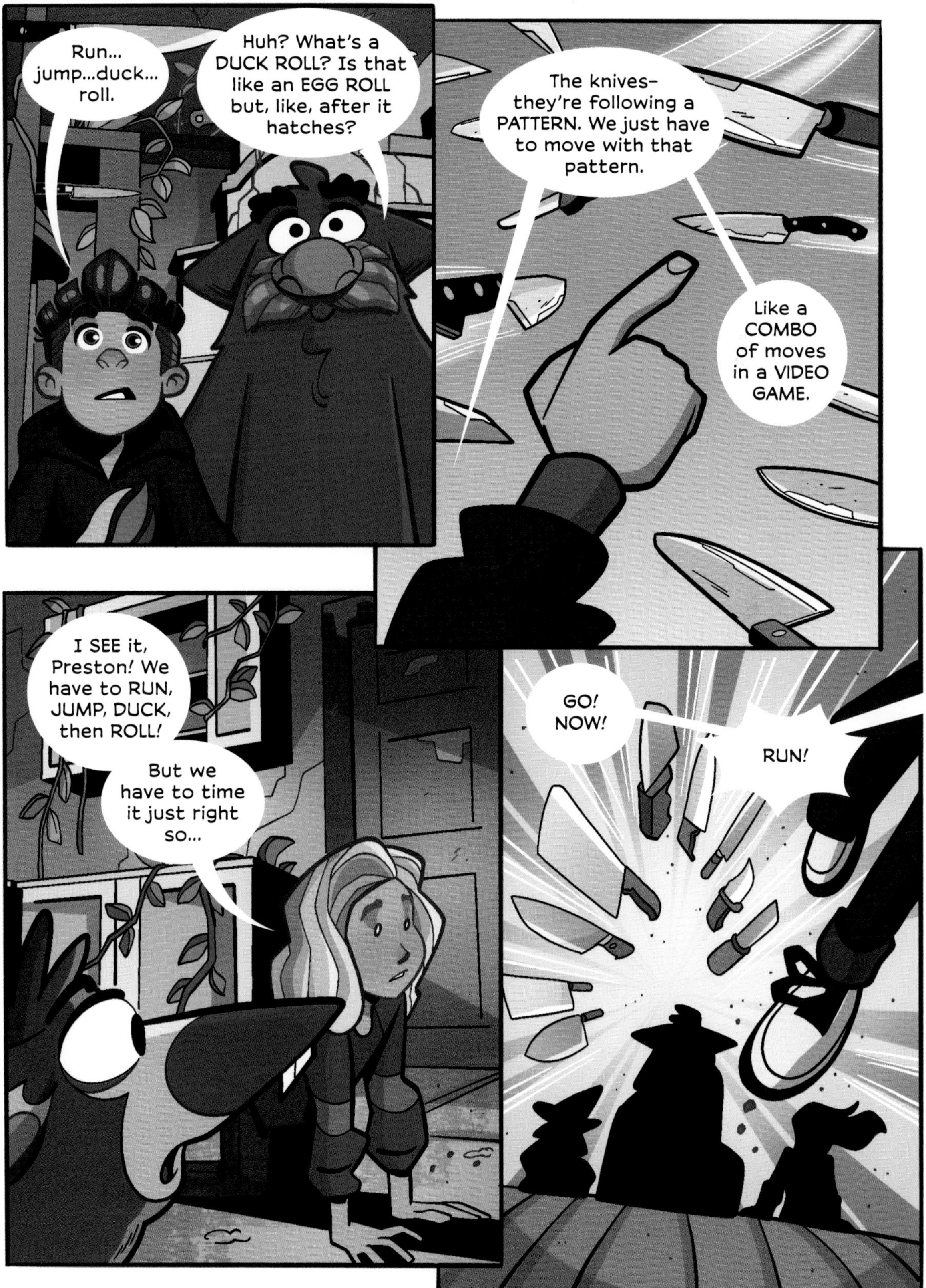
Run... jump...duck... roll.
Huh? What's a DUCK ROLL? Is that like an EGG ROLL but, like, after it hatches?
The knives– they're following a PATTERN. We just have to move with that pattern.
Like a COMBO of moves in a VIDEO GAME.
I SEE it, Preston! We have to RUN, JUMP, DUCK, then ROLL!
But we have to time it just right so...
GO! NOW!
RUN!

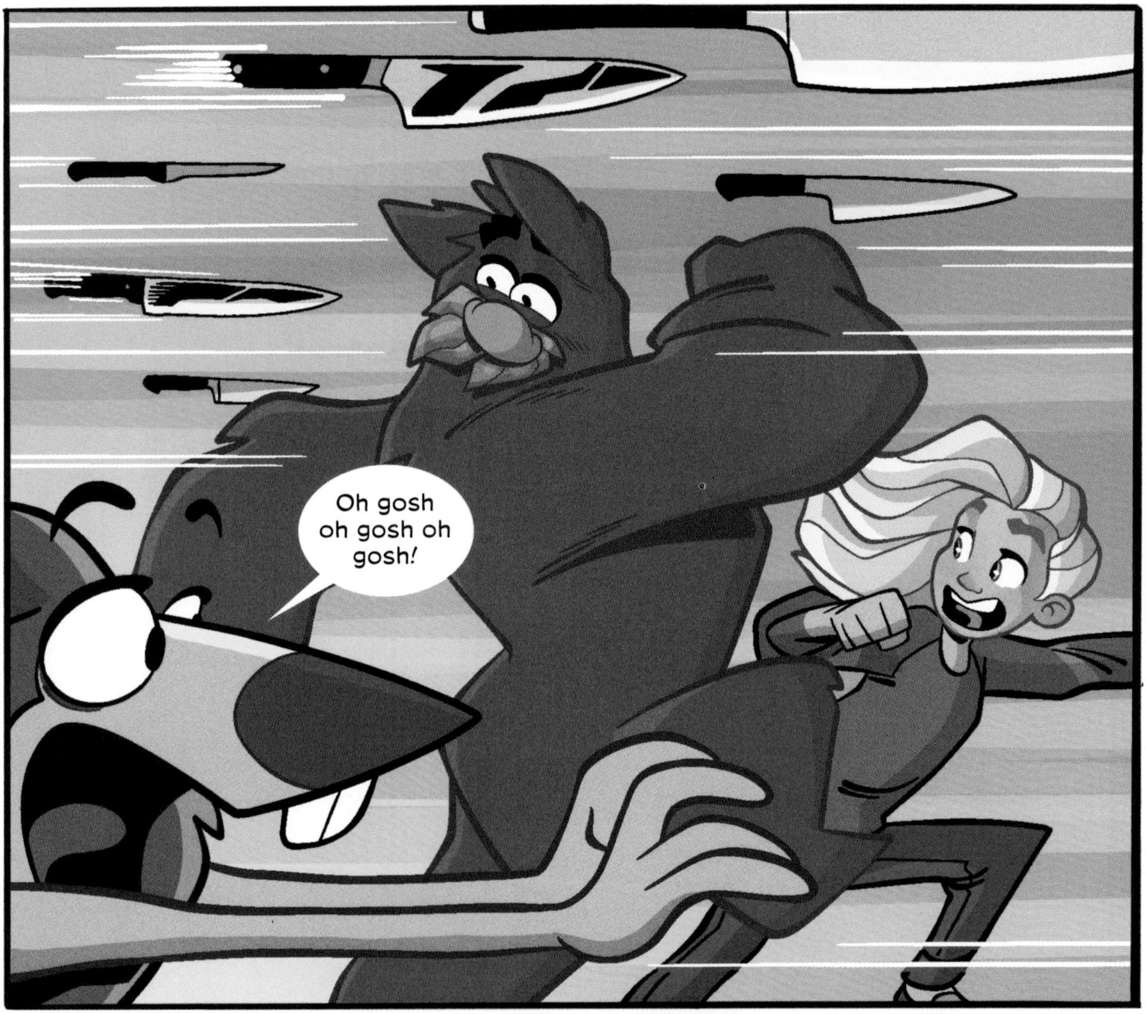
Oh gosh oh gosh oh gosh!

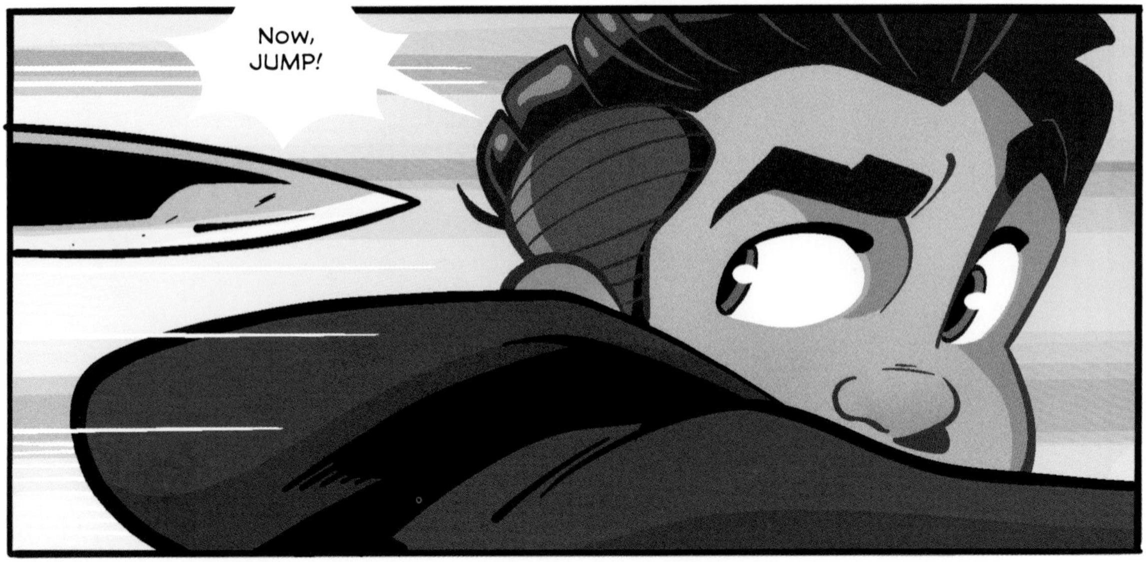
Now, JUMP!

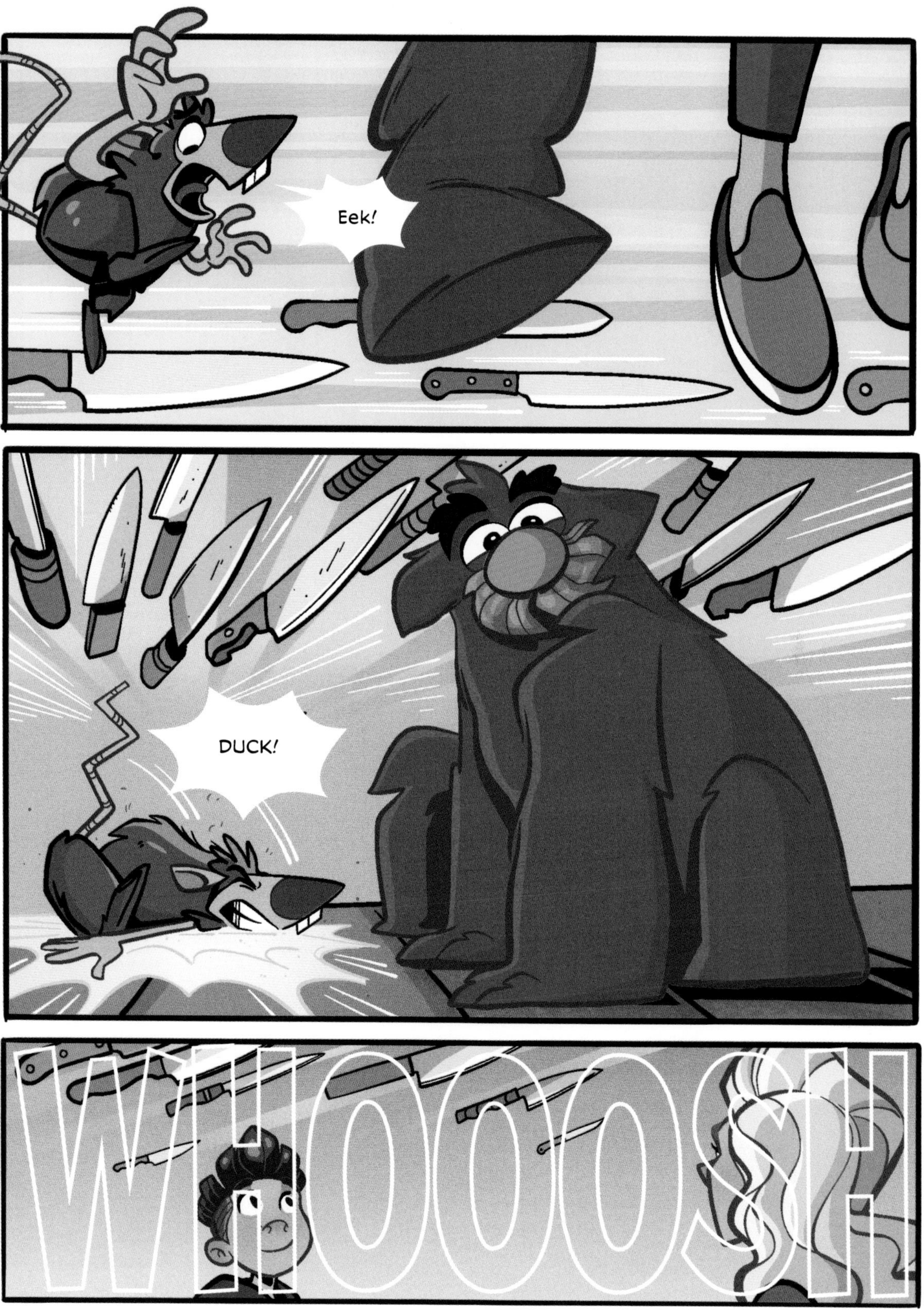
Eek!
DUCK!
WHOOOSH

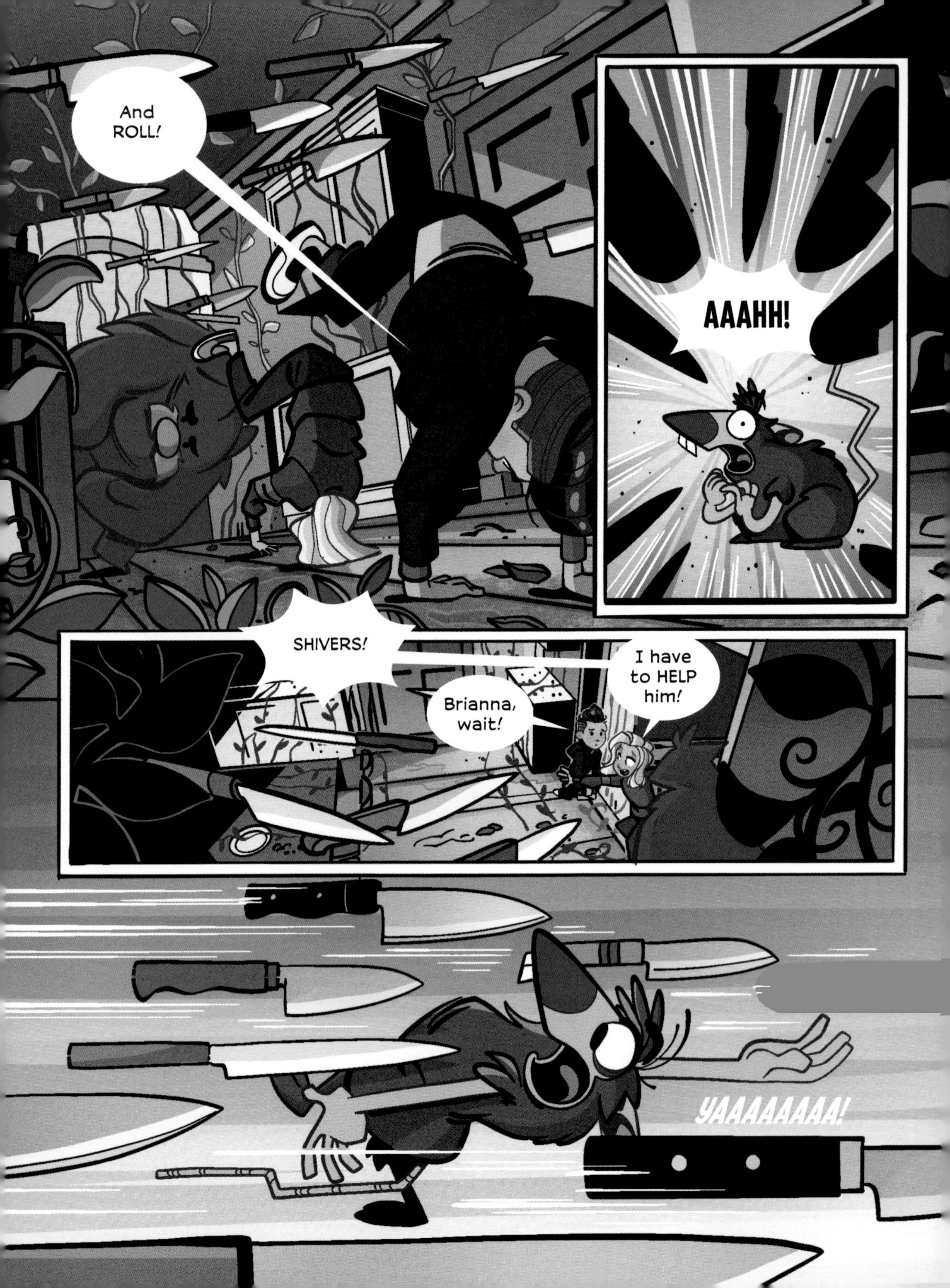

And ROLL!
AAAHH!
SHIVERS!
Brianna, wait!
I have to HELP him!
YAAAAAAAA!

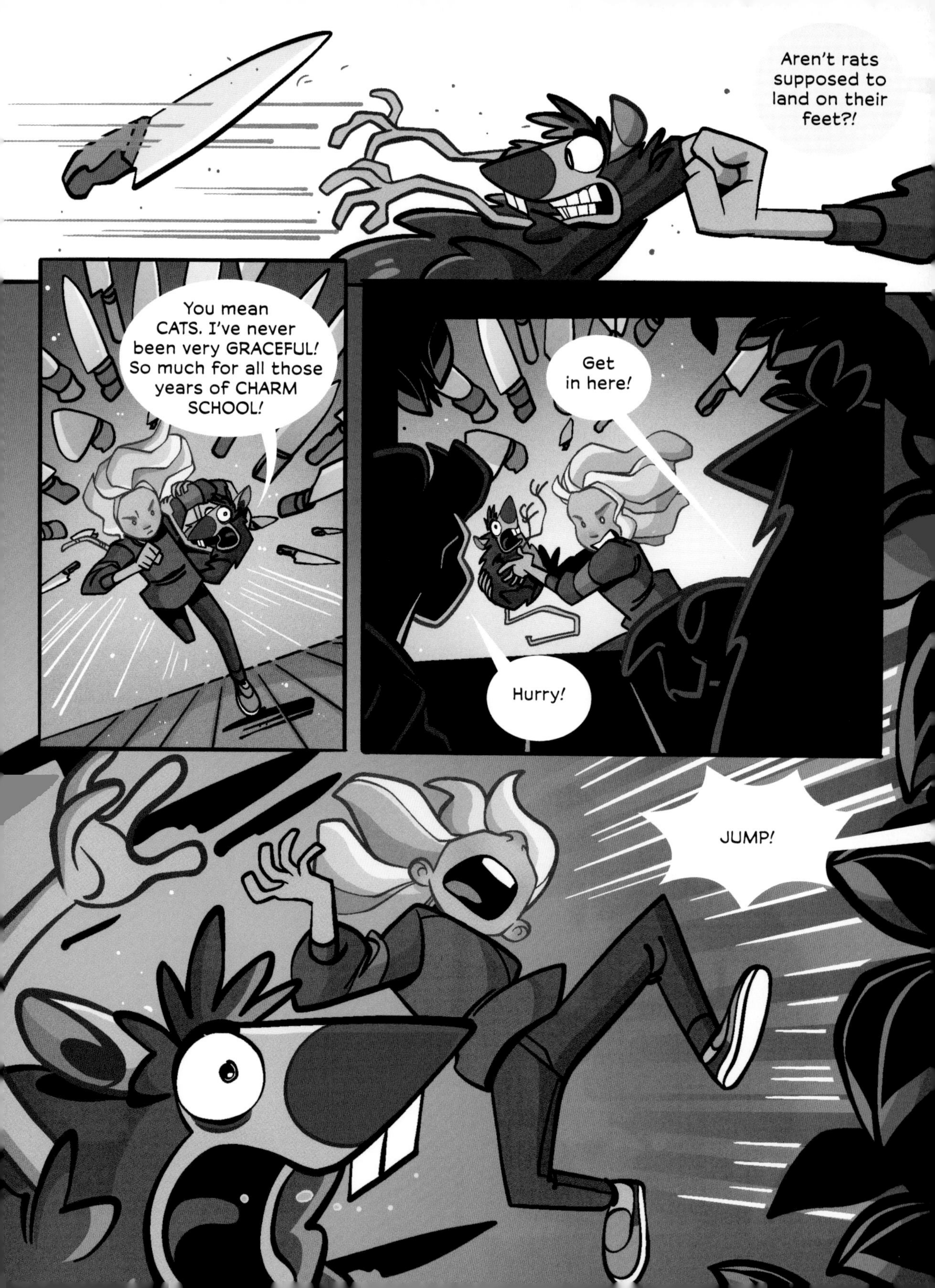

Aren't rats supposed to land on their feet?!
You mean CATS. I've never been very GRACEFUL! So much for all those years of CHARM SCHOOL!
Get in here!
Hurry!
JUMP!

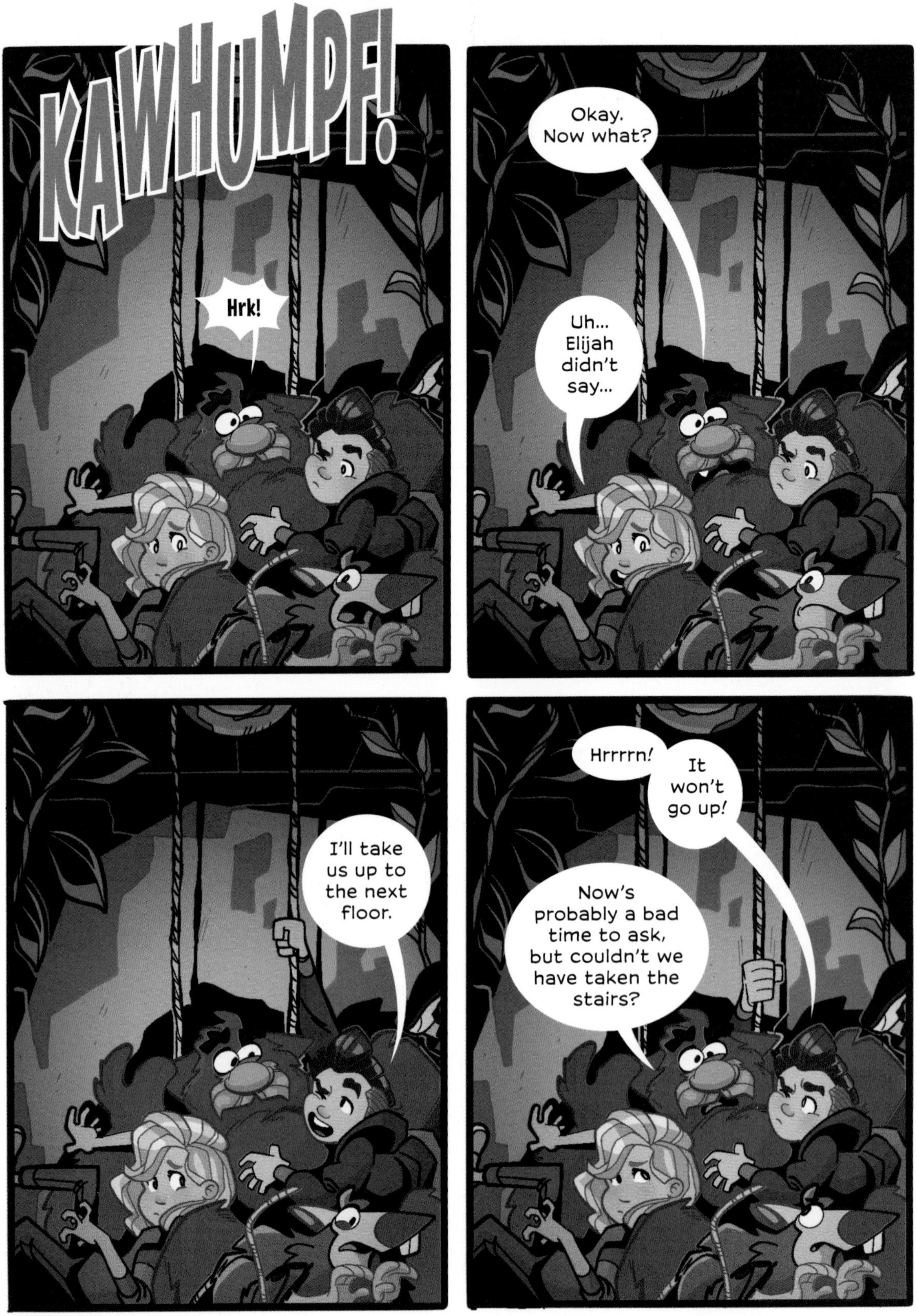
KAWHUMPF!
Hrk!
Okay. Now what?
Uh... Elijah didn't say...
I'll take us up to the next floor.
Hrrrrn!
It won't go up!
Now's probably a bad time to ask, but couldn't we have taken the stairs?

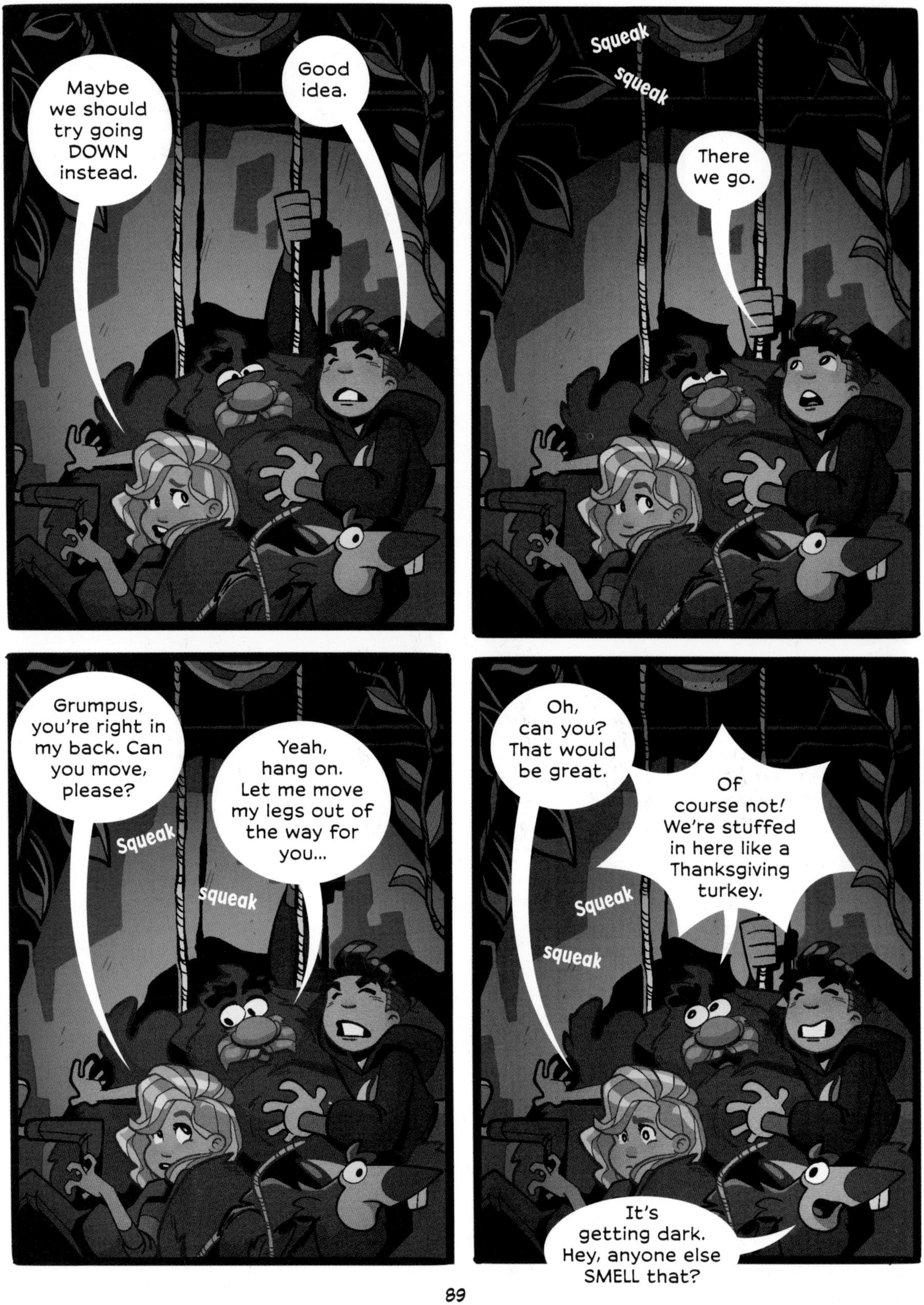
Maybe we should try going DOWN instead.
Good idea.
Squeak
squeak
There we go.
Grumpus, you're right in my back. Can you move, please?
Squeak
squeak
Yeah, hang on. Let me move my legs out of the way for you...
Oh, can you? That would be great.
Of course not! We're stuffed in here like a Thanksgiving turkey.
Squeak
squeak
It's getting dark. Hey, anyone else SMELL that?

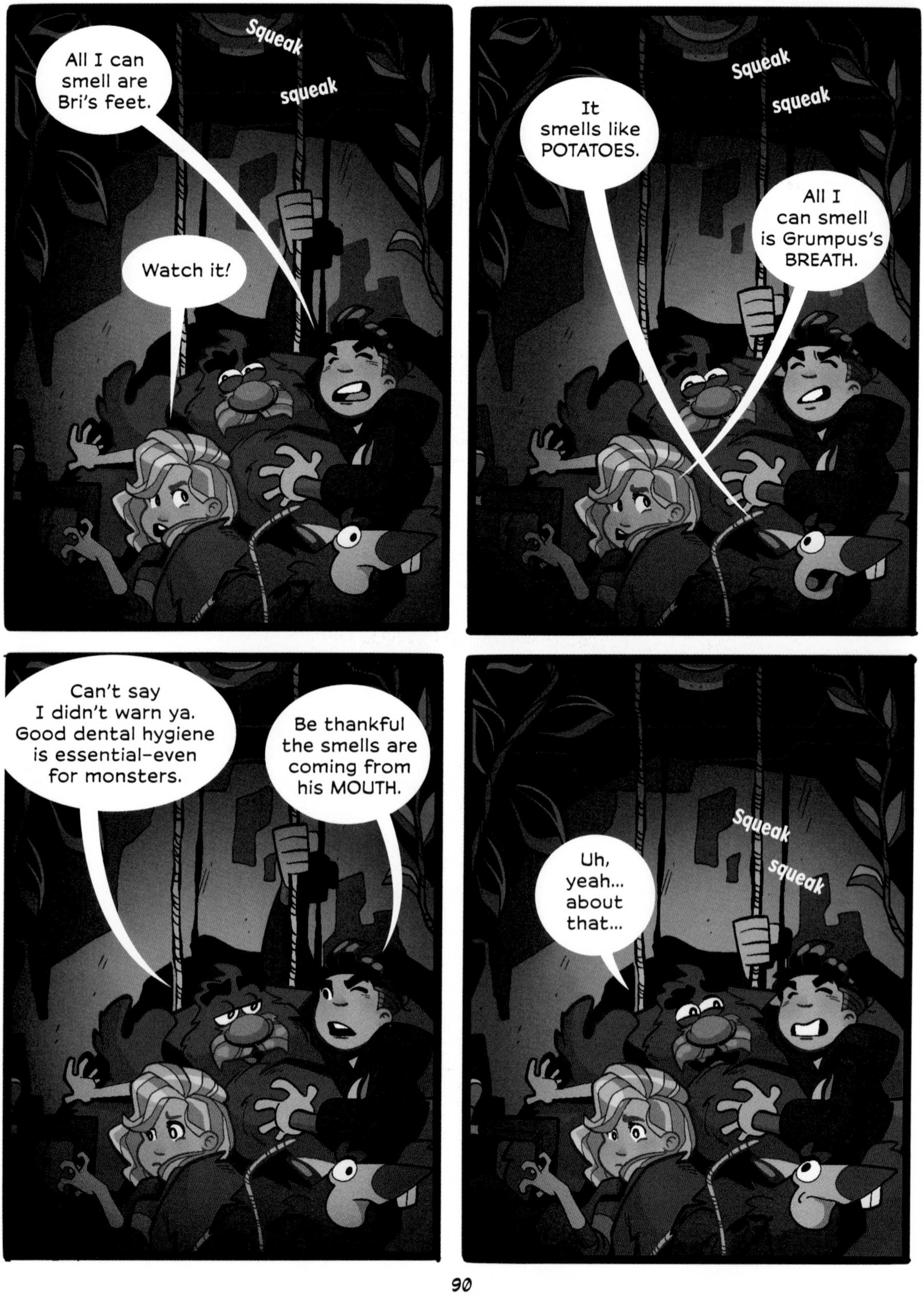
Squeak
squeak
All I can smell are Bri's feet.
Watch it!
Squeak
squeak
It smells like POTATOES.
All I can smell is Grumpus's BREATH.
Can't say I didn't warn ya. Good dental hygiene is essential—even for monsters.
Be thankful the smells are coming from his MOUTH.
Squeak
squeak
Uh, yeah... about that...

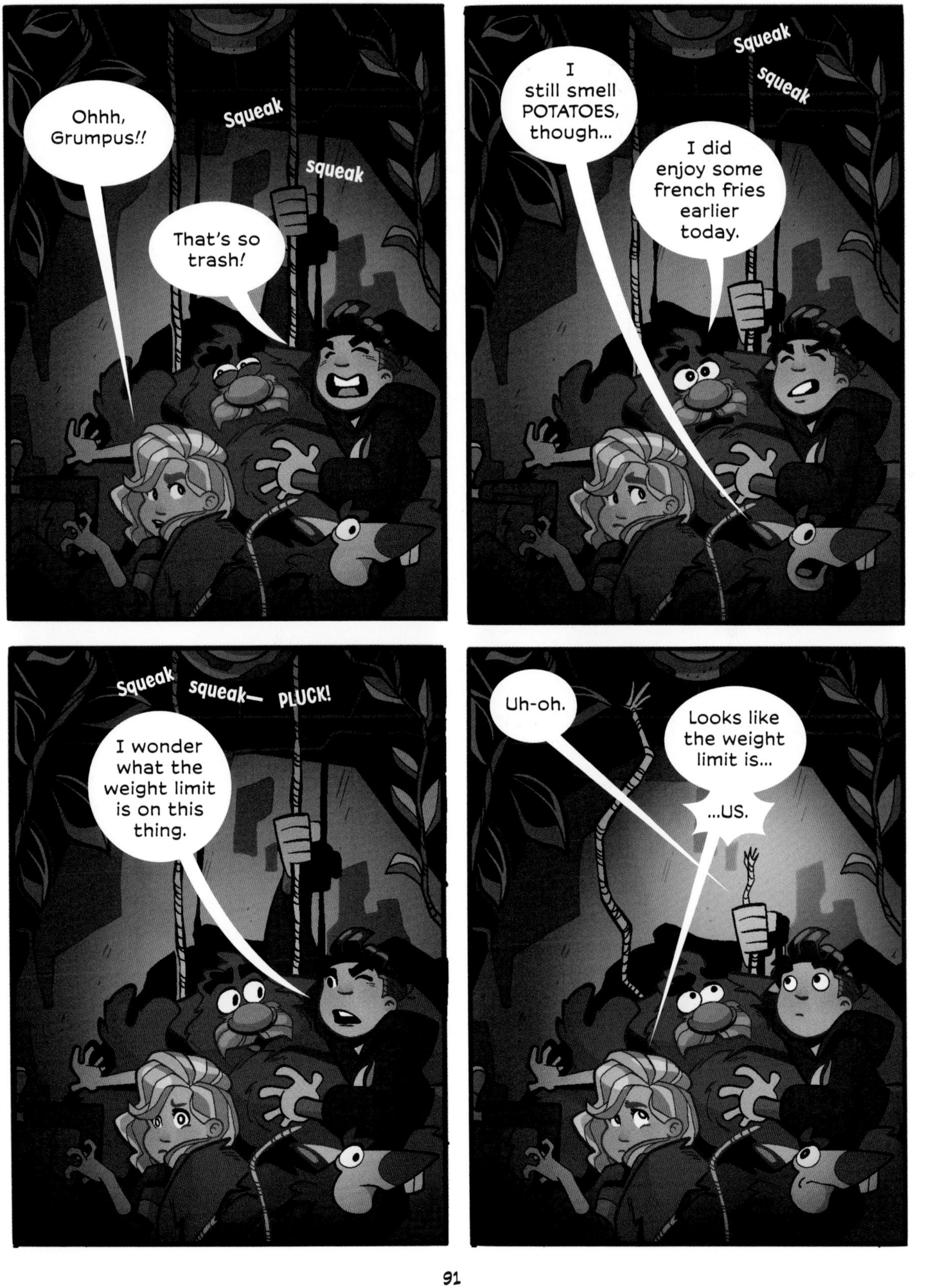
Ohhh, Grumpus!!
Squeak
squeak
That's so trash!
I still smell POTATOES, though...
Squeak
squeak
I did enjoy some french fries earlier today.
Squeak
squeak—
PLUCK!
I wonder what the weight limit is on this thing.
Uh-oh.
Looks like the weight limit is...
...US.

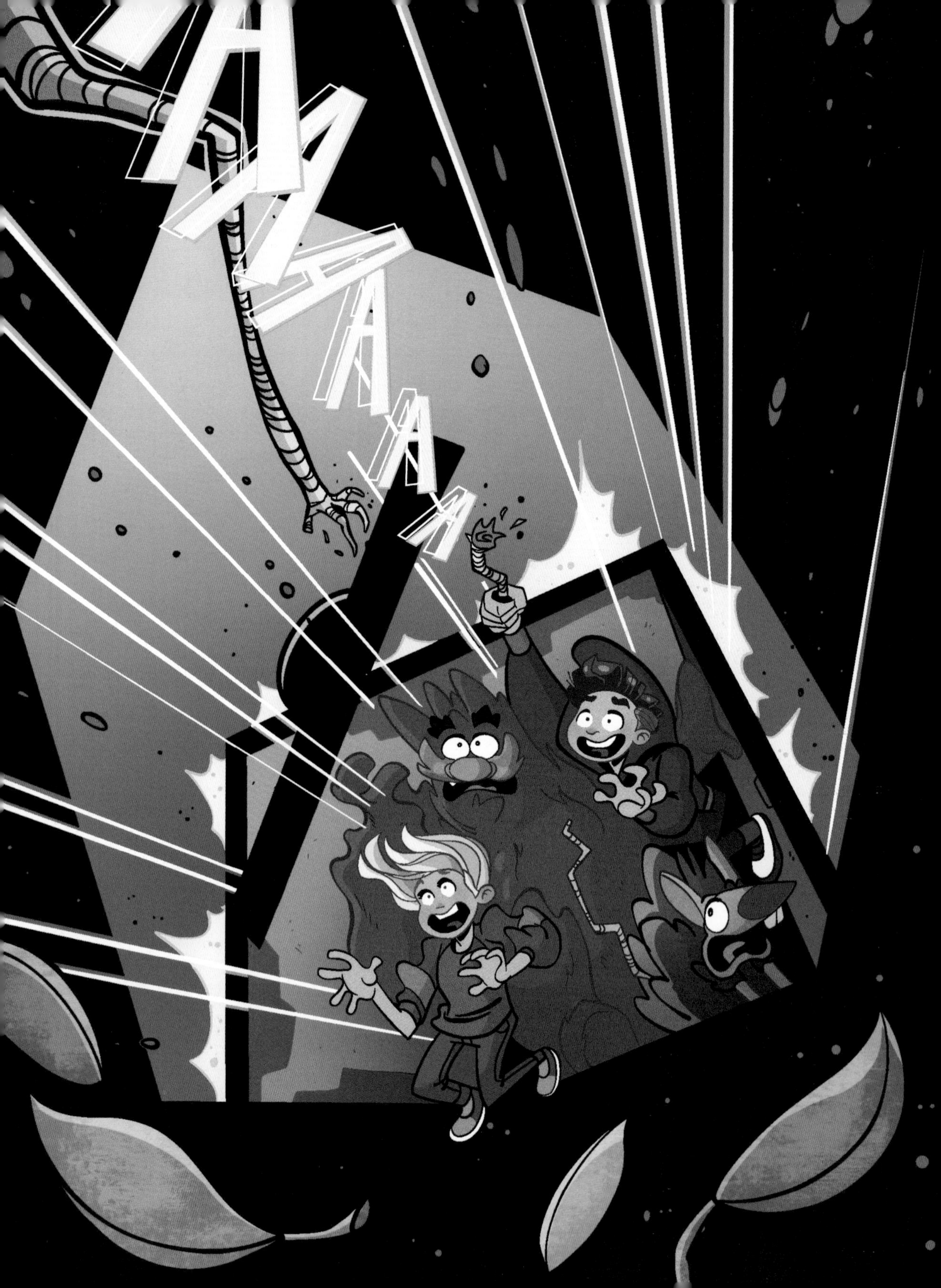
AAAAAAAA

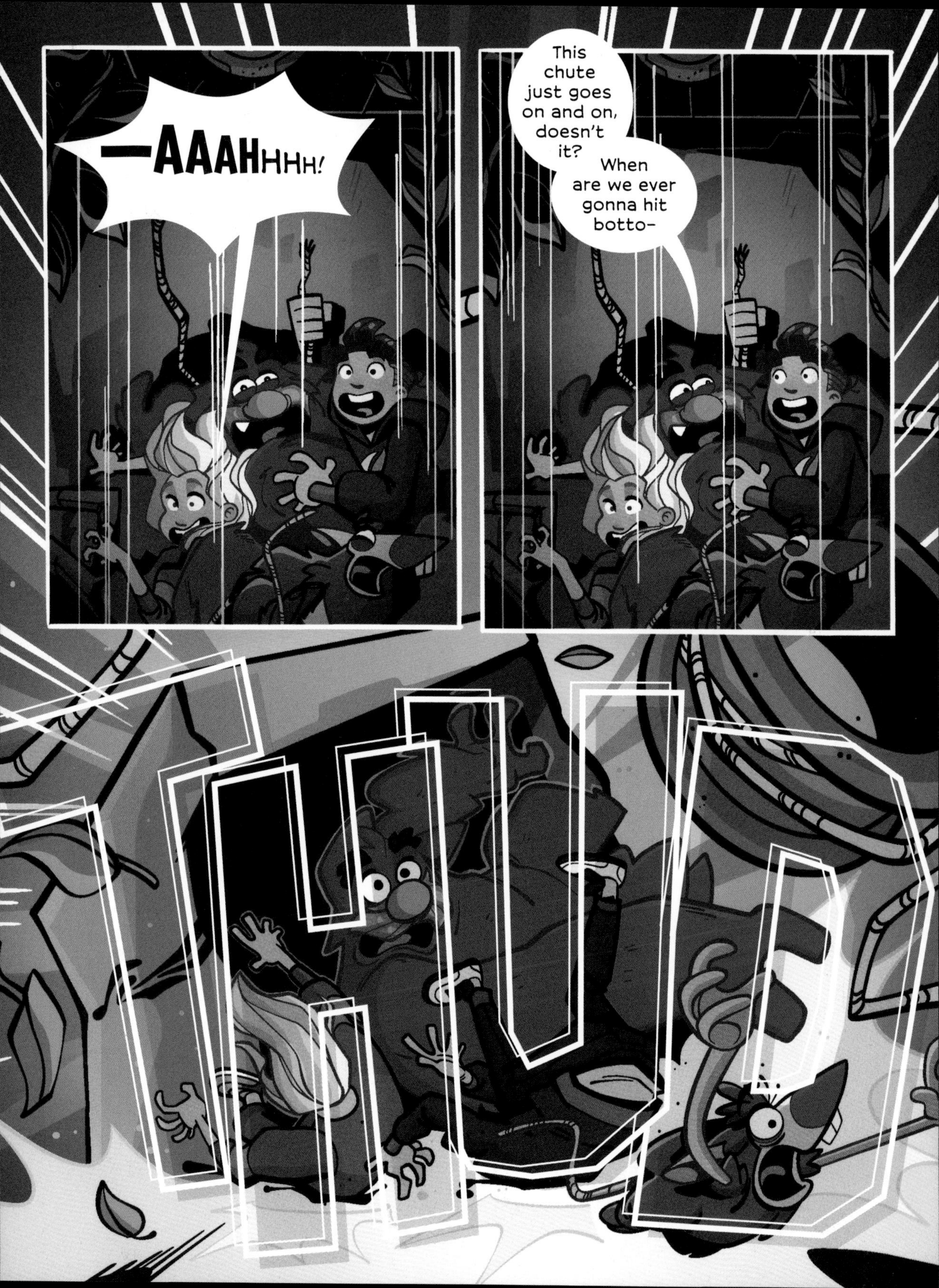
—AAAHHHH!
This chute just goes on and on, doesn't it?
When are we ever gonna hit botto–
THUD

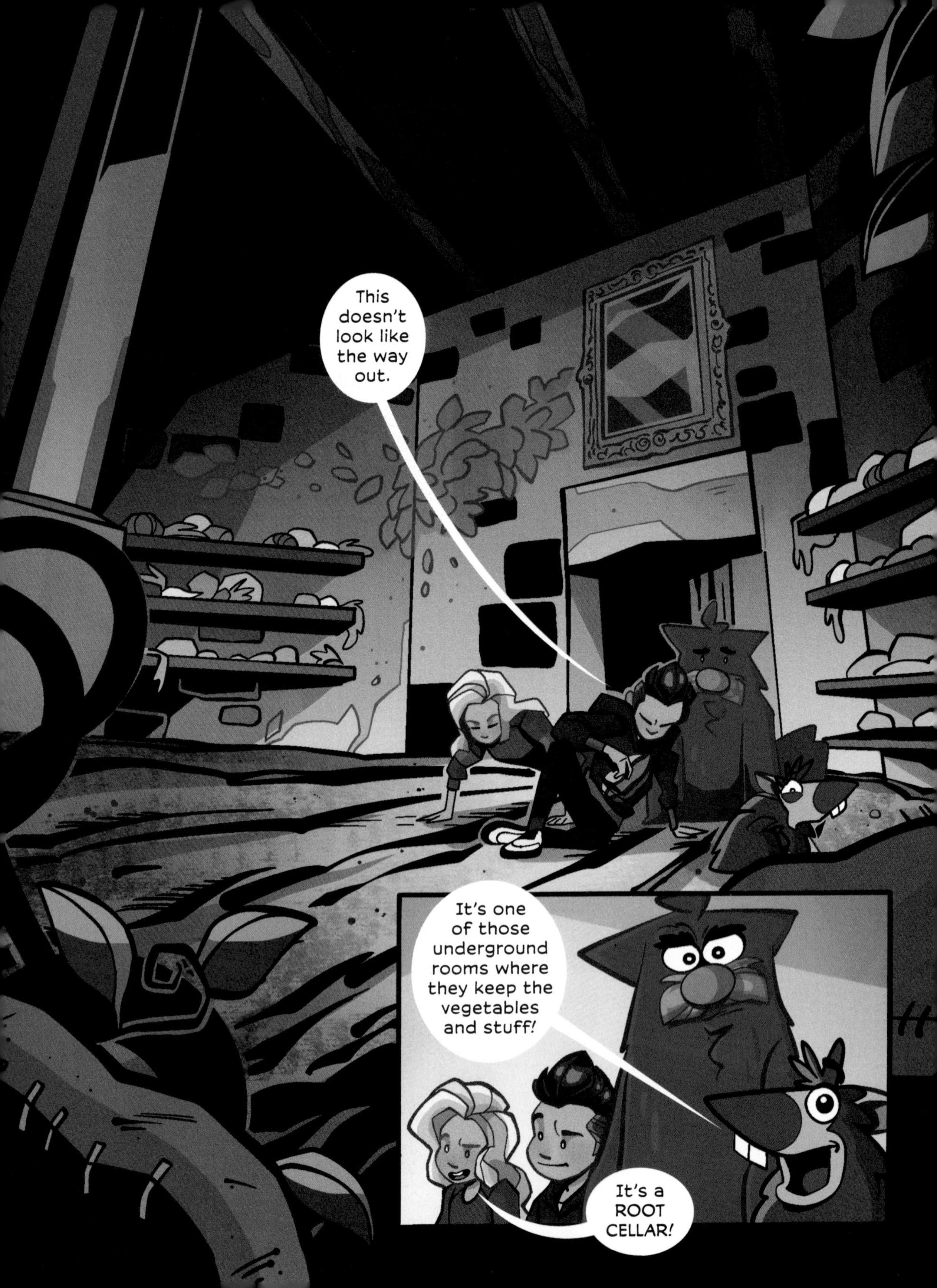
This doesn't look like the way out.
It's one of those underground rooms where they keep the vegetables and stuff!
It's a ROOT CELLAR!

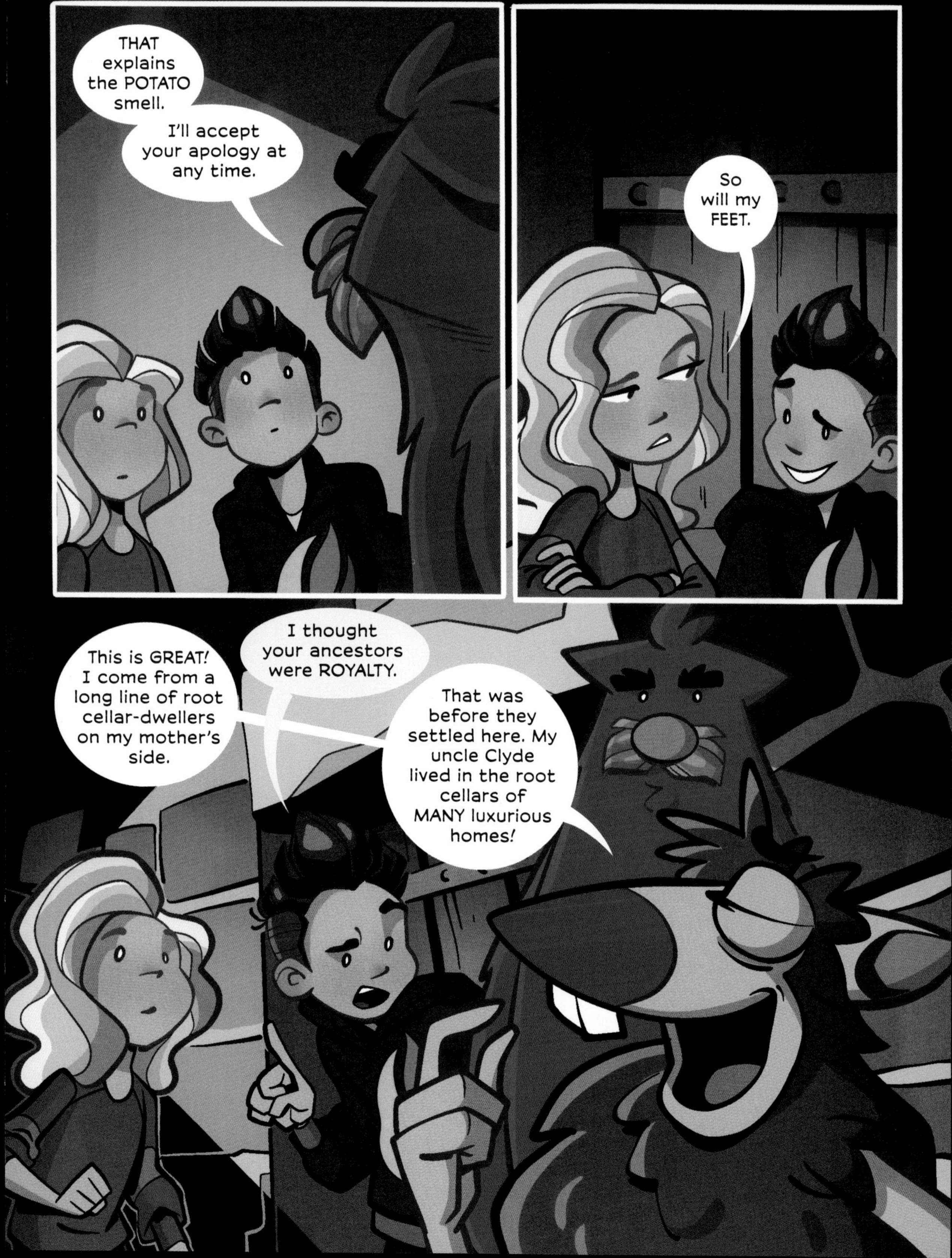
THAT explains the POTATO smell.
I'll accept your apology at any time.
So will my FEET.
This is GREAT! I come from a long line of root cellar-dwellers on my mother's side.
I thought your ancestors were ROYALTY.
That was before they settled here. My uncle Clyde lived in the root cellars of MANY luxurious homes!

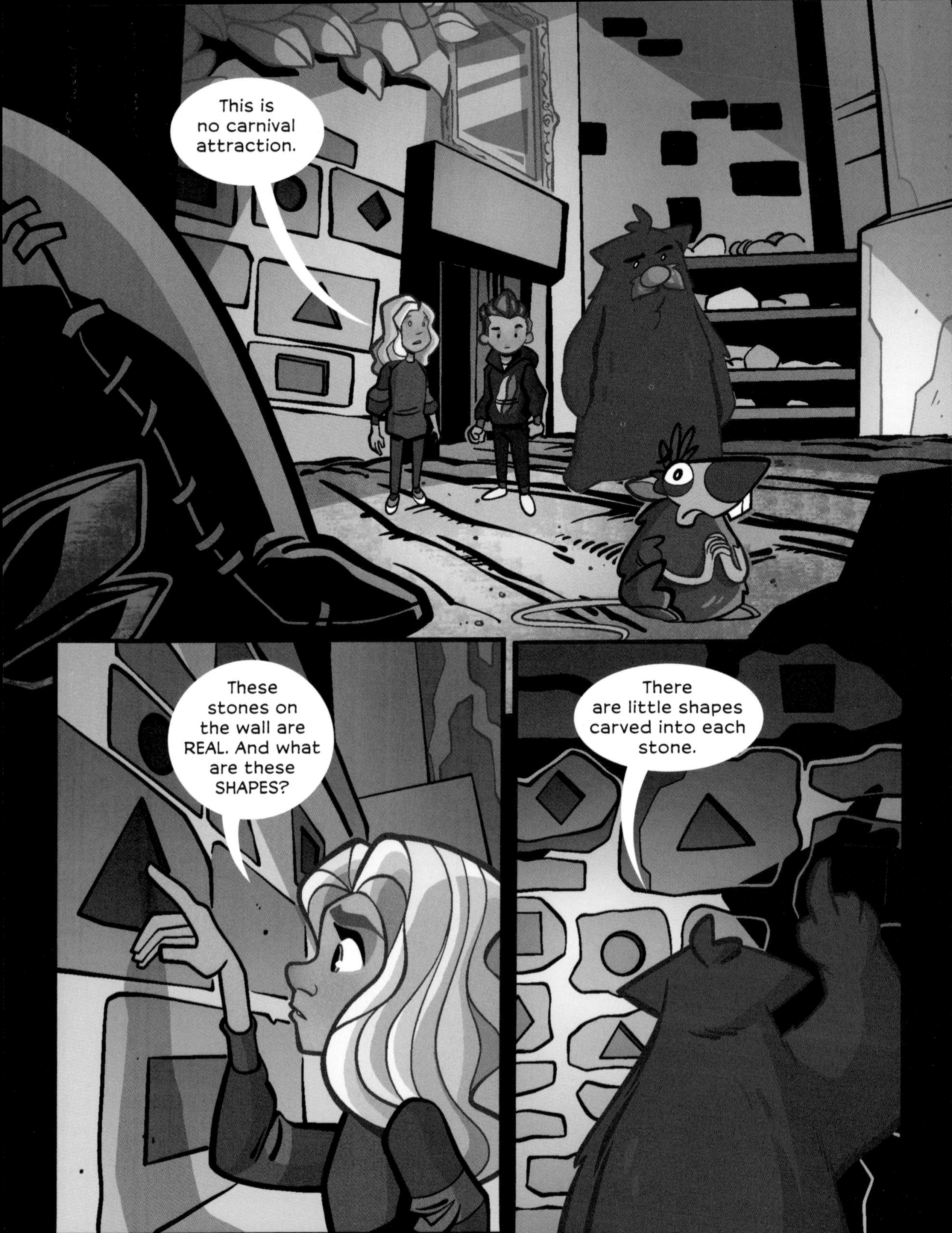
This is no carnival attraction.
These stones on the wall are REAL. And what are these SHAPES?
There are little shapes carved into each stone.

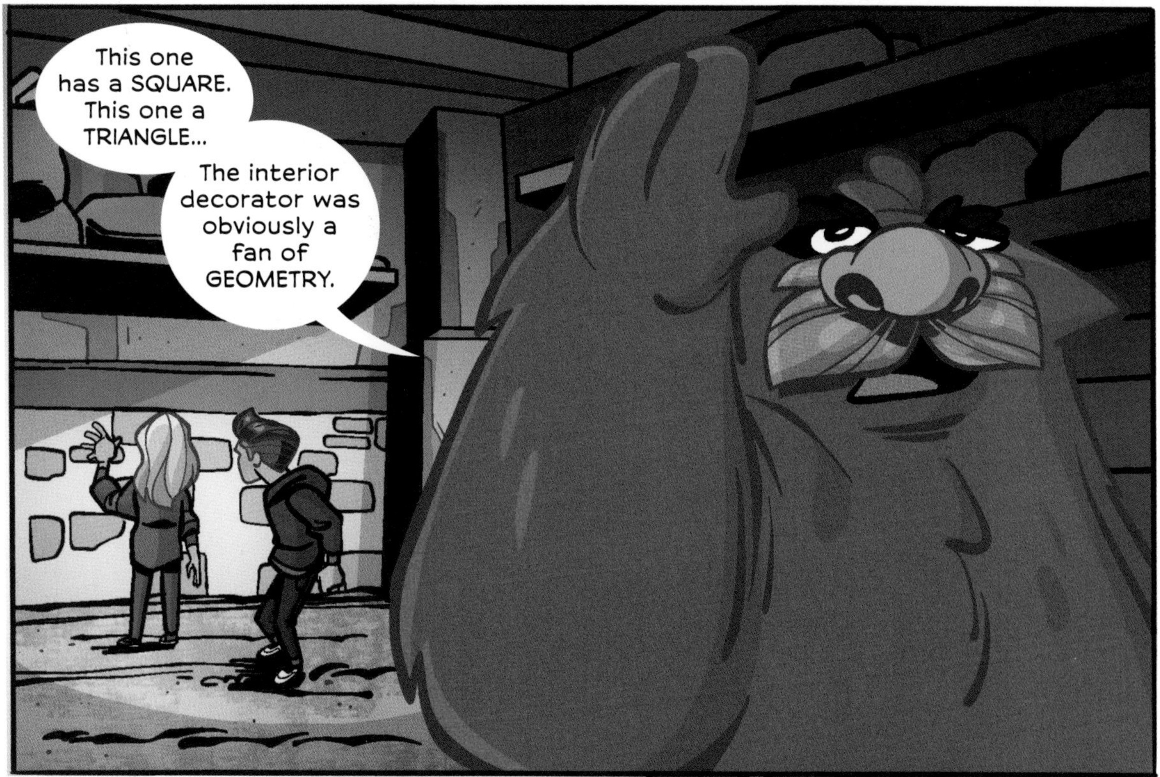

This one has a SQUARE. This one a TRIANGLE...
The interior decorator was obviously a fan of GEOMETRY.

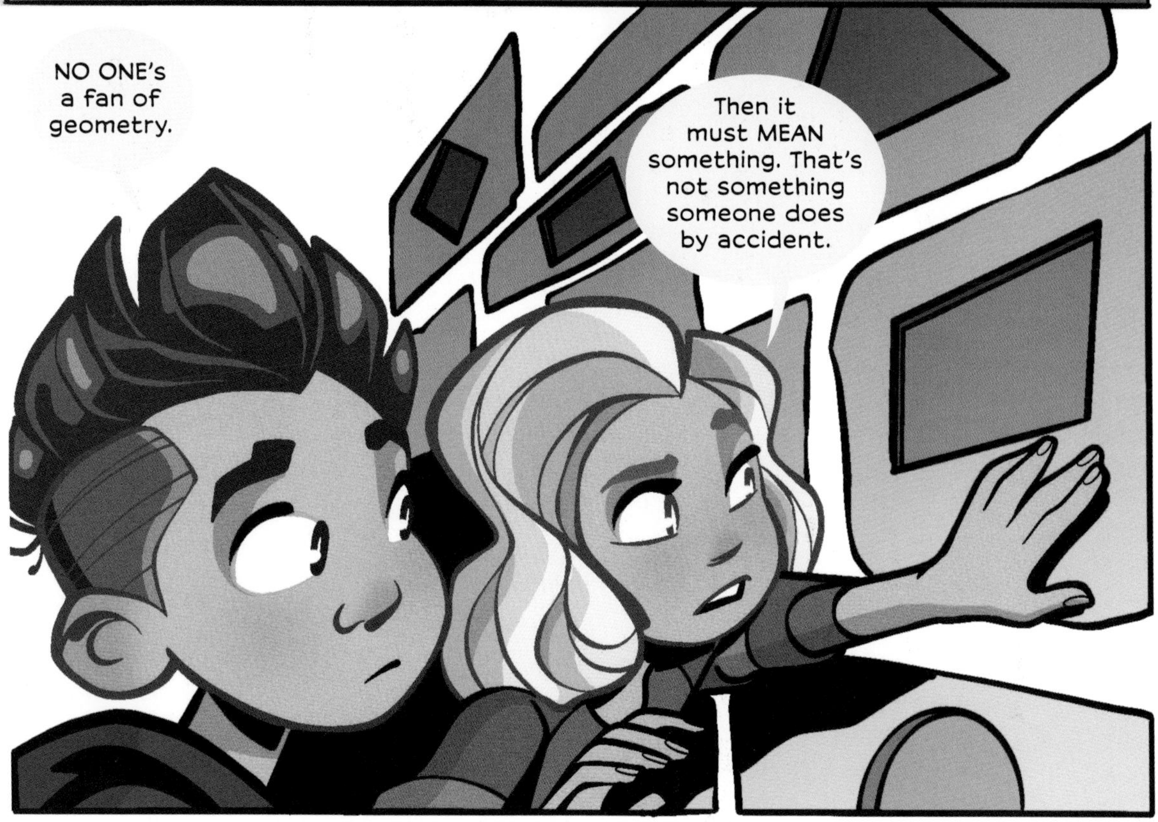

NO ONE's a fan of geometry.
Then it must MEAN something. That's not something someone does by accident.

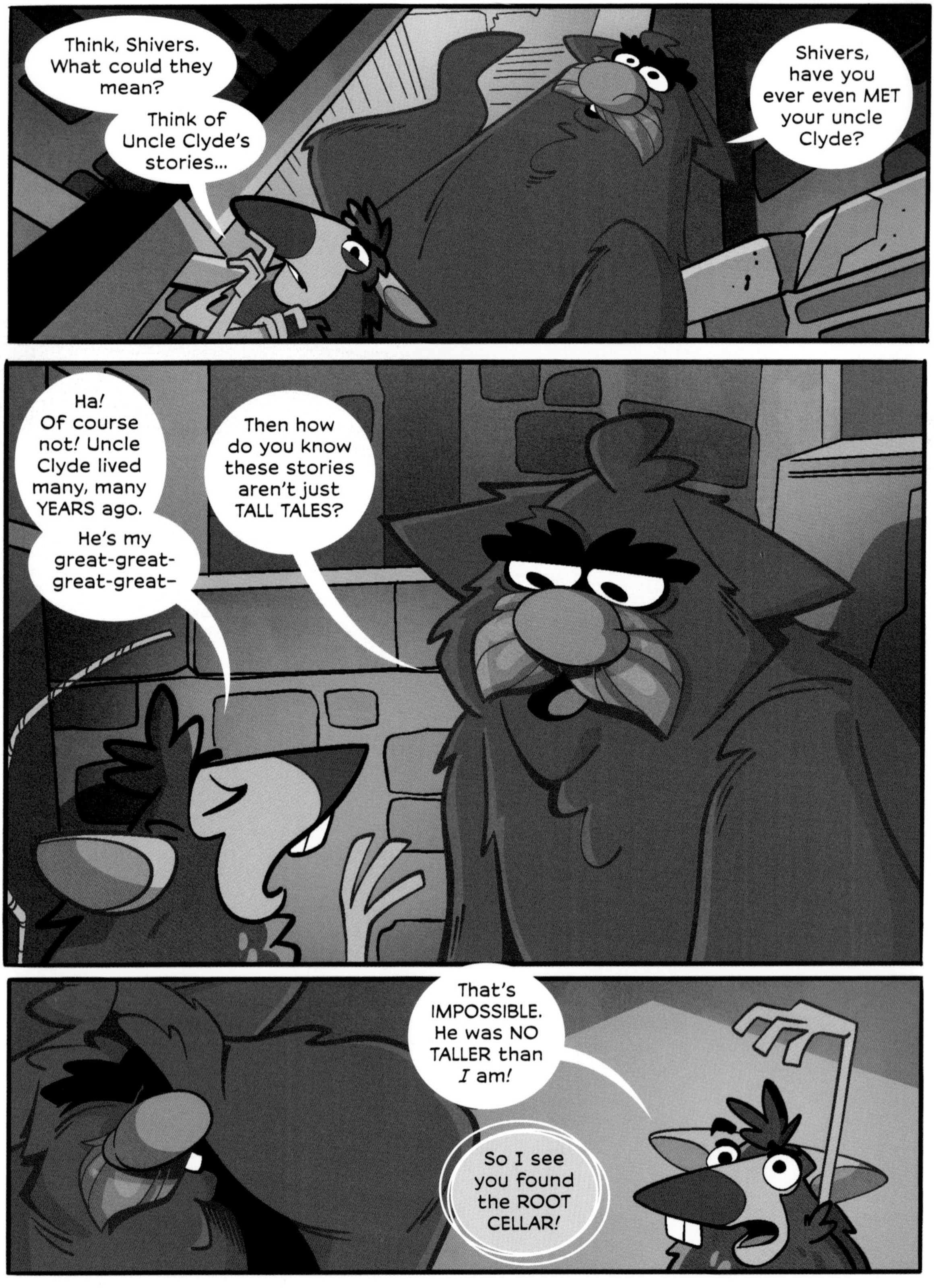
Think, Shivers. What could they mean?
Think of Uncle Clyde's stories...
Shivers, have you ever even MET your uncle Clyde?
Ha! Of course not! Uncle Clyde lived many, many YEARS ago.
He's my great-great-great-great-
Then how do you know these stories aren't just TALL TALES?
That's IMPOSSIBLE. He was NO TALLER than *I* am!
So I see you found the ROOT CELLAR!

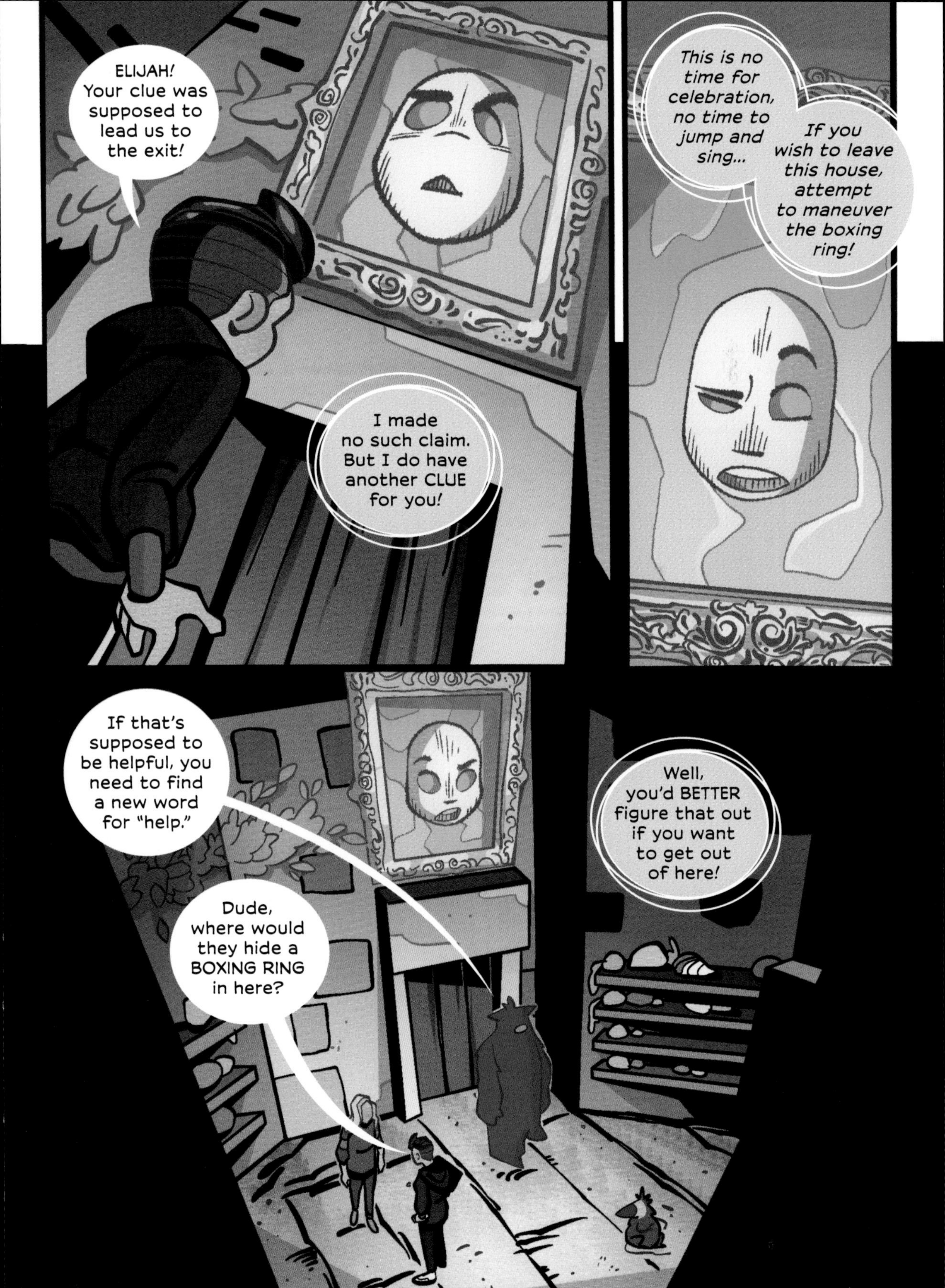
ELIJAH! Your clue was supposed to lead us to the exit!
I made no such claim. But I do have another CLUE for you!
This is no time for celebration, no time to jump and sing...
If you wish to leave this house, attempt to maneuver the boxing ring!
If that's supposed to be helpful, you need to find a new word for "help."
Well, you'd BETTER figure that out if you want to get out of here!
Dude, where would they hide a BOXING RING in here?

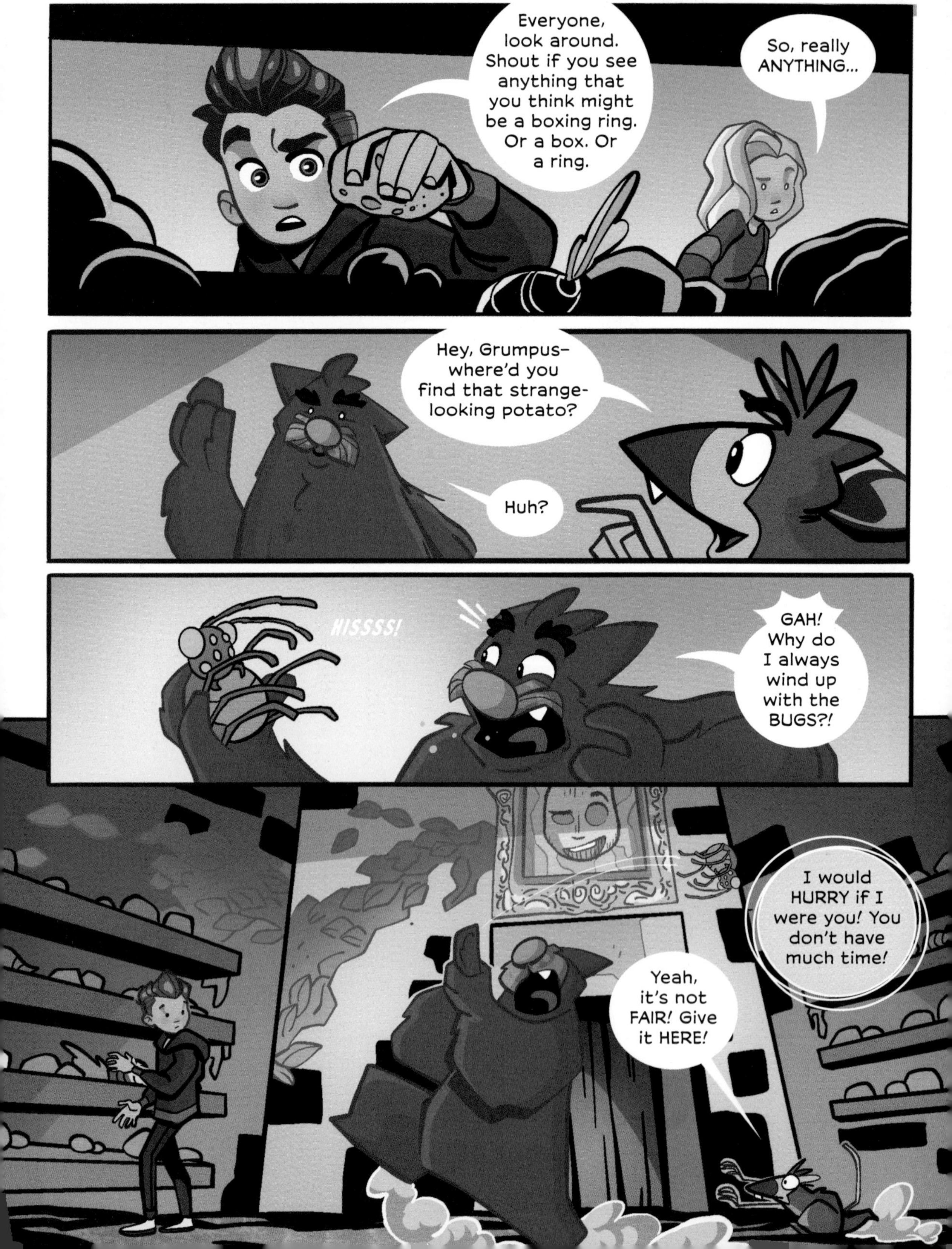
Everyone, look around. Shout if you see anything that you think might be a boxing ring. Or a box. Or a ring.
So, really ANYTHING...
Hey, Grumpus– where'd you find that strange-looking potato?
Huh?
HISSSS!
GAH! Why do I always wind up with the BUGS?!
I would HURRY if I were you! You don't have much time!
Yeah, it's not FAIR! Give it HERE!

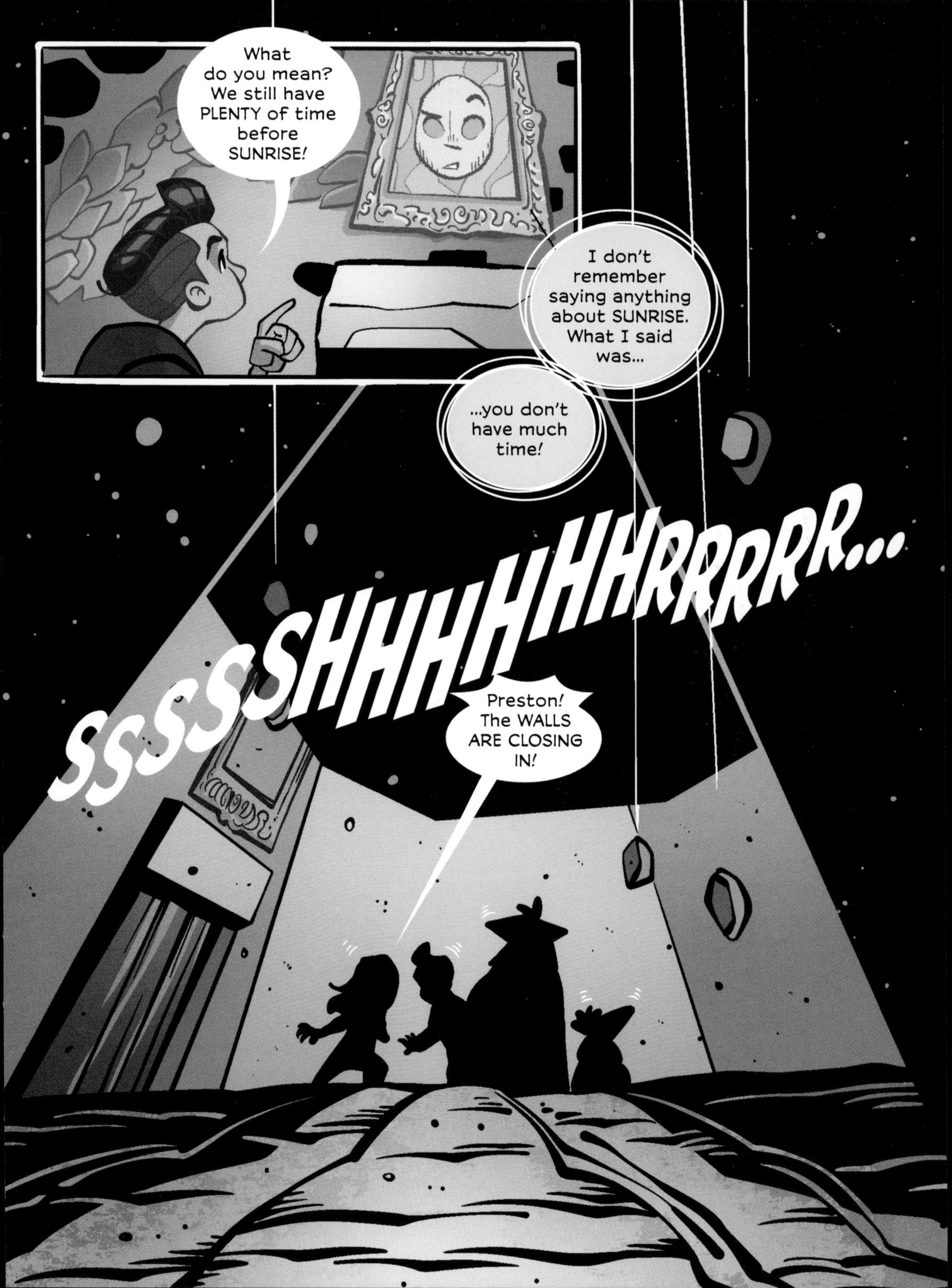
What do you mean? We still have PLENTY of time before SUNRISE!
I don't remember saying anything about SUNRISE. What I said was...
...you don't have much time!
SSSSSHHHHHHHRRRRRR...
Preston! The WALLS ARE CLOSING IN!

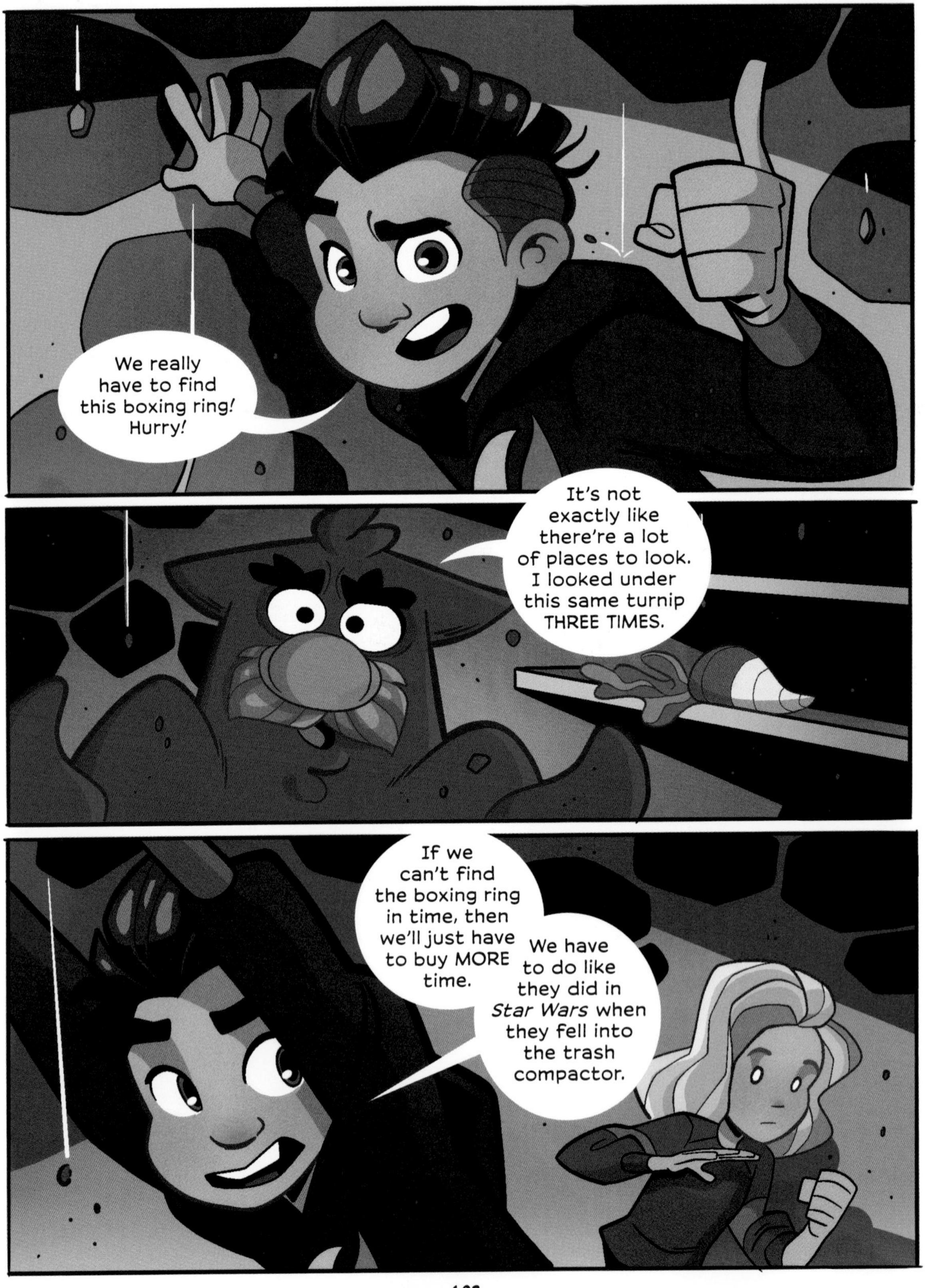
We really have to find this boxing ring! Hurry!
It's not exactly like there're a lot of places to look. I looked under this same turnip THREE TIMES.
If we can't find the boxing ring in time, then we'll just have to buy MORE time.
We have to do like they did in *Star Wars* when they fell into the trash compactor.

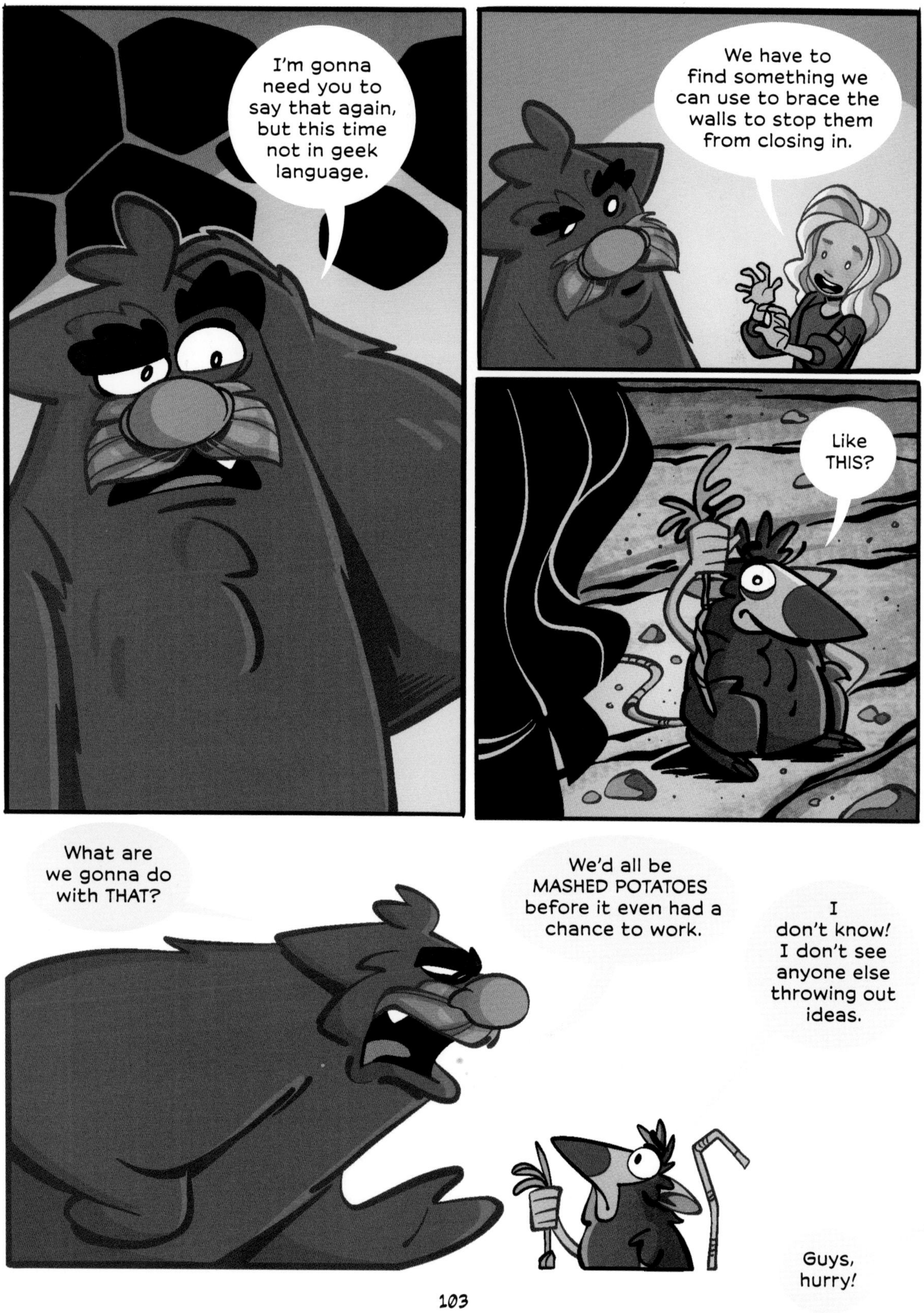
I'm gonna need you to say that again, but this time not in geek language.
We have to find something we can use to brace the walls to stop them from closing in.
Like THIS?
What are we gonna do with THAT?
We'd all be MASHED POTATOES before it even had a chance to work.
I don't know! I don't see anyone else throwing out ideas.
Guys, hurry!

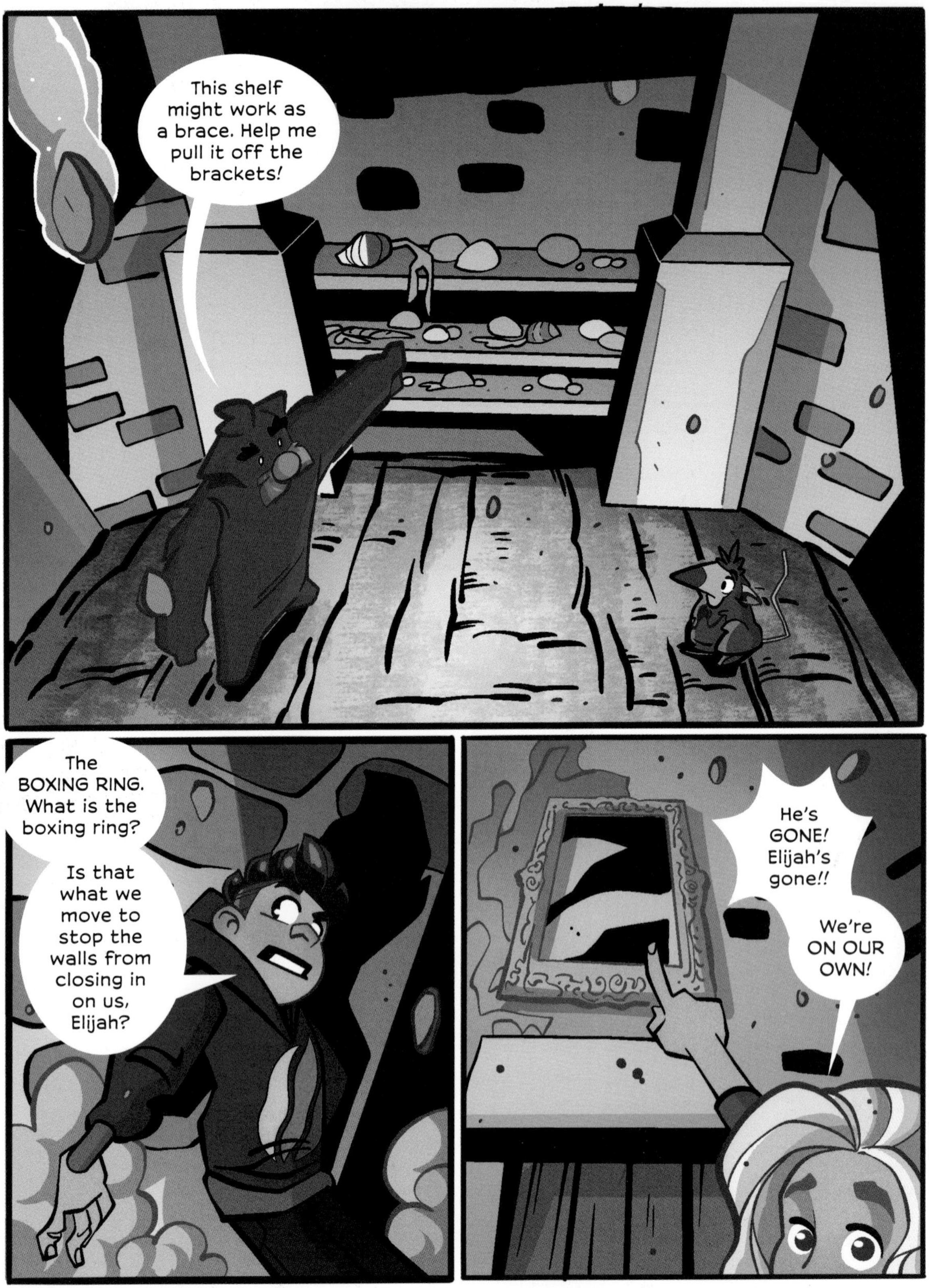
This shelf might work as a brace. Help me pull it off the brackets!
The BOXING RING. What is the boxing ring?
Is that what we move to stop the walls from closing in on us, Elijah?
He's GONE! Elijah's gone!!
We're ON OUR OWN!

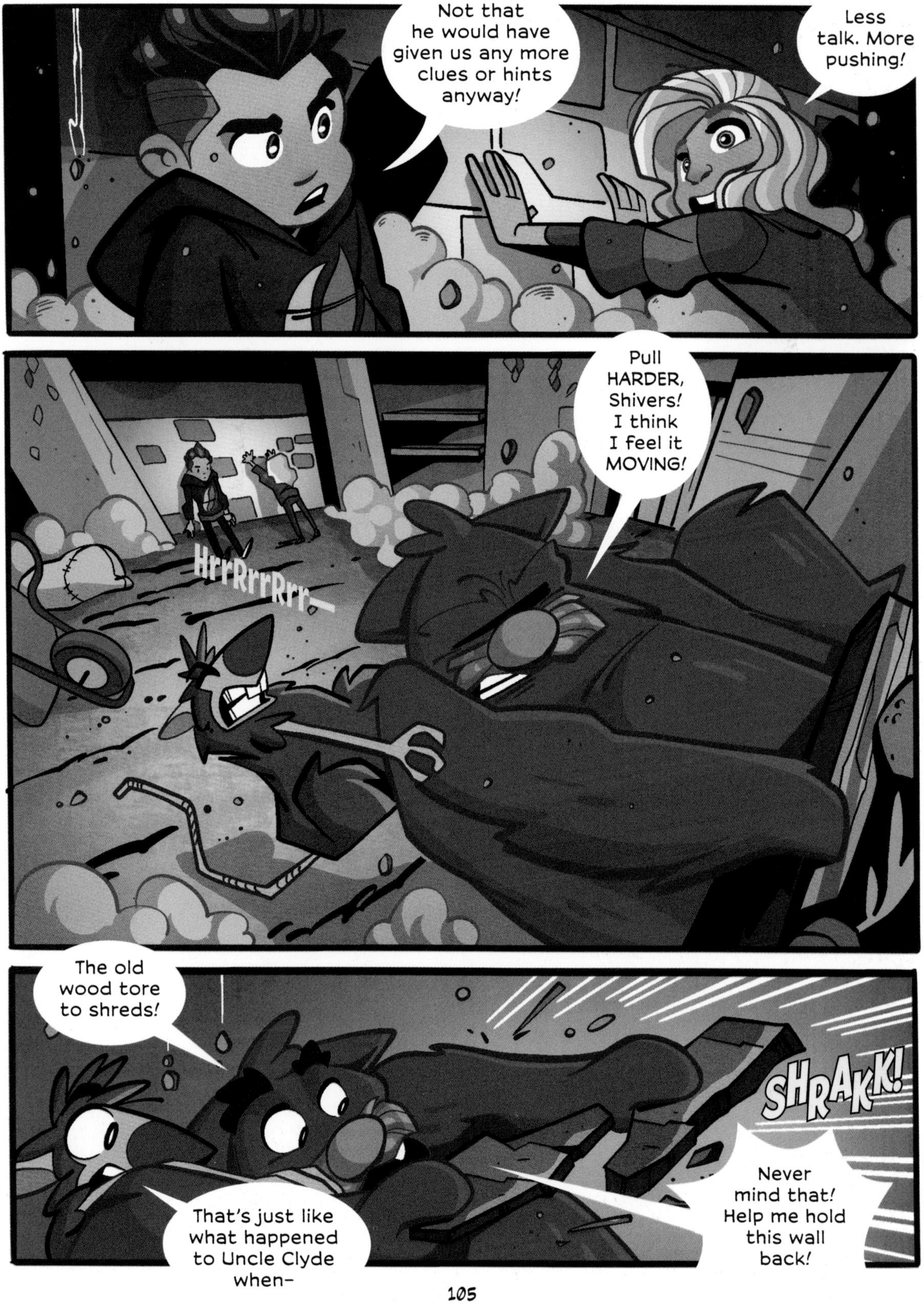
Not that he would have given us any more clues or hints anyway!
Less talk. More pushing!
Pull HARDER, Shivers! I think I feel it MOVING!
HrrRrrRrr–
The old wood tore to shreds!
SHRAKK!
That's just like what happened to Uncle Clyde when–
Never mind that! Help me hold this wall back!

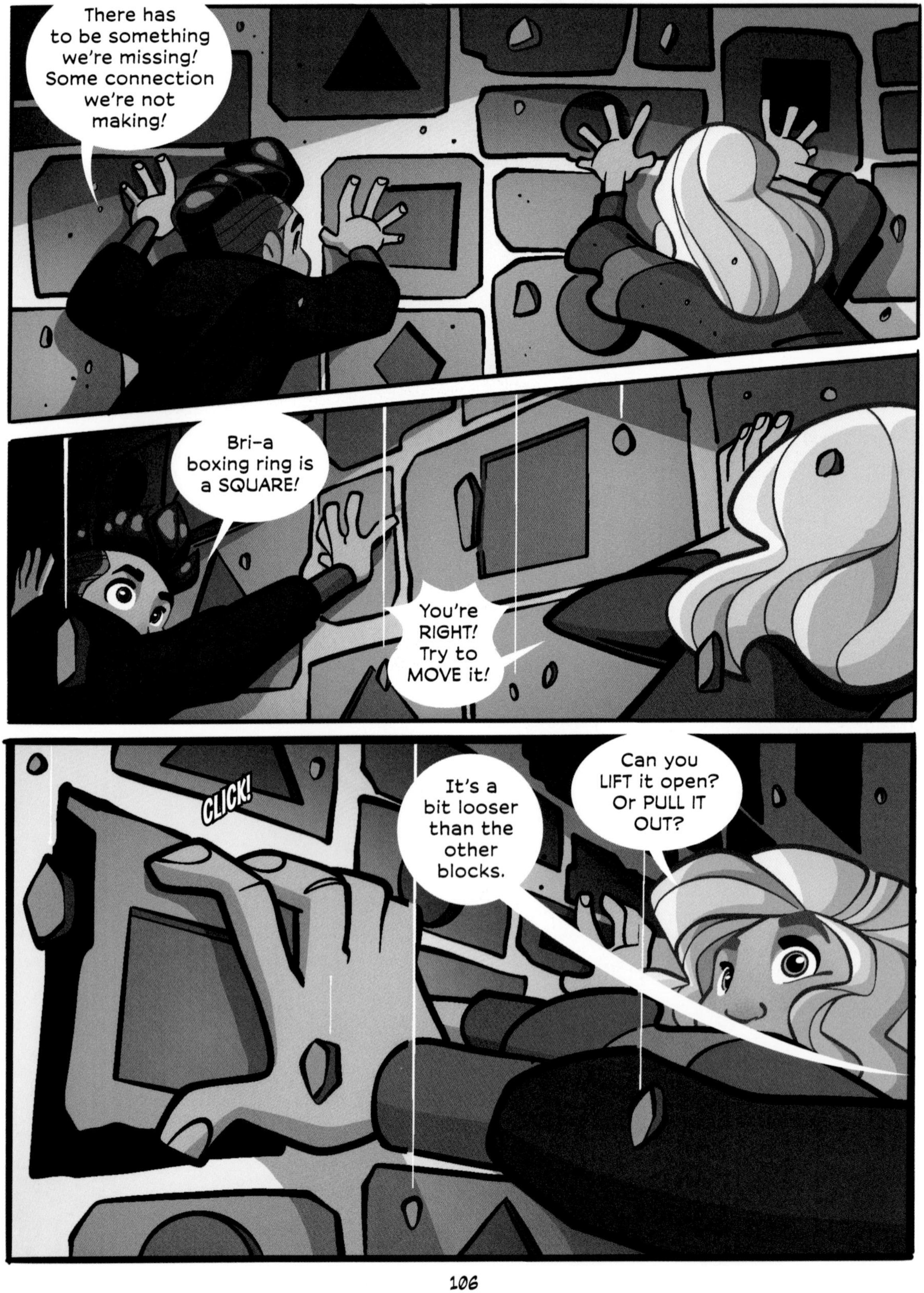
There has to be something we're missing! Some connection we're not making!
Bri—a boxing ring is a SQUARE!
You're RIGHT! Try to MOVE it!
CLICK!
It's a bit looser than the other blocks.
Can you LIFT it open? Or PULL IT OUT?

...and Uncle Clyde warned them that the old boat wouldn't hold, but they took their chances and went over the waterfall anyway!

Shivers, no one wants to hear your stories right now!

...Well? What happened next?

Huh?

To UNCLE CLYDE! What happened?

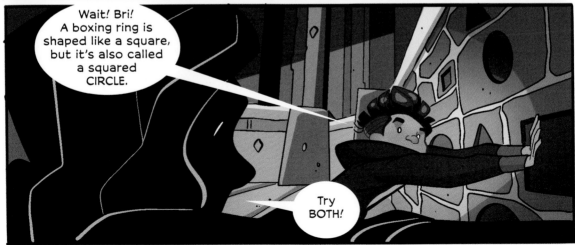

Wait! Bri! A boxing ring is shaped like a square, but it's also called a squared CIRCLE.

Try BOTH!

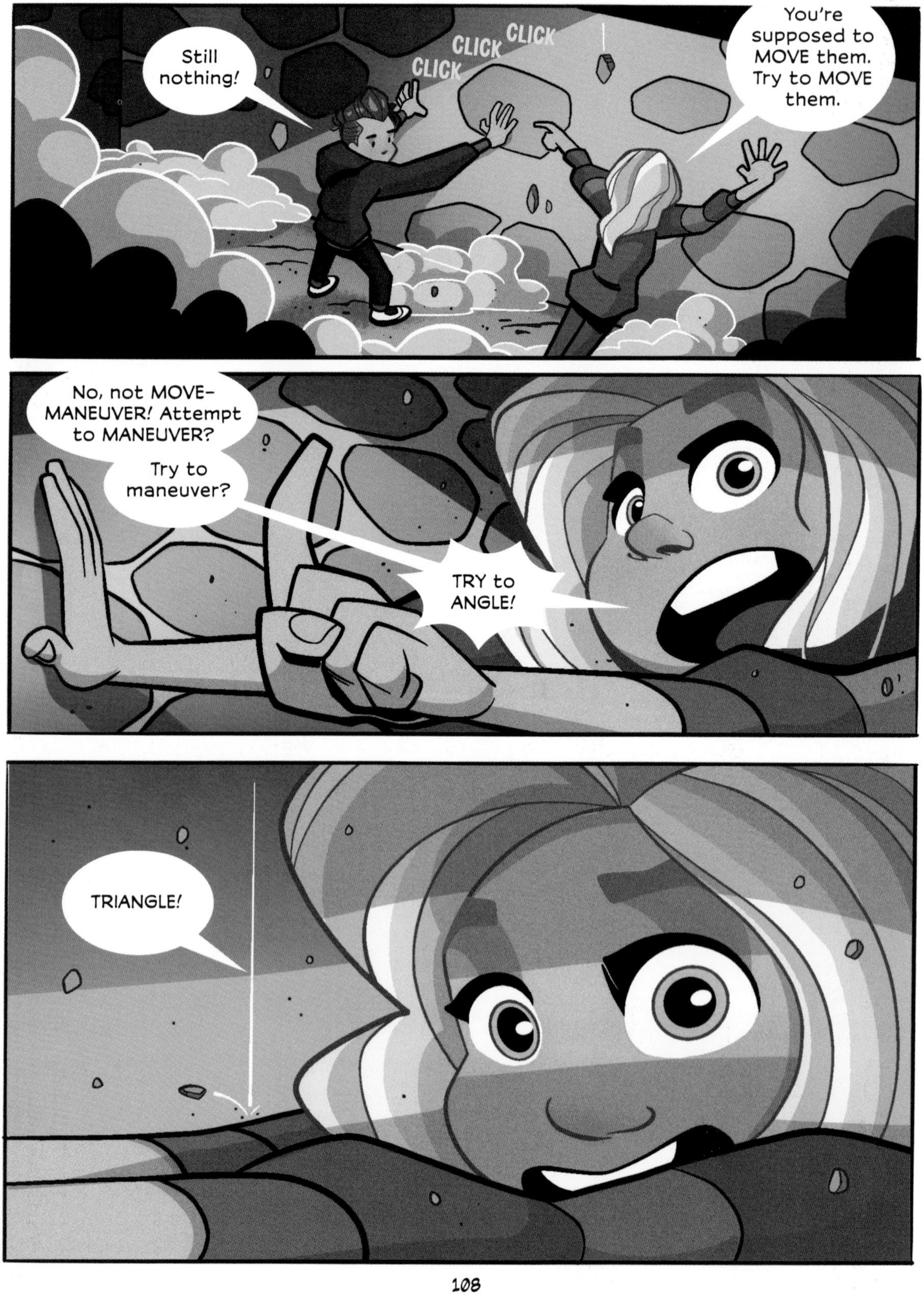
CLICK
CLICK
CLICK
Still nothing!
You're supposed to MOVE them. Try to MOVE them.
No, not MOVE–MANEUVER! Attempt to MANEUVER?
Try to maneuver?
TRY to ANGLE!
TRIANGLE!

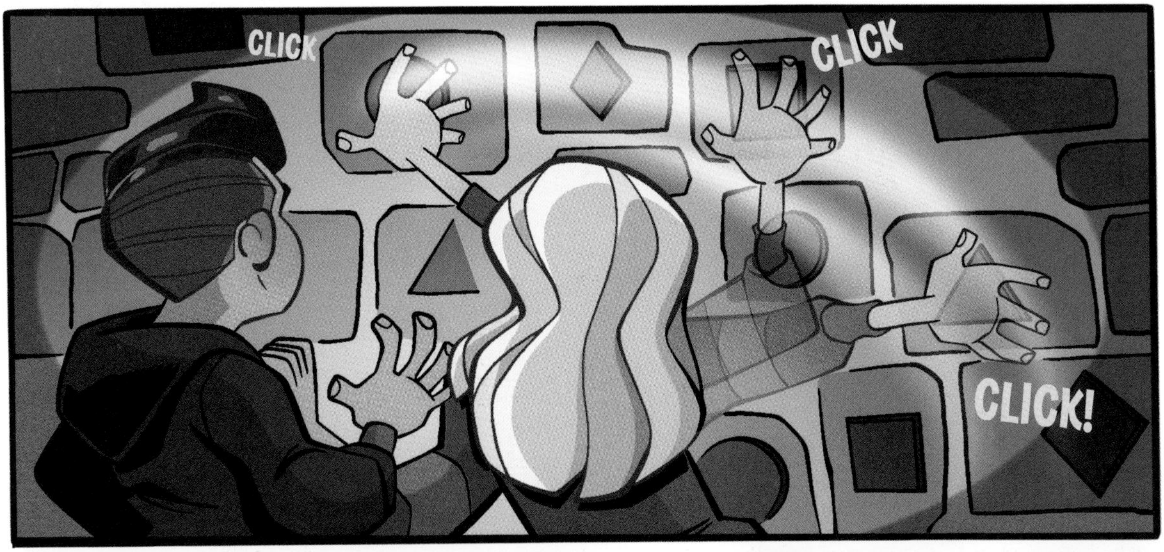
CLICK
CLICK
CLICK!

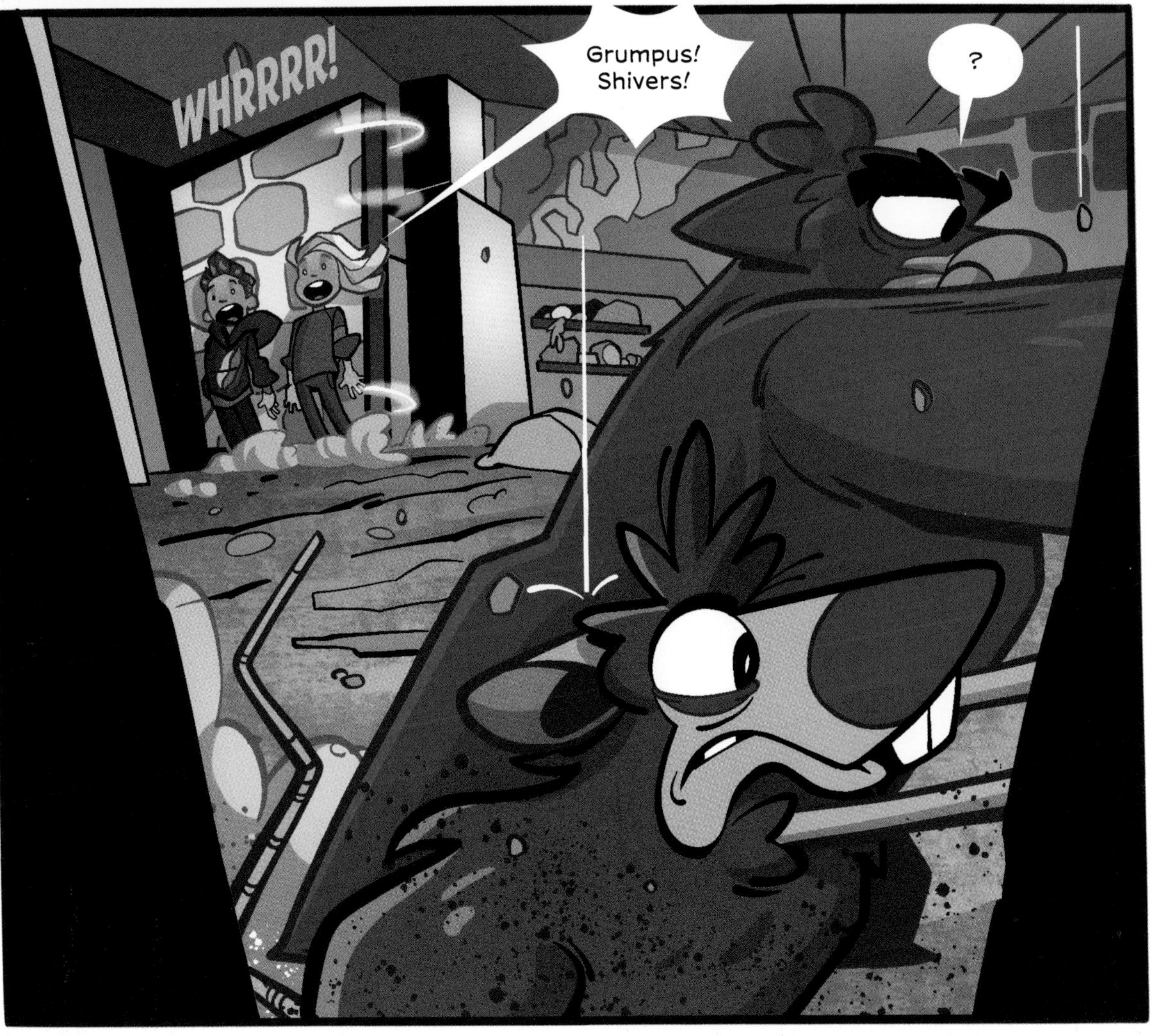
WHRRRR!
Grumpus! Shivers!
?

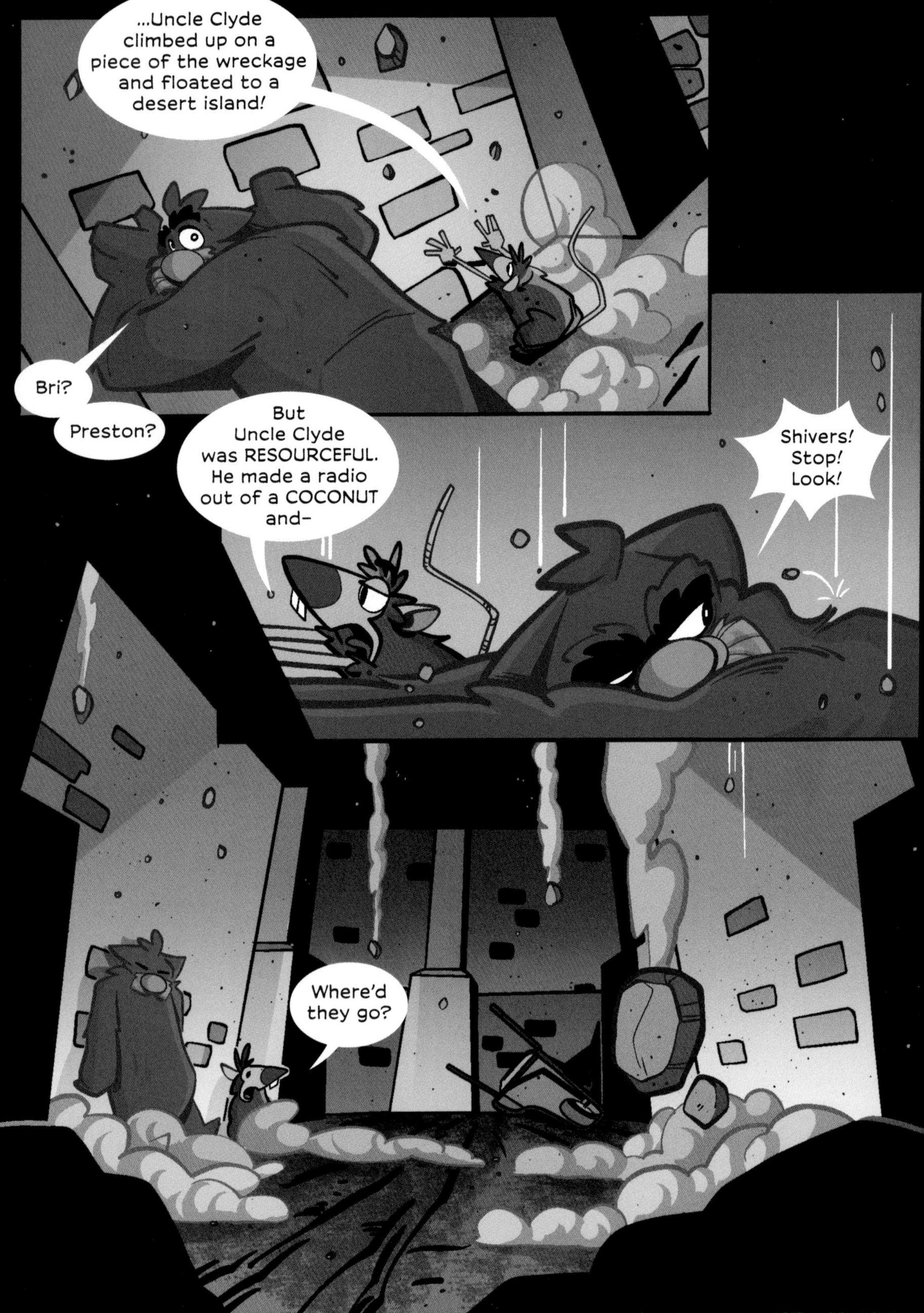

...Uncle Clyde climbed up on a piece of the wreckage and floated to a desert island!
Bri?
Preston?
But Uncle Clyde was RESOURCEFUL. He made a radio out of a COCONUT and–
Shivers! Stop! Look!
Where'd they go?

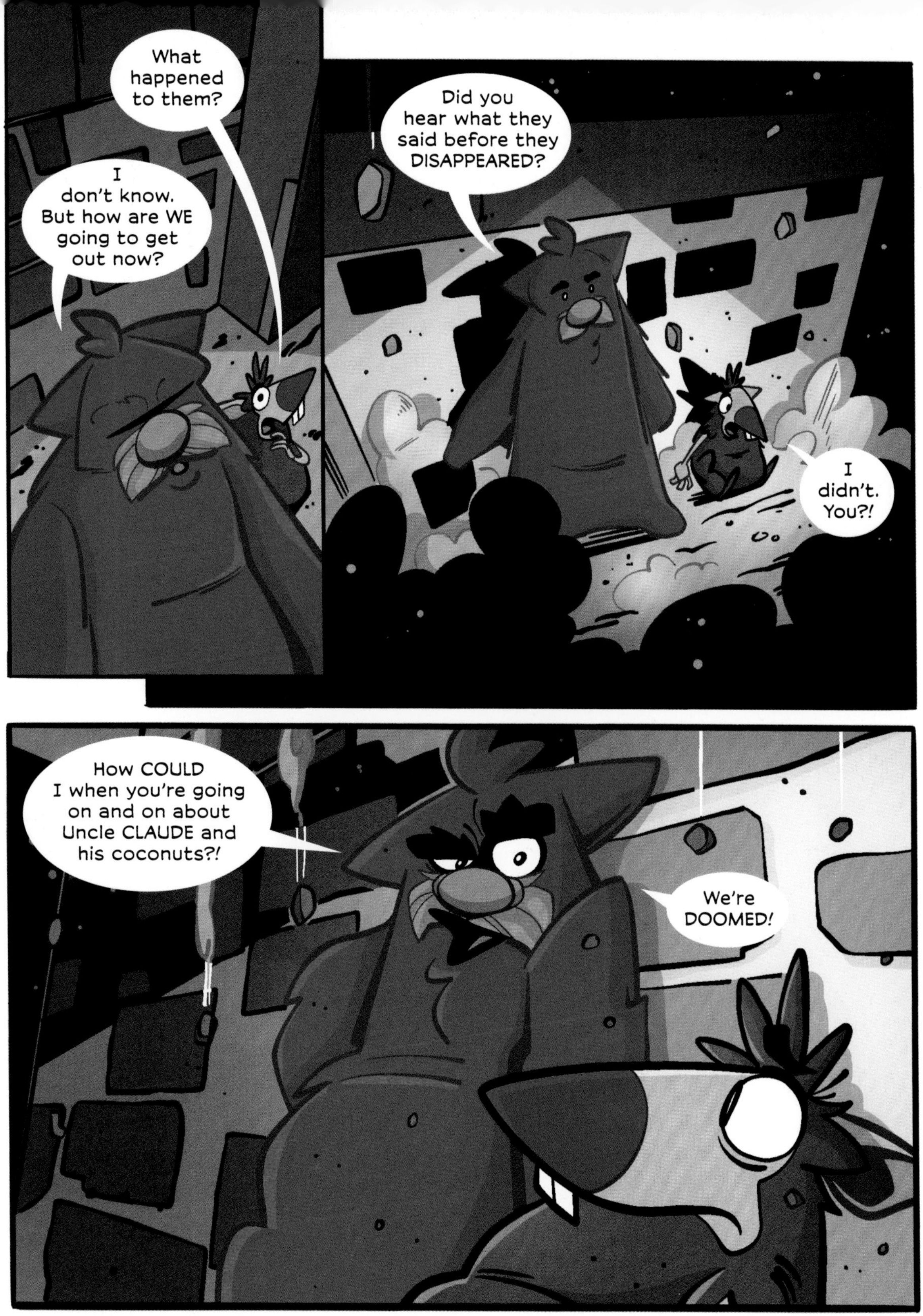
What happened to them?
I don't know. But how are WE going to get out now?
Did you hear what they said before they DISAPPEARED?
I didn't. You?!
How COULD I when you're going on and on about Uncle CLAUDE and his coconuts?!
We're DOOMED!

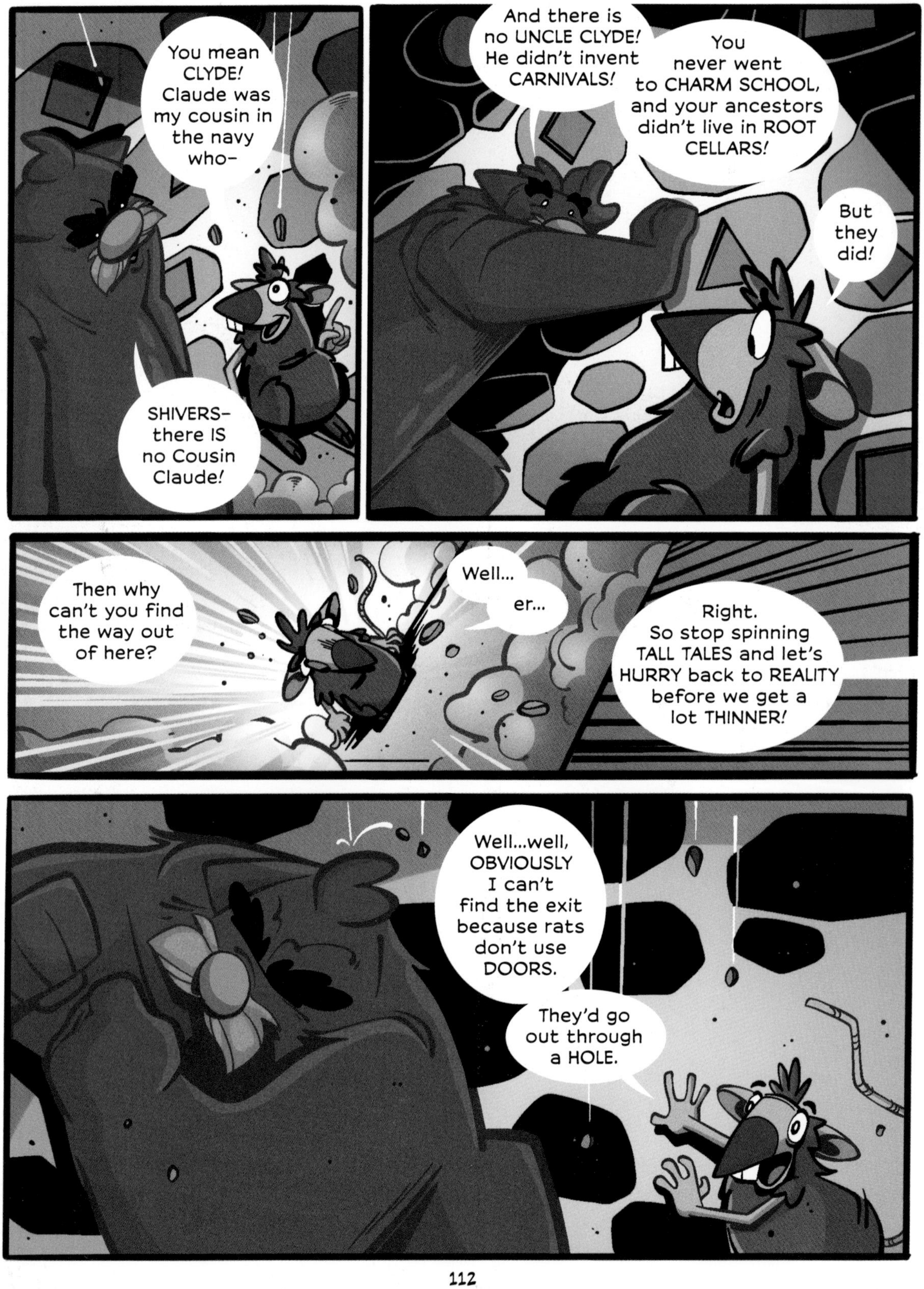
You mean CLYDE! Claude was my cousin in the navy who–
SHIVERS– there IS no Cousin Claude!
And there is no UNCLE CLYDE! He didn't invent CARNIVALS!
You never went to CHARM SCHOOL, and your ancestors didn't live in ROOT CELLARS!
But they did!
Then why can't you find the way out of here?
Well...
er...
Right. So stop spinning TALL TALES and let's HURRY back to REALITY before we get a lot THINNER!
Well...well, OBVIOUSLY I can't find the exit because rats don't use DOORS.
They'd go out through a HOLE.

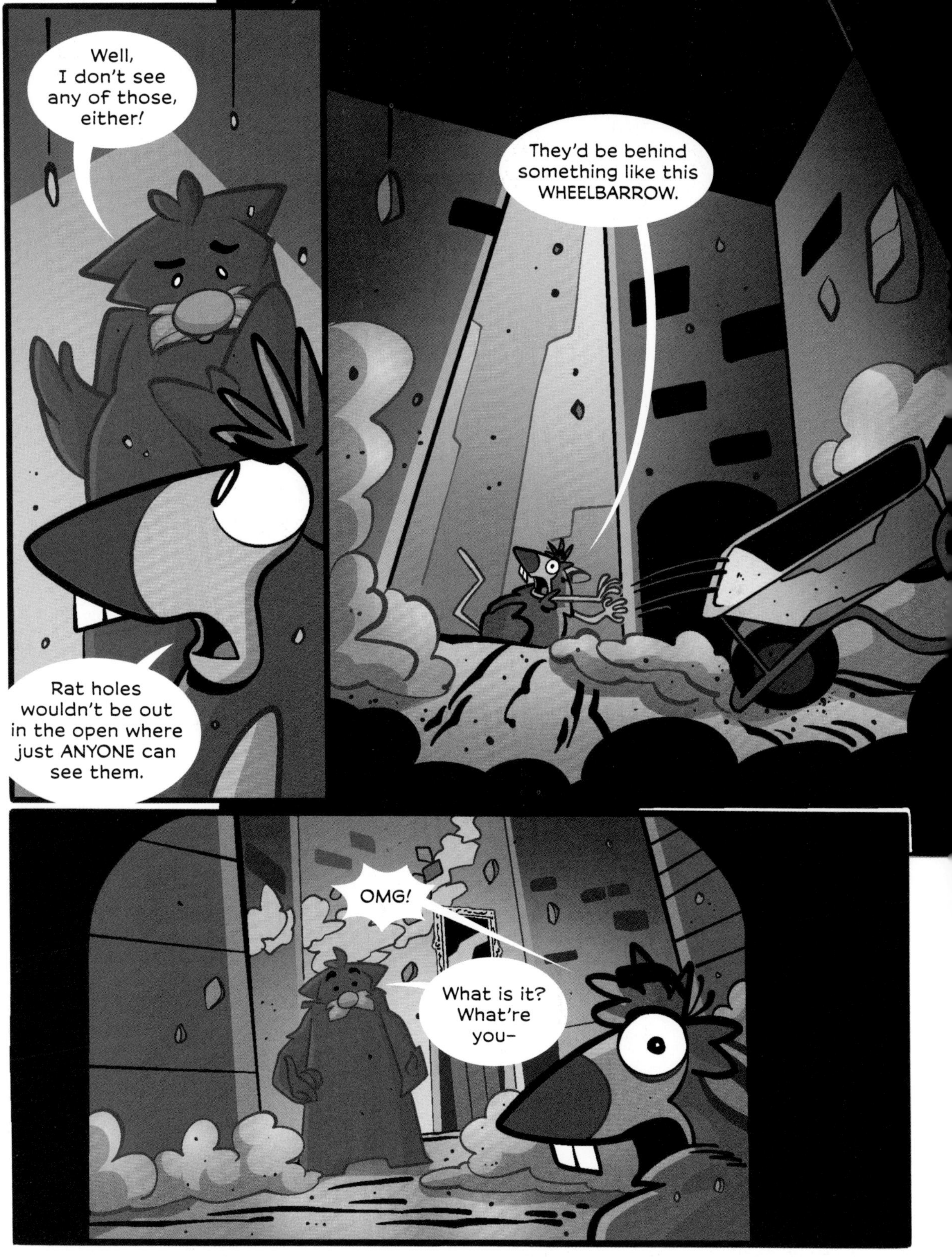

Well, I don't see any of those, either!
Rat holes wouldn't be out in the open where just ANYONE can see them.
They'd be behind something like this WHEELBARROW.
OMG!
What is it? What're you-

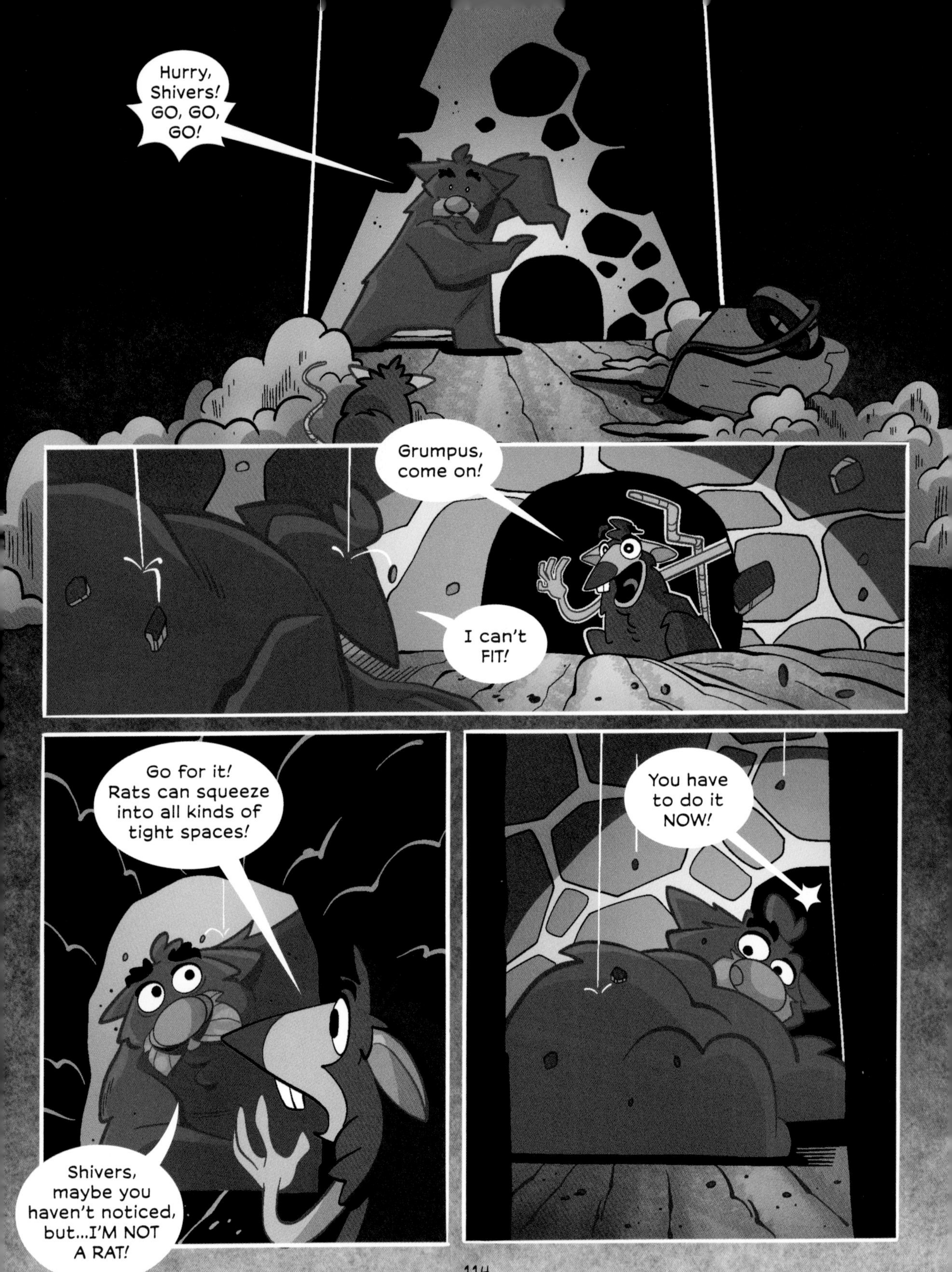
Hurry, Shivers! GO, GO, GO!
Grumpus, come on!
I can't FIT!
Go for it! Rats can squeeze into all kinds of tight spaces!
Shivers, maybe you haven't noticed, but...I'M NOT A RAT!
You have to do it NOW!

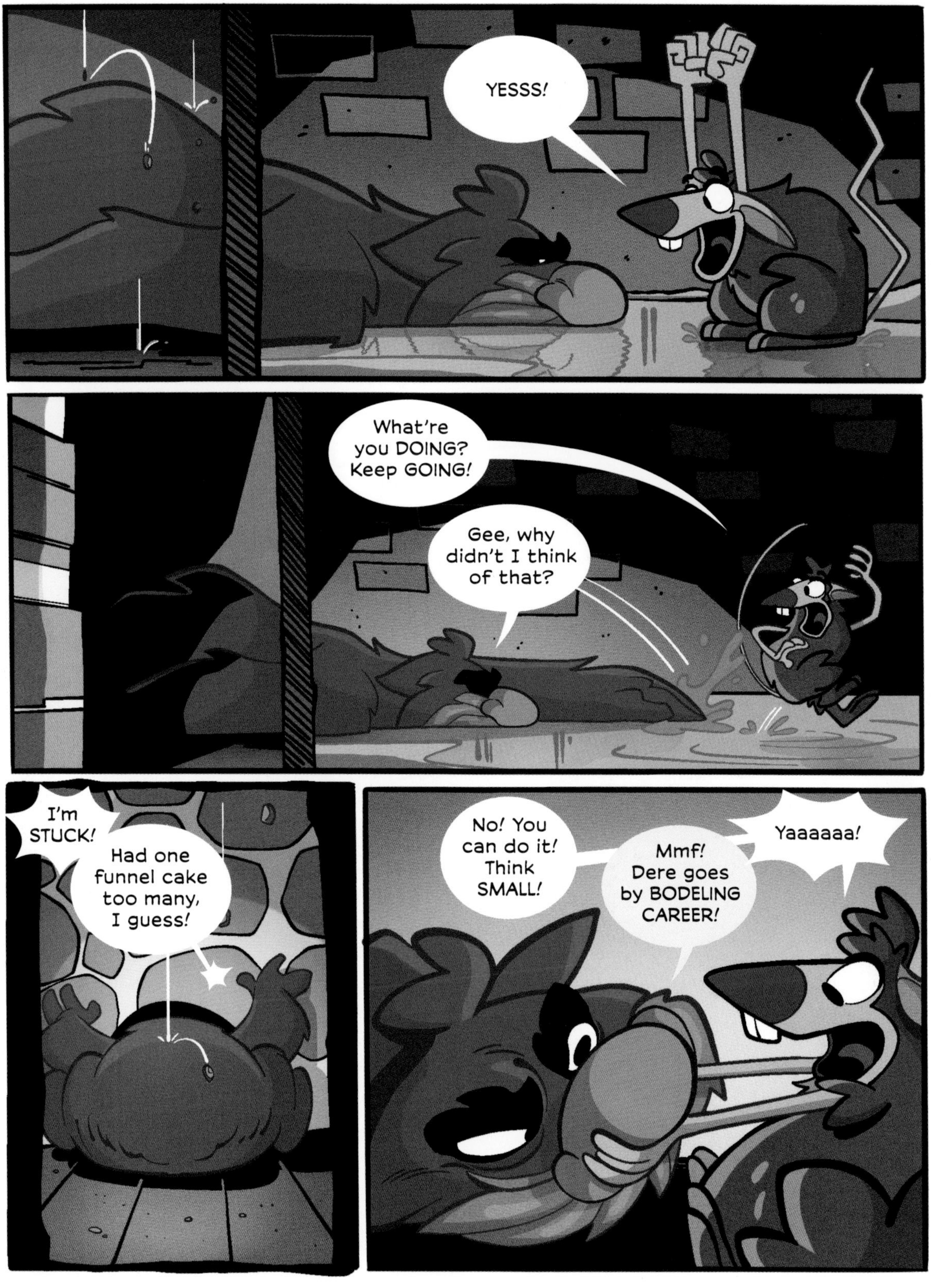
YESSS!
What're you DOING? Keep GOING!
Gee, why didn't I think of that?
I'm STUCK!
Had one funnel cake too many, I guess!
No! You can do it! Think SMALL!
Mmf! Dere goes by BODELING CAREER!
Yaaaaaa!

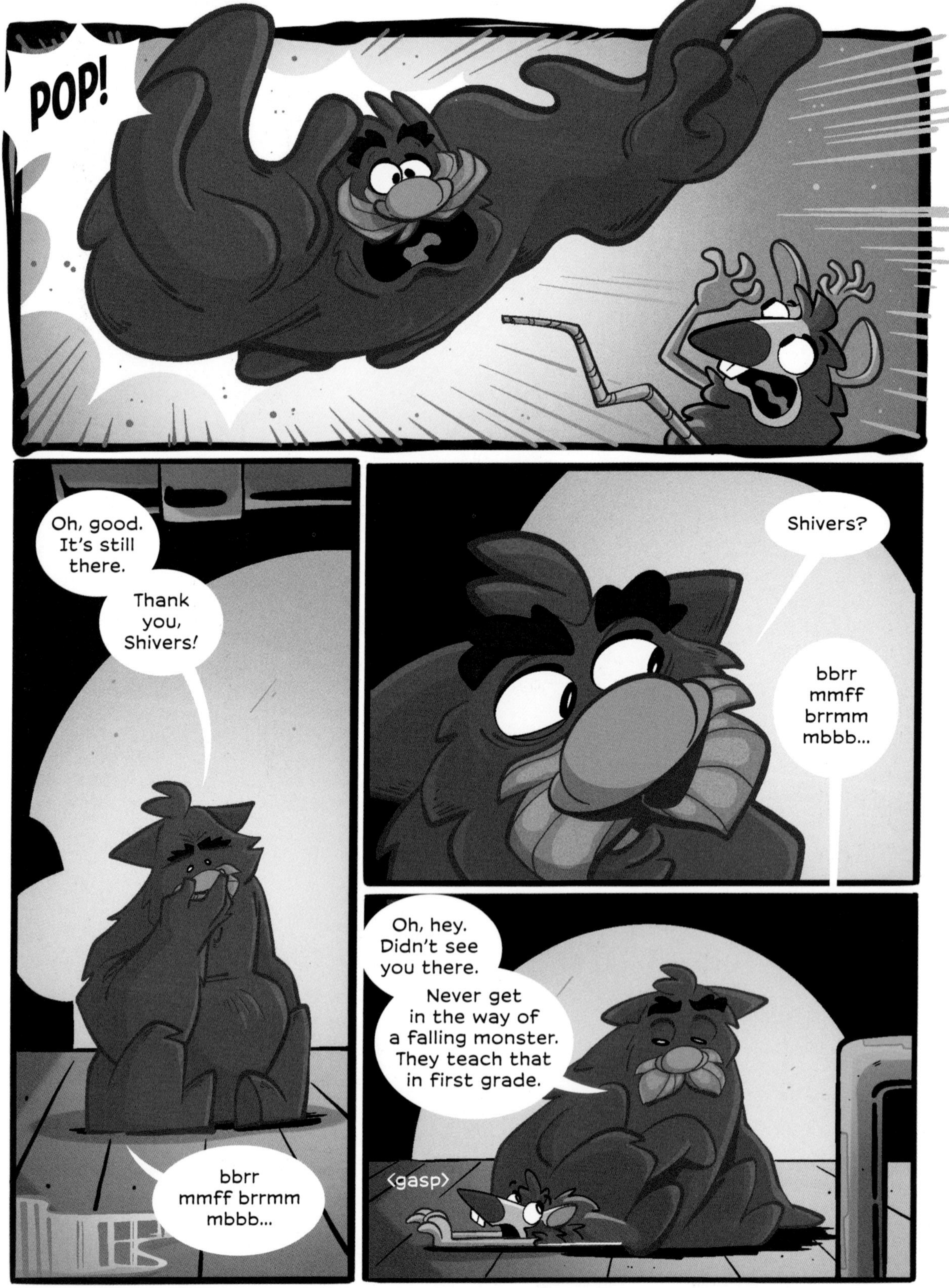
POP!
Oh, good. It's still there.
Thank you, Shivers!
bbrr mmff brrmm mbbb...
Shivers?
bbrr mmff brrmm mbbb...
Oh, hey. Didn't see you there.
Never get in the way of a falling monster. They teach that in first grade.
<gasp>

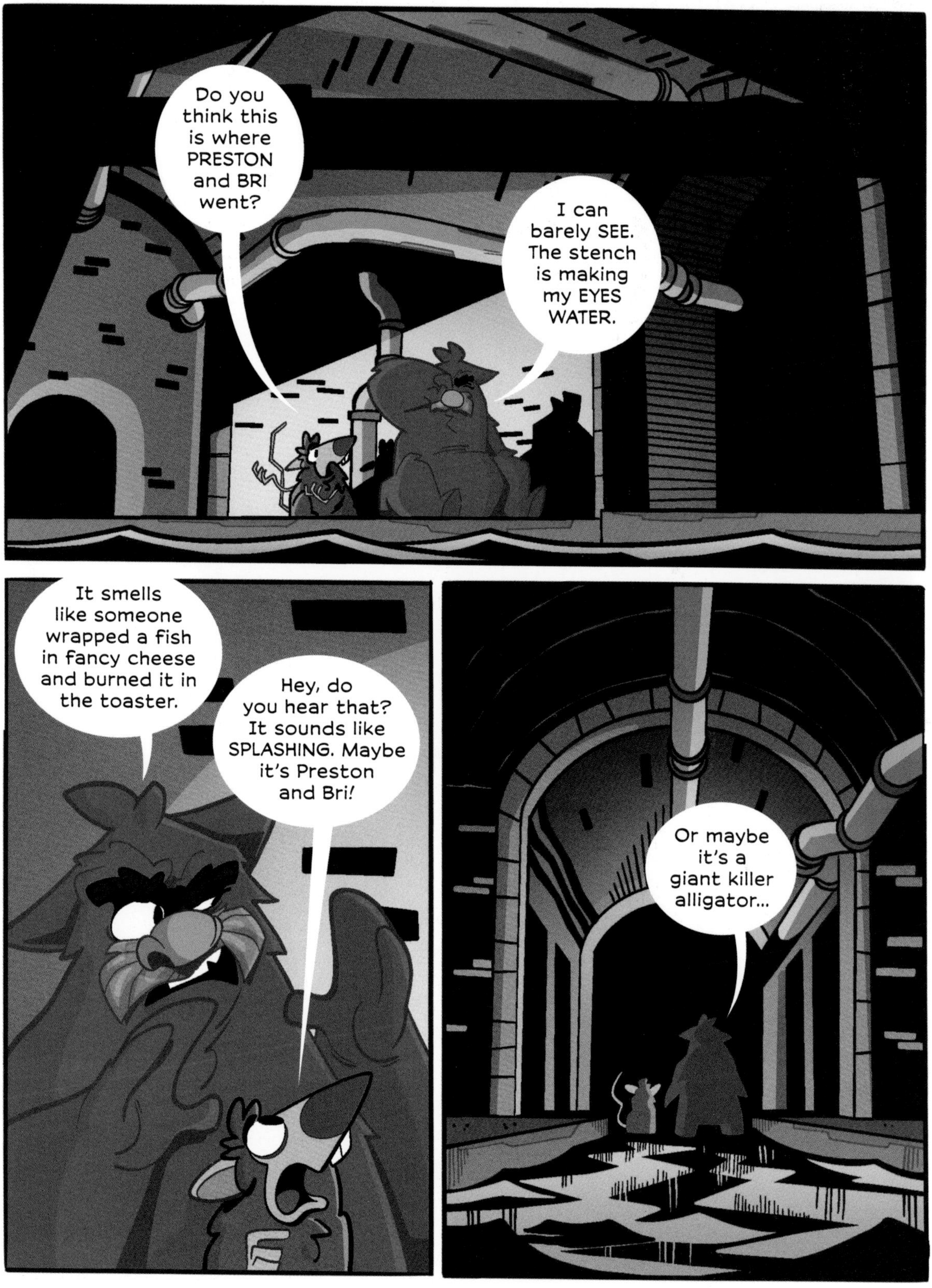
Do you think this is where PRESTON and BRI went?
I can barely SEE. The stench is making my EYES WATER.
It smells like someone wrapped a fish in fancy cheese and burned it in the toaster.
Hey, do you hear that? It sounds like SPLASHING. Maybe it's Preston and Bri!
Or maybe it's a giant killer alligator...

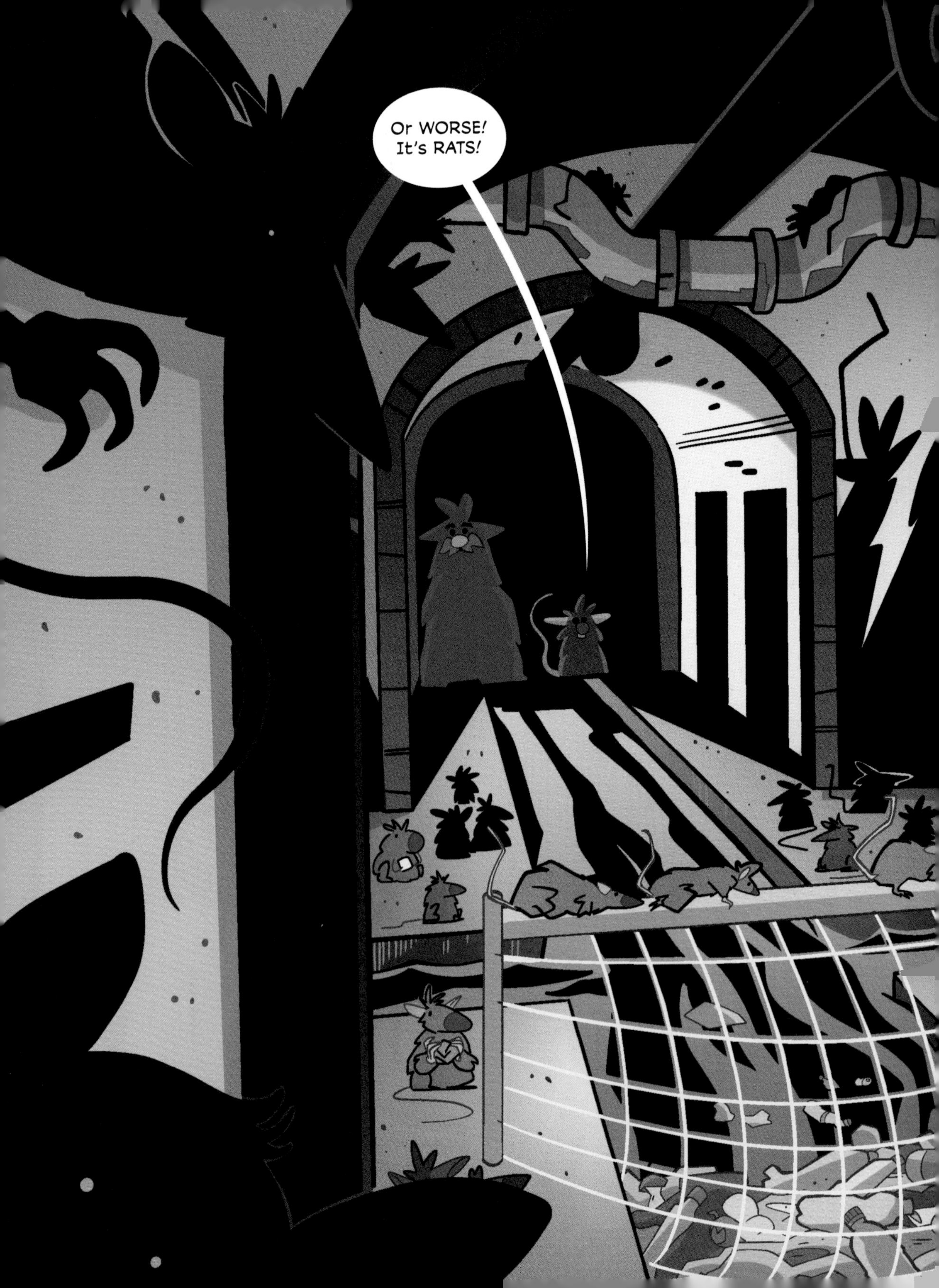
Or WORSE!
It's RATS!

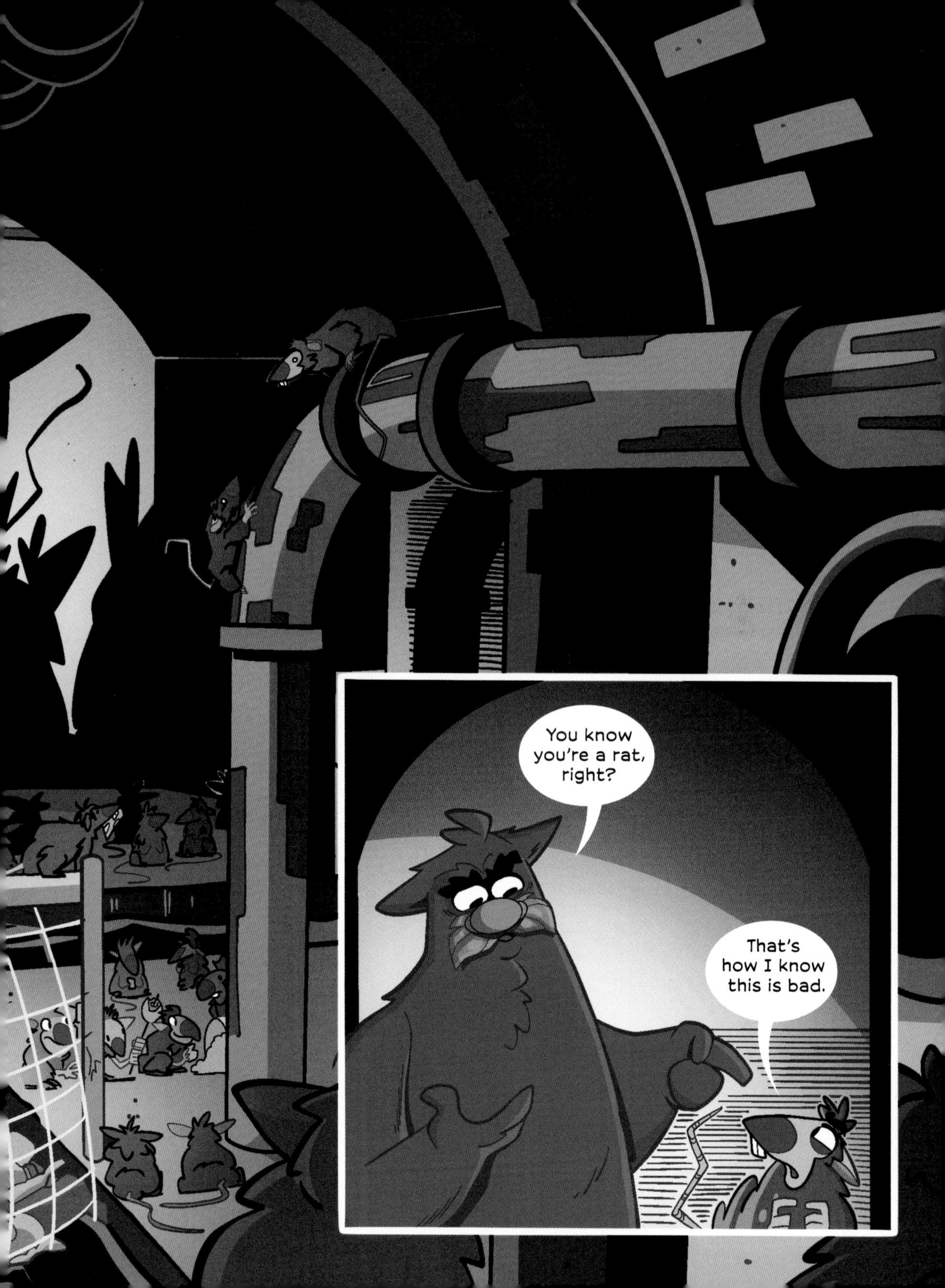
You know you're a rat, right?
That's how I know this is bad.

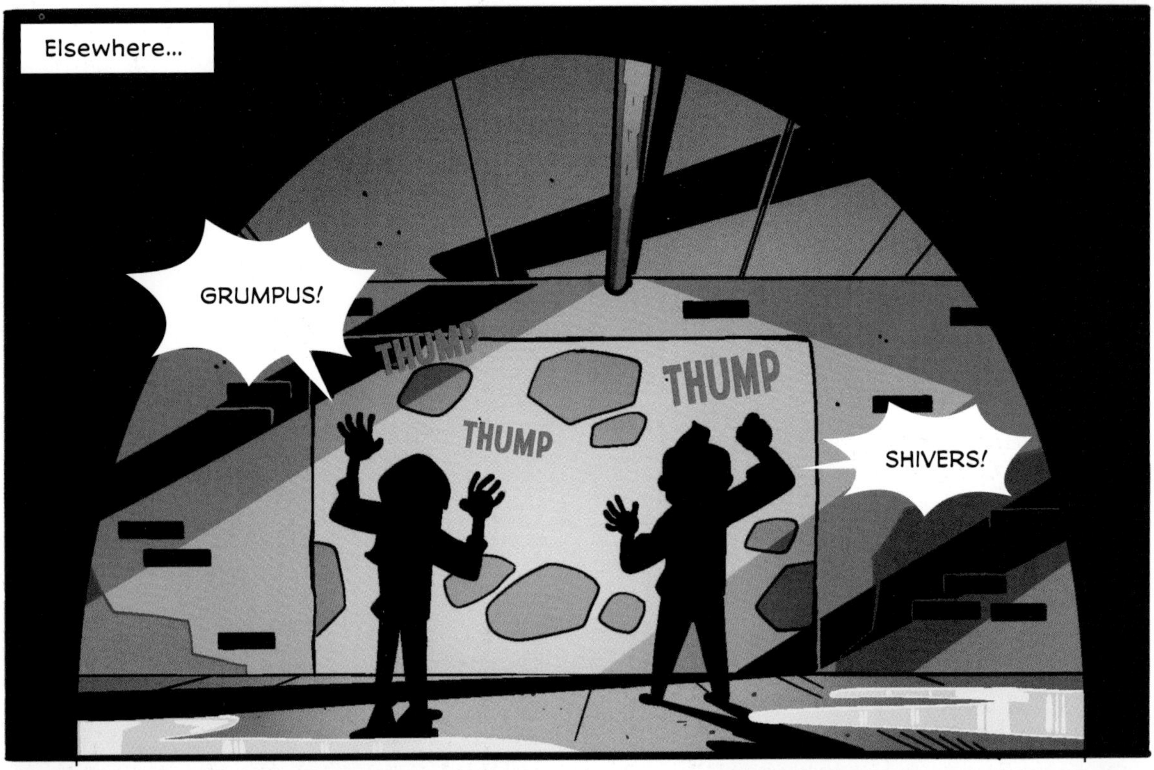
Elsewhere...
GRUMPUS!
THUMP
THUMP
THUMP
SHIVERS!

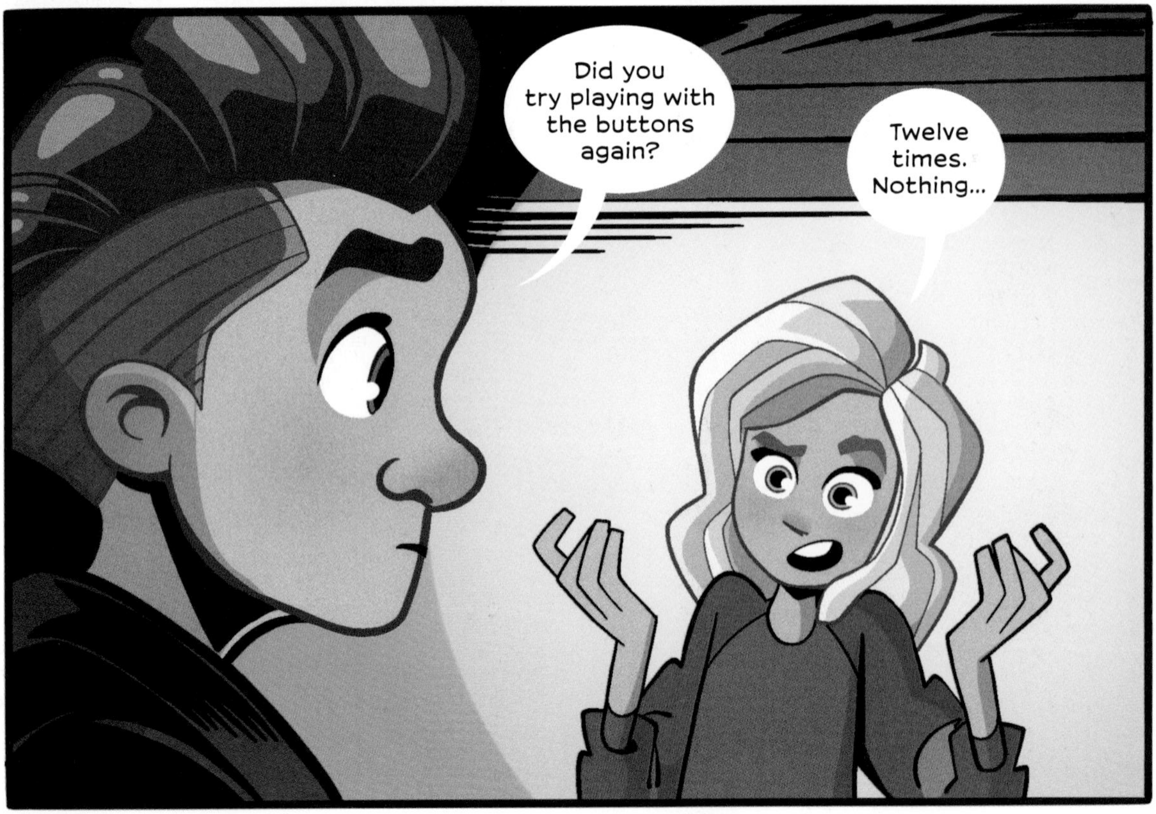
Did you try playing with the buttons again?
Twelve times. Nothing...

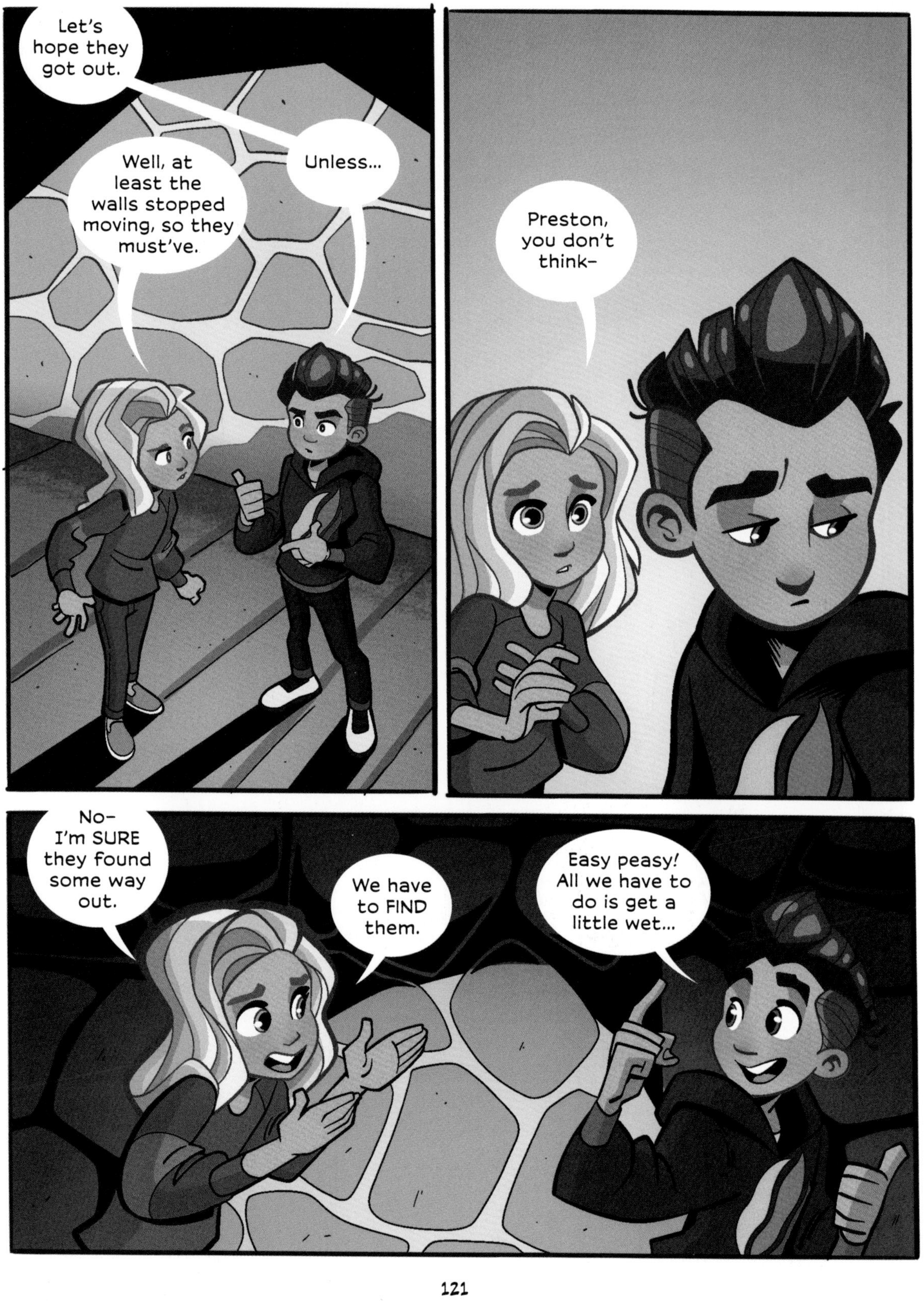

Let's hope they got out.
Well, at least the walls stopped moving, so they must've.
Unless...
Preston, you don't think–
No– I'm SURE they found some way out.
We have to FIND them.
Easy peasy! All we have to do is get a little wet...

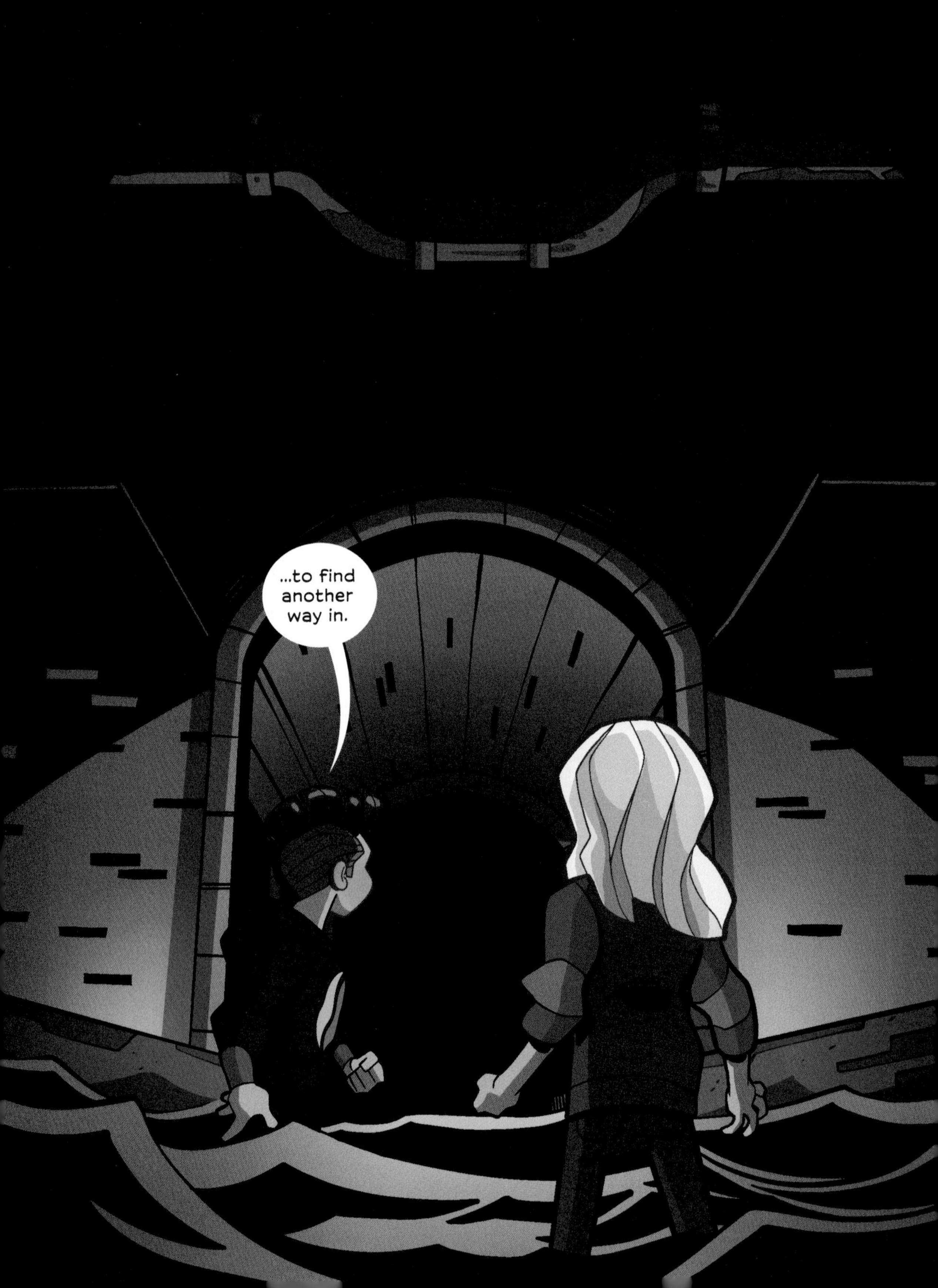
...to find another way in.

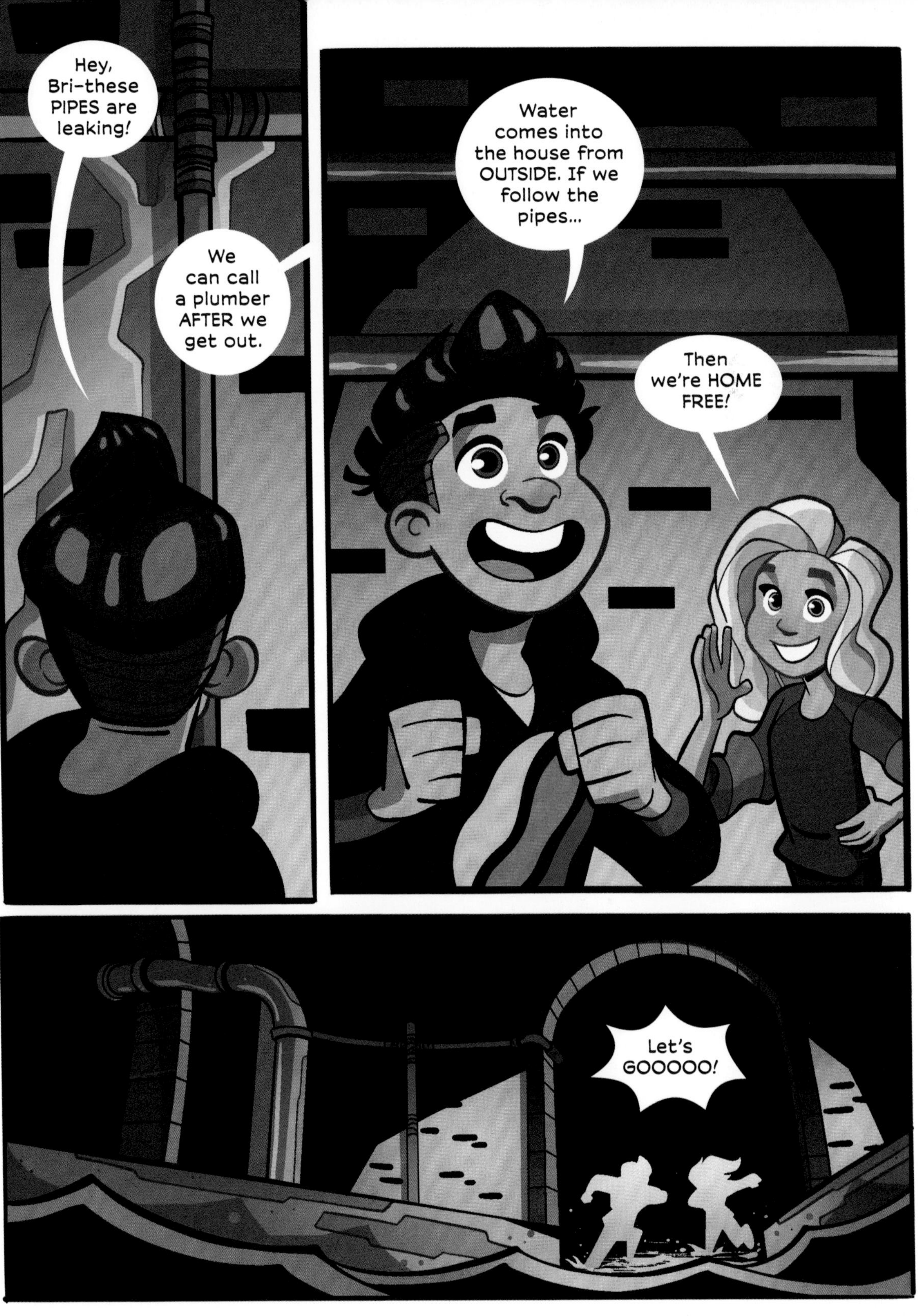
Hey, Bri–these PIPES are leaking!
We can call a plumber AFTER we get out.
Water comes into the house from OUTSIDE. If we follow the pipes...
Then we're HOME FREE!
Let's GOOOOO!

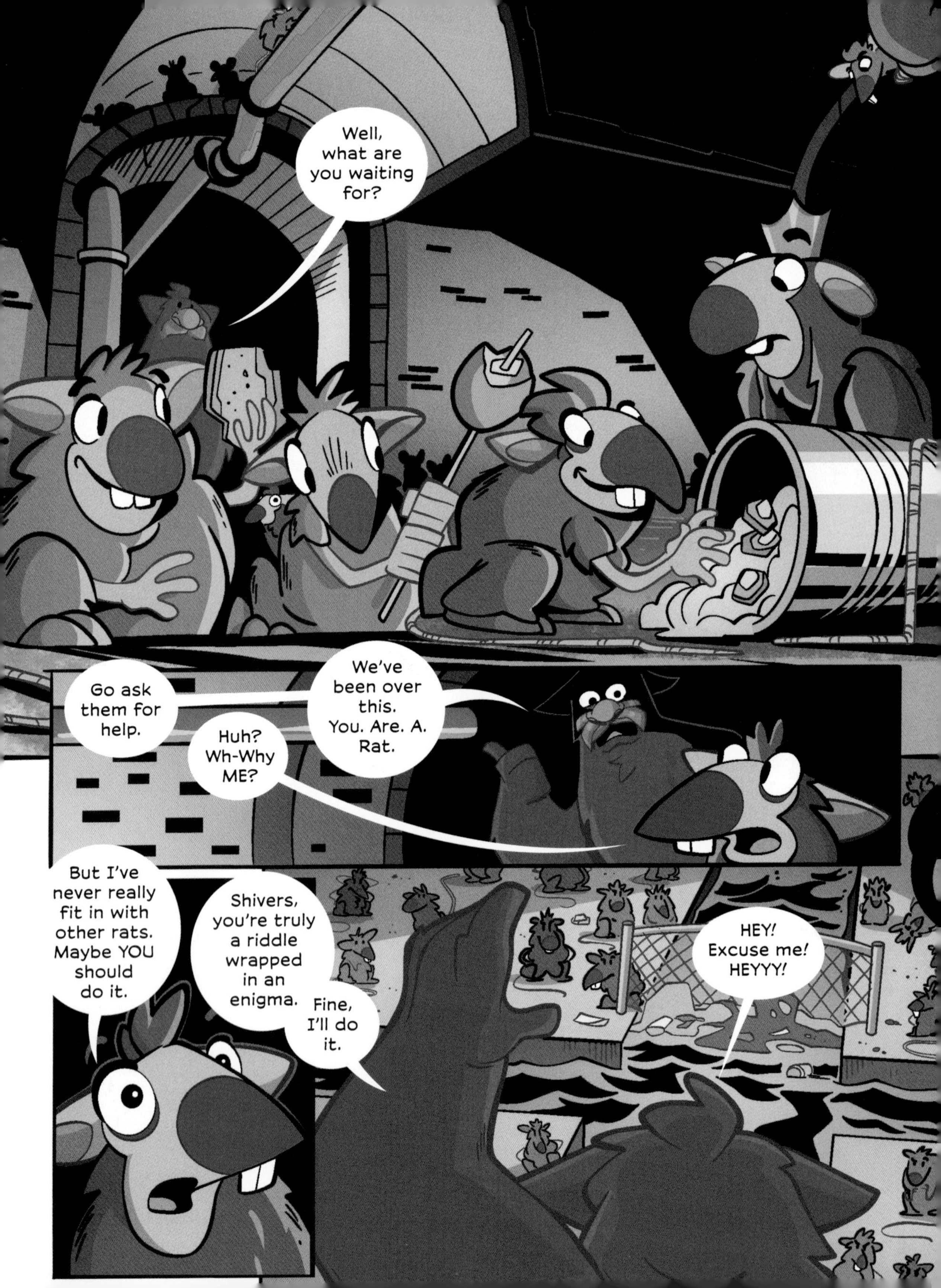
Well, what are you waiting for?
Go ask them for help.
Huh? Wh-Why ME?
We've been over this. You. Are. A. Rat.
But I've never really fit in with other rats. Maybe YOU should do it.
Shivers, you're truly a riddle wrapped in an enigma.
Fine, I'll do it.
HEY! Excuse me! HEYYY!

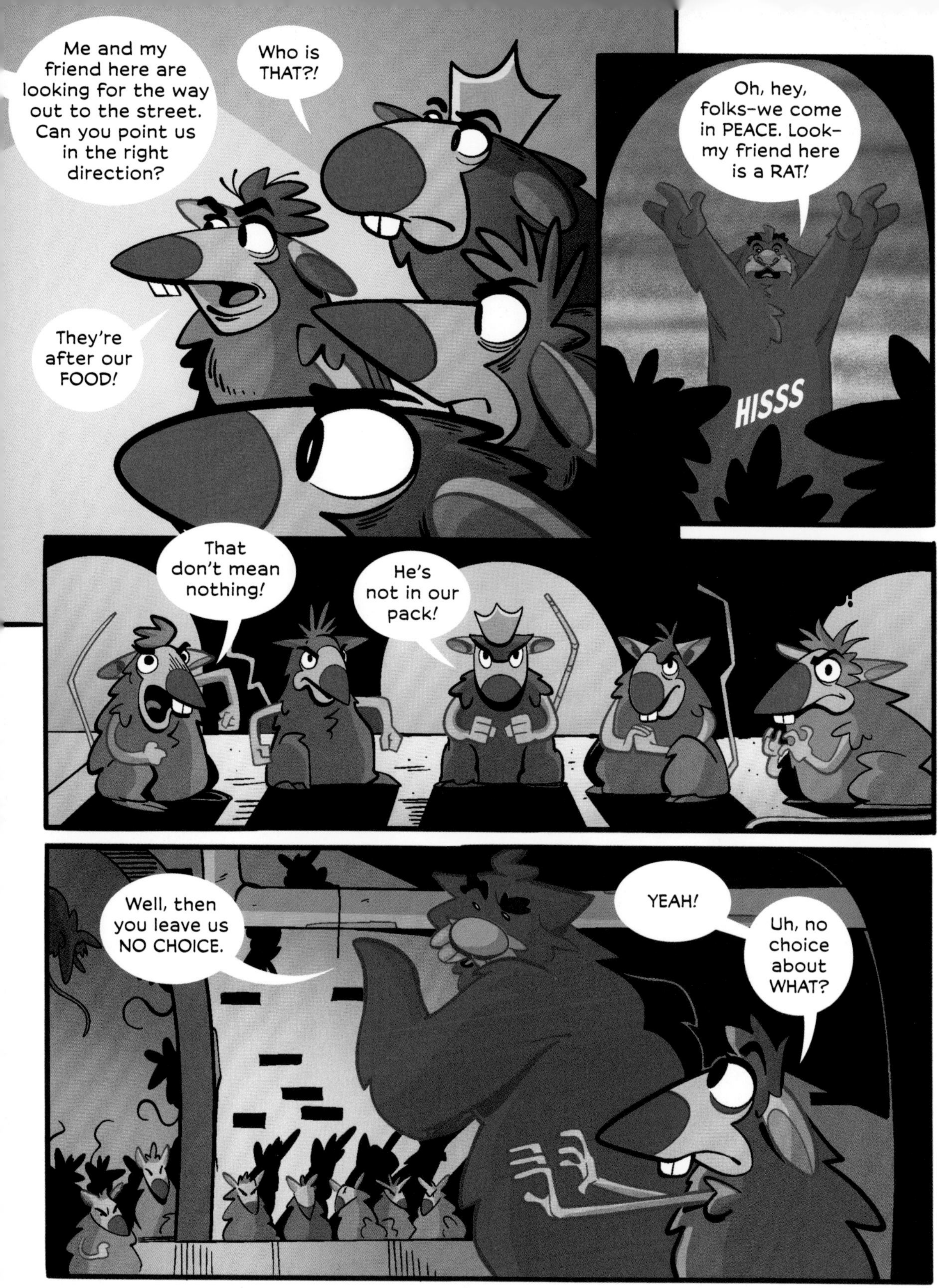
Me and my friend here are looking for the way out to the street. Can you point us in the right direction?
Who is THAT?!
They're after our FOOD!
Oh, hey, folks—we come in PEACE. Look—my friend here is a RAT!
HISSS
That don't mean nothing!
He's not in our pack!
Well, then you leave us NO CHOICE.
YEAH!
Uh, no choice about WHAT?

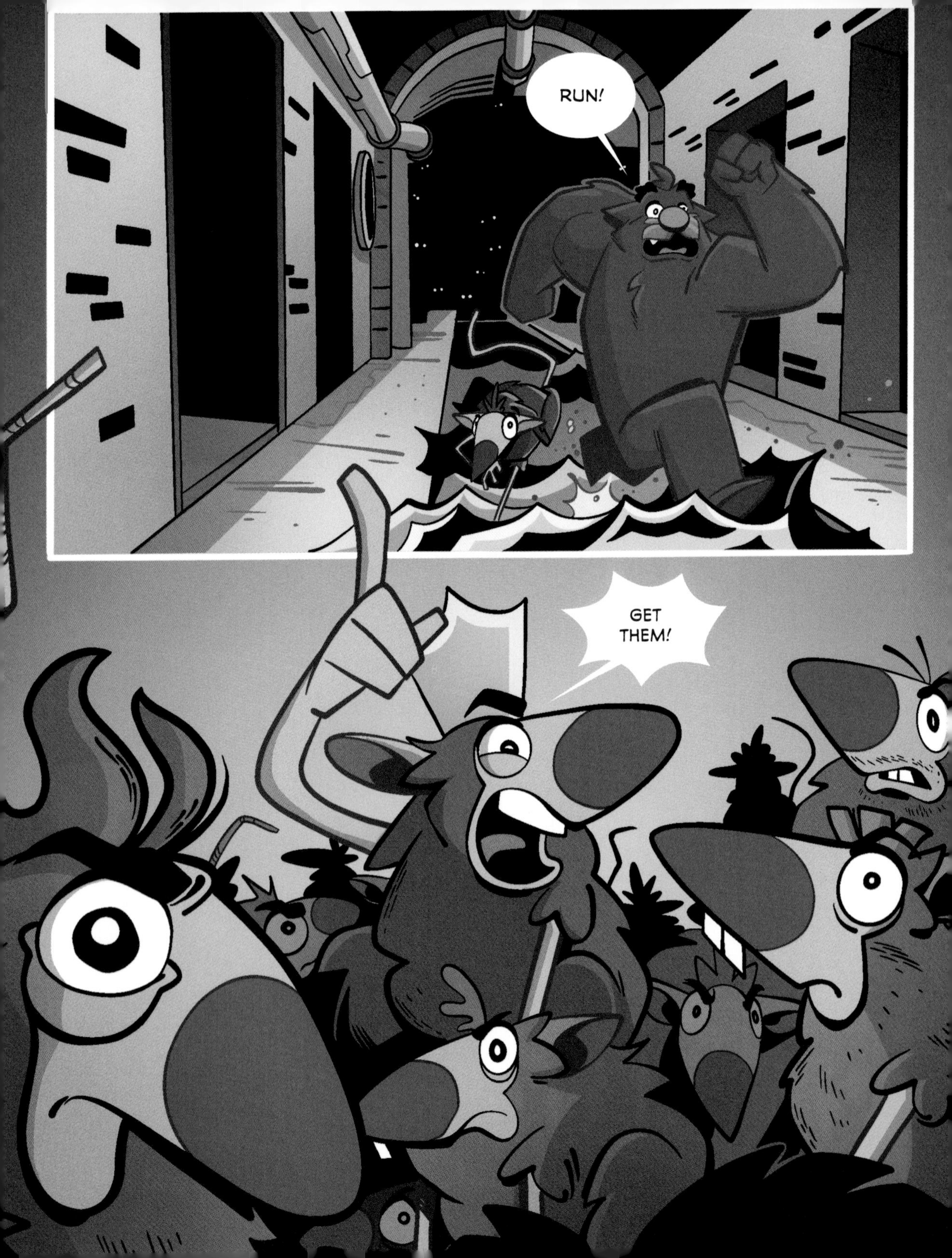
RUN!
GET THEM!

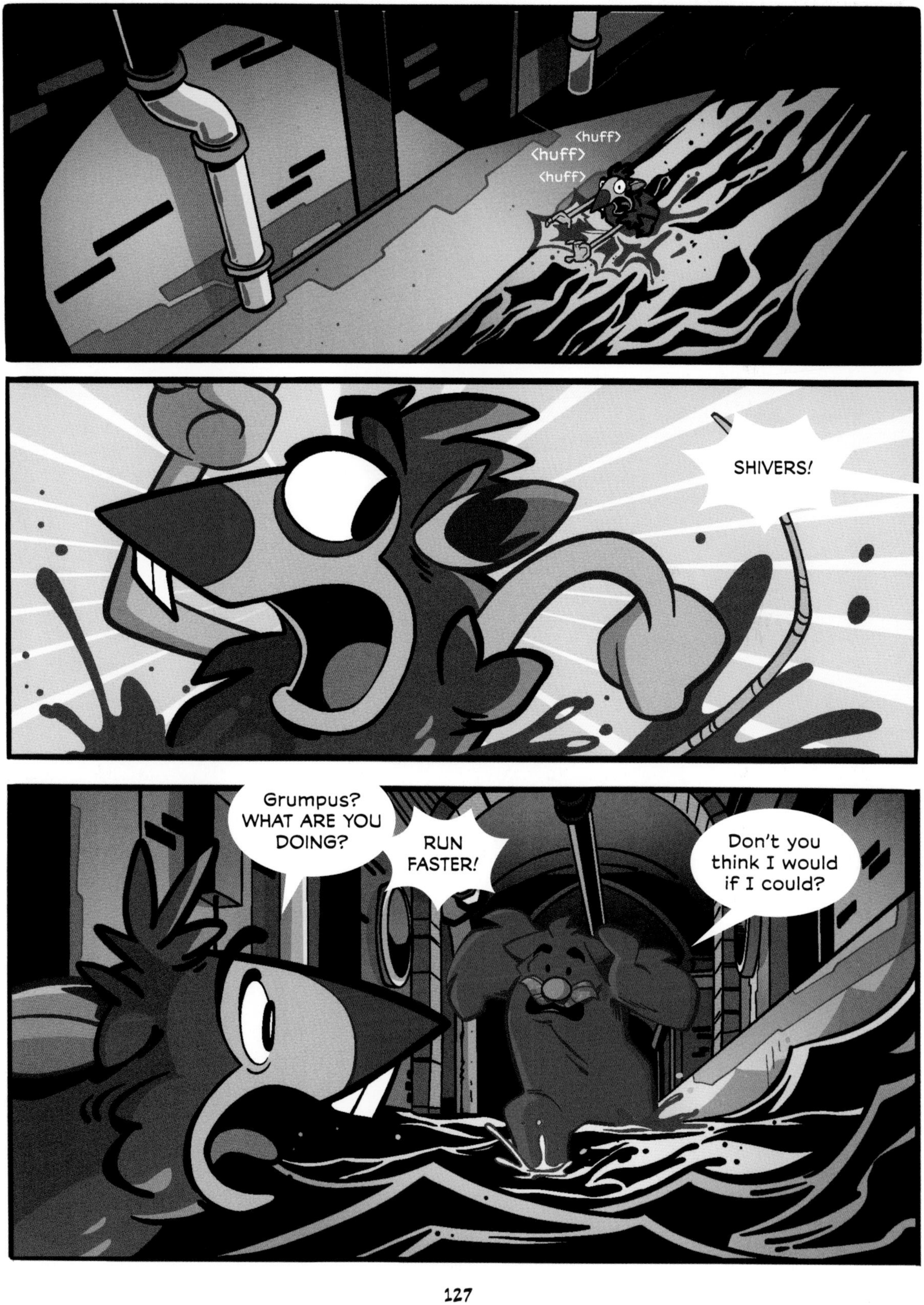
<huff>
<huff>
<huff>
SHIVERS!
Grumpus? WHAT ARE YOU DOING?
RUN FASTER!
Don't you think I would if I could?

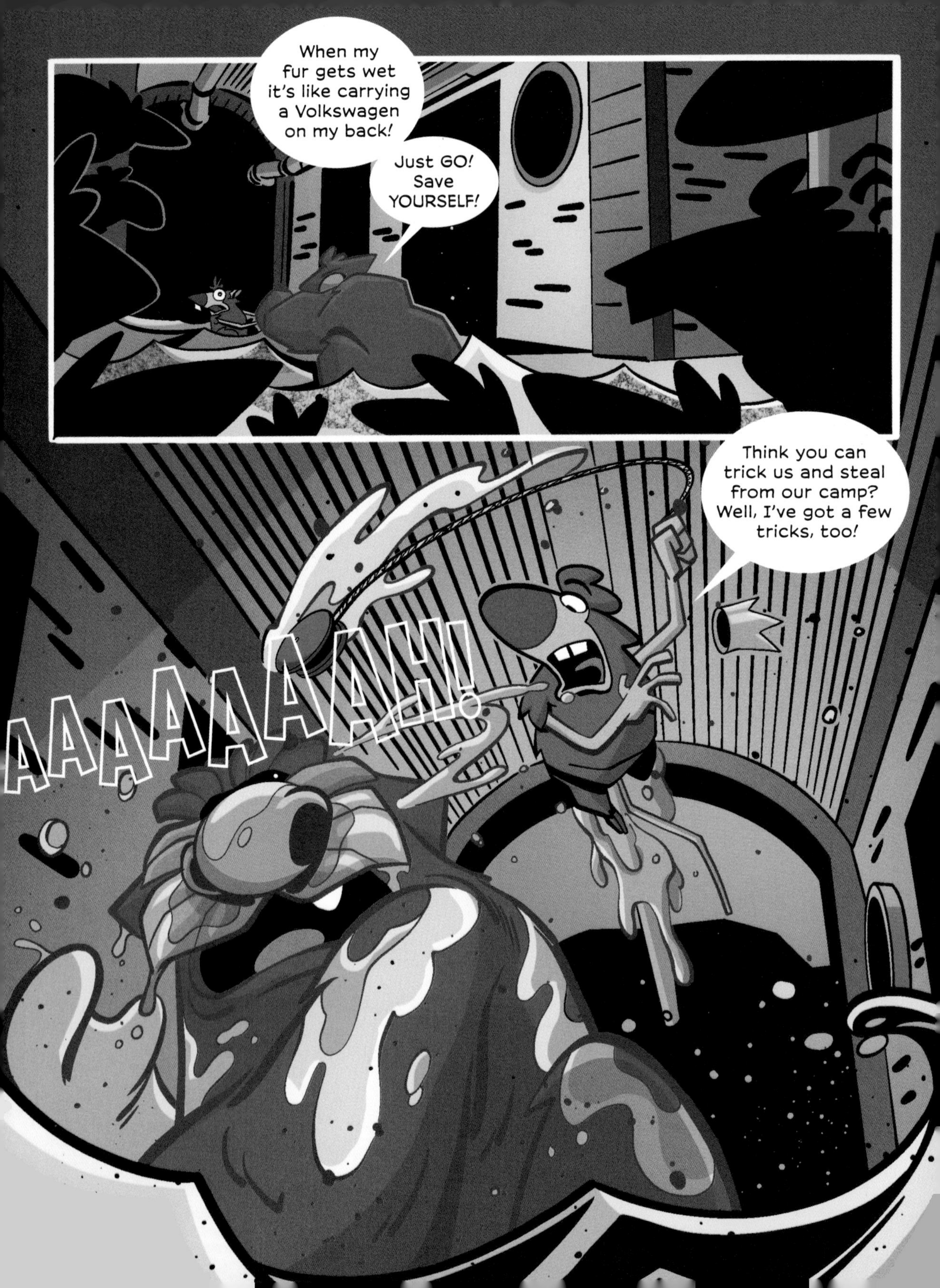
When my fur gets wet it's like carrying a Volkswagen on my back!
Just GO! Save YOURSELF!
Think you can trick us and steal from our camp? Well, I've got a few tricks, too!
AAAAAAAAH!

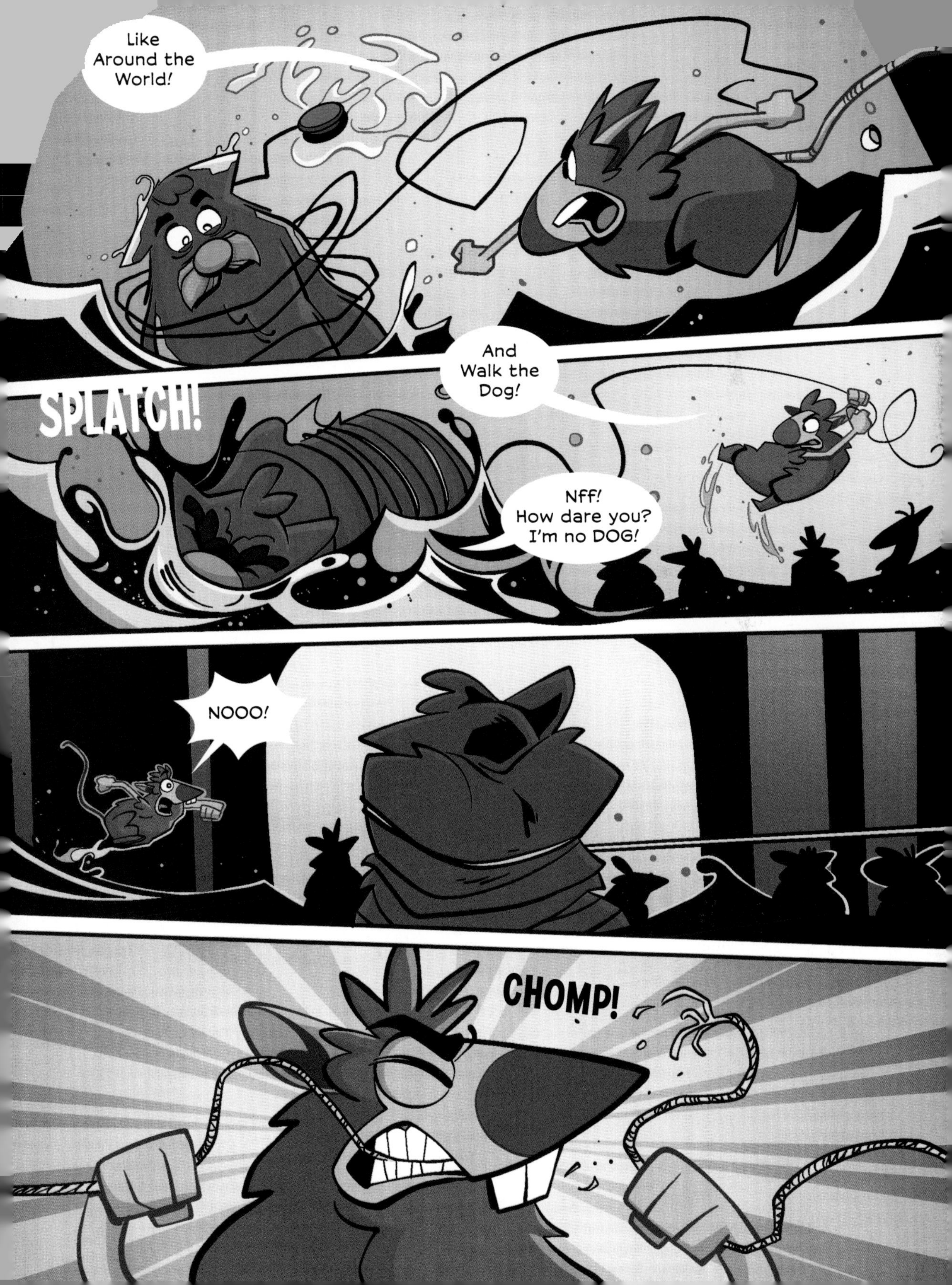
Like Around the World!
SPLATCH!
And Walk the Dog!
Nff! How dare you? I'm no DOG!
NOOO!
CHOMP!

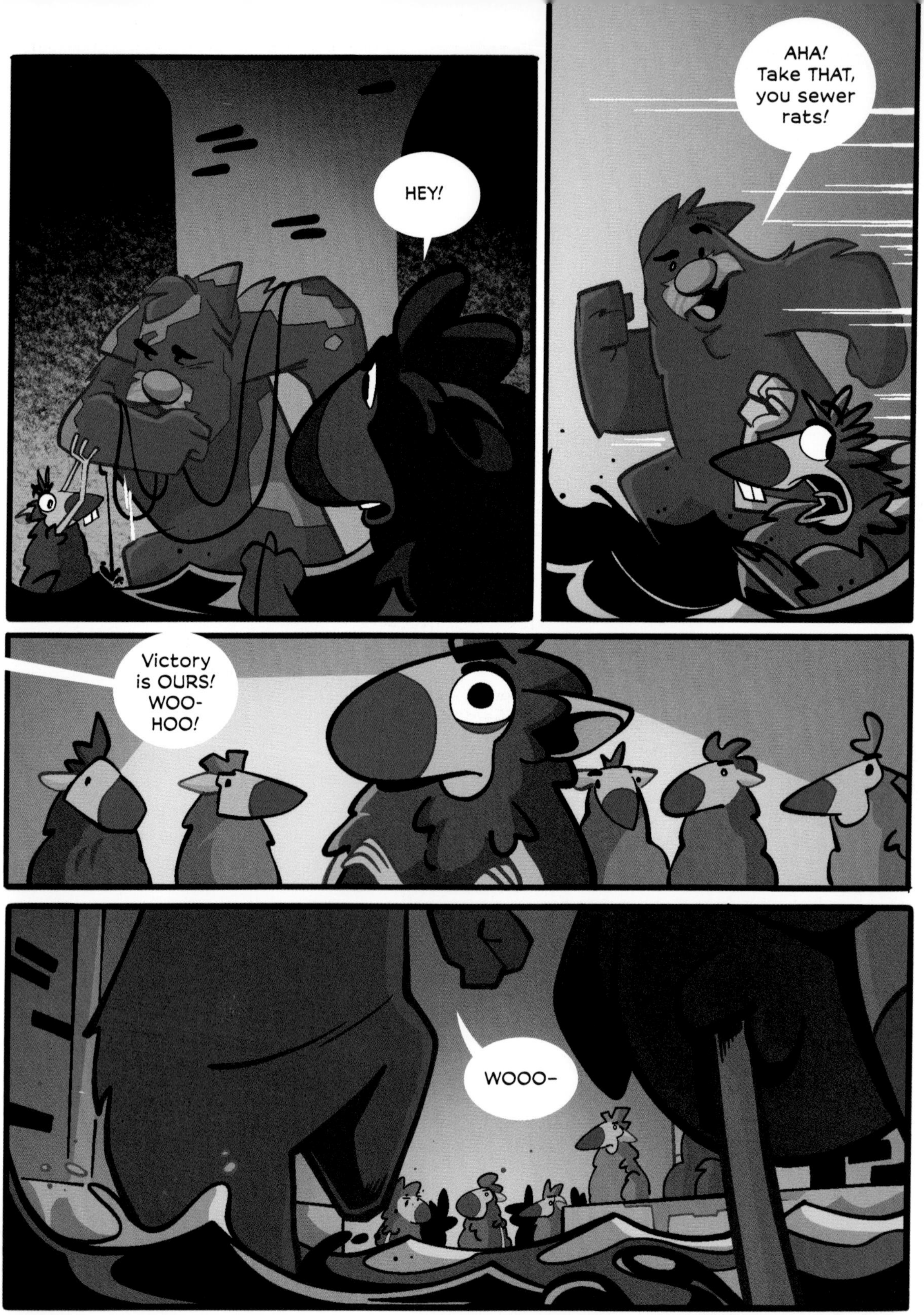
HEY!
AHA! Take THAT, you sewer rats!
Victory is OURS! WOO-HOO!
WOOO-

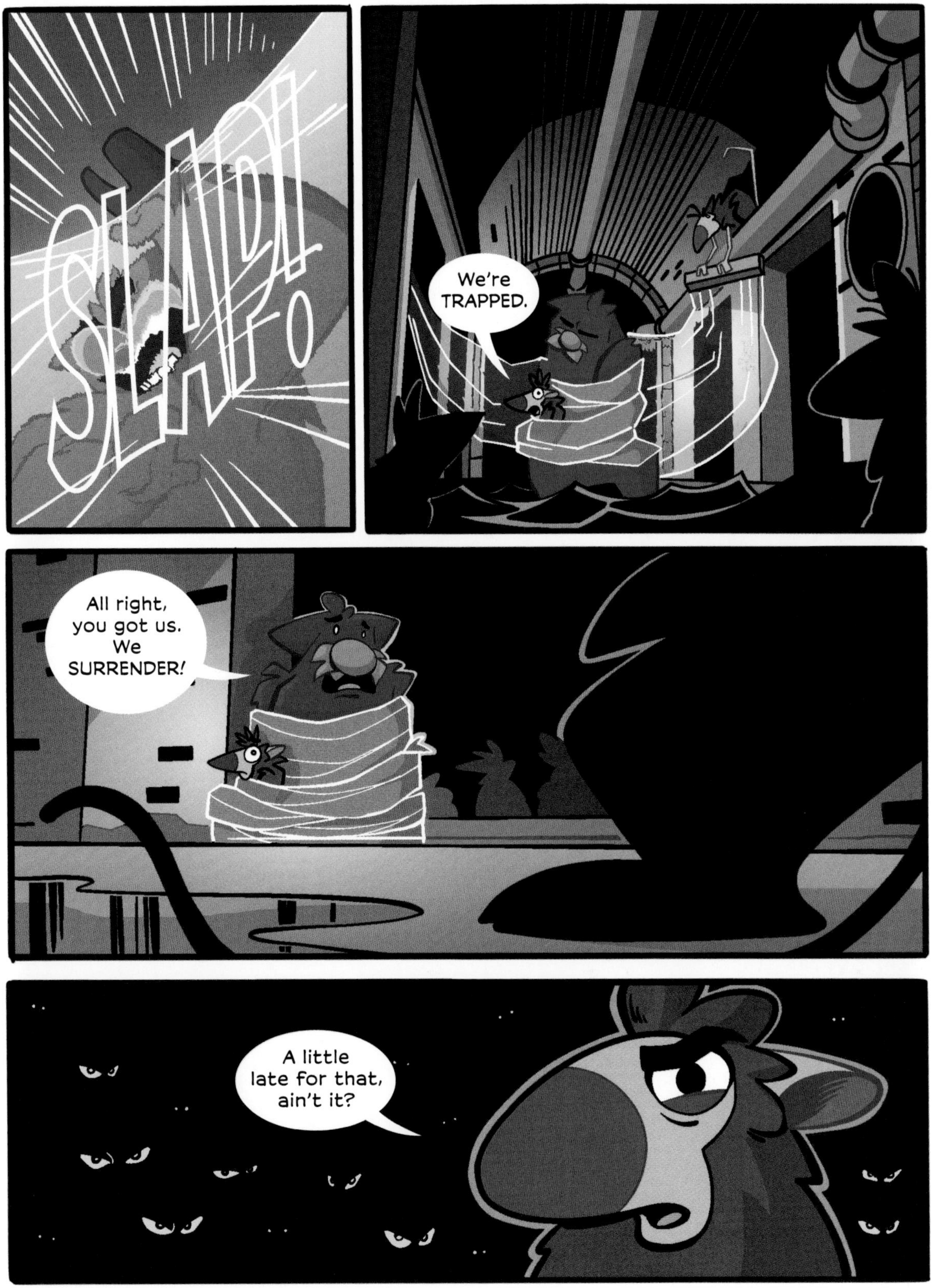
SLAP!
We're TRAPPED.
All right, you got us. We SURRENDER!
A little late for that, ain't it?

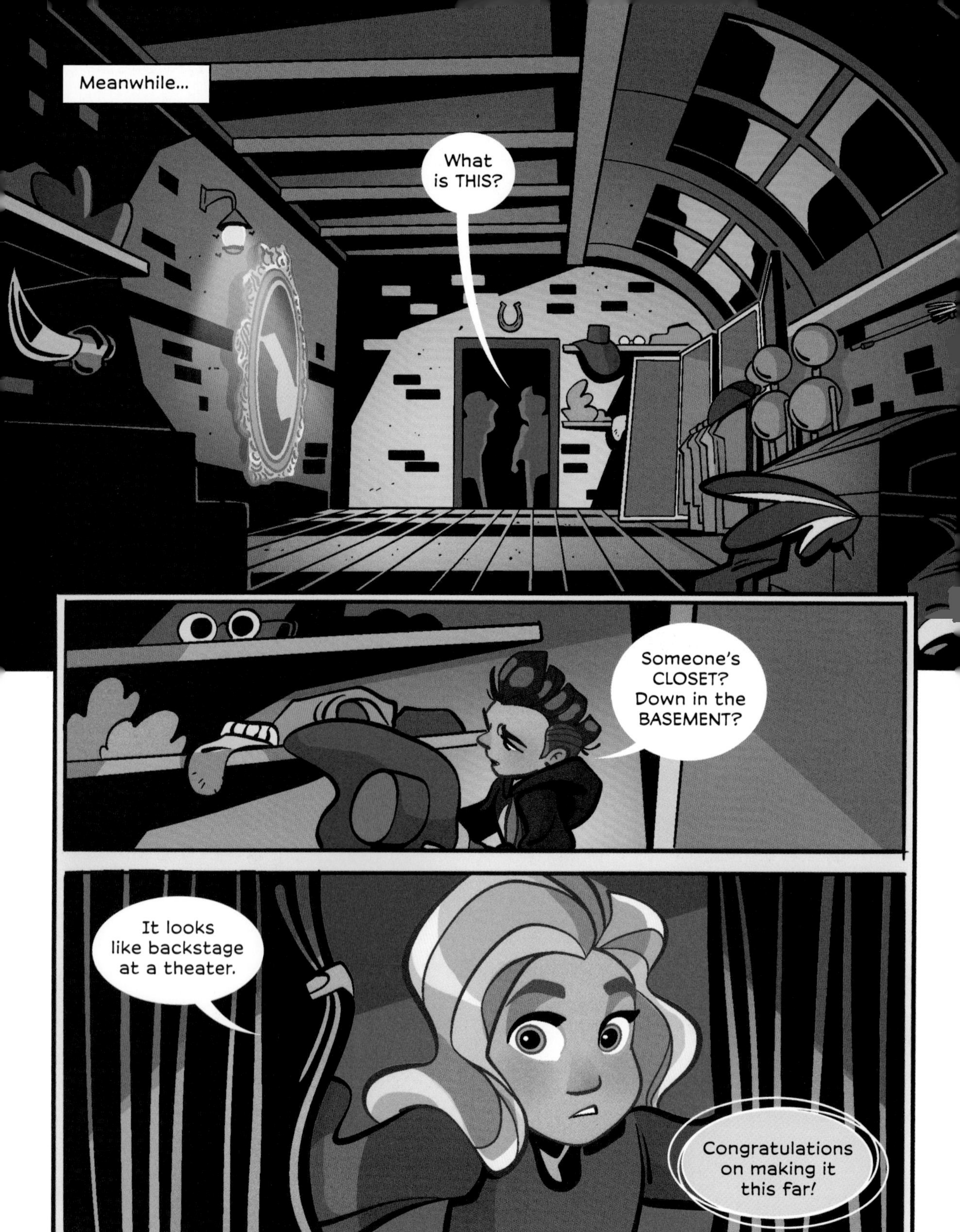
Meanwhile...
What is THIS?
Someone's CLOSET? Down in the BASEMENT?
It looks like backstage at a theater.
Congratulations on making it this far!

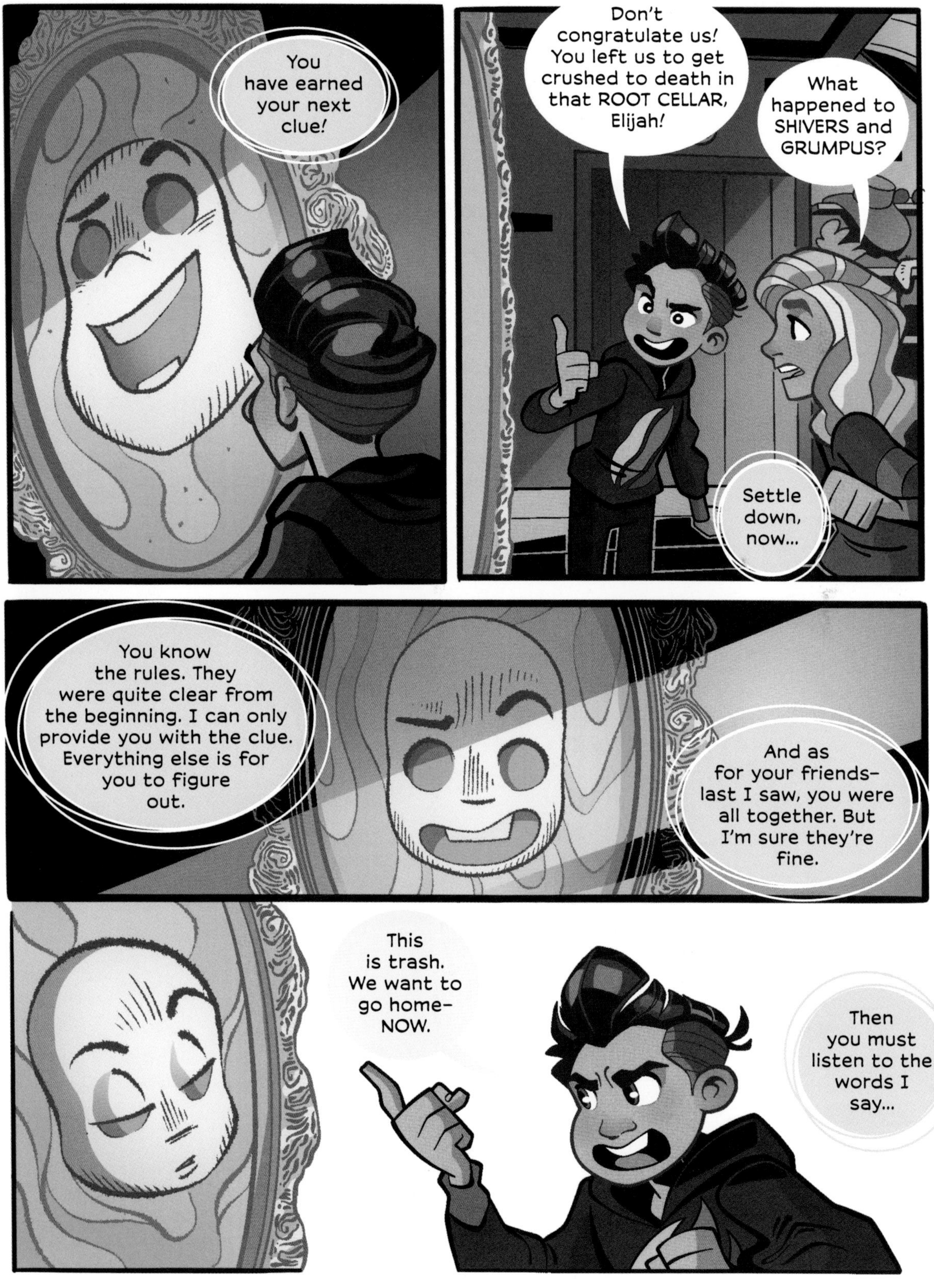
You have earned your next clue!
Don't congratulate us! You left us to get crushed to death in that ROOT CELLAR, Elijah!
What happened to SHIVERS and GRUMPUS?
Settle down, now...
You know the rules. They were quite clear from the beginning. I can only provide you with the clue. Everything else is for you to figure out.
And as for your friends– last I saw, you were all together. But I'm sure they're fine.
This is trash. We want to go home– NOW.
Then you must listen to the words I say...

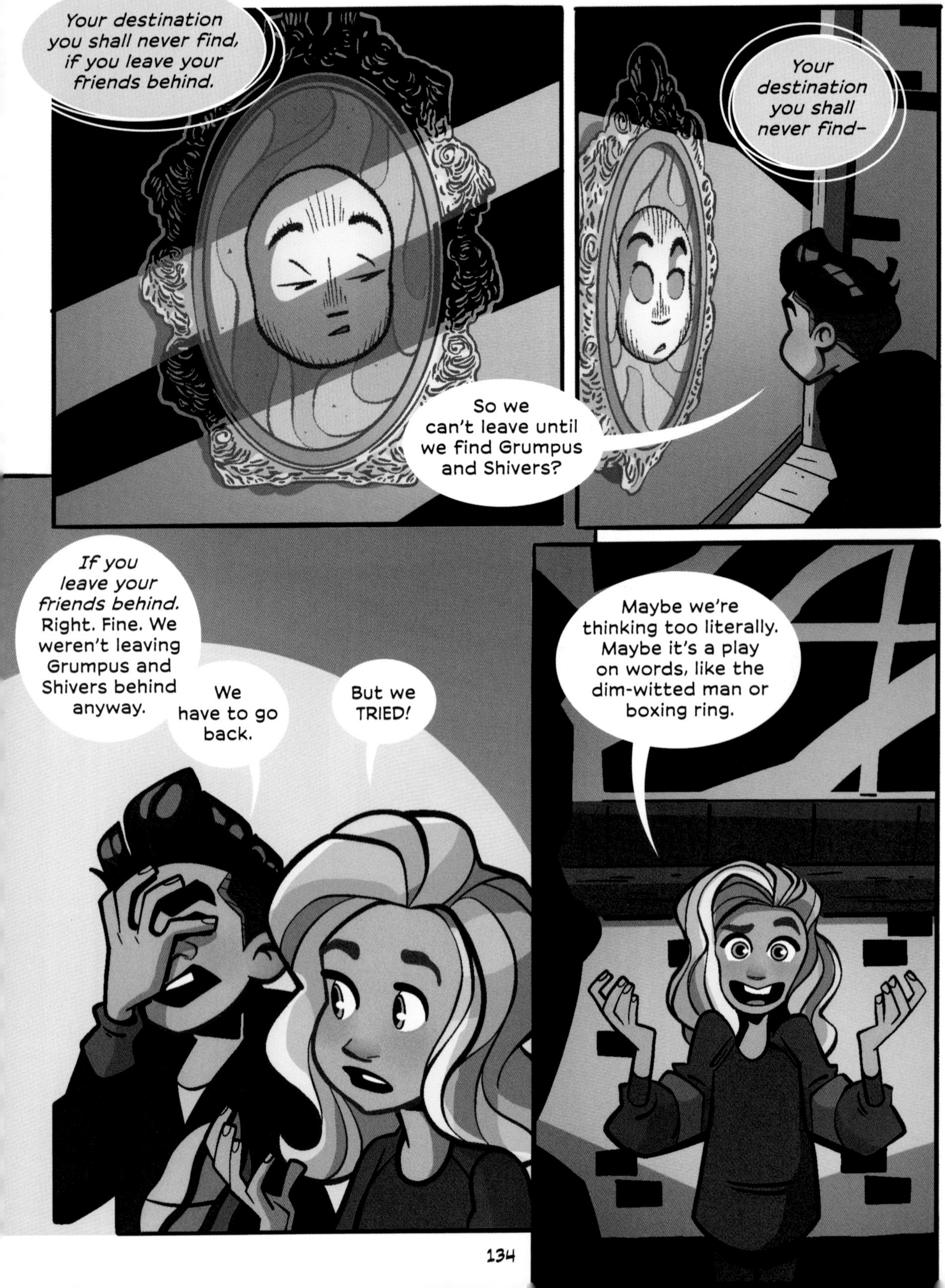
Your destination you shall never find, if you leave your friends behind.
Your destination you shall never find–
So we can't leave until we find Grumpus and Shivers?
If you leave your friends behind. Right. Fine. We weren't leaving Grumpus and Shivers behind anyway.
We have to go back.
But we TRIED!
Maybe we're thinking too literally. Maybe it's a play on words, like the dim-witted man or boxing ring.

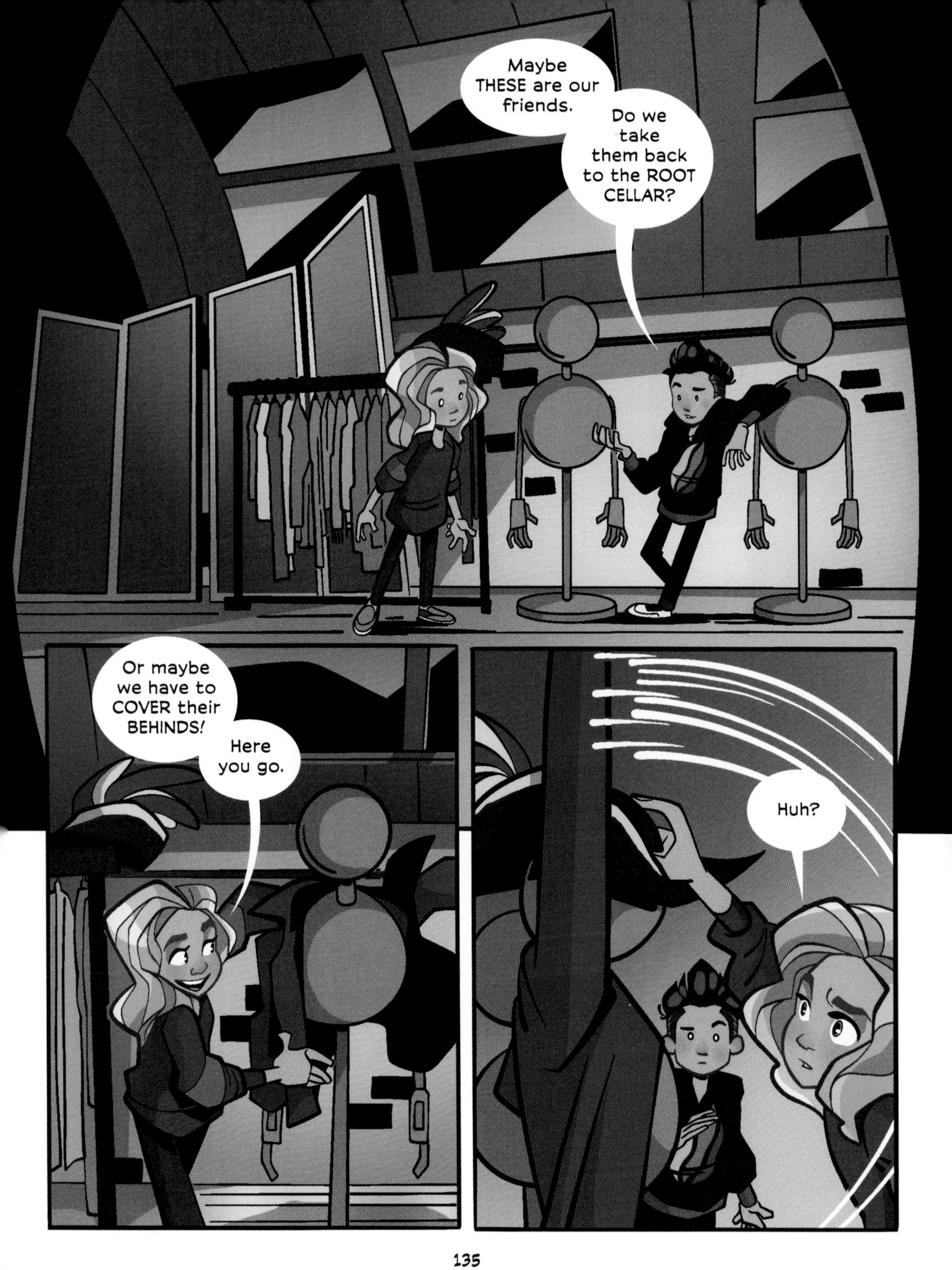
Maybe THESE are our friends.
Do we take them back to the ROOT CELLAR?
Or maybe we have to COVER their BEHINDS!
Here you go.
Huh?

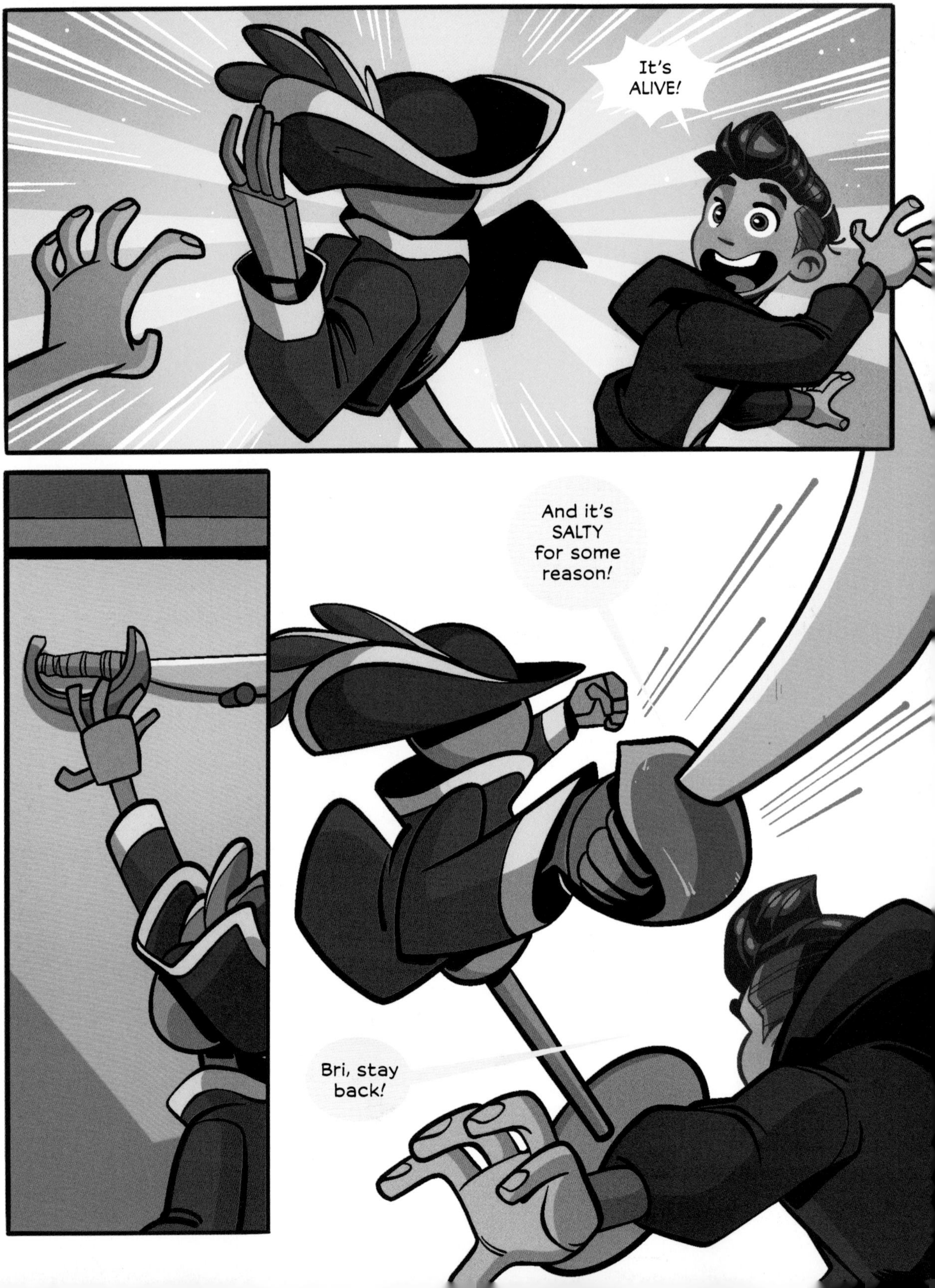
It's ALIVE!
And it's SALTY for some reason!
Bri, stay back!

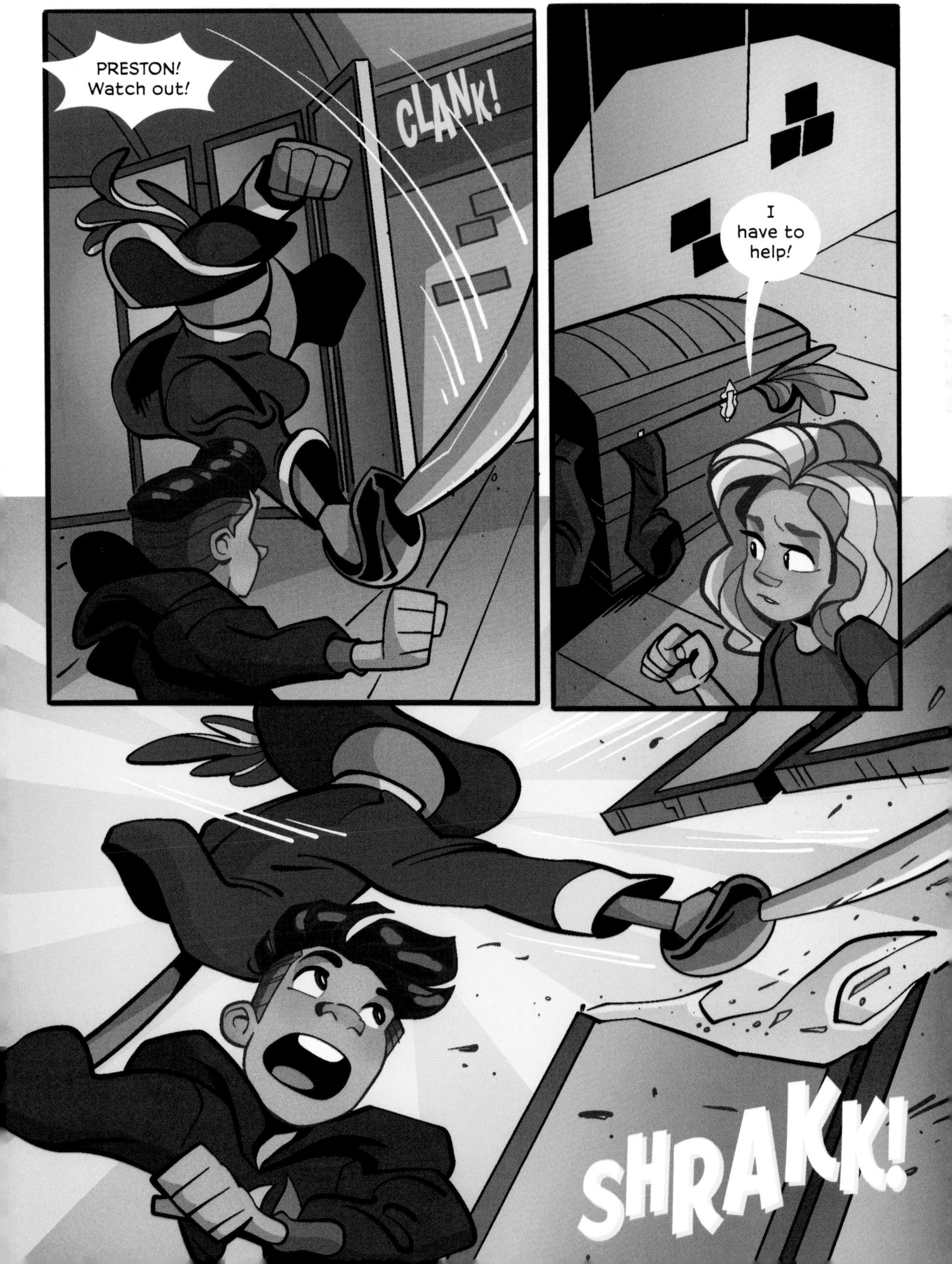
PRESTON! Watch out!
CLANK!
I have to help!
SHRAKK!

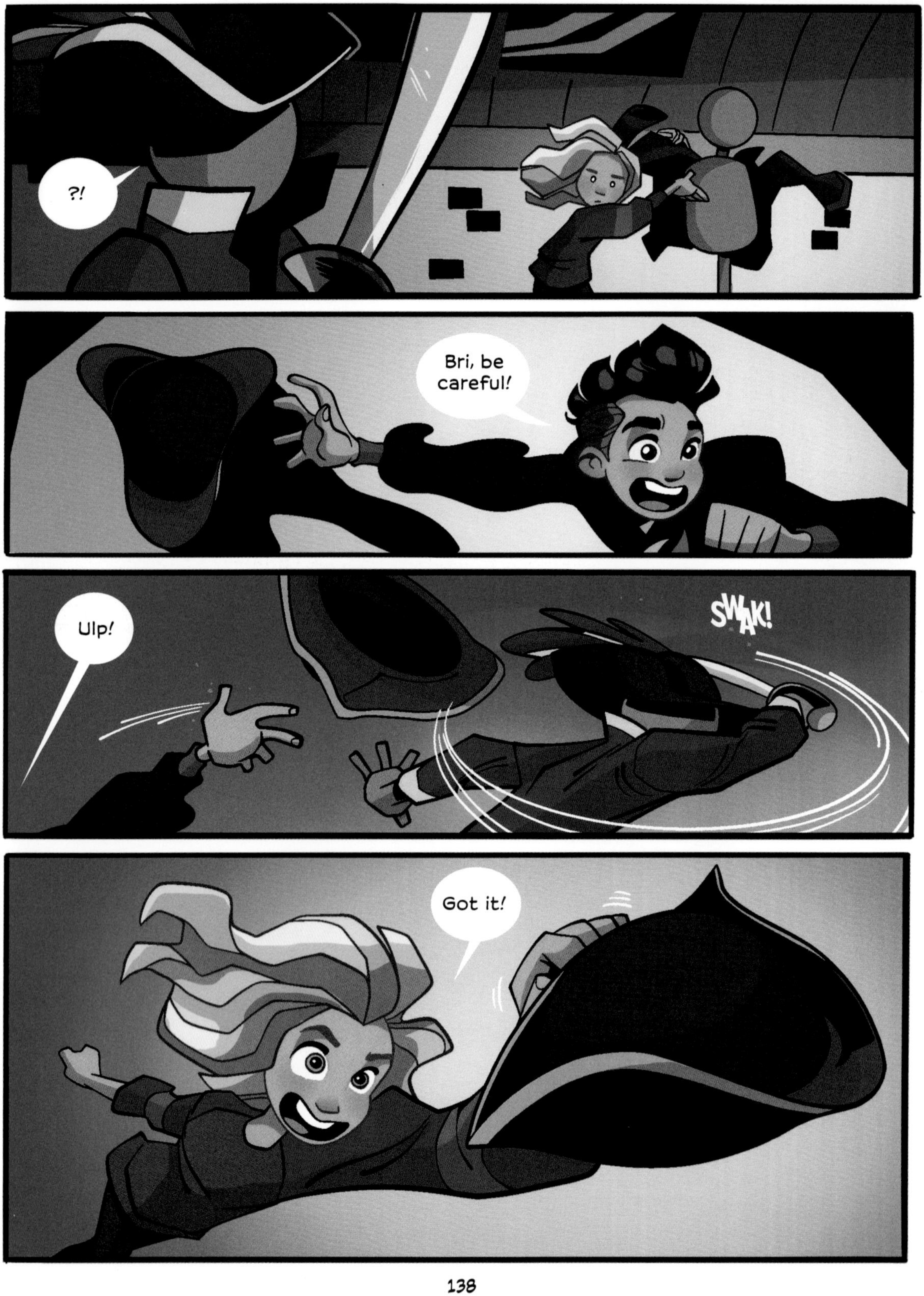
?!
Bri, be careful!
Ulp!
SWAK!
Got it!

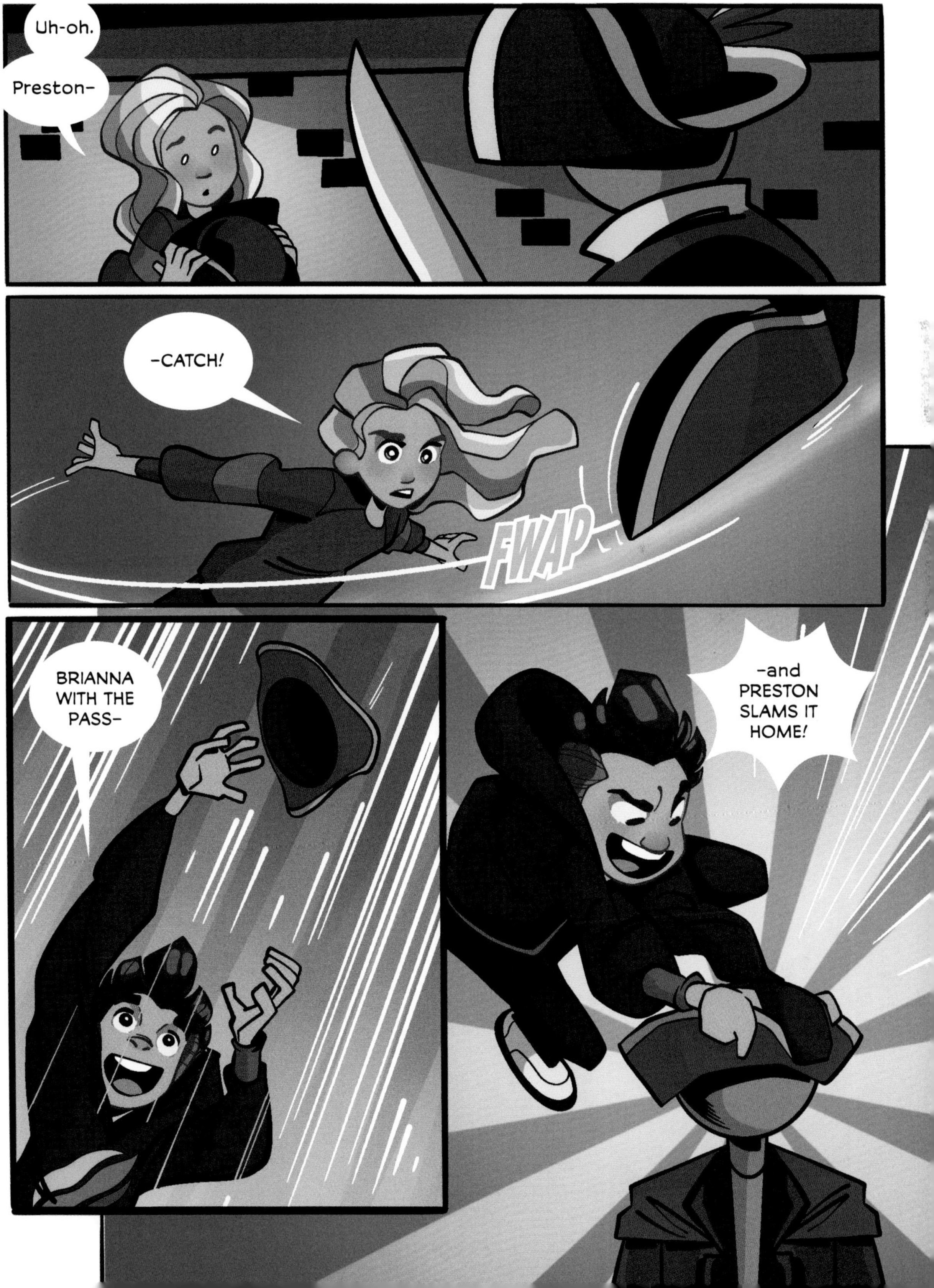
Uh-oh.
Preston-
-CATCH!
FWAP
BRIANNA WITH THE PASS-
-and PRESTON SLAMS IT HOME!

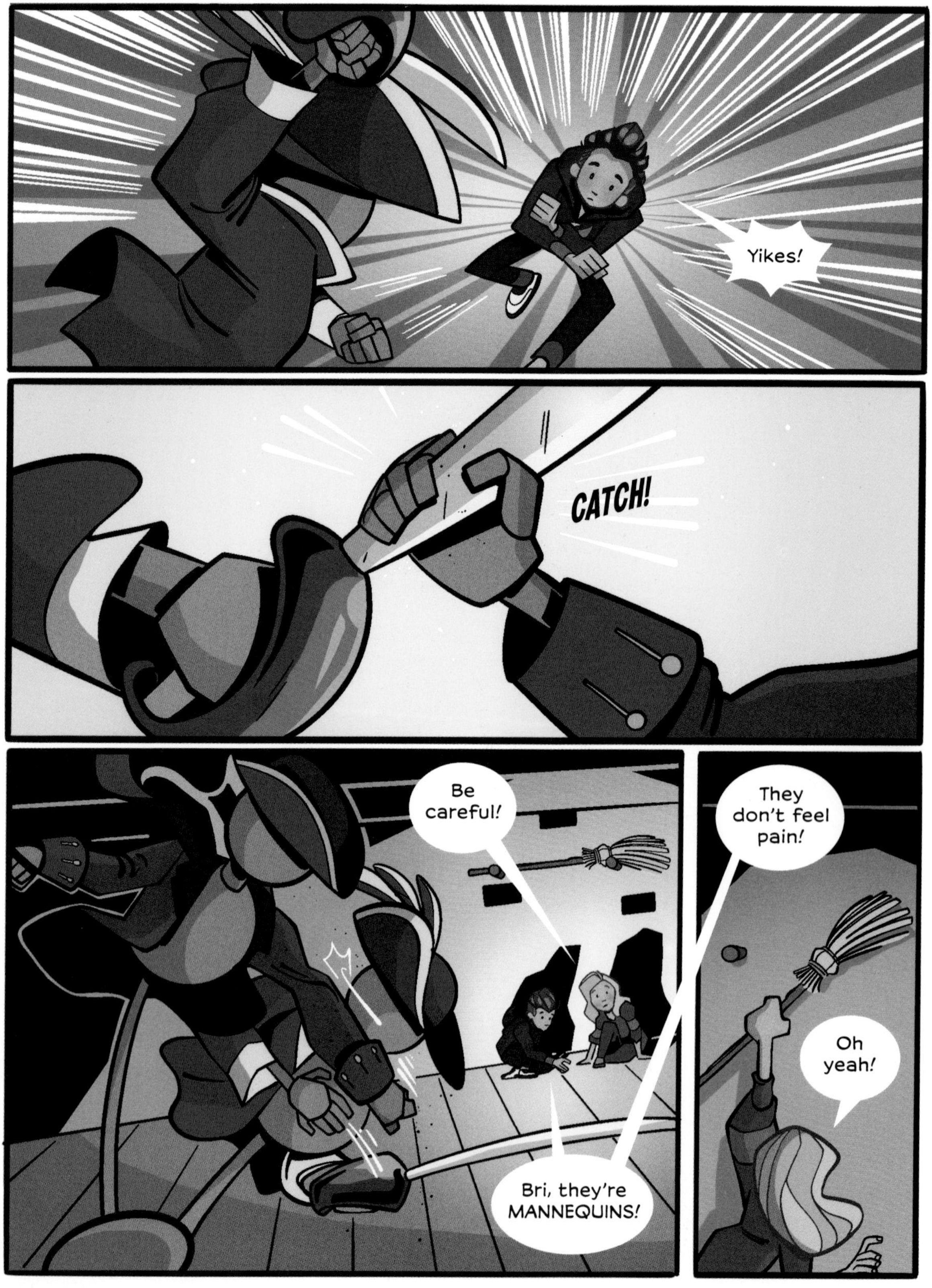
Yikes!
CATCH!
Be careful!
They don't feel pain!
Bri, they're MANNEQUINS!
Oh yeah!

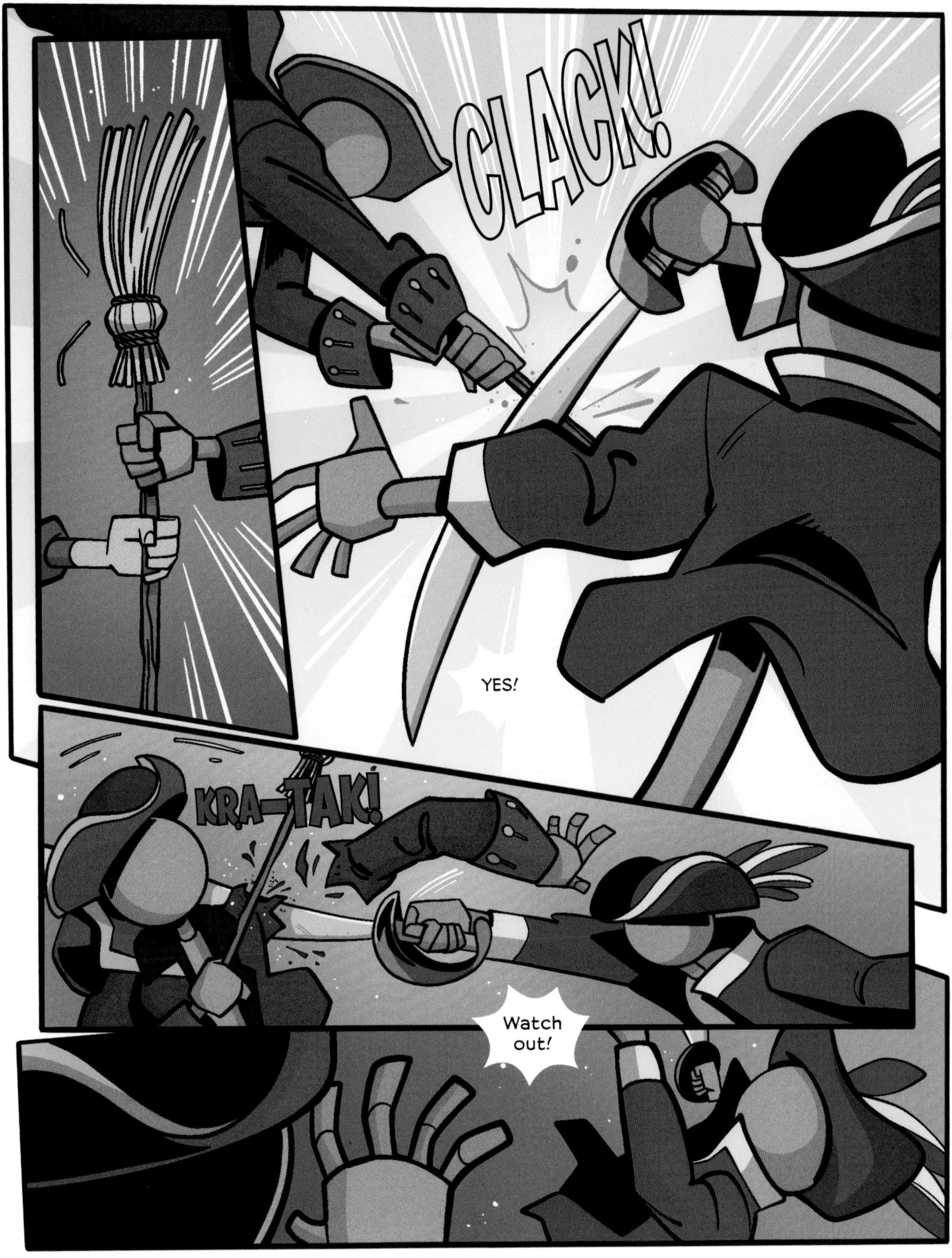
CLACK!
YES!
KRA-TAK!
Watch out!

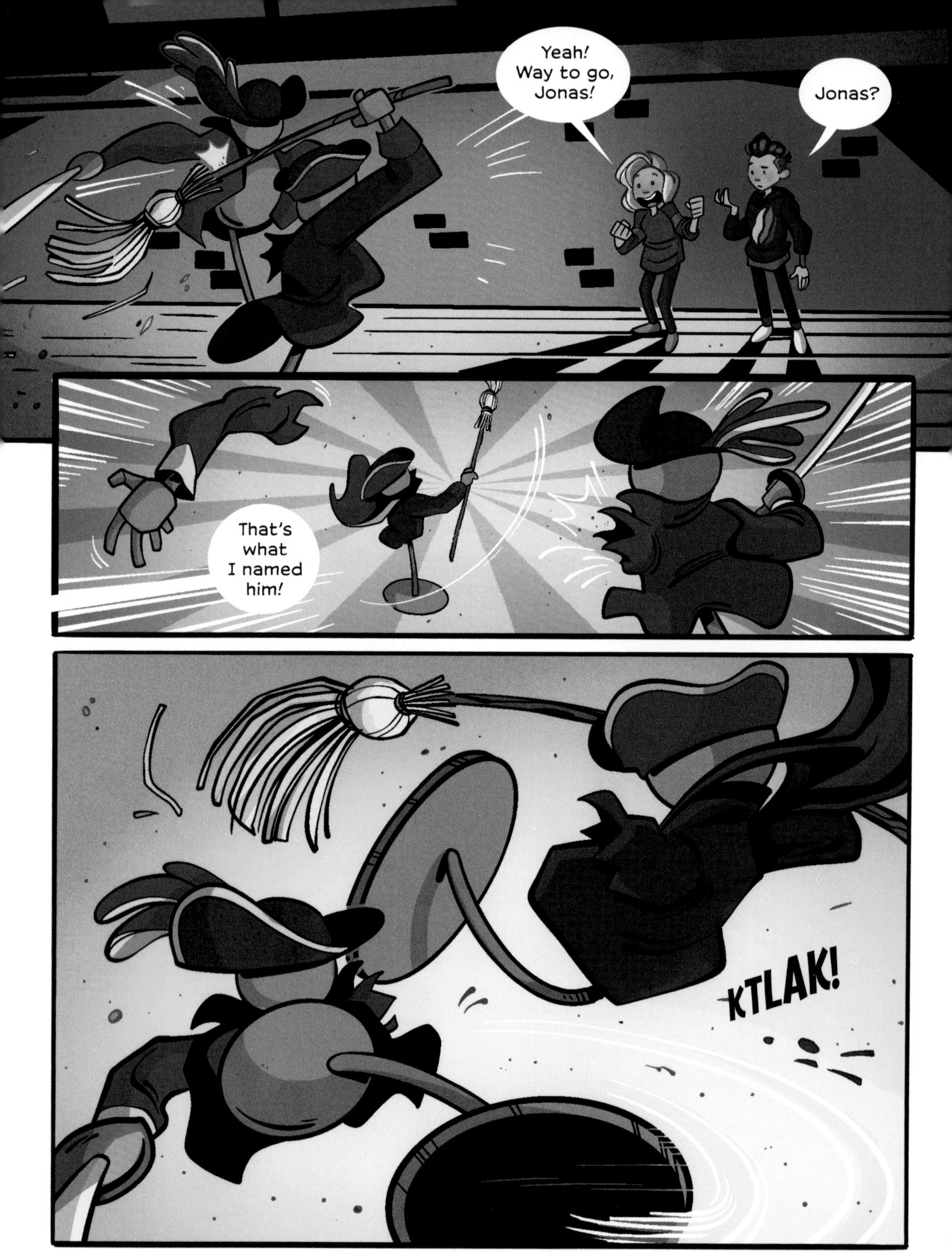
Yeah! Way to go, Jonas!
Jonas?
That's what I named him!
KTLAK!

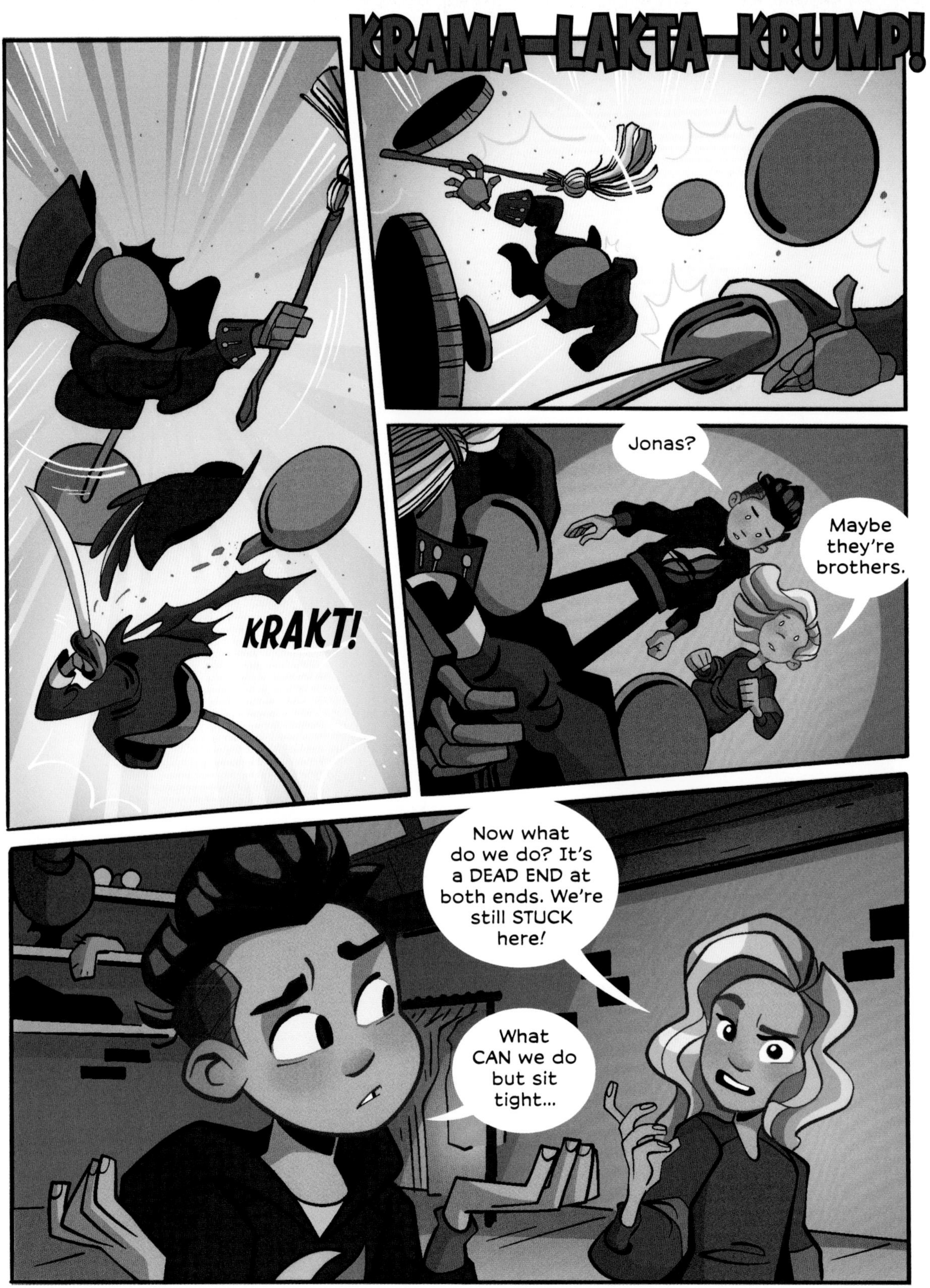
KRAMA-LAKTA-KRUMP!
KRAKT!
Jonas?
Maybe they're brothers.
Now what do we do? It's a DEAD END at both ends. We're still STUCK here!
What CAN we do but sit tight...

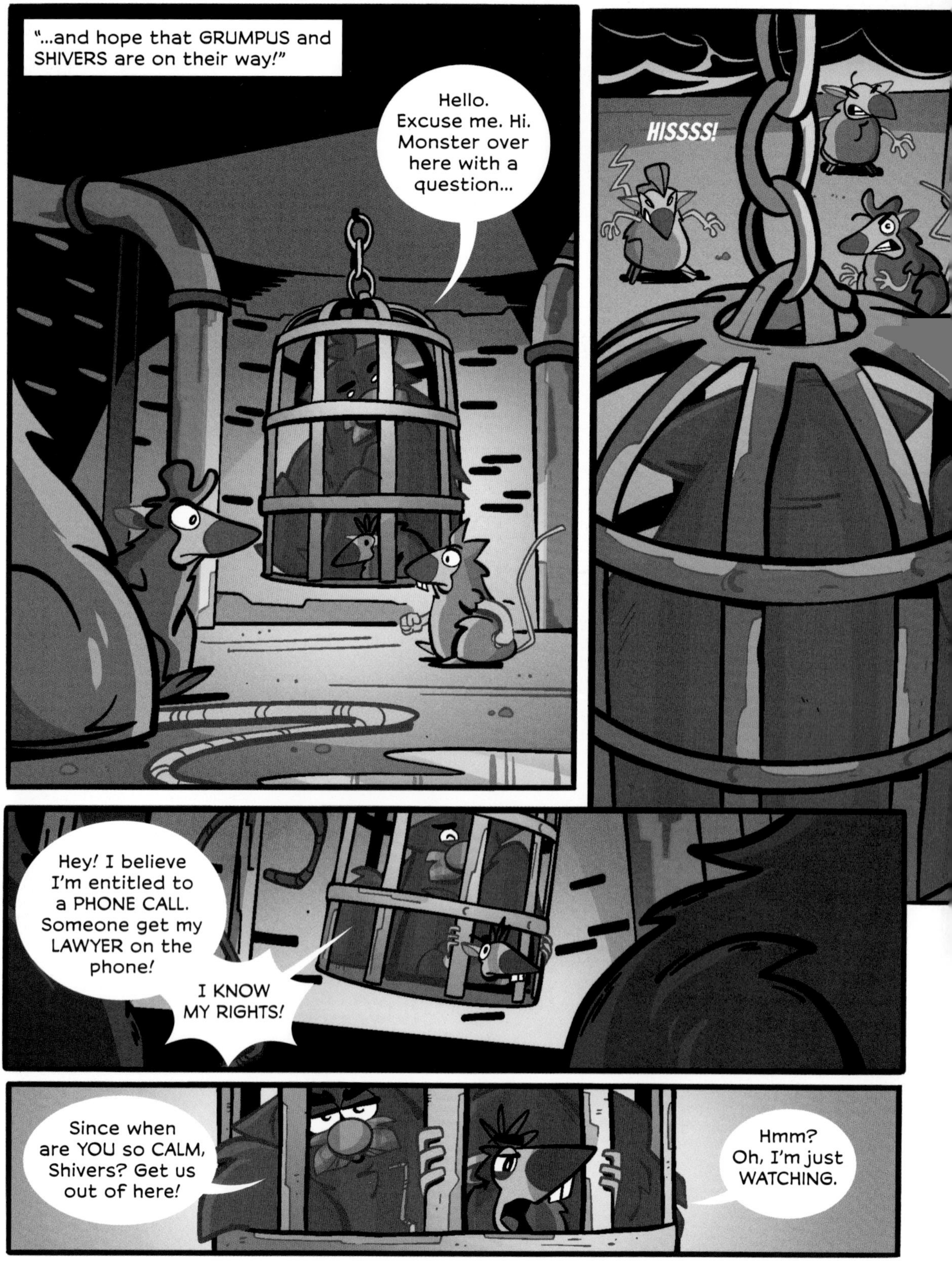
"...and hope that GRUMPUS and SHIVERS are on their way!"
Hello. Excuse me. Hi. Monster over here with a question...
HISSSS!
Hey! I believe I'm entitled to a PHONE CALL. Someone get my LAWYER on the phone!
I KNOW MY RIGHTS!
Since when are YOU so CALM, Shivers? Get us out of here!
Hmm? Oh, I'm just WATCHING.

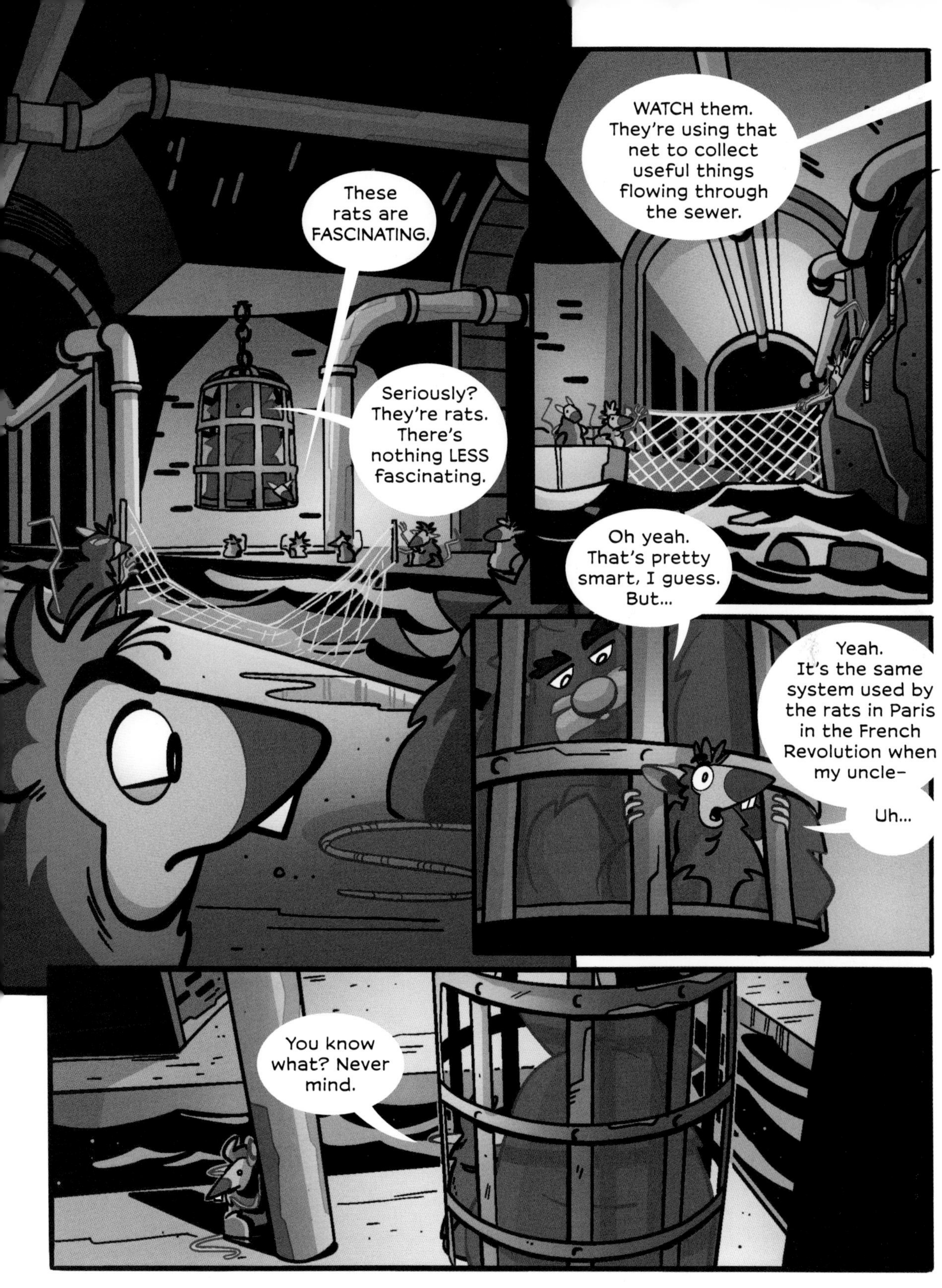
These rats are FASCINATING.
Seriously? They're rats. There's nothing LESS fascinating.
WATCH them. They're using that net to collect useful things flowing through the sewer.
Oh yeah. That's pretty smart, I guess. But...
Yeah. It's the same system used by the rats in Paris in the French Revolution when my uncle-
Uh...
You know what? Never mind.

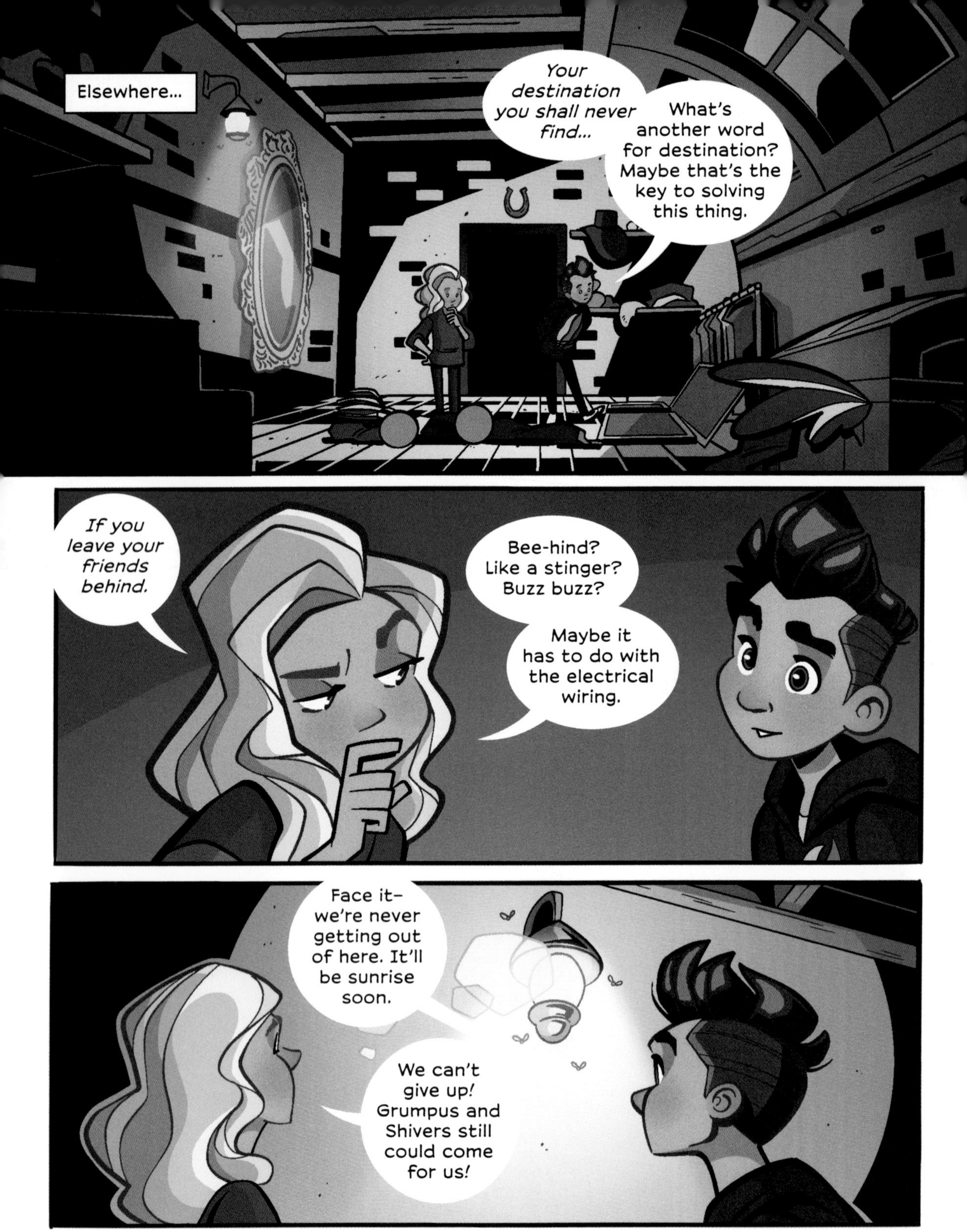
Elsewhere...
Your destination you shall never find...
What's another word for destination? Maybe that's the key to solving this thing.
If you leave your friends behind.
Bee-hind? Like a stinger? Buzz buzz?
Maybe it has to do with the electrical wiring.
Face it— we're never getting out of here. It'll be sunrise soon.
We can't give up! Grumpus and Shivers still could come for us!

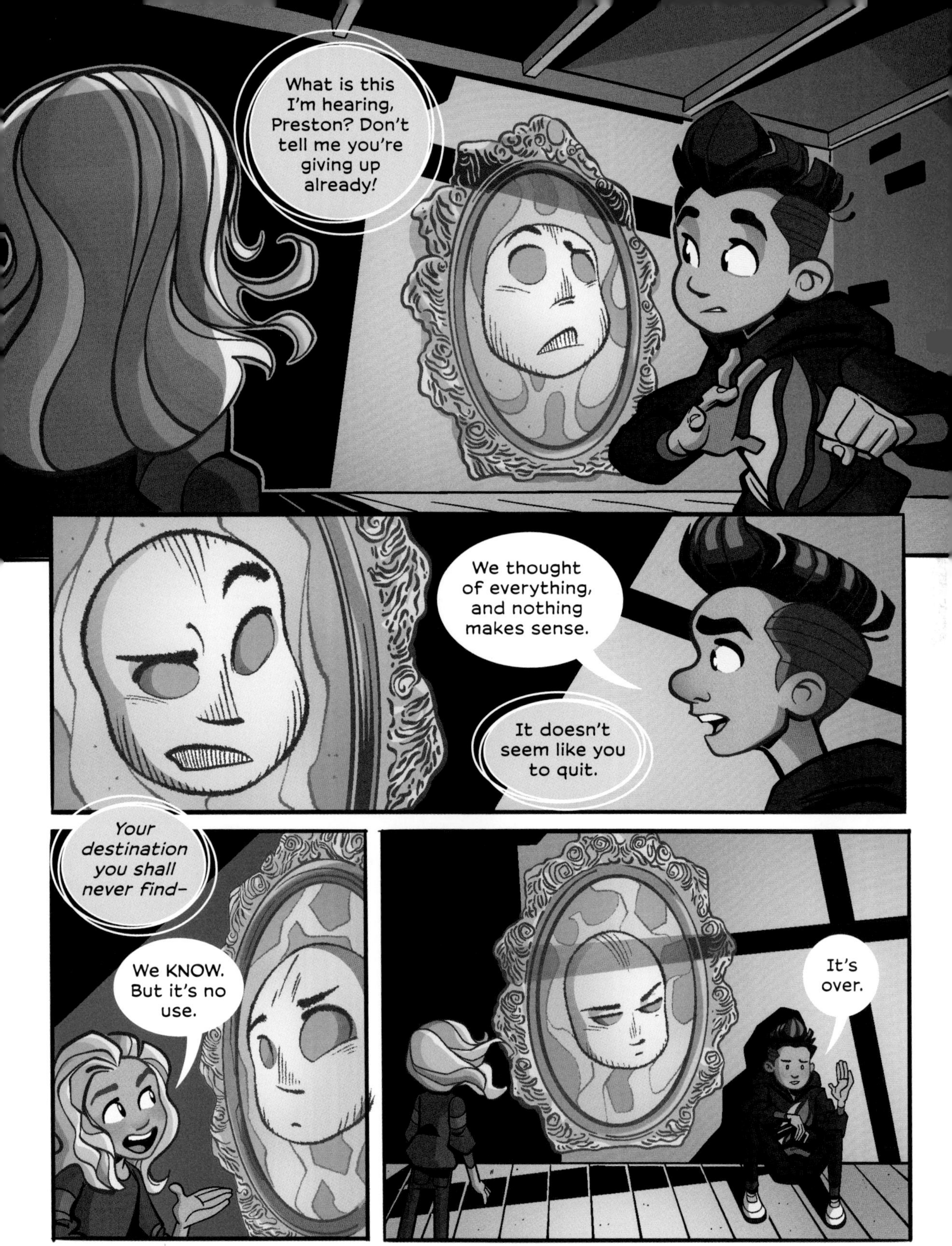
What is this I'm hearing, Preston? Don't tell me you're giving up already!
We thought of everything, and nothing makes sense.
It doesn't seem like you to quit.
Your destination you shall never find–
We KNOW. But it's no use.
It's over.

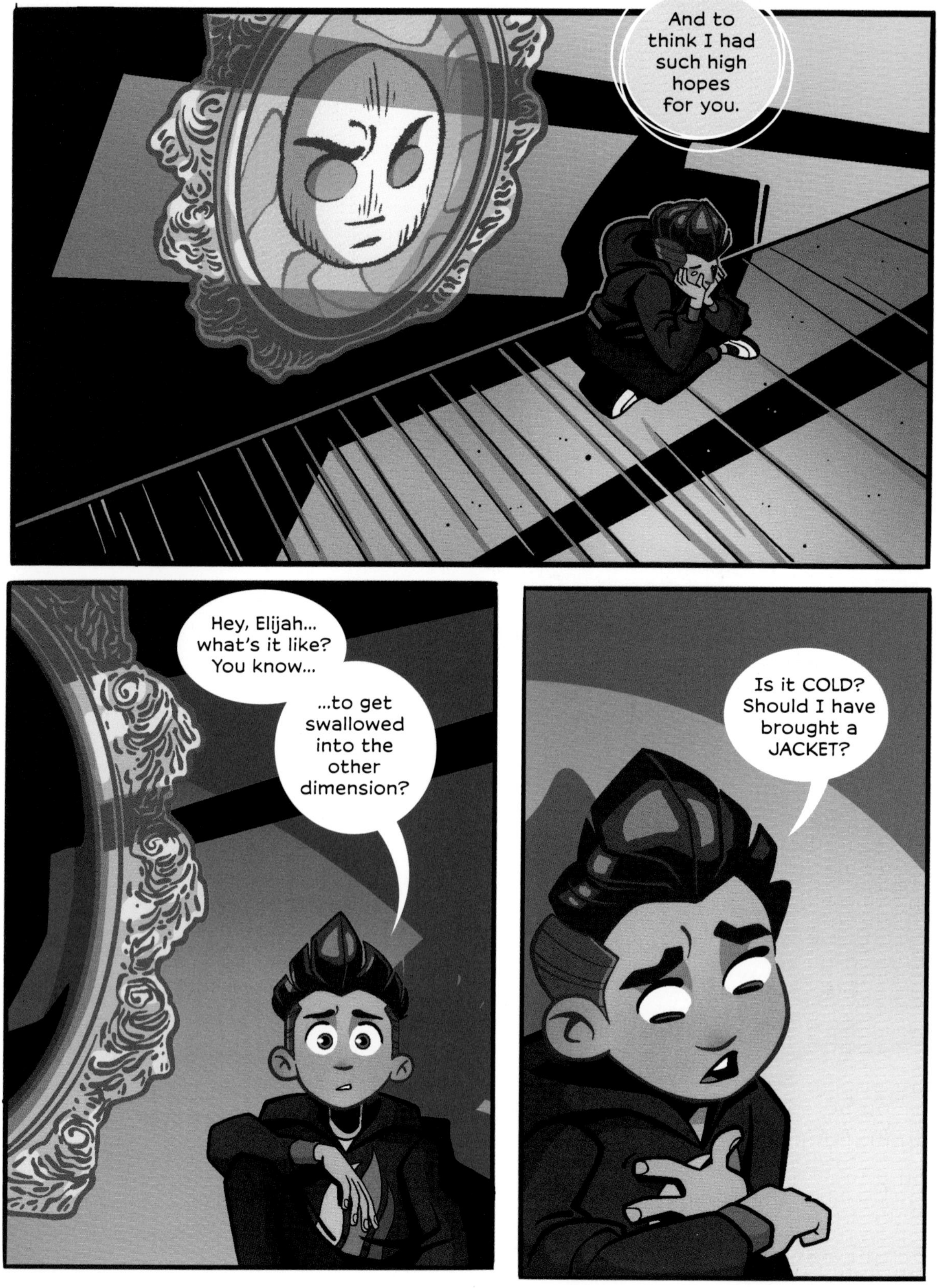
And to think I had such high hopes for you.
Hey, Elijah... what's it like? You know...
...to get swallowed into the other dimension?
Is it COLD? Should I have brought a JACKET?

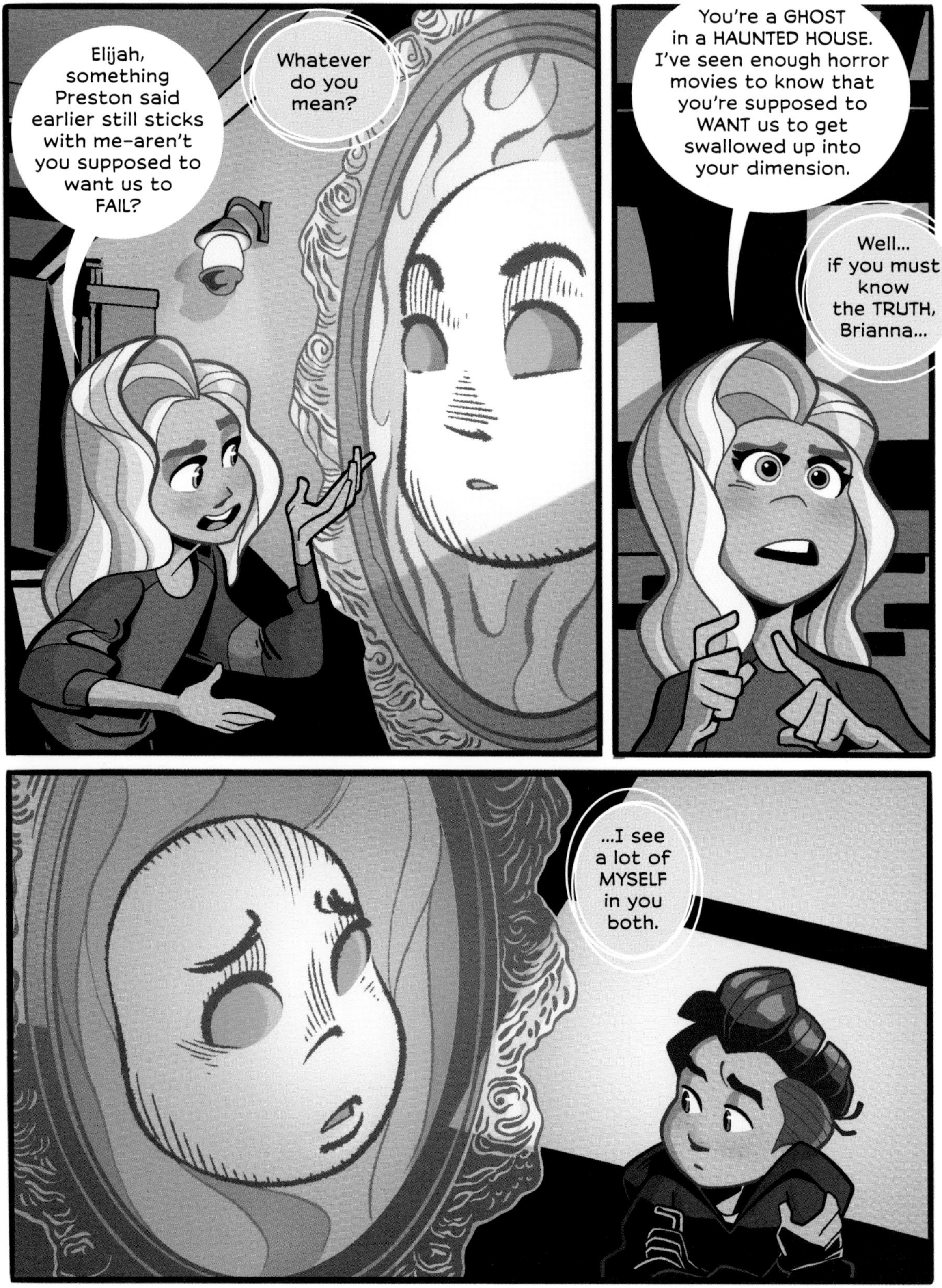
Elijah, something Preston said earlier still sticks with me–aren't you supposed to want us to FAIL?
Whatever do you mean?
You're a GHOST in a HAUNTED HOUSE. I've seen enough horror movies to know that you're supposed to WANT us to get swallowed up into your dimension.
Well... if you must know the TRUTH, Brianna...
...I see a lot of MYSELF in you both.

I was once like you–young and AMBITIOUS, full of ENERGY and IDEAS.

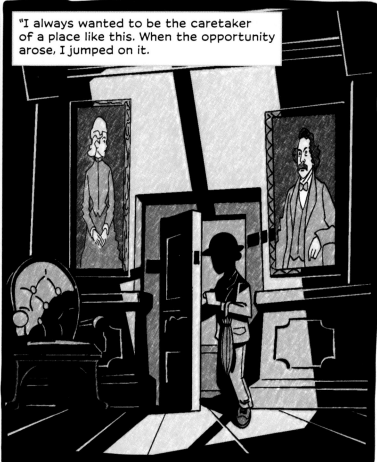

"I always wanted to be the caretaker of a place like this. When the opportunity arose, I jumped on it.

"Like you, I was warned against spending too much time here. Warned that I'd be swallowed up by an alternate dimension. I wasn't scared. It seemed EXCITING to me.

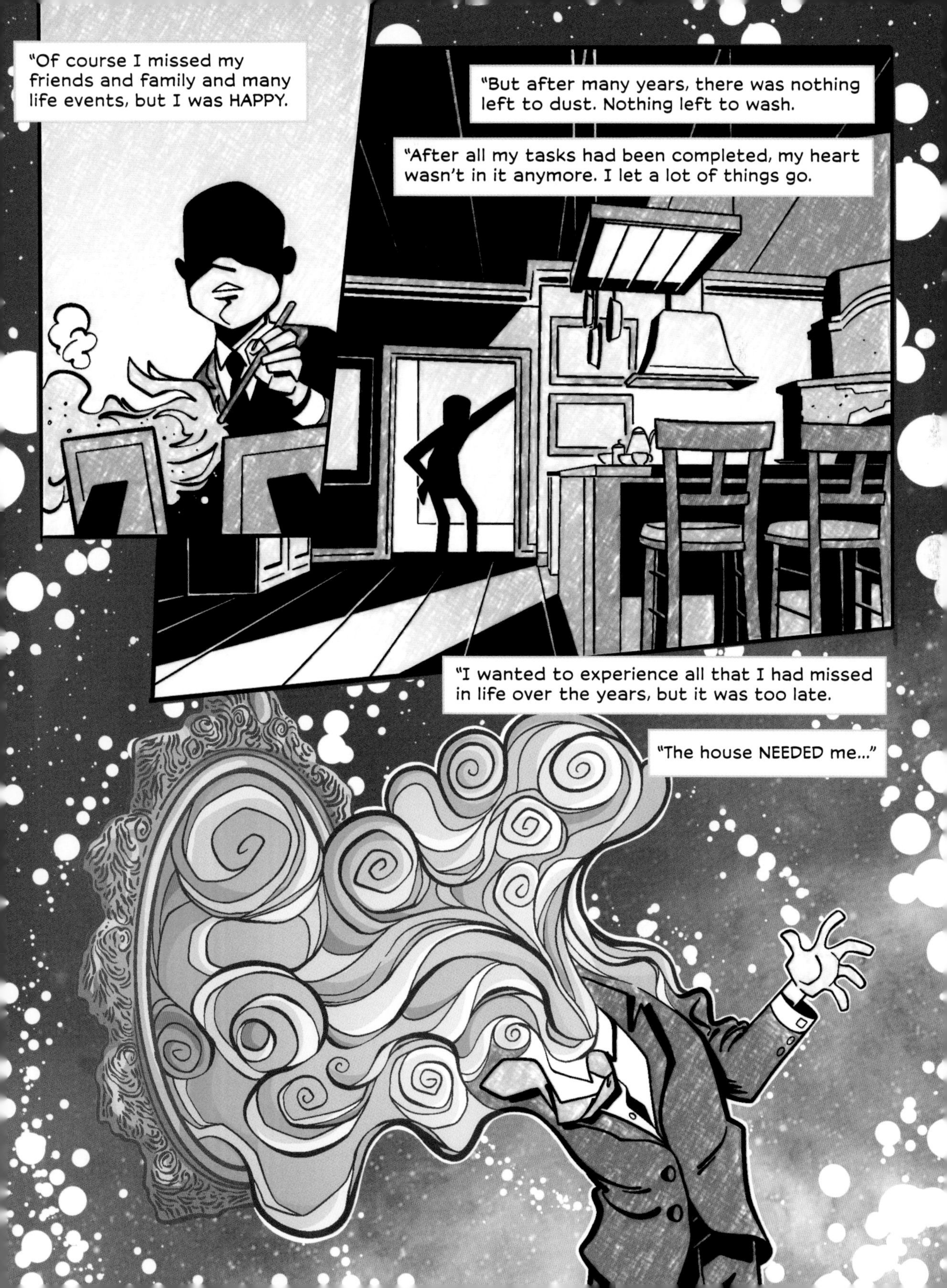
"Of course I missed my friends and family and many life events, but I was HAPPY.
"But after many years, there was nothing left to dust. Nothing left to wash.
"After all my tasks had been completed, my heart wasn't in it anymore. I let a lot of things go.
"I wanted to experience all that I had missed in life over the years, but it was too late.
"The house NEEDED me..."

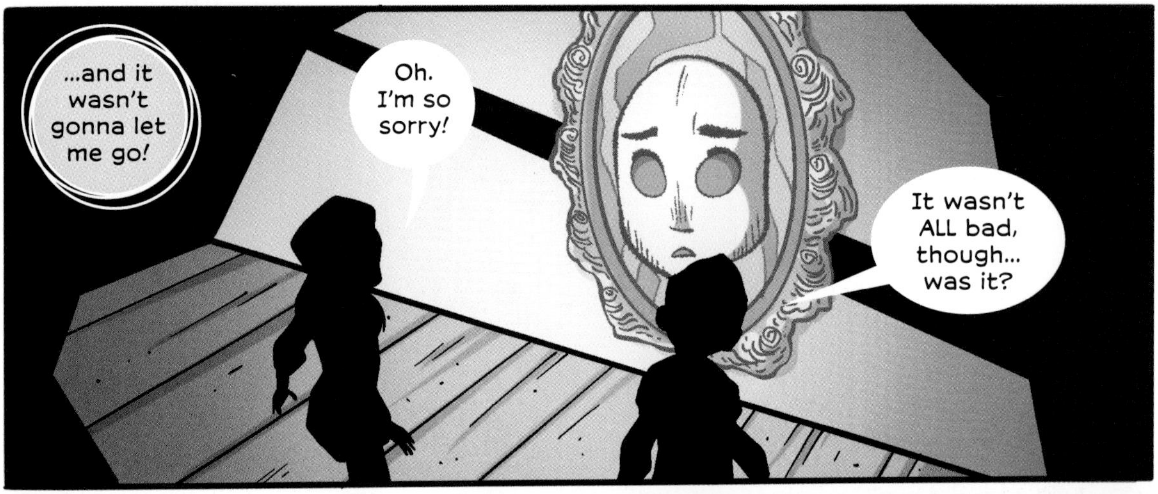
...and it wasn't gonna let me go!
Oh. I'm so sorry!
It wasn't ALL bad, though... was it?
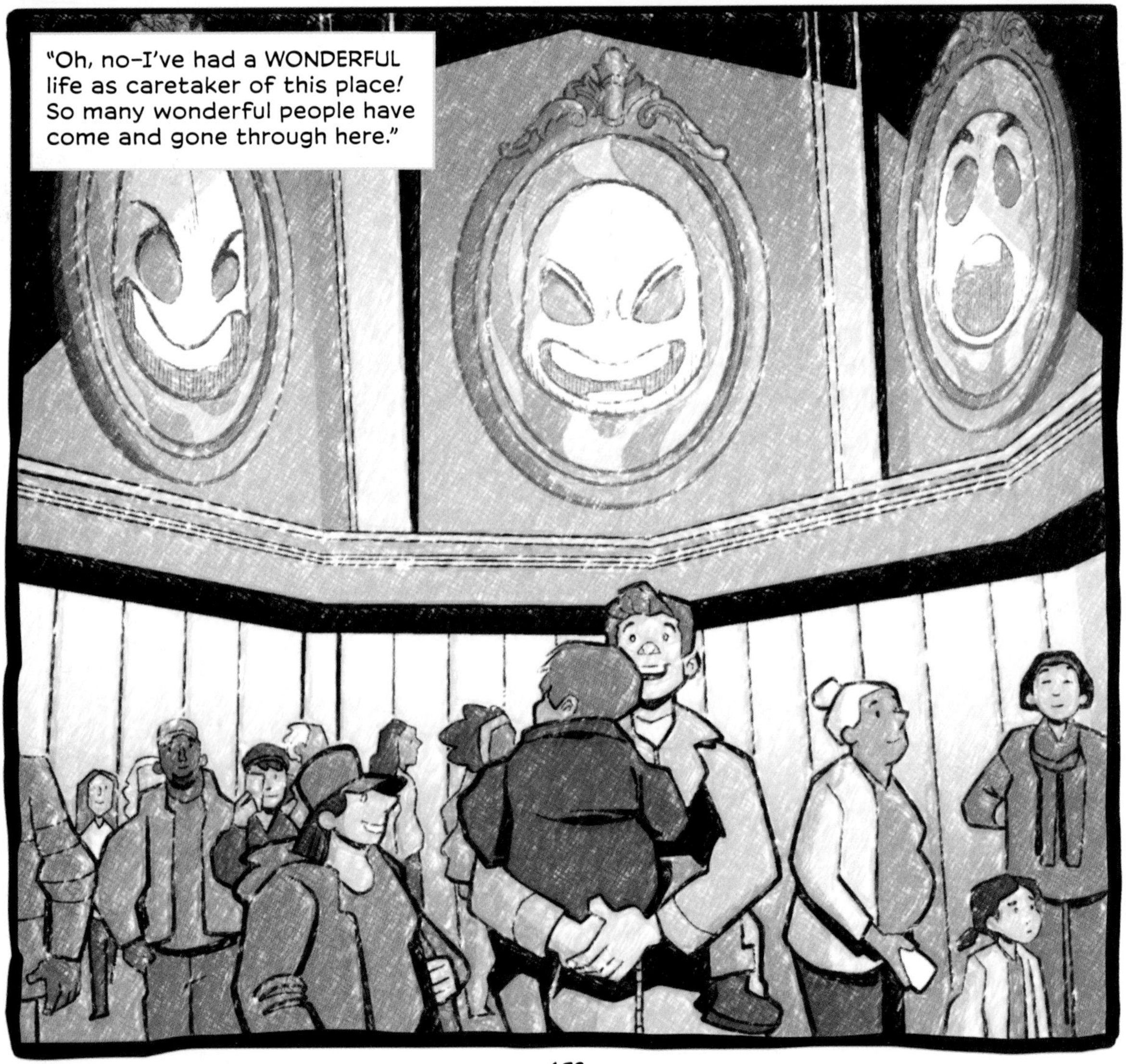
"Oh, no–I've had a WONDERFUL life as caretaker of this place! So many wonderful people have come and gone through here."

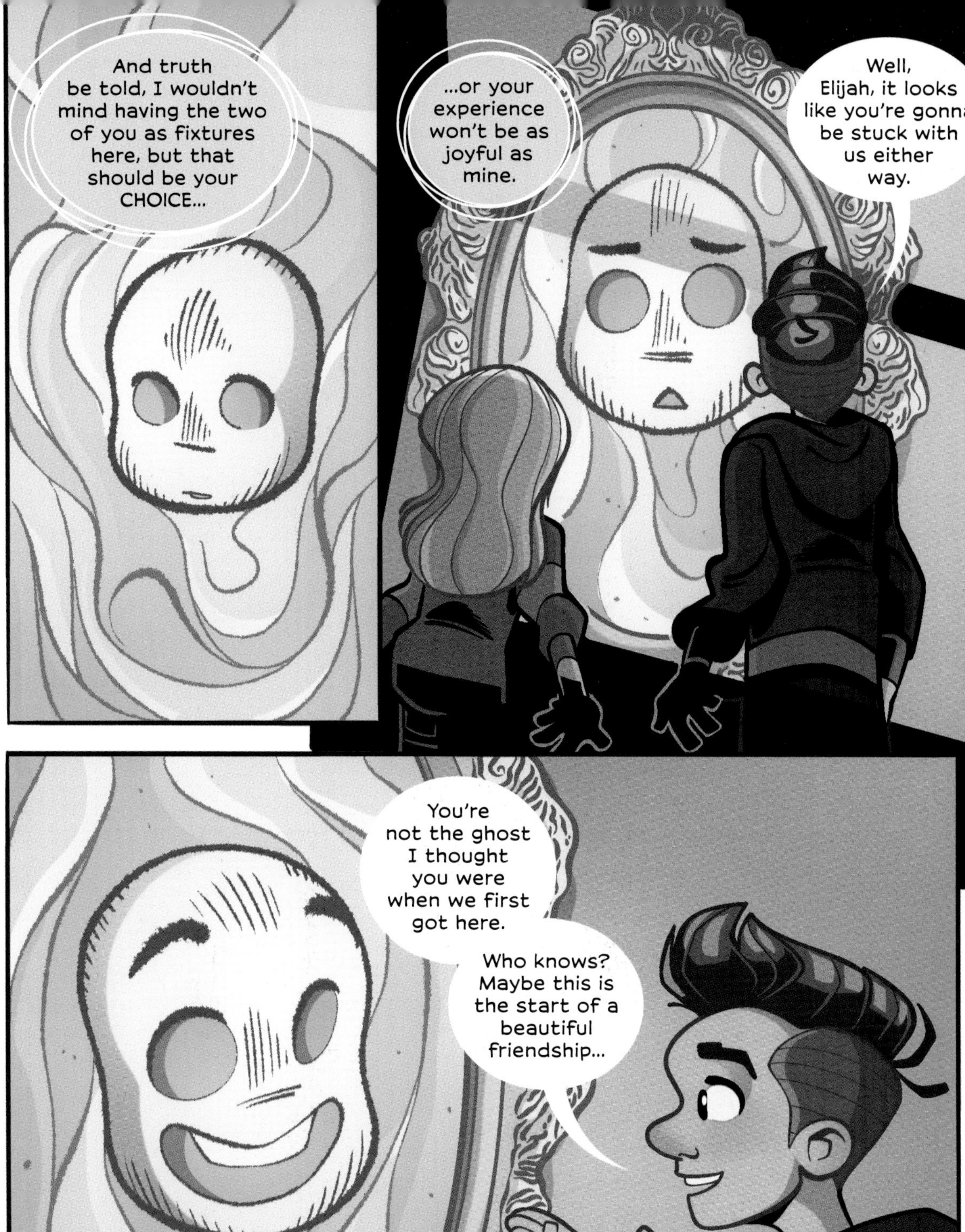
And truth be told, I wouldn't mind having the two of you as fixtures here, but that should be your CHOICE...
...or your experience won't be as joyful as mine.
Well, Elijah, it looks like you're gonna be stuck with us either way.
You're not the ghost I thought you were when we first got here.
Who knows? Maybe this is the start of a beautiful friendship...

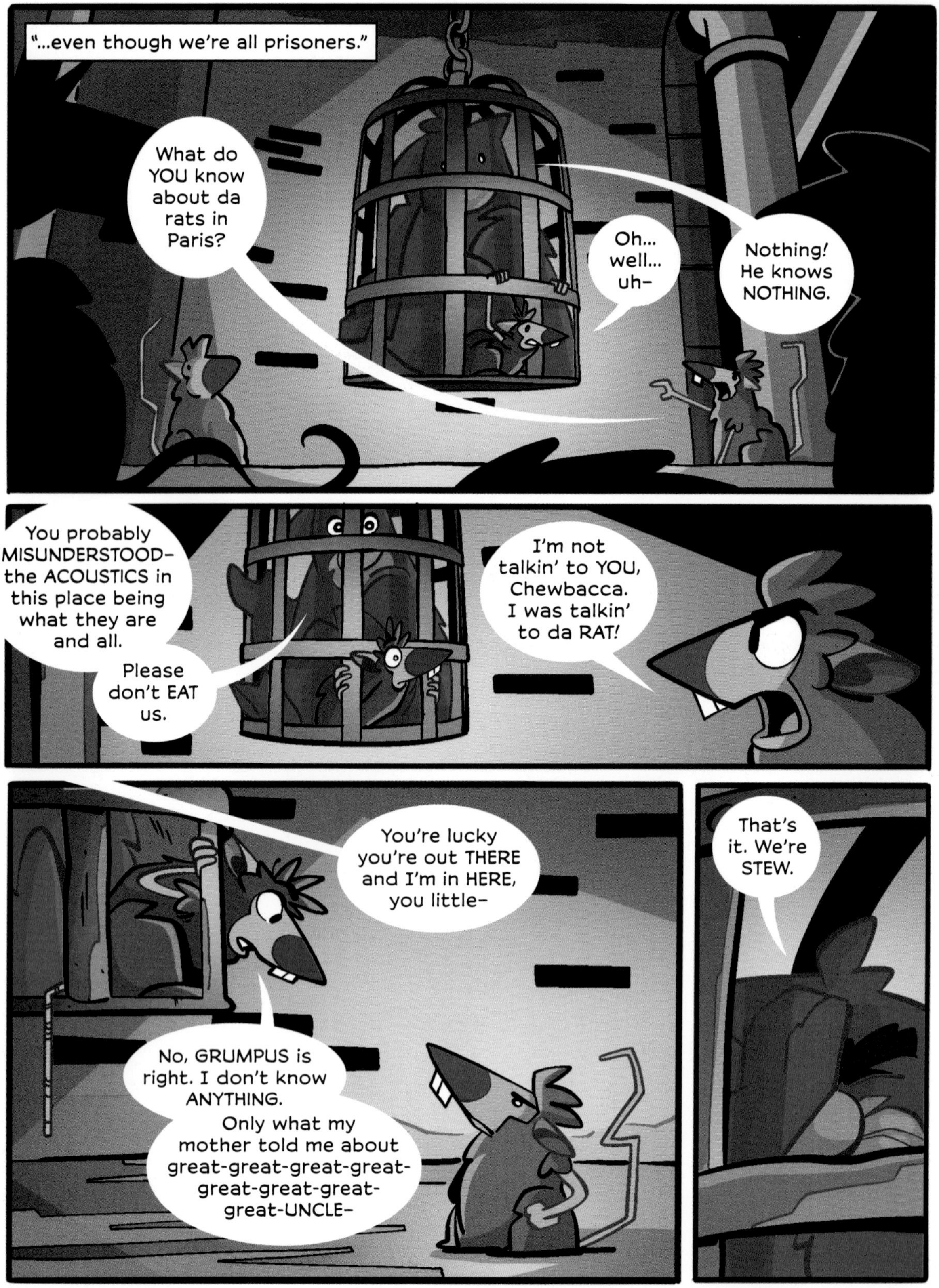
"...even though we're all prisoners."
What do YOU know about da rats in Paris?
Oh... well... uh–
Nothing! He knows NOTHING.
You probably MISUNDERSTOOD– the ACOUSTICS in this place being what they are and all.
Please don't EAT us.
I'm not talkin' to YOU, Chewbacca. I was talkin' to da RAT!
You're lucky you're out THERE and I'm in HERE, you little–
No, GRUMPUS is right. I don't know ANYTHING.
Only what my mother told me about great-great-great-great-great-great-great-great-UNCLE–
That's it. We're STEW.

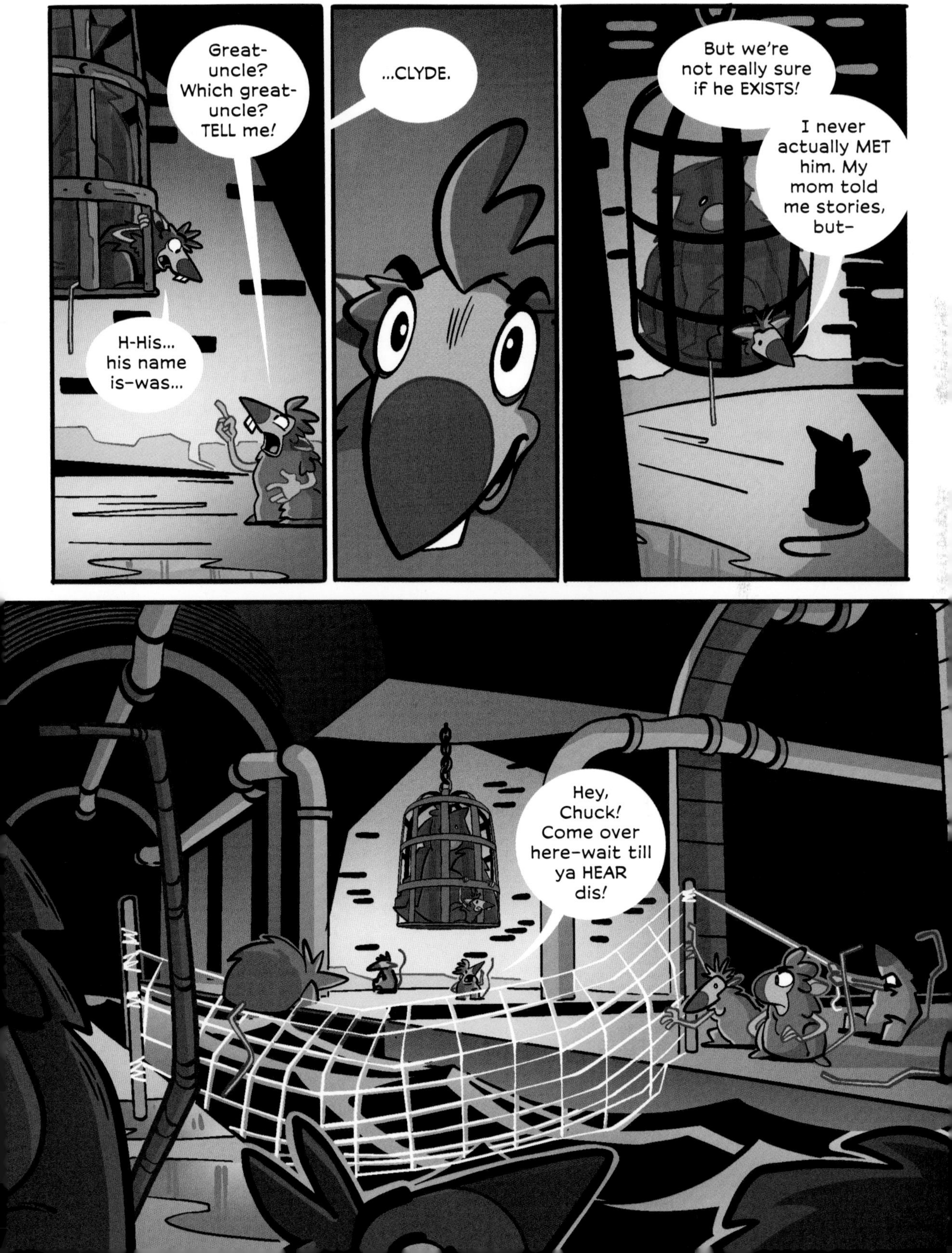
Great-uncle? Which great-uncle? TELL me!
H-His... his name is-was...
...CLYDE.
But we're not really sure if he EXISTS!
I never actually MET him. My mom told me stories, but-
Hey, Chuck! Come over here-wait till ya HEAR dis!

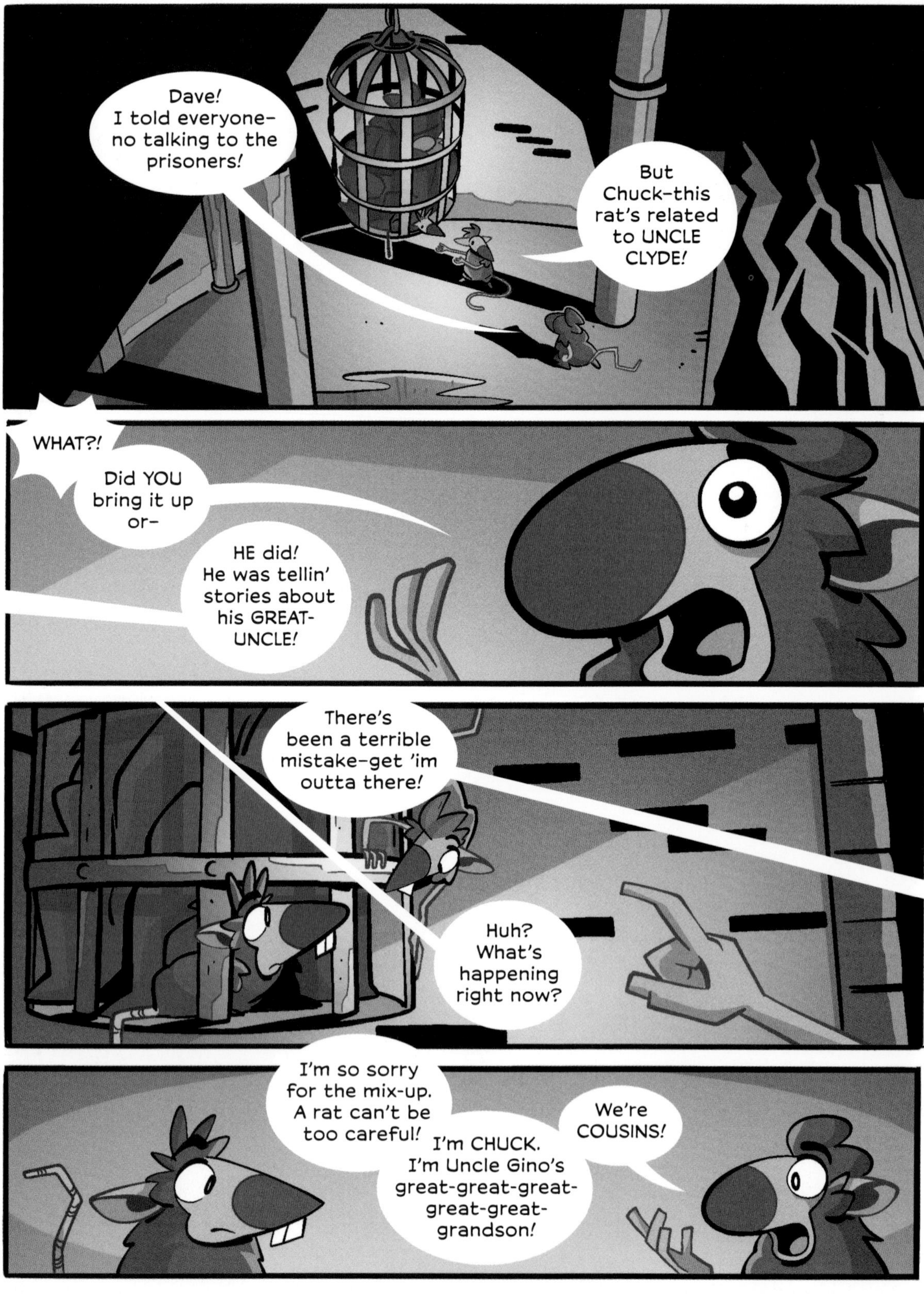

Dave! I told everyone– no talking to the prisoners!
But Chuck–this rat's related to UNCLE CLYDE!
WHAT?!
Did YOU bring it up or–
HE did! He was tellin' stories about his GREAT-UNCLE!
There's been a terrible mistake–get 'im outta there!
Huh? What's happening right now?
I'm so sorry for the mix-up. A rat can't be too careful!
I'm CHUCK. I'm Uncle Gino's great-great-great-great-great-grandson!
We're COUSINS!

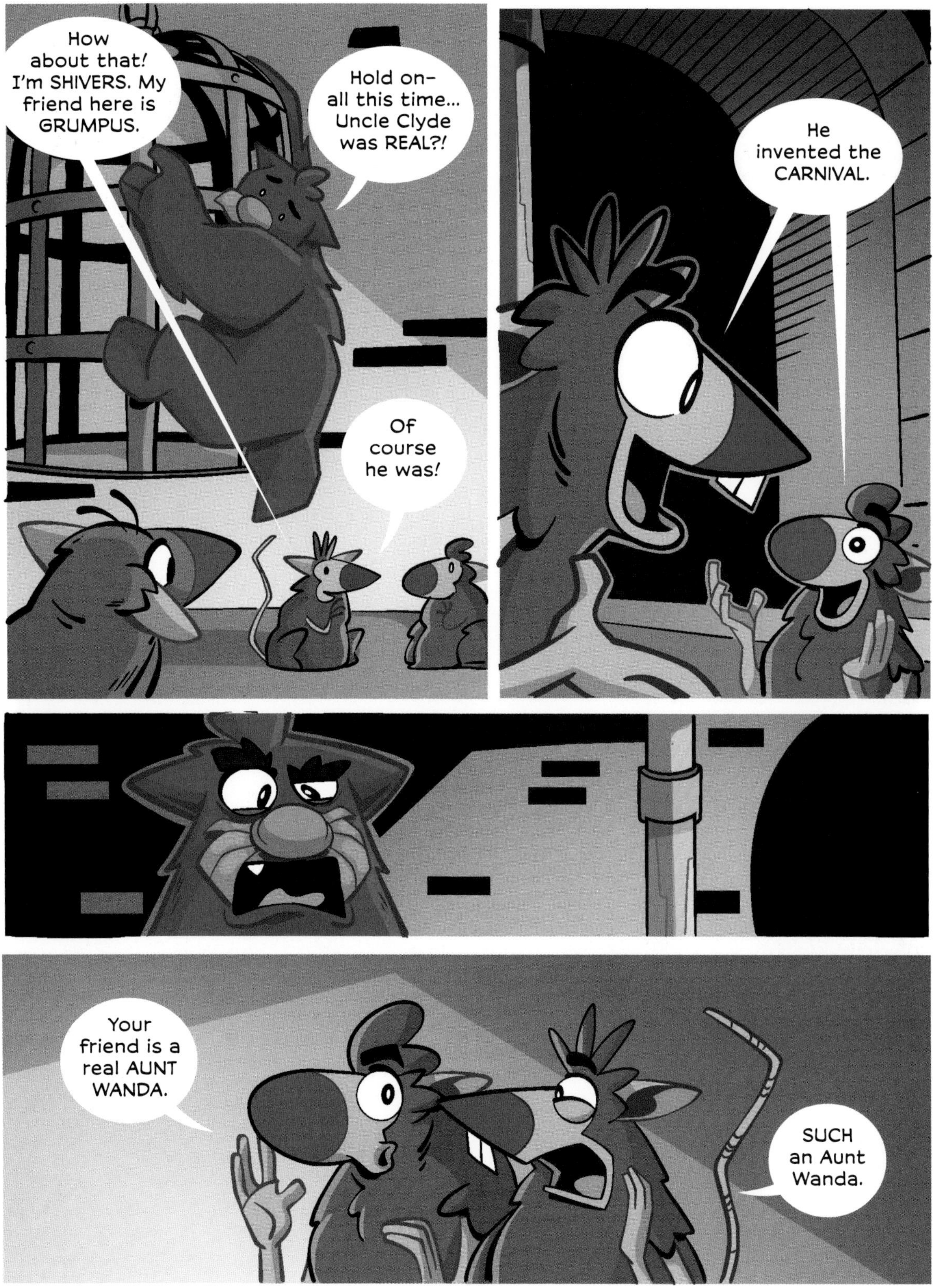
How about that! I'm SHIVERS. My friend here is GRUMPUS.
Hold on– all this time... Uncle Clyde was REAL?!
Of course he was!
He invented the CARNIVAL.
Your friend is a real AUNT WANDA.
SUCH an Aunt Wanda.

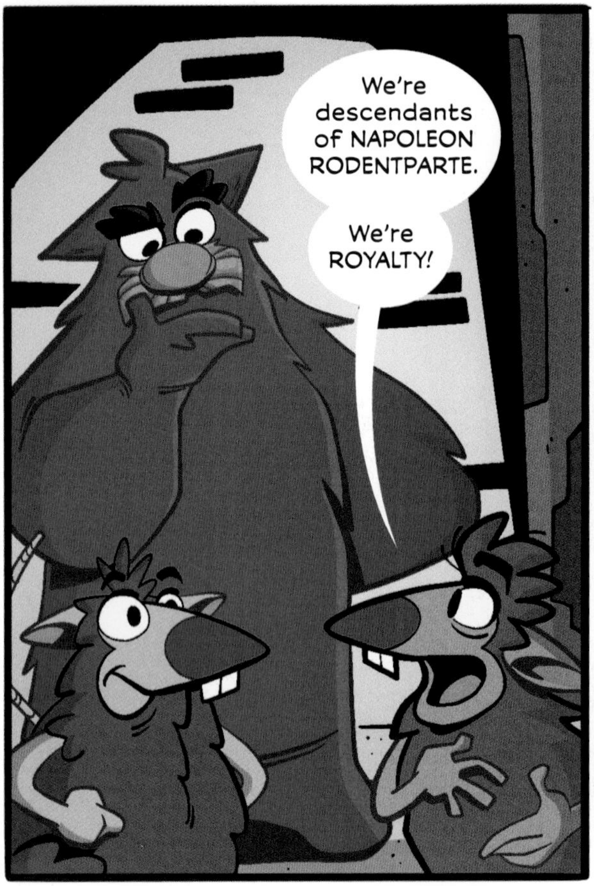
We're descendants of NAPOLEON RODENTPARTE.
We're ROYALTY!

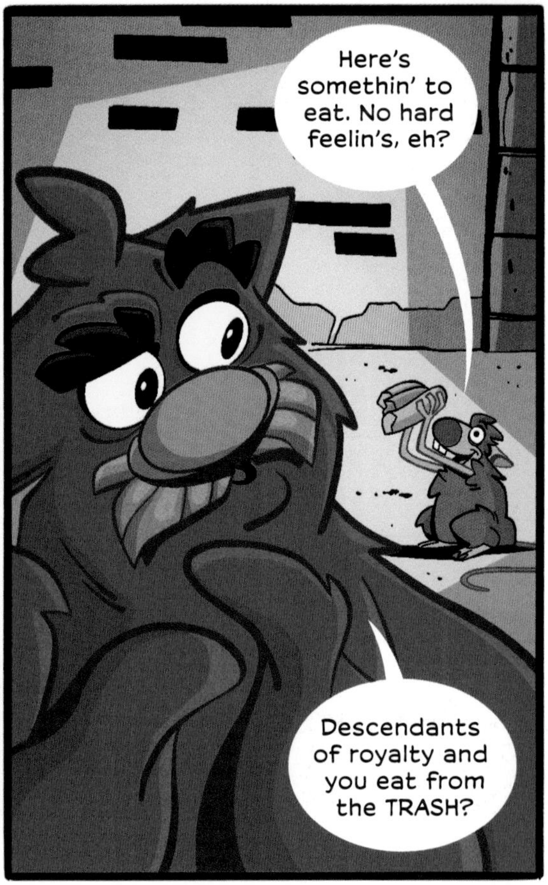
Here's somethin' to eat. No hard feelin's, eh?
Descendants of royalty and you eat from the TRASH?

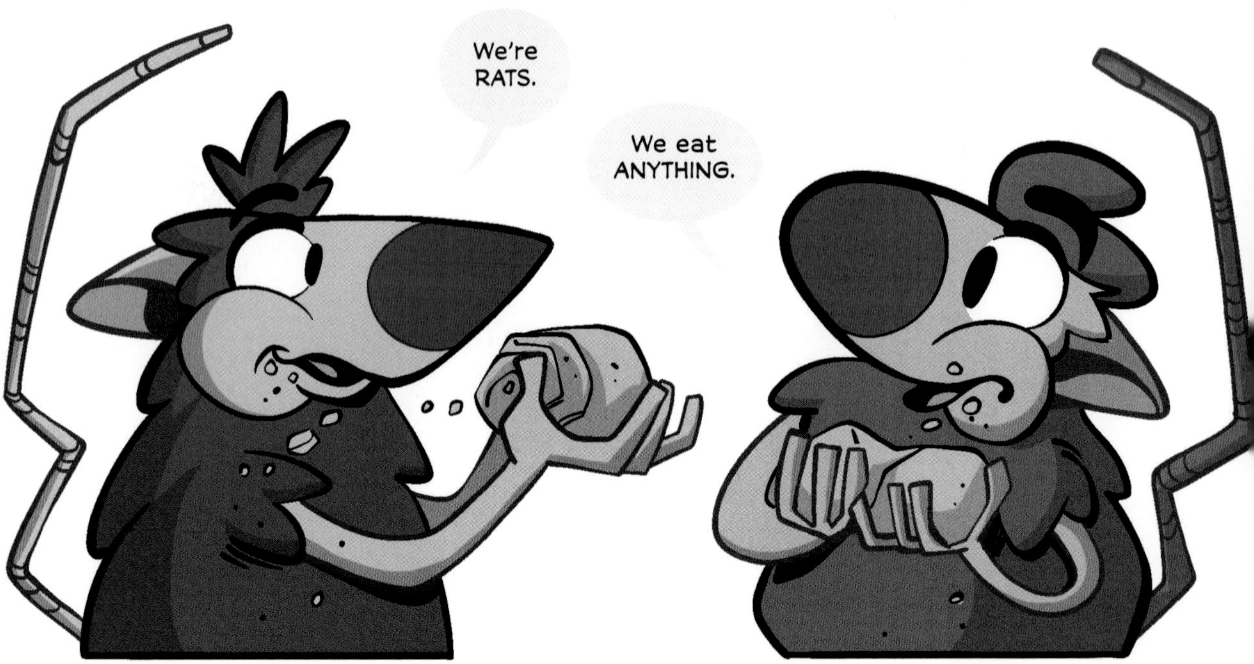
We're RATS.
We eat ANYTHING.

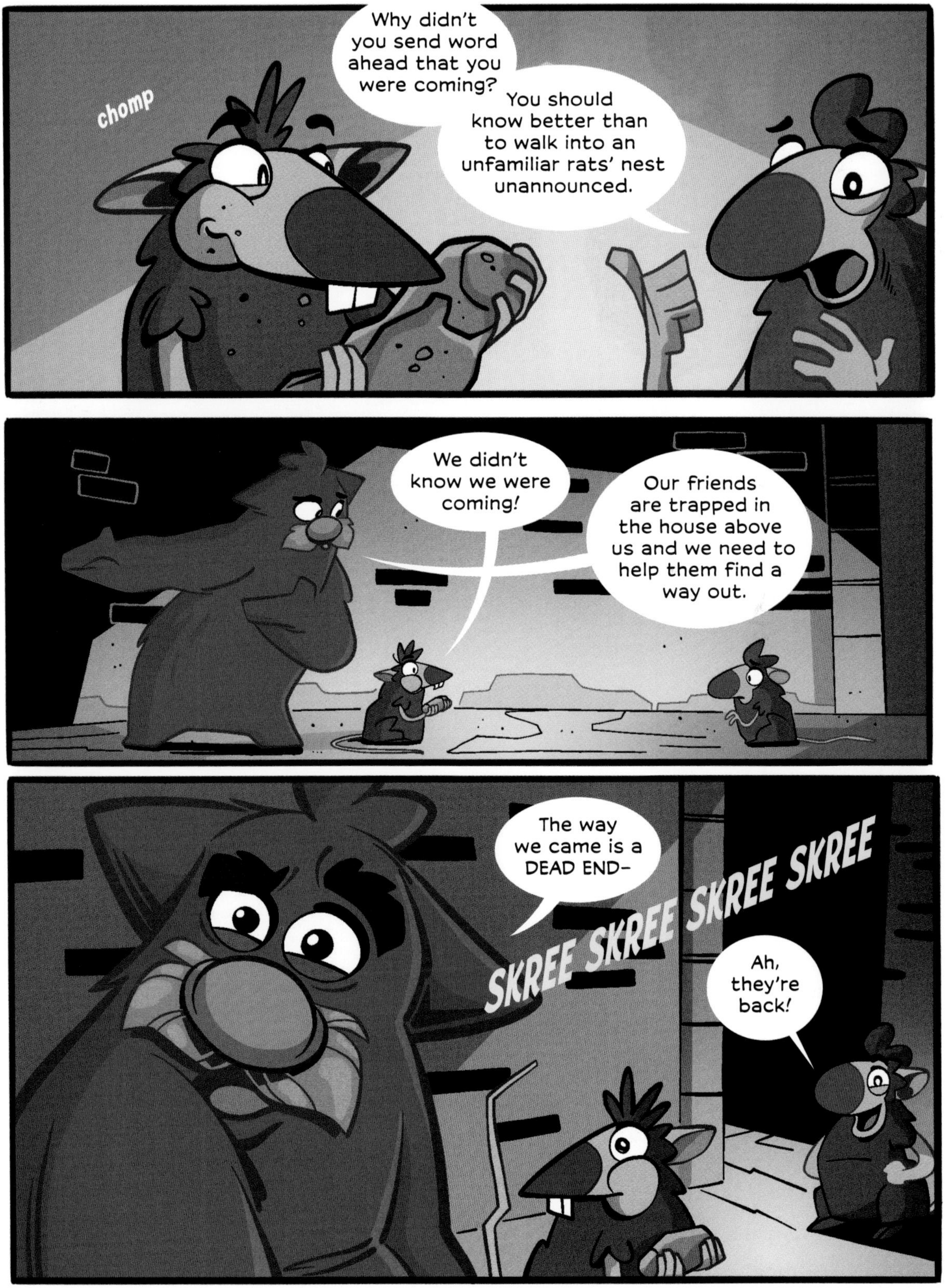
chomp
Why didn't you send word ahead that you were coming?
You should know better than to walk into an unfamiliar rats' nest unannounced.
We didn't know we were coming!
Our friends are trapped in the house above us and we need to help them find a way out.
The way we came is a DEAD END–
SKREE SKREE SKREE SKREE
Ah, they're back!

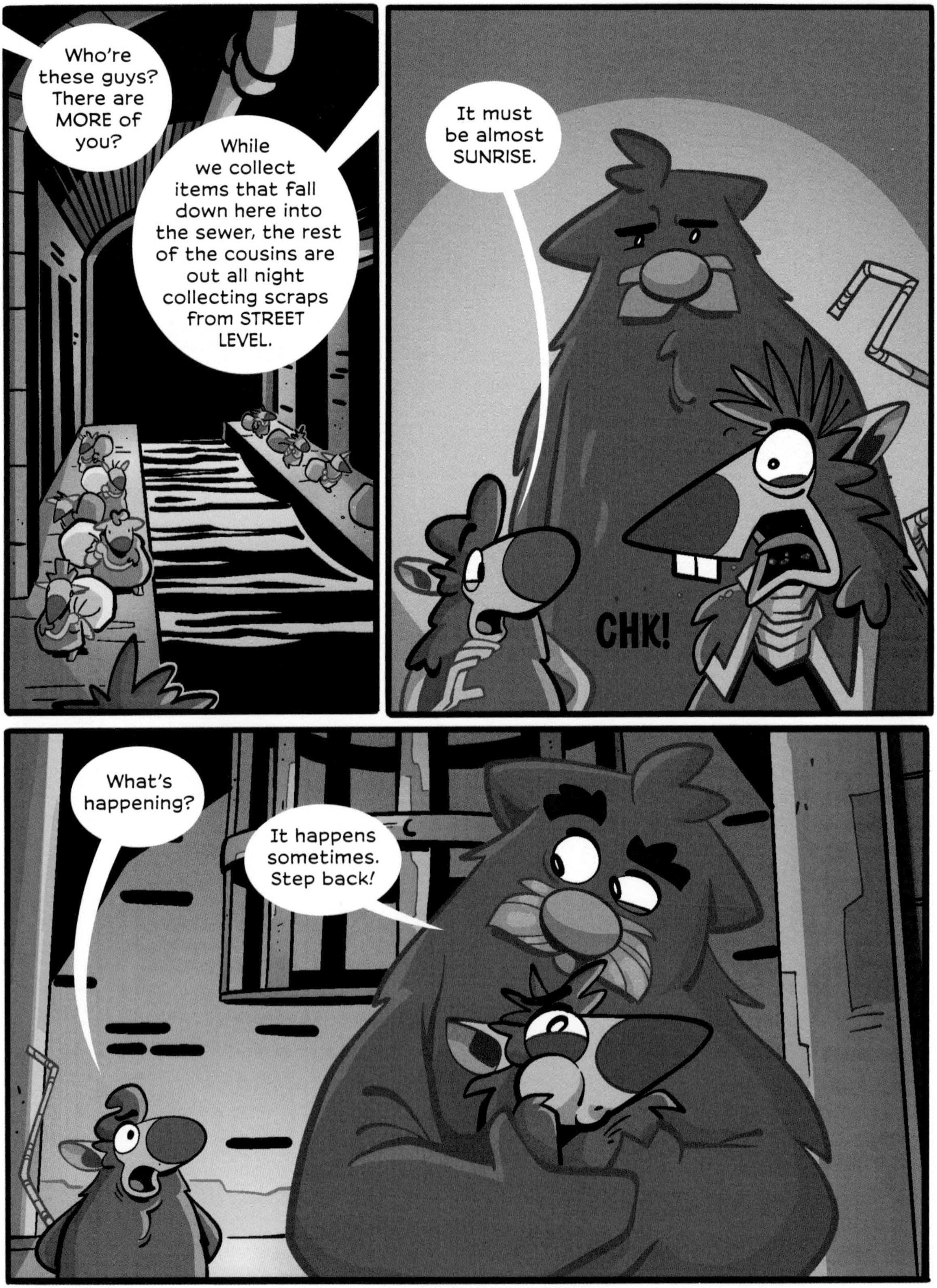
Who're these guys? There are MORE of you?
While we collect items that fall down here into the sewer, the rest of the cousins are out all night collecting scraps from STREET LEVEL.
It must be almost SUNRISE.
CHK!
What's happening?
It happens sometimes. Step back!

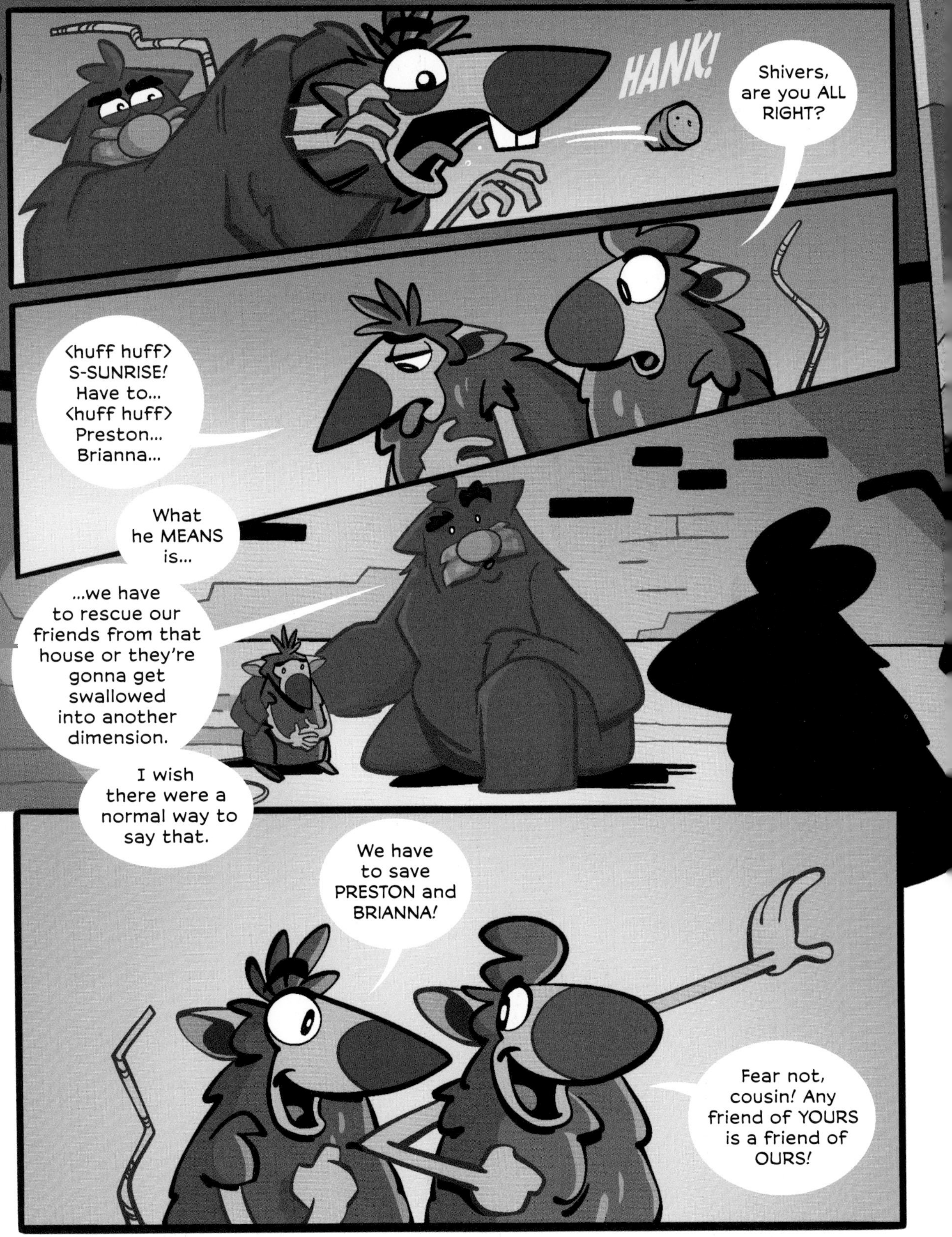
HANK!
Shivers, are you ALL RIGHT?
<huff huff> S-SUNRISE! Have to... <huff huff> Preston... Brianna...
What he MEANS is...
...we have to rescue our friends from that house or they're gonna get swallowed into another dimension.
I wish there were a normal way to say that.
We have to save PRESTON and BRIANNA!
Fear not, cousin! Any friend of YOURS is a friend of OURS!

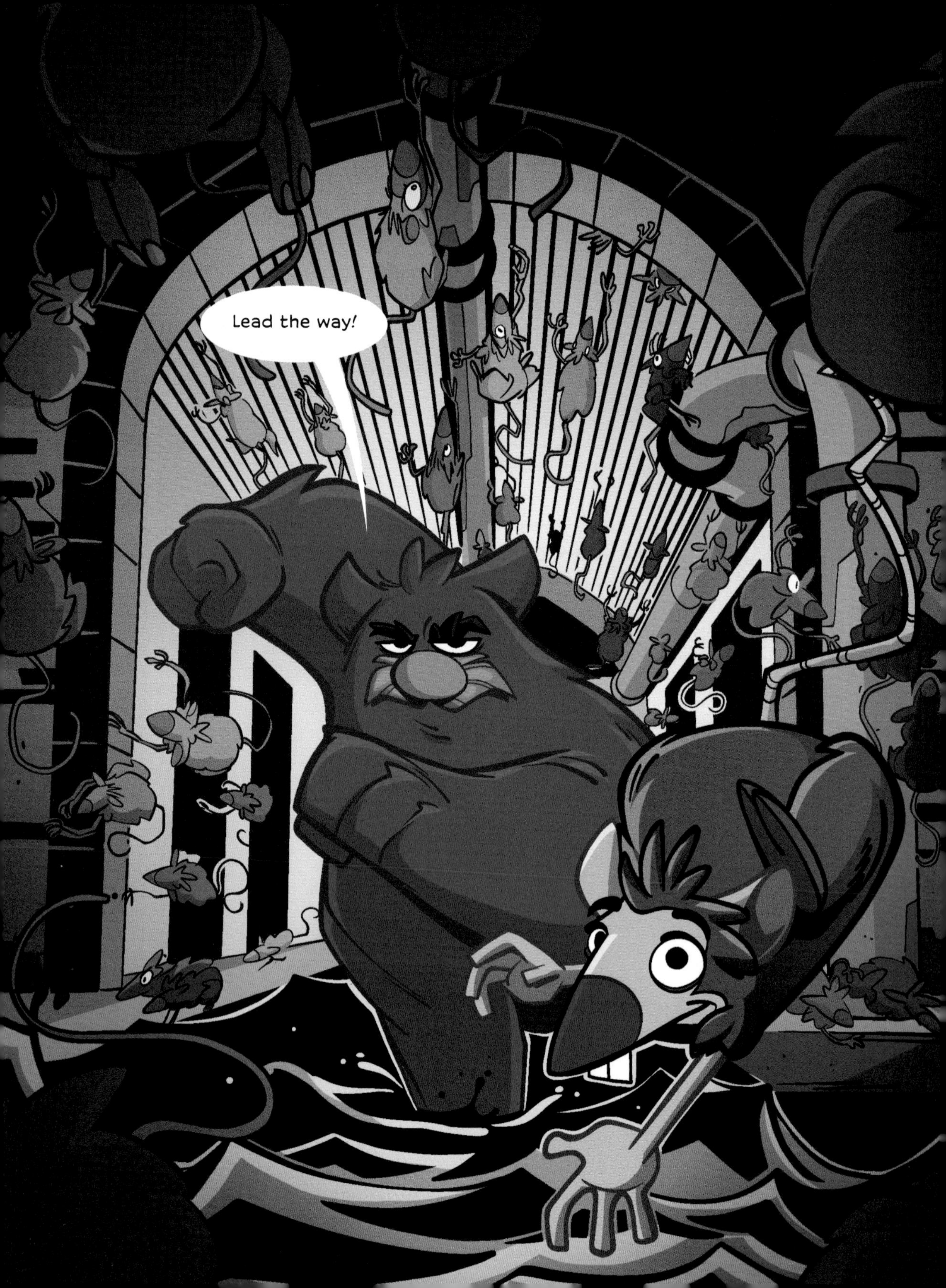
Lead the way!

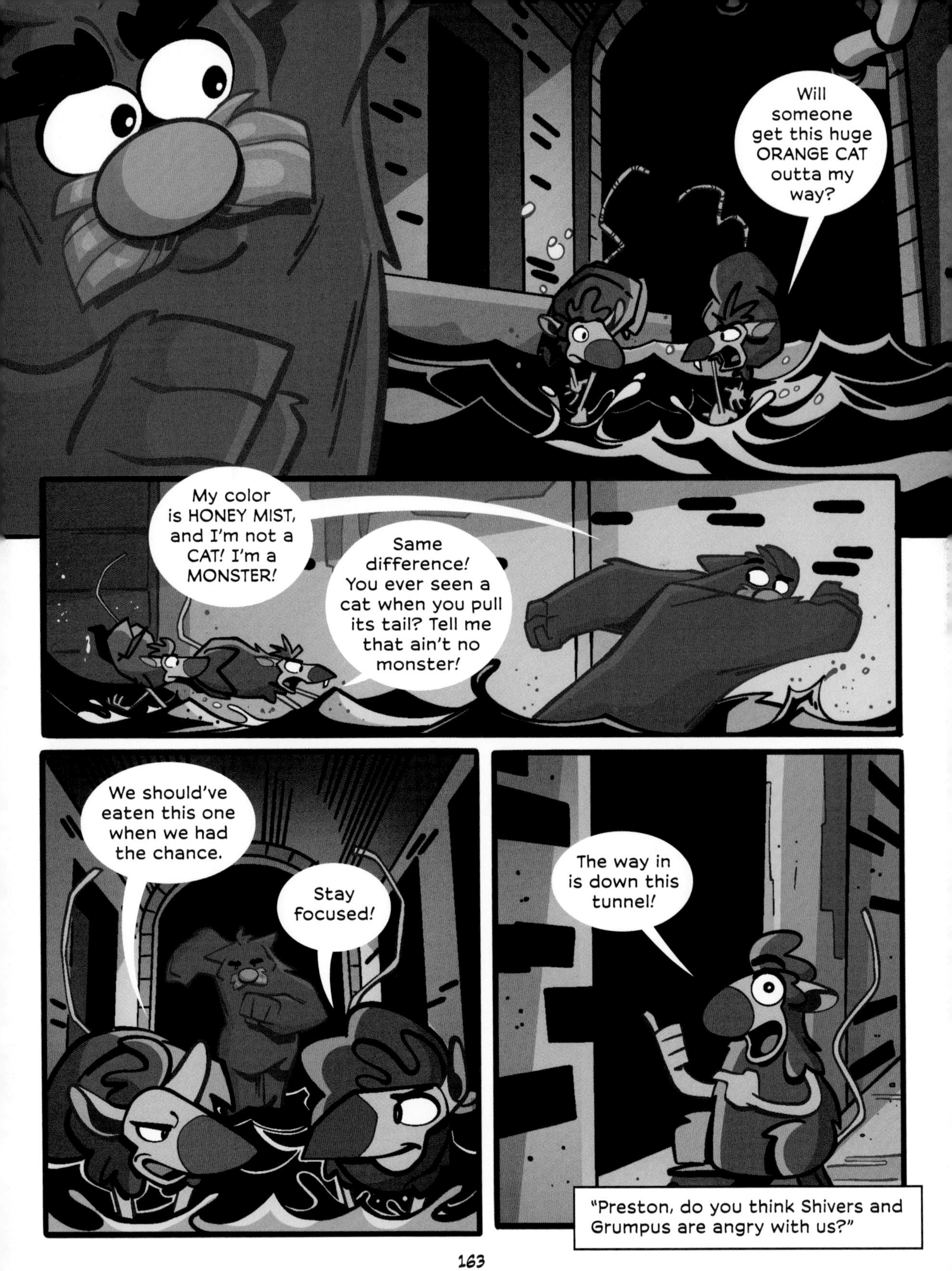

Will someone get this huge ORANGE CAT outta my way?
My color is HONEY MIST, and I'm not a CAT! I'm a MONSTER!
Same difference! You ever seen a cat when you pull its tail? Tell me that ain't no monster!
We should've eaten this one when we had the chance.
Stay focused!
The way in is down this tunnel!
"Preston, do you think Shivers and Grumpus are angry with us?"

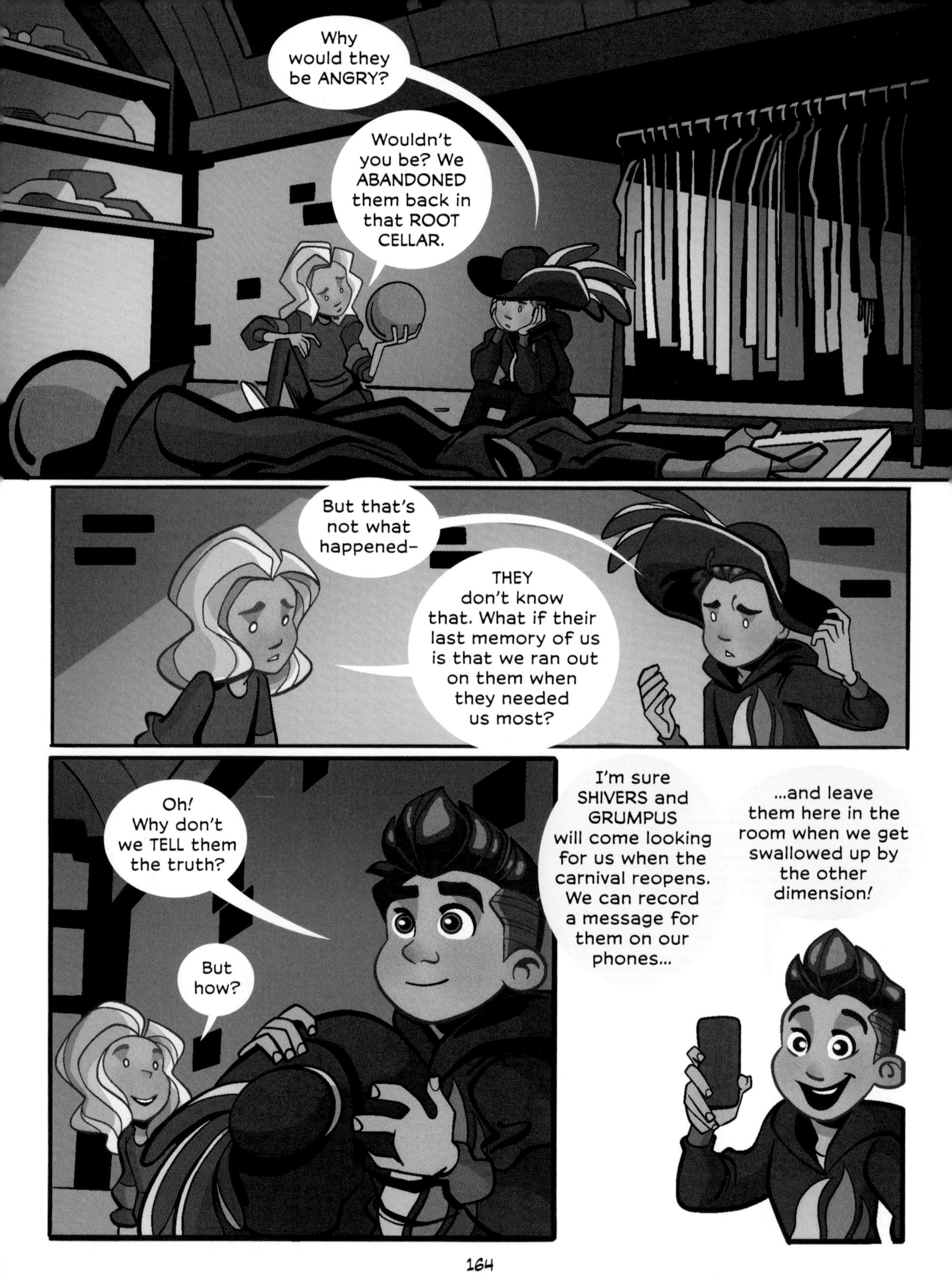

Why would they be ANGRY?
Wouldn't you be? We ABANDONED them back in that ROOT CELLAR.
But that's not what happened–
THEY don't know that. What if their last memory of us is that we ran out on them when they needed us most?
Oh! Why don't we TELL them the truth?
But how?
I'm sure SHIVERS and GRUMPUS will come looking for us when the carnival reopens. We can record a message for them on our phones...
...and leave them here in the room when we get swallowed up by the other dimension!

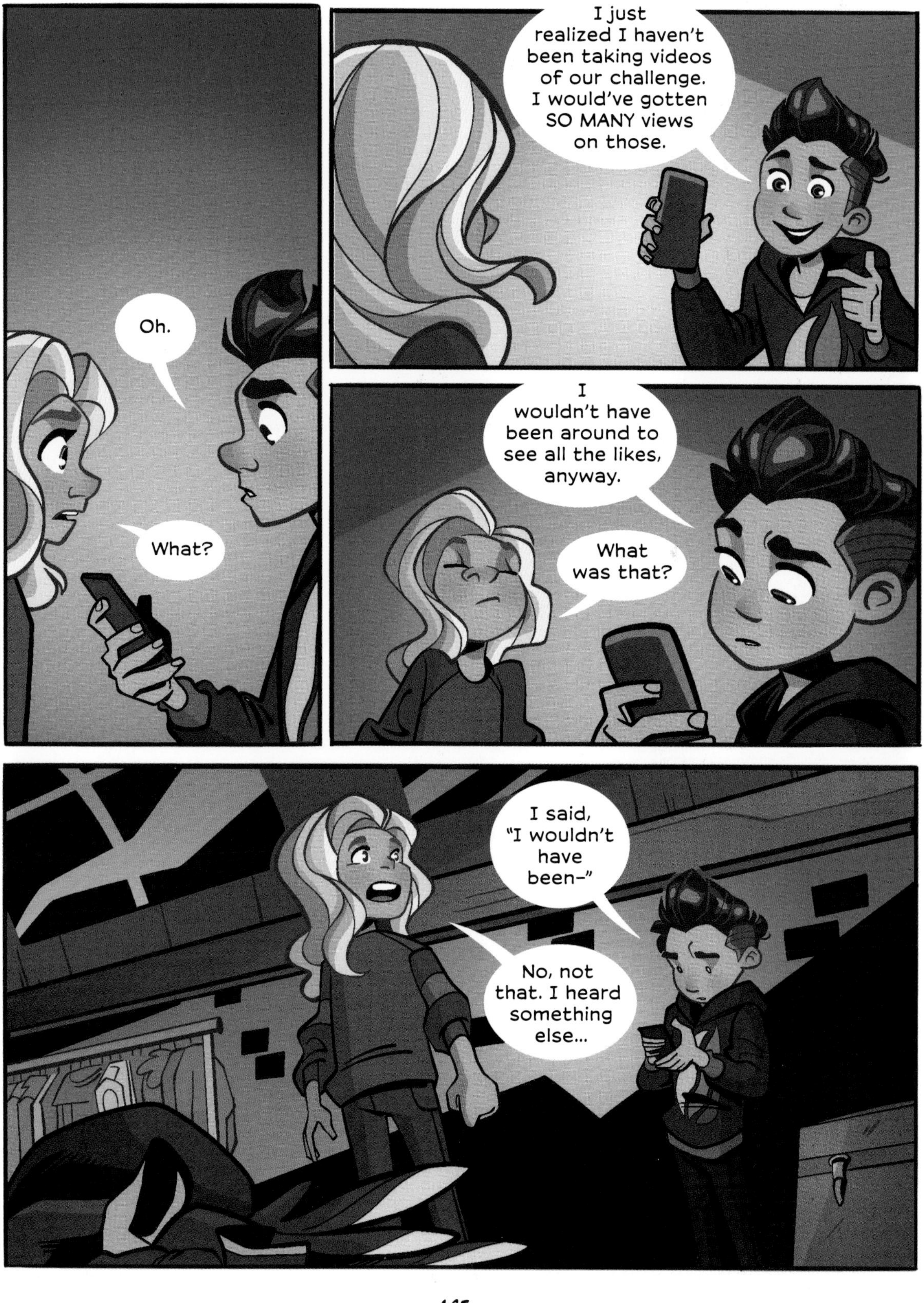
Oh.
What?
I just realized I haven't been taking videos of our challenge. I would've gotten SO MANY views on those.
I wouldn't have been around to see all the likes, anyway.
What was that?
I said, "I wouldn't have been–"
No, not that. I heard something else...

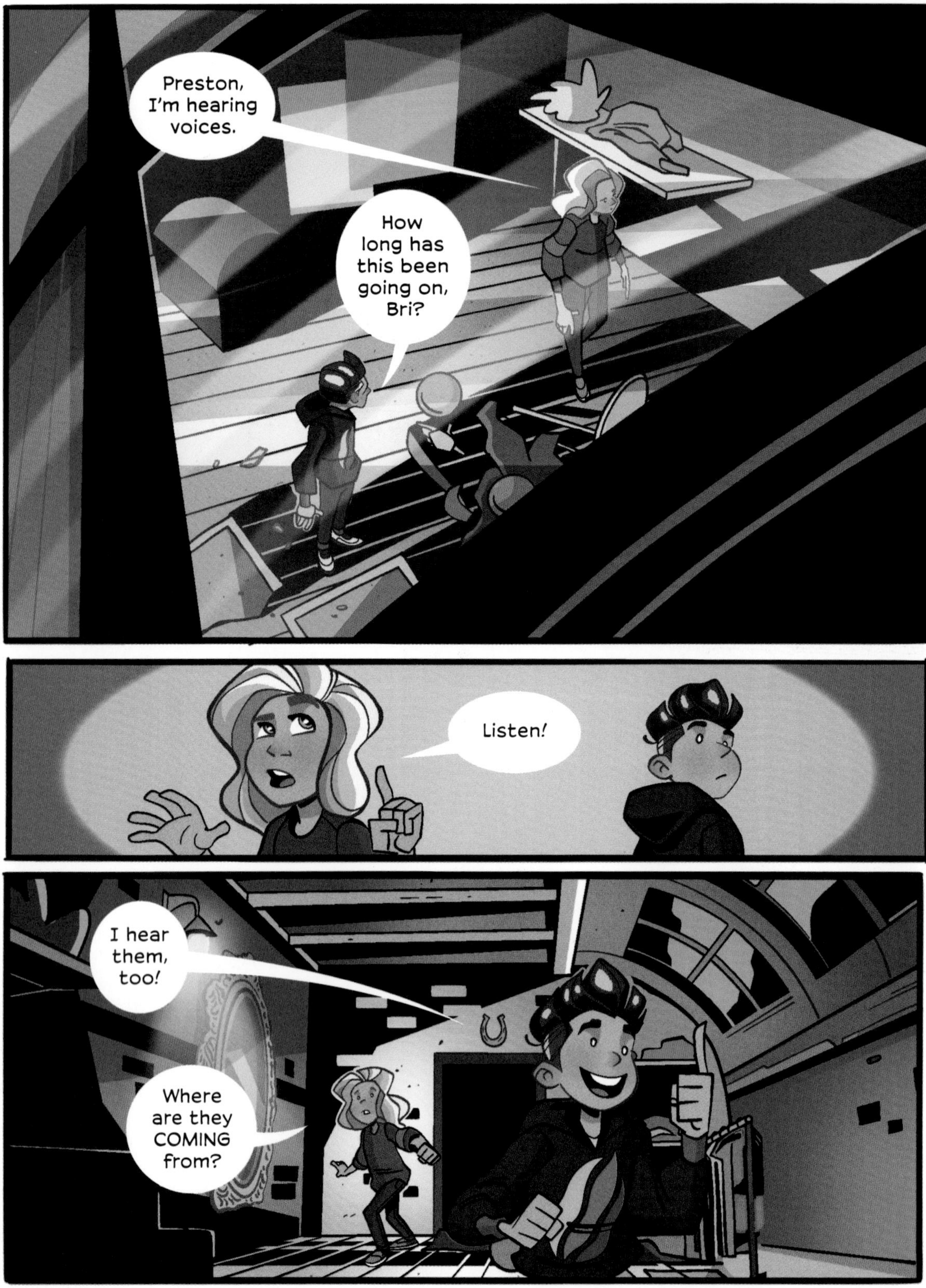
Preston, I'm hearing voices.
How long has this been going on, Bri?
Listen!
I hear them, too!
Where are they COMING from?

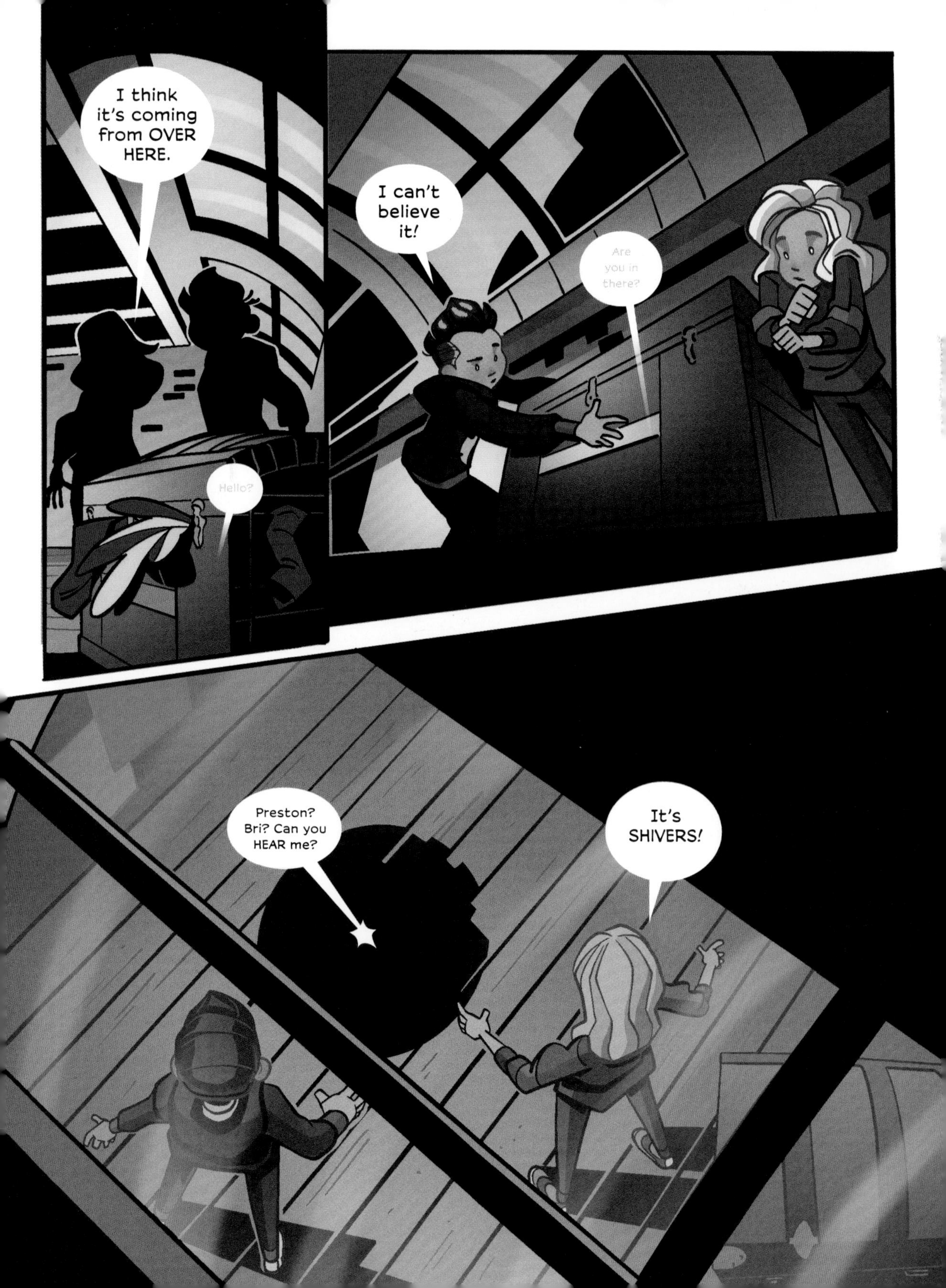
I think it's coming from OVER HERE.
Hello?
I can't believe it!
Are you in there?
Preston? Bri? Can you HEAR me?
It's SHIVERS!

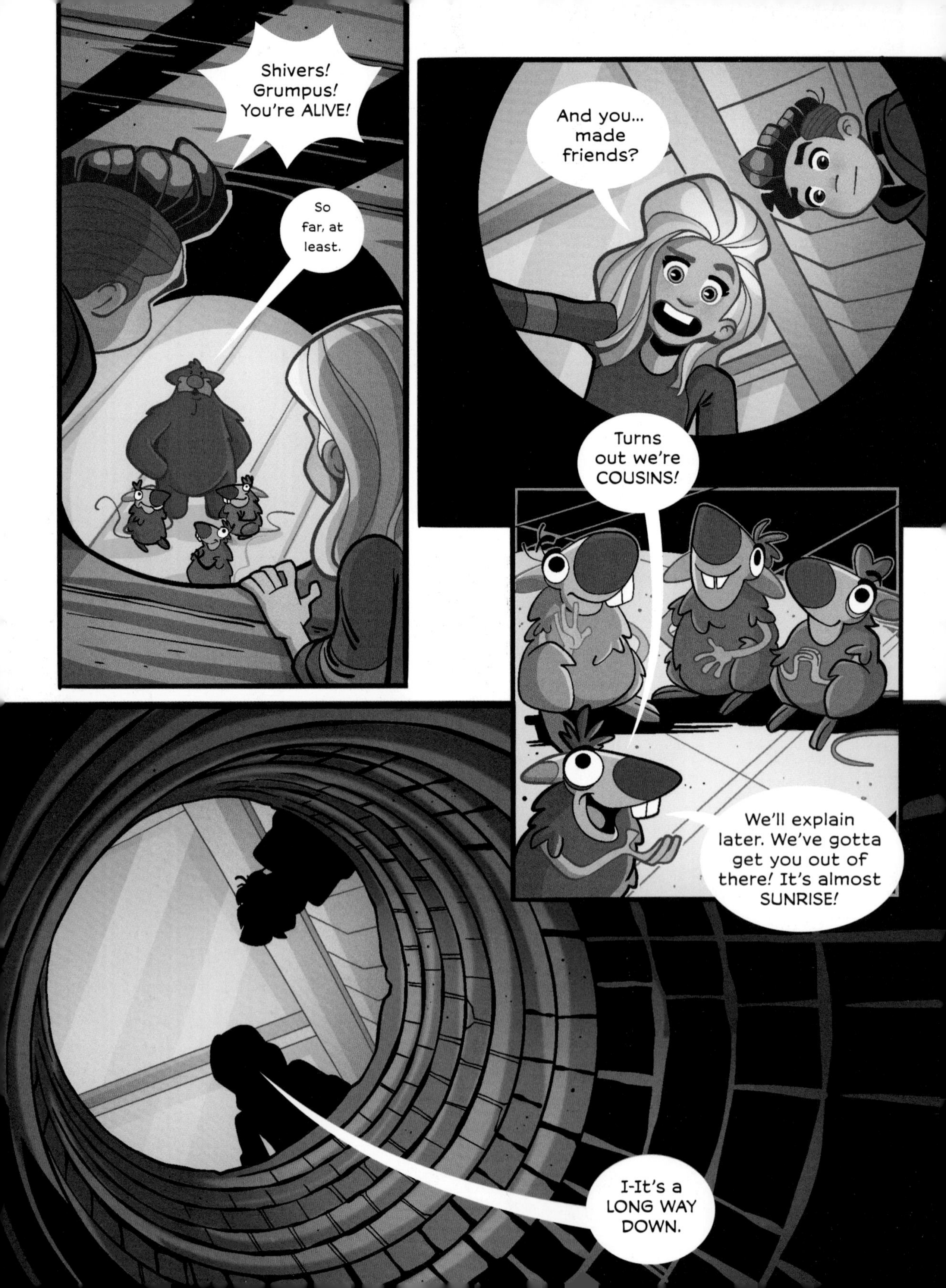

Shivers! Grumpus! You're ALIVE!
So far, at least.
And you... made friends?
Turns out we're COUSINS!
We'll explain later. We've gotta get you out of there! It's almost SUNRISE!
I-It's a LONG WAY DOWN.

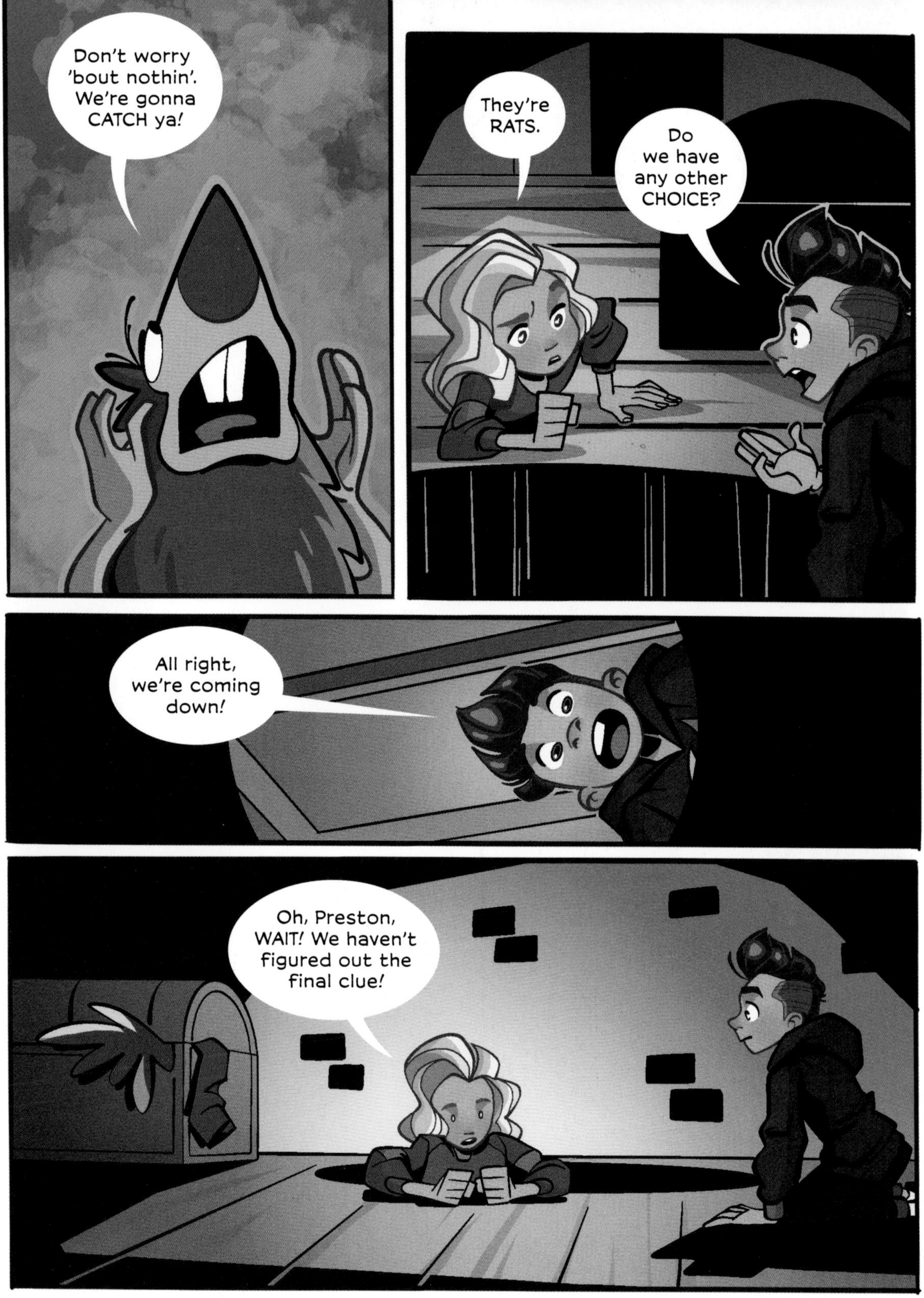

Don't worry 'bout nothin'. We're gonna CATCH ya!
They're RATS.
Do we have any other CHOICE?
All right, we're coming down!
Oh, Preston, WAIT! We haven't figured out the final clue!

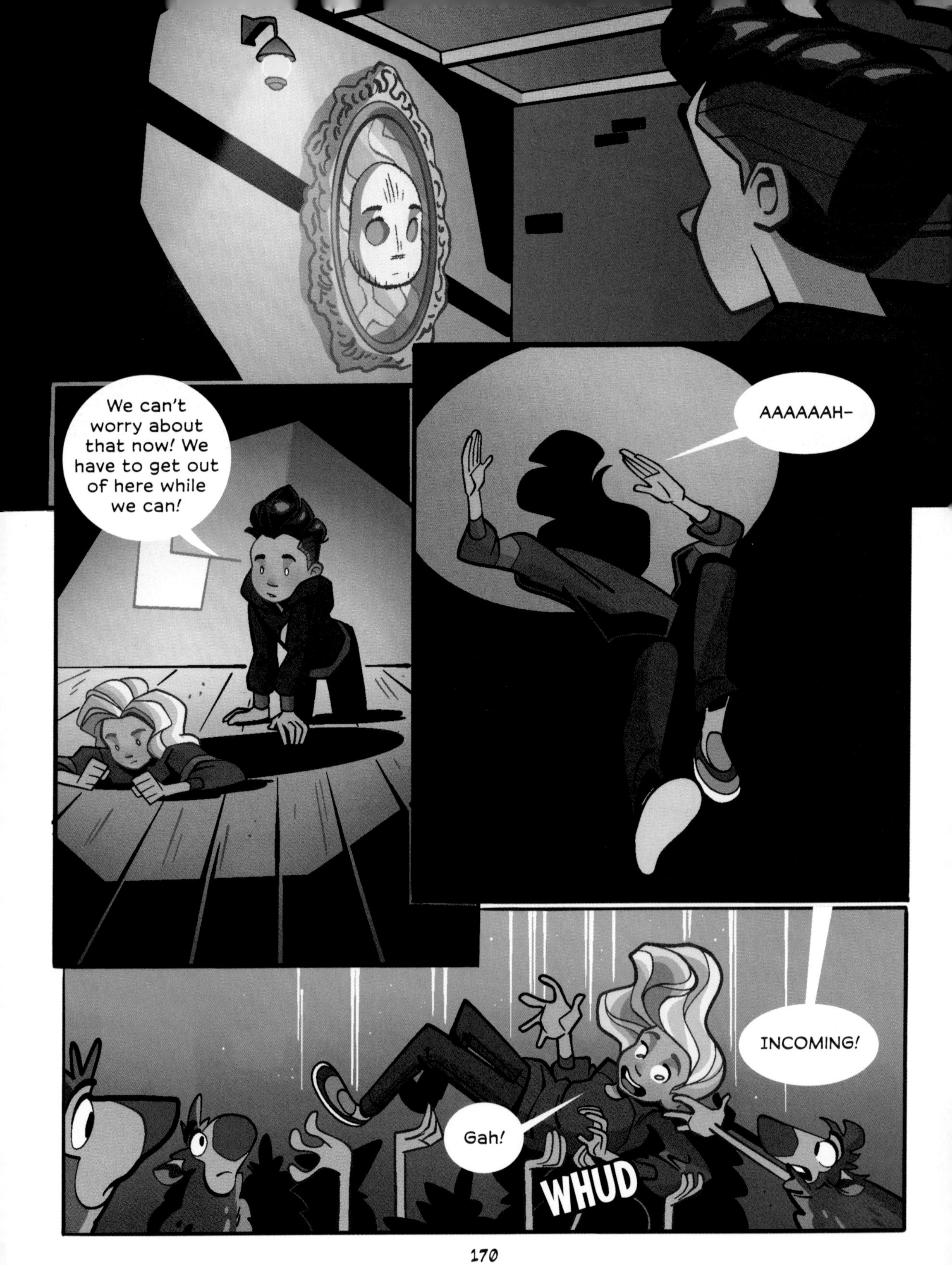
We can't worry about that now! We have to get out of here while we can!
AAAAAAH-
INCOMING!
Gah!
WHUD

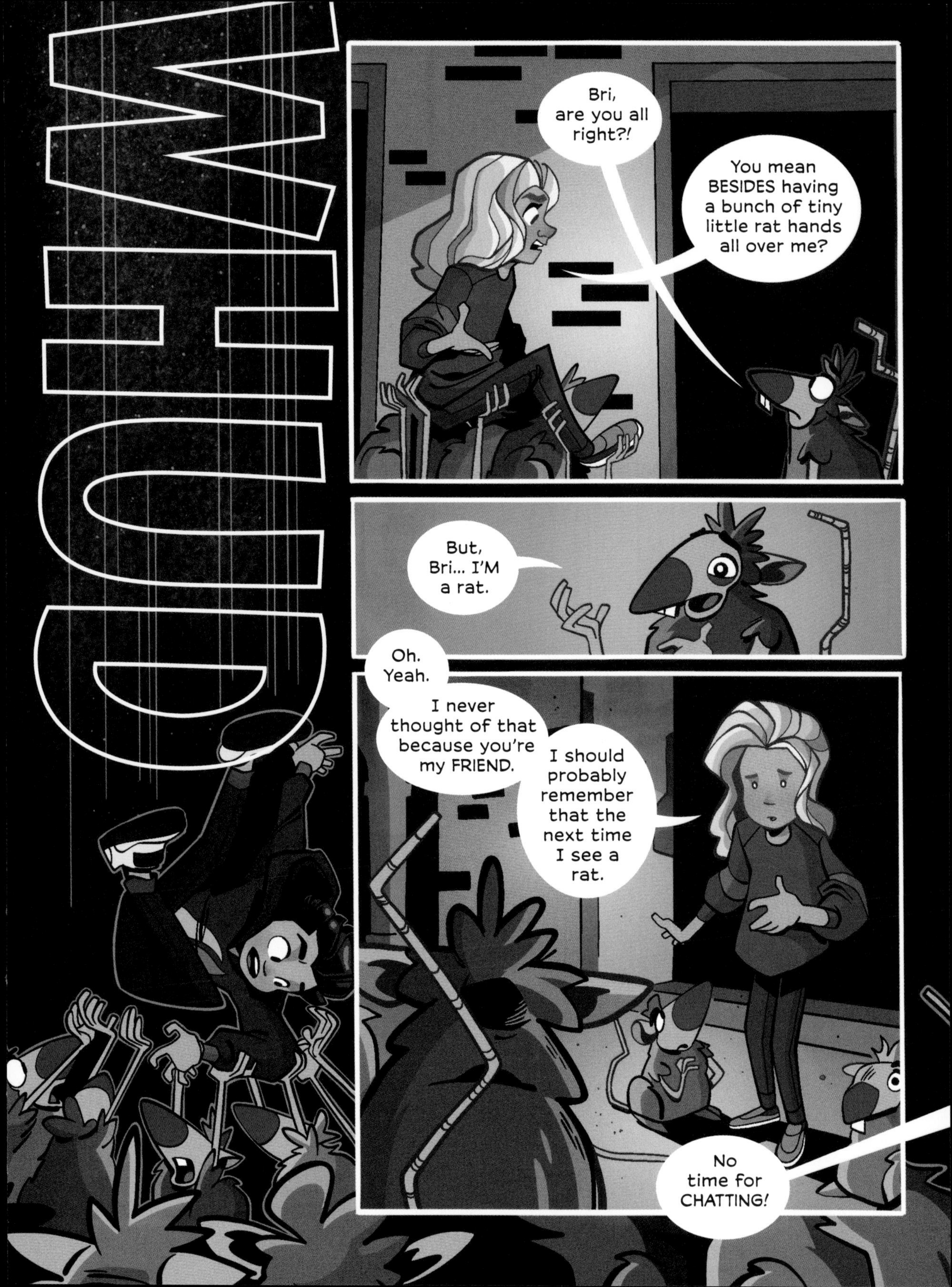
WHUD
Bri, are you all right?!
You mean BESIDES having a bunch of tiny little rat hands all over me?
But, Bri... I'M a rat.
Oh. Yeah.
I never thought of that because you're my FRIEND.
I should probably remember that the next time I see a rat.
No time for CHATTING!

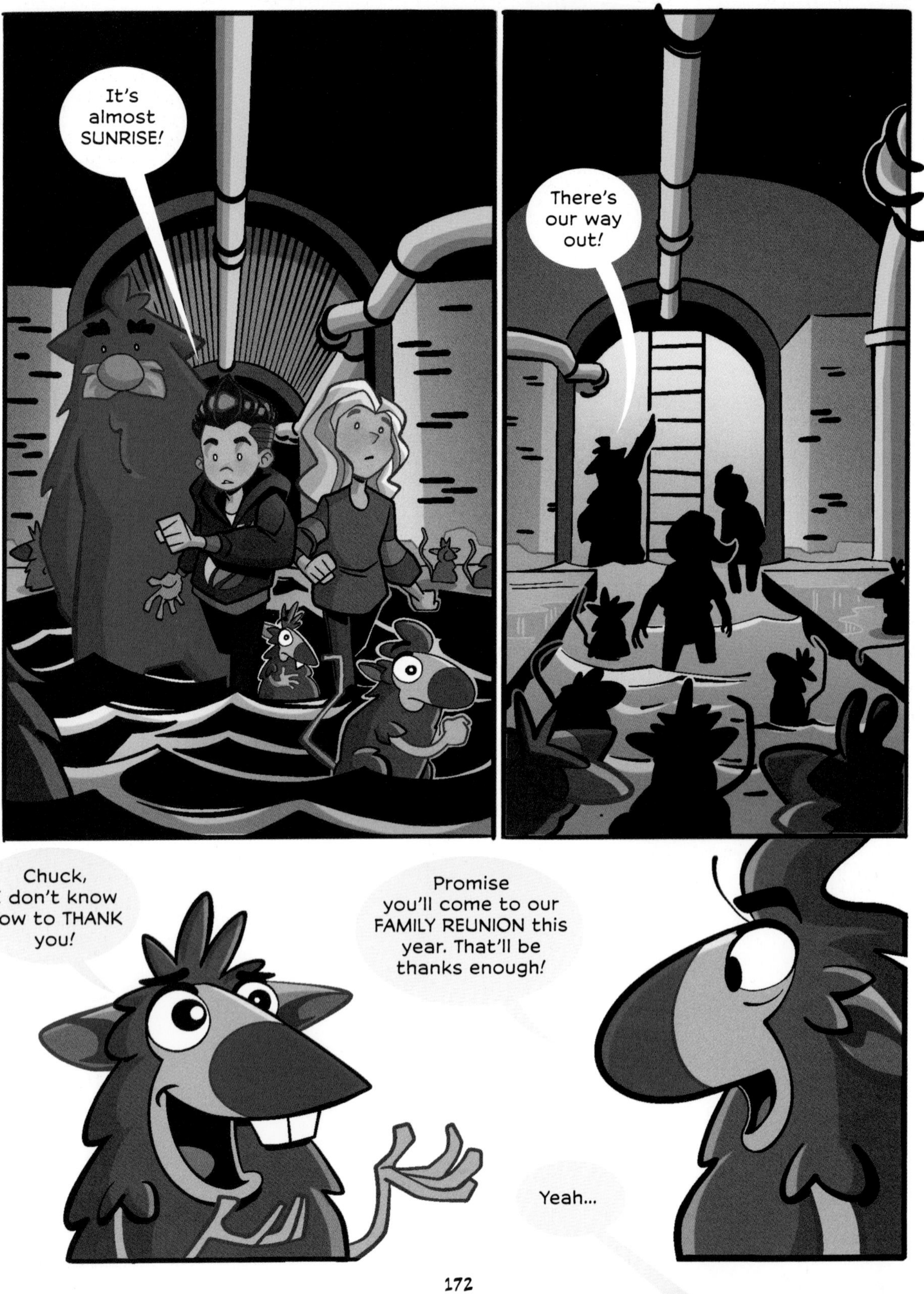
It's almost SUNRISE!
There's our way out!
Chuck, I don't know how to THANK you!
Promise you'll come to our FAMILY REUNION this year. That'll be thanks enough!
Yeah...

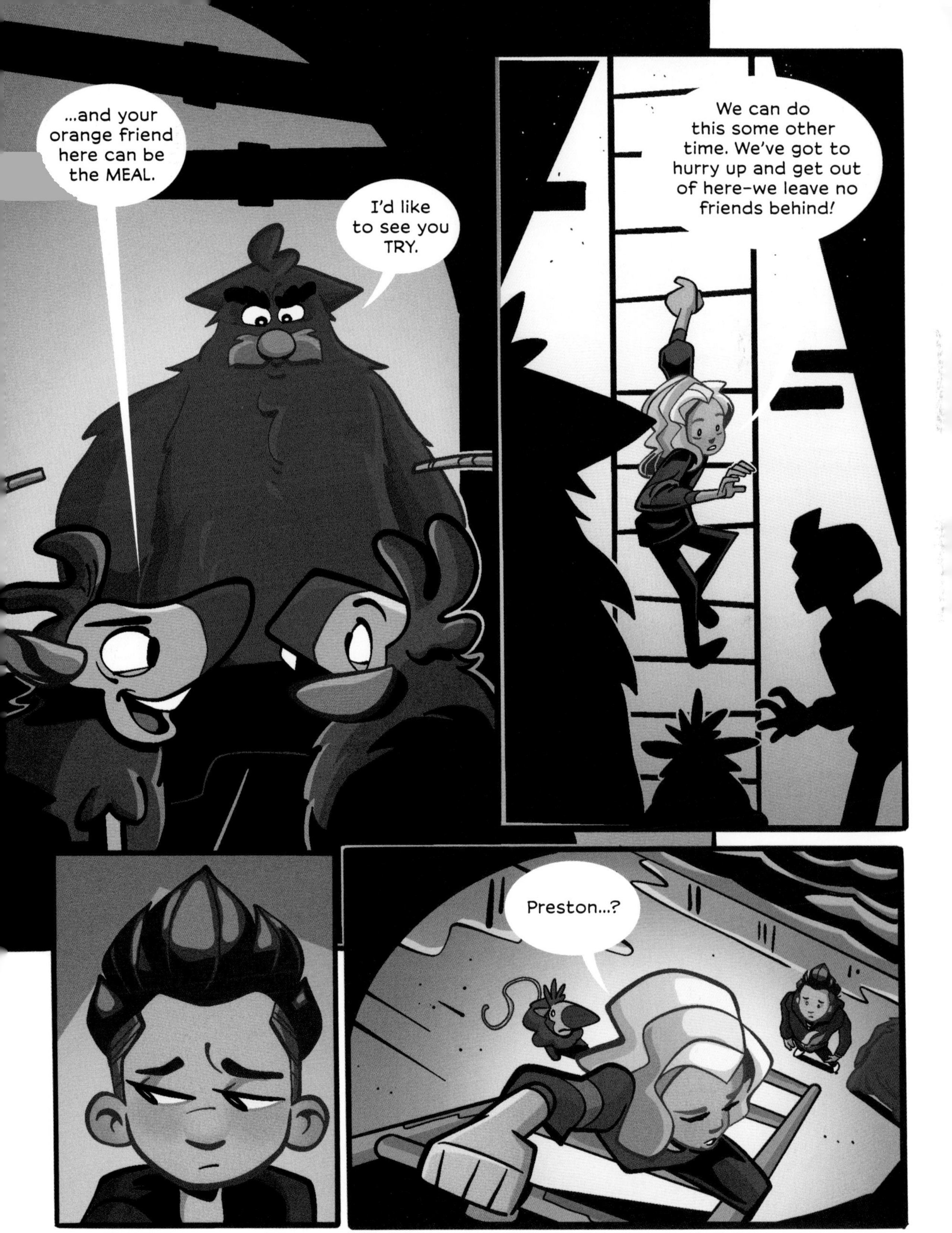
...and your orange friend here can be the MEAL.
I'd like to see you TRY.
We can do this some other time. We've got to hurry up and get out of here–we leave no friends behind!
Preston...?

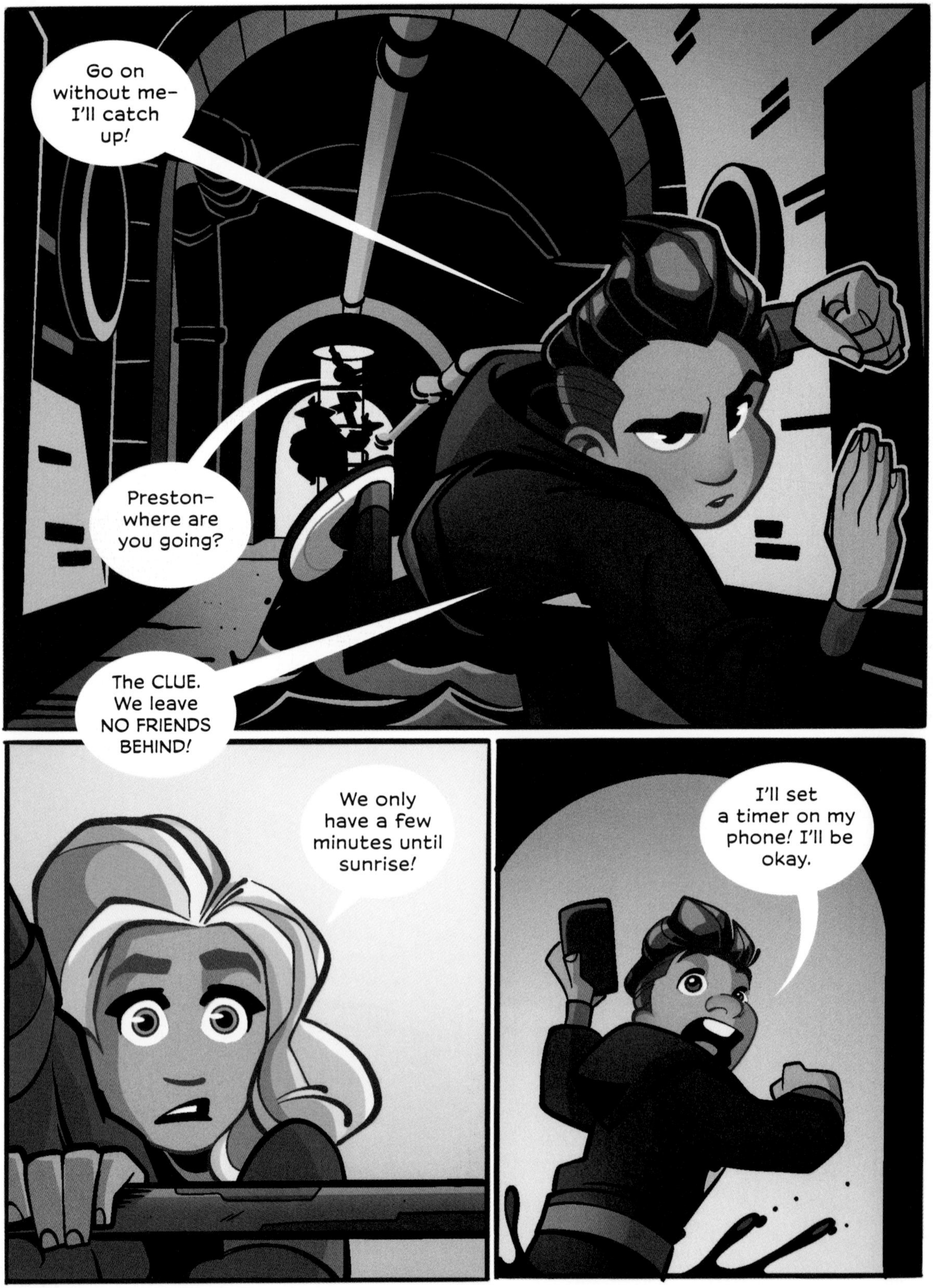
Go on without me– I'll catch up!
Preston– where are you going?
The CLUE. We leave NO FRIENDS BEHIND!
We only have a few minutes until sunrise!
I'll set a timer on my phone! I'll be okay.

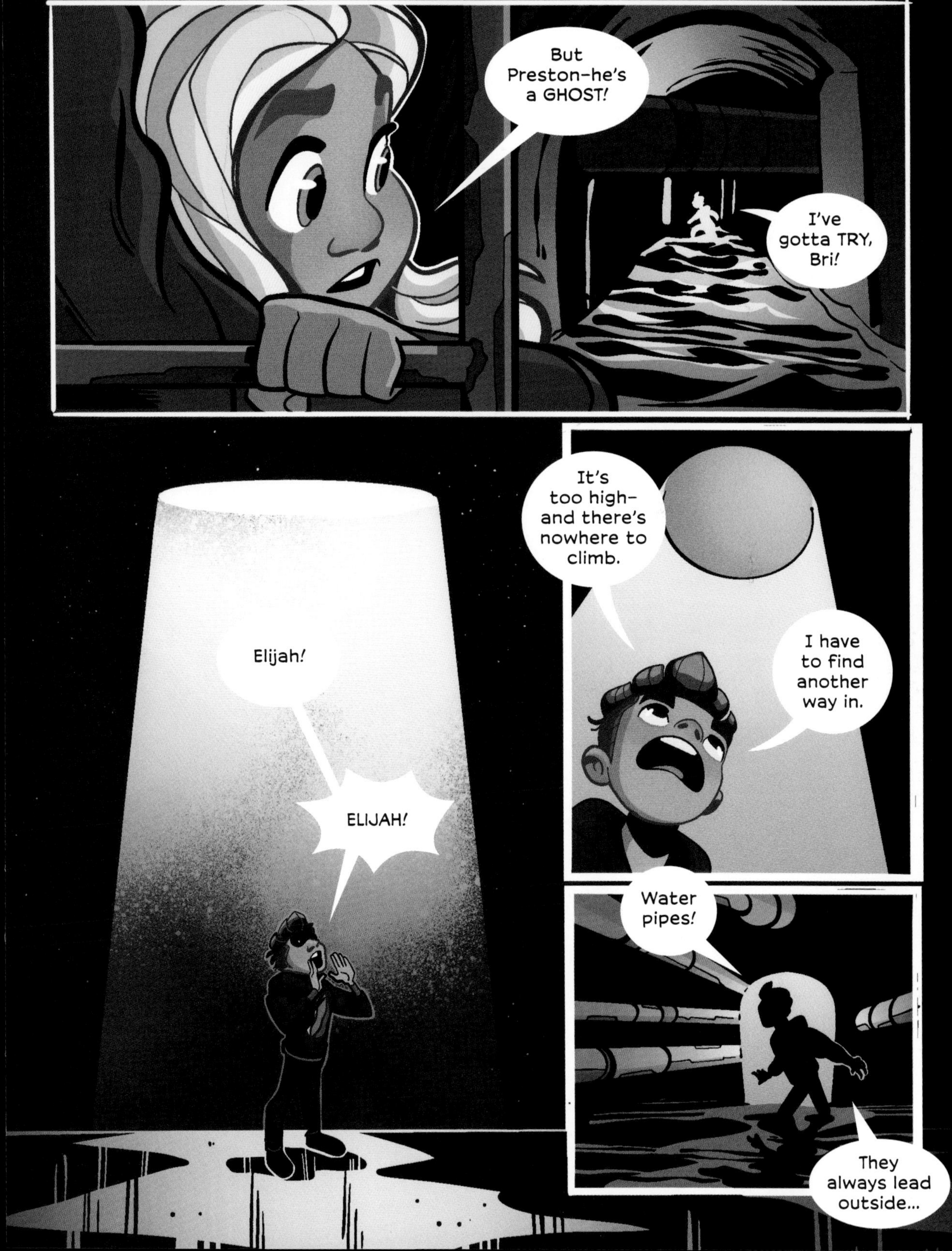
But Preston–he's a GHOST!
I've gotta TRY, Bri!
Elijah!
ELIJAH!
It's too high–and there's nowhere to climb.
I have to find another way in.
Water pipes!
They always lead outside...

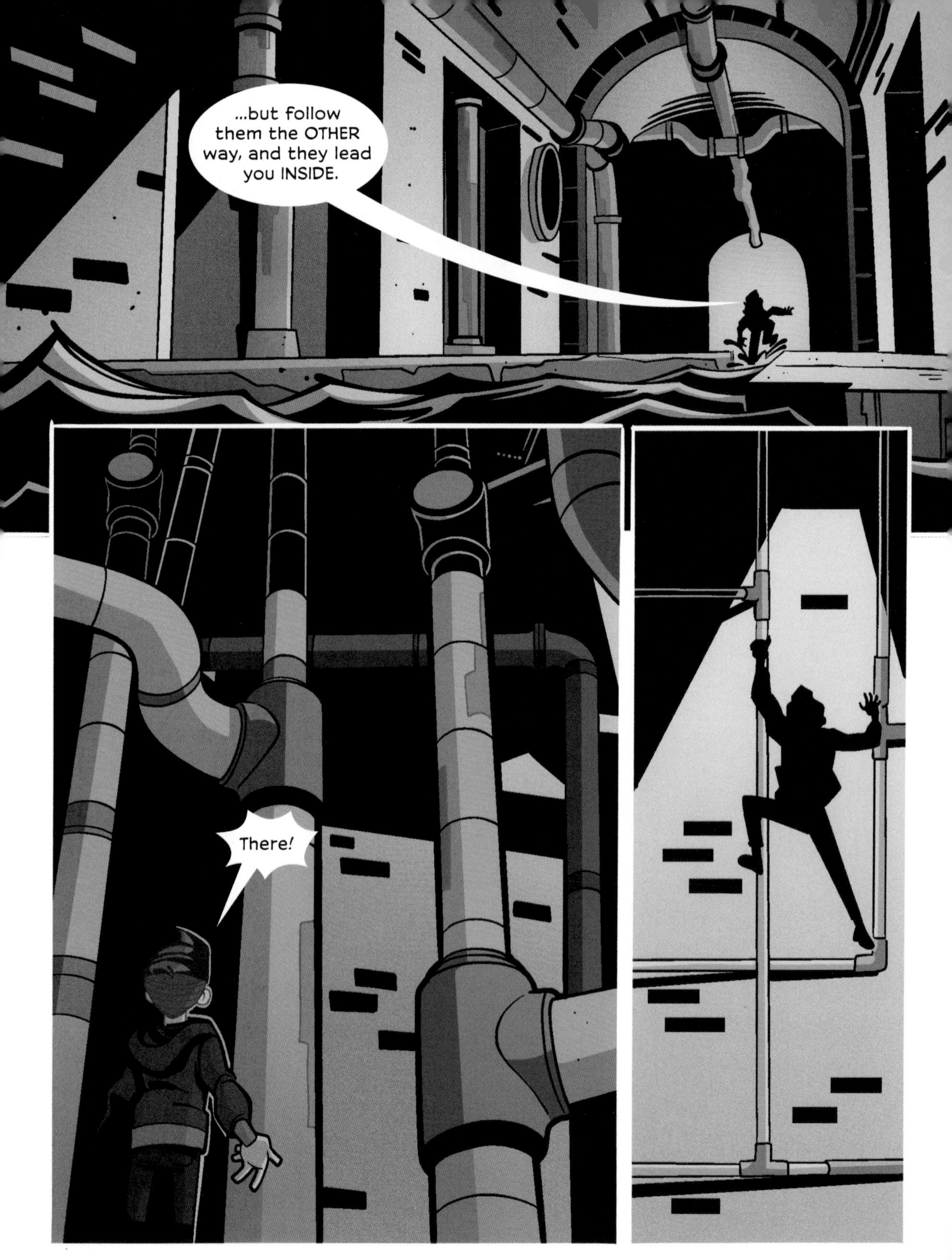
...but follow them the OTHER way, and they lead you INSIDE.
There!

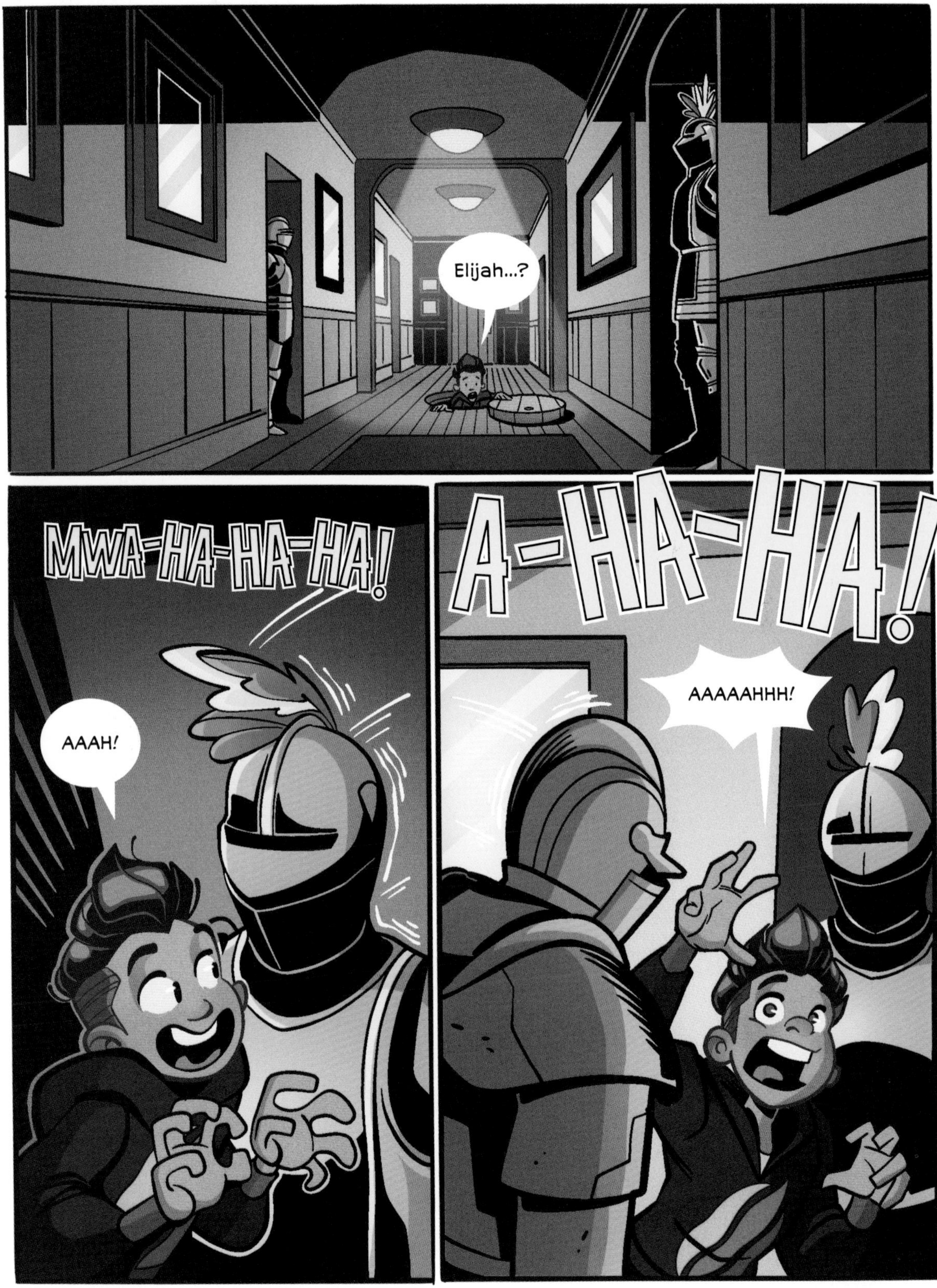

Elijah...?
MWA-HA-HA-HA!
AAAH!
A-HA-HA!
AAAAAHHH!

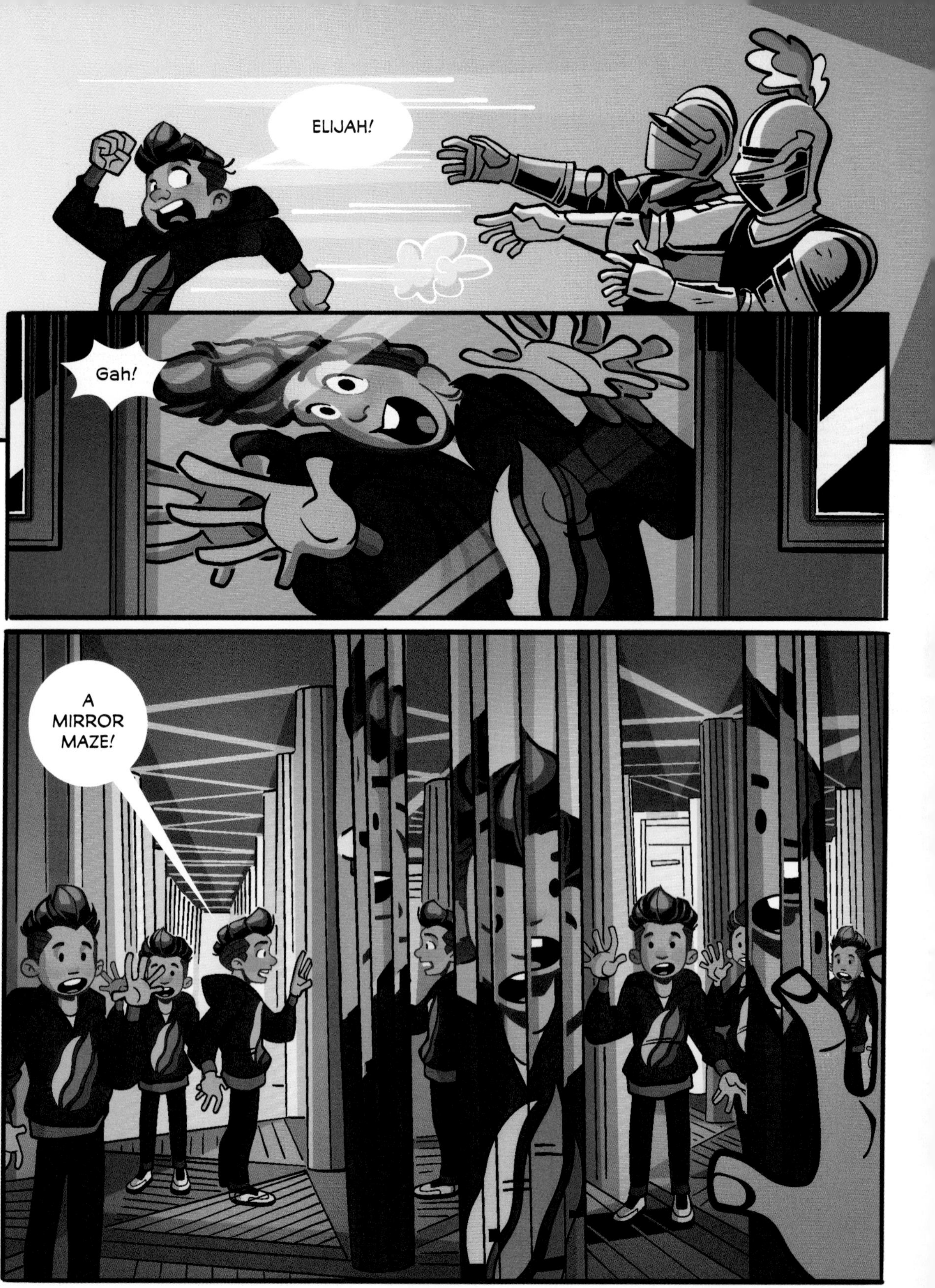
ELIJAH!
Gah!
A MIRROR MAZE!

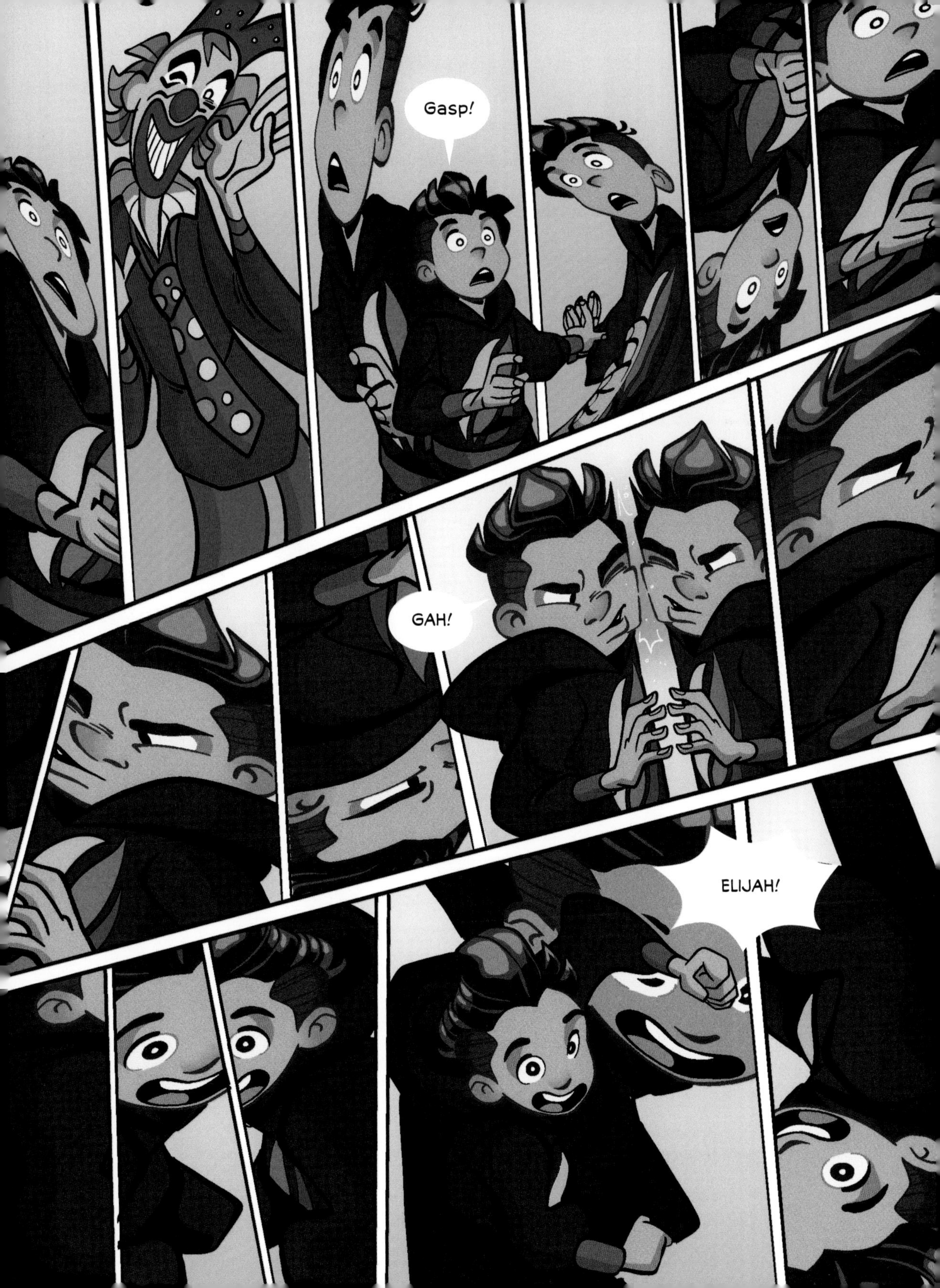
Gasp!
GAH!
ELIJAH!

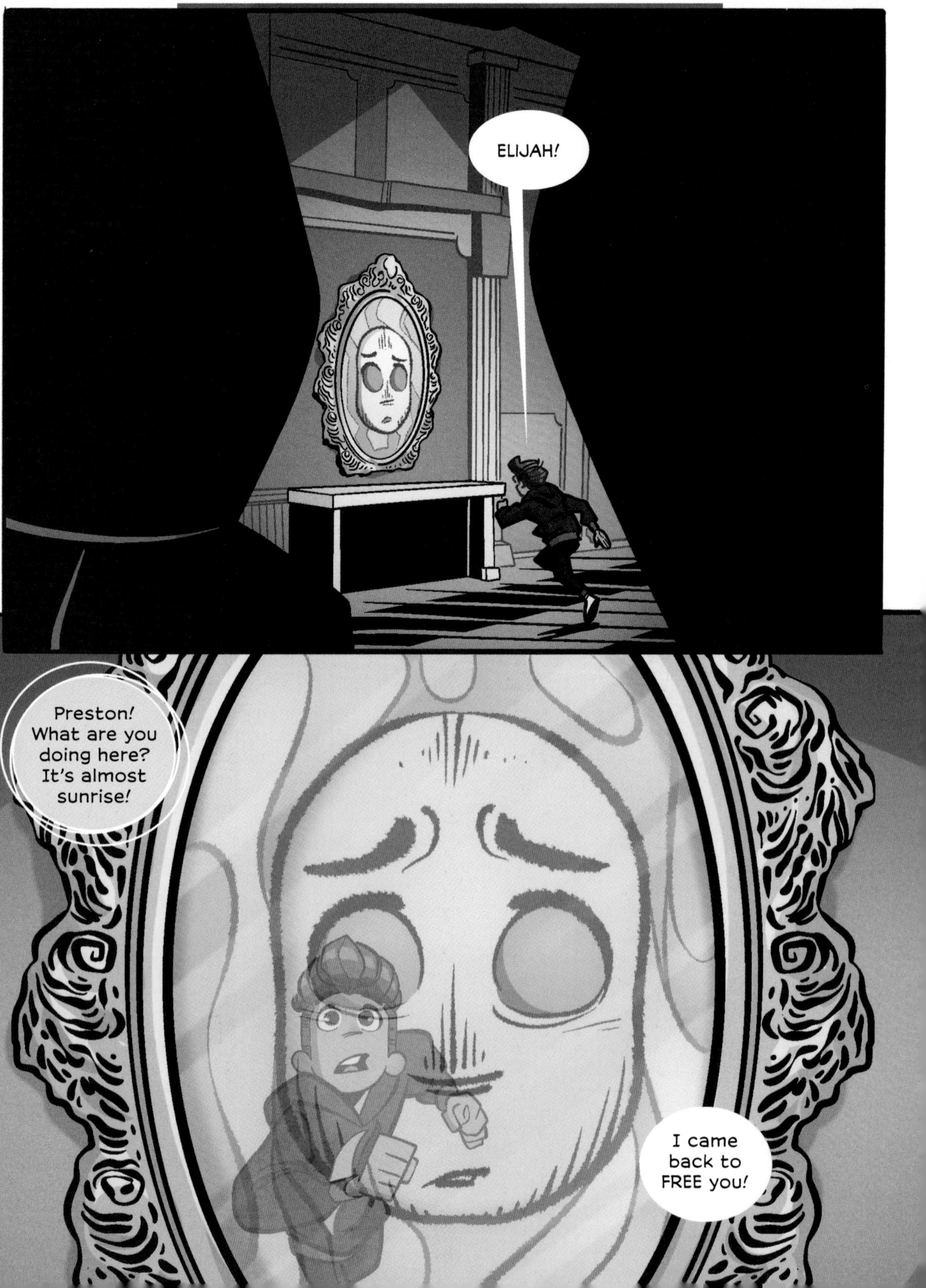
ELIJAH!
Preston! What are you doing here? It's almost sunrise!
I came back to FREE you!

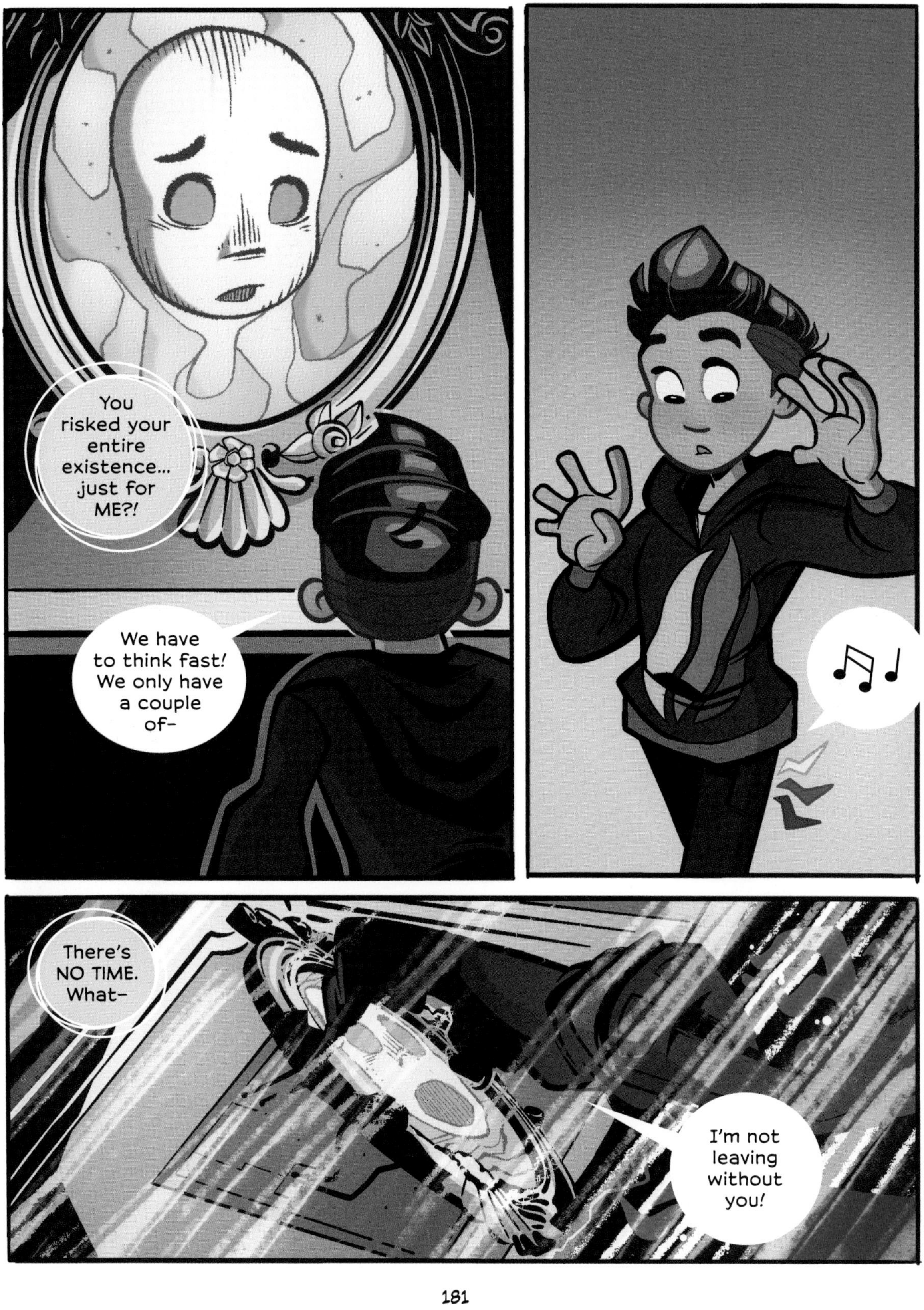
You risked your entire existence... just for ME?!
We have to think fast! We only have a couple of-
♫♩
There's NO TIME. What-
I'm not leaving without you!

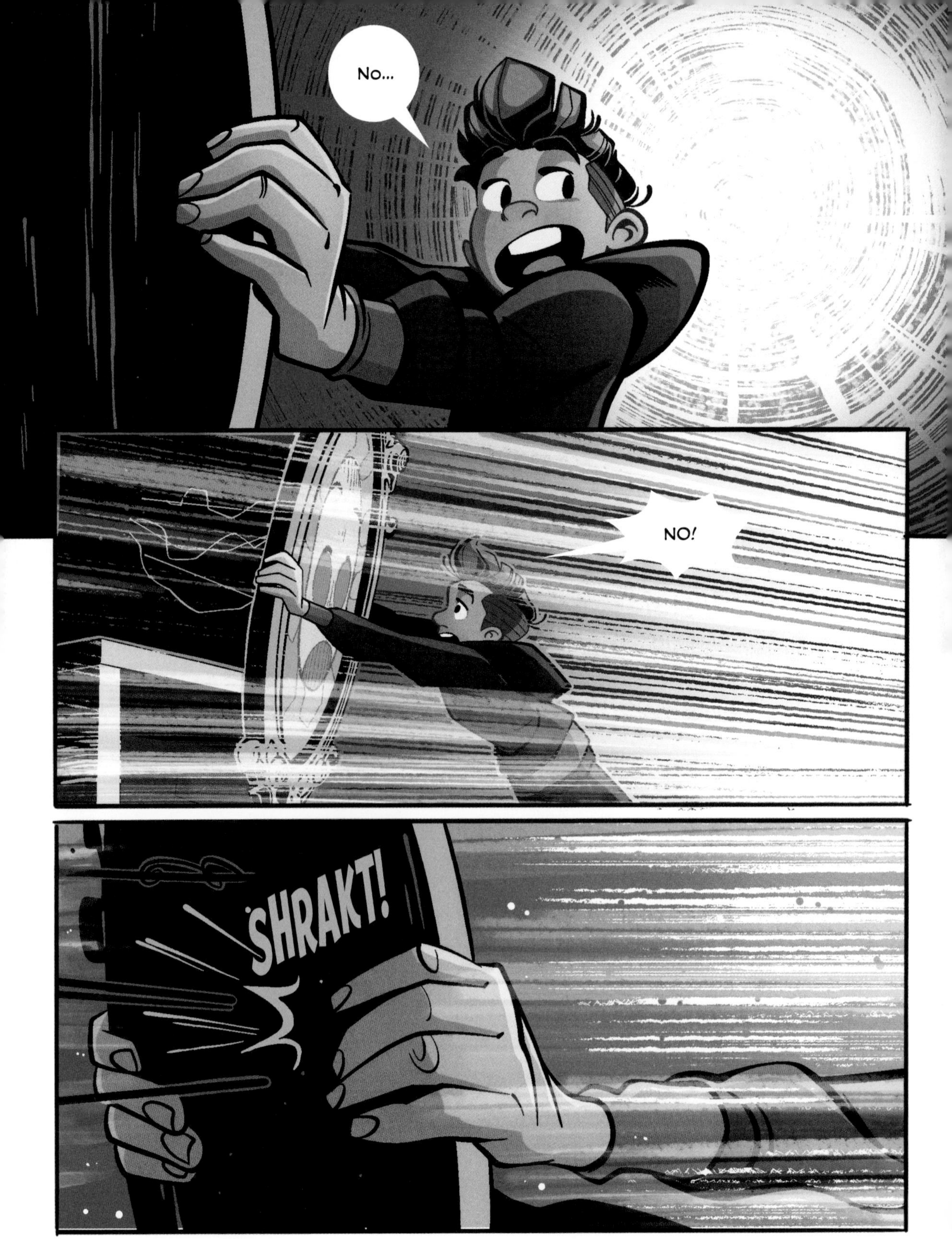
No...
NO!
SHRAKT!

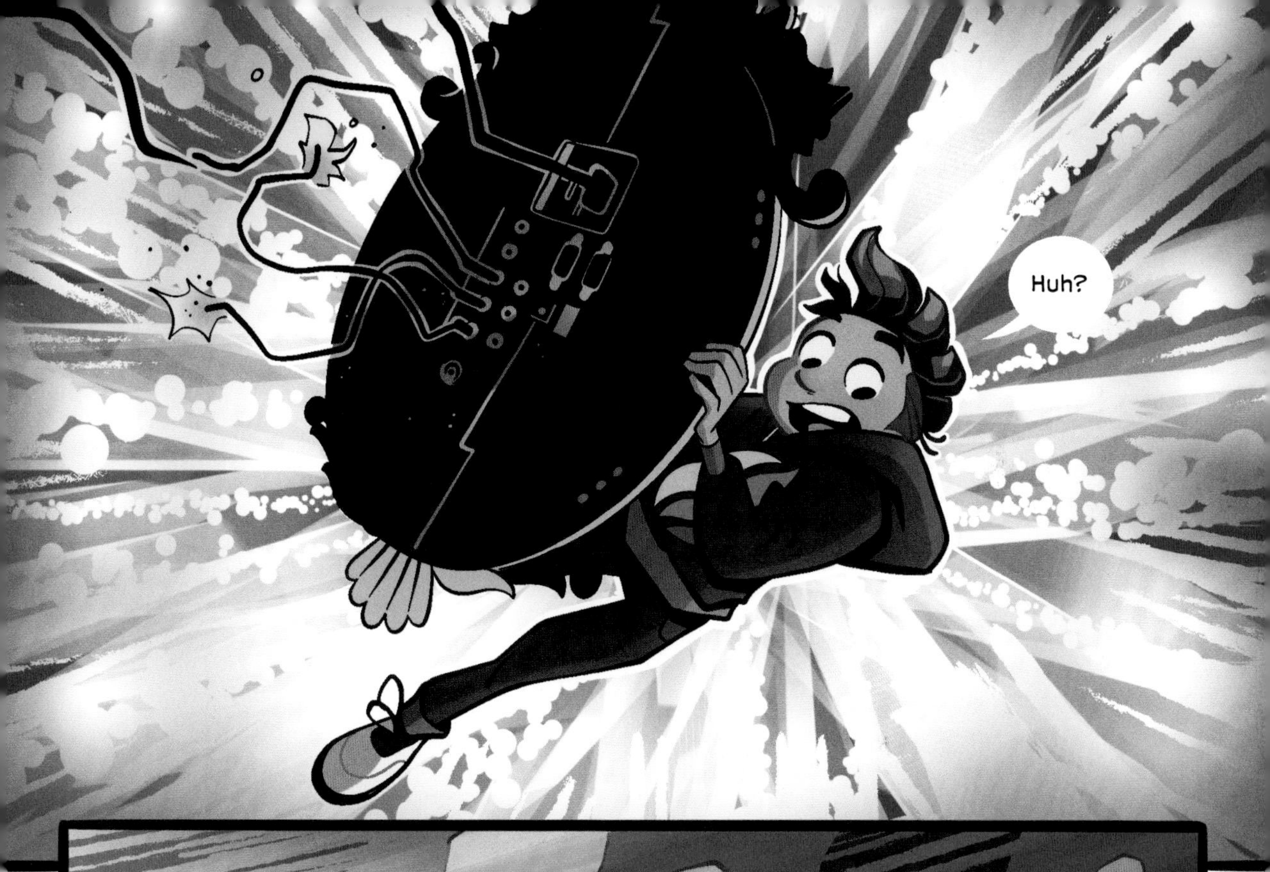
Huh?

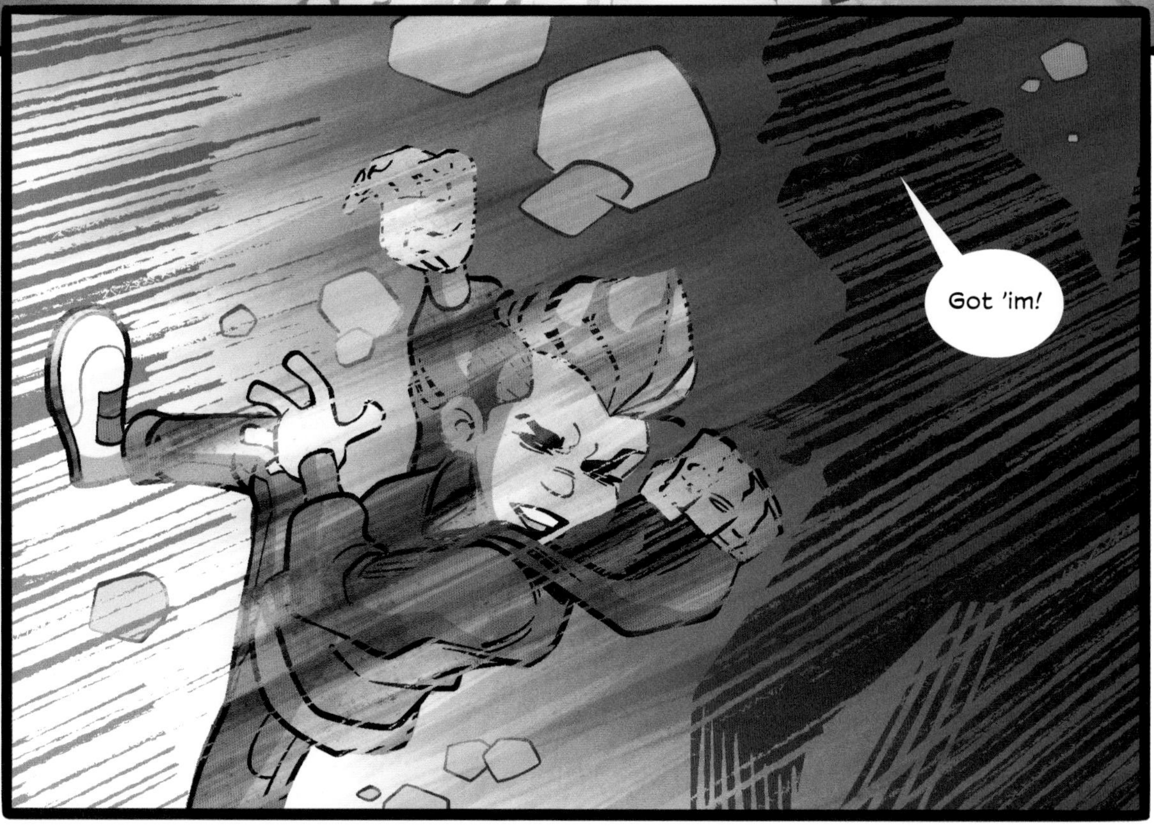
Got 'im!

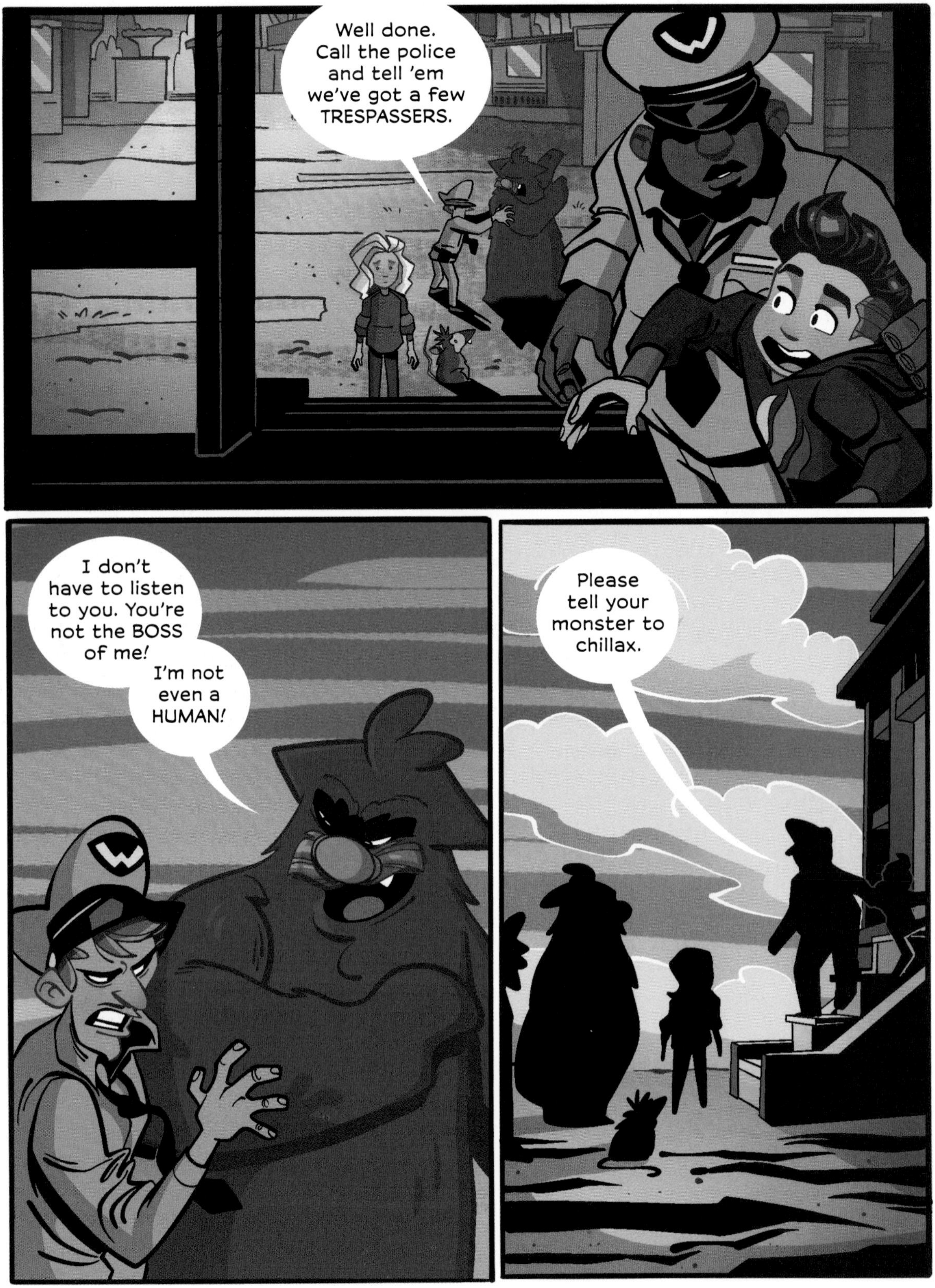
Well done. Call the police and tell 'em we've got a few TRESPASSERS.
I don't have to listen to you. You're not the BOSS of me!
I'm not even a HUMAN!
Please tell your monster to chillax.

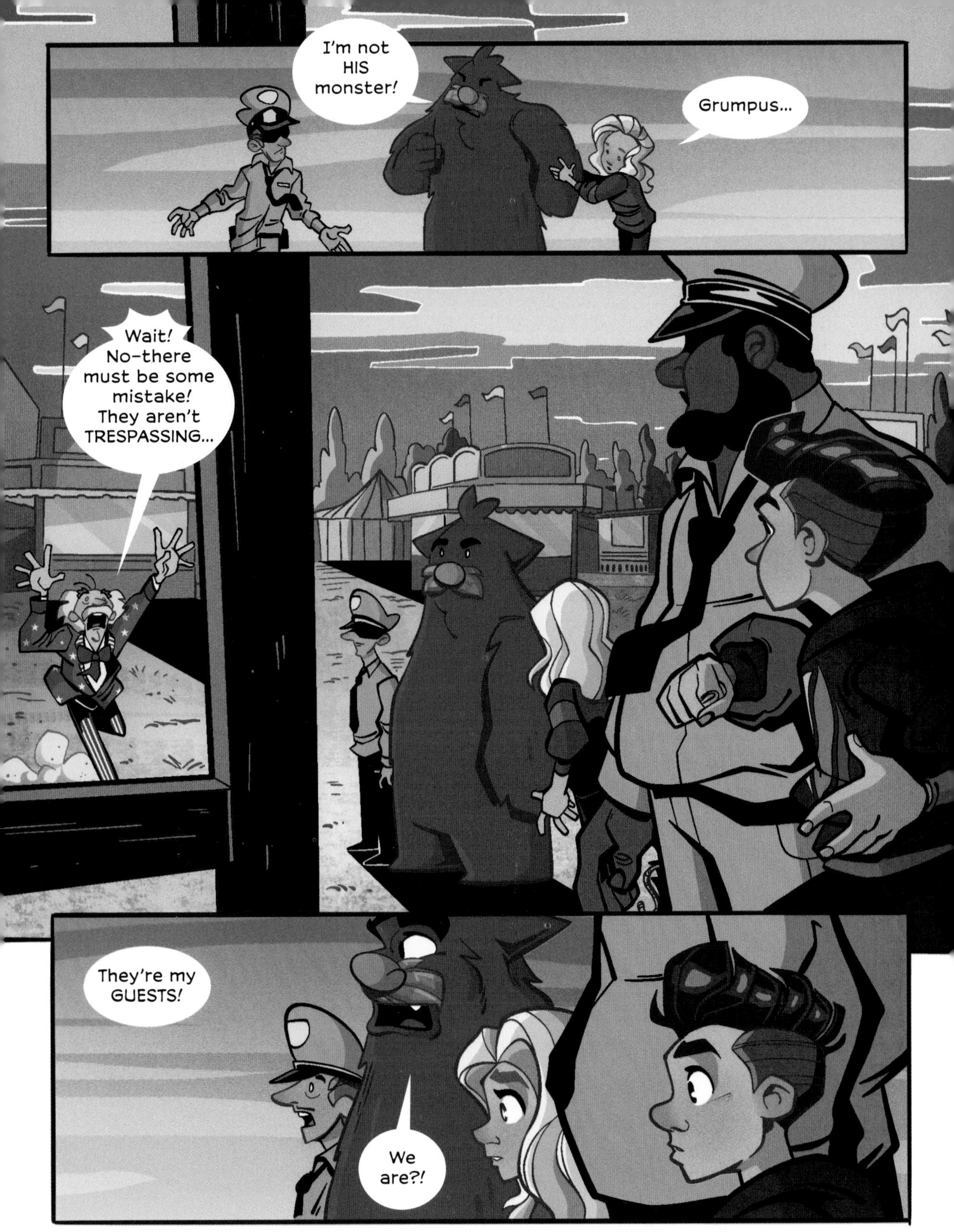
I'm not HIS monster!
Grumpus...
Wait! No-there must be some mistake! They aren't TRESPASSING...
They're my GUESTS!
We are?!

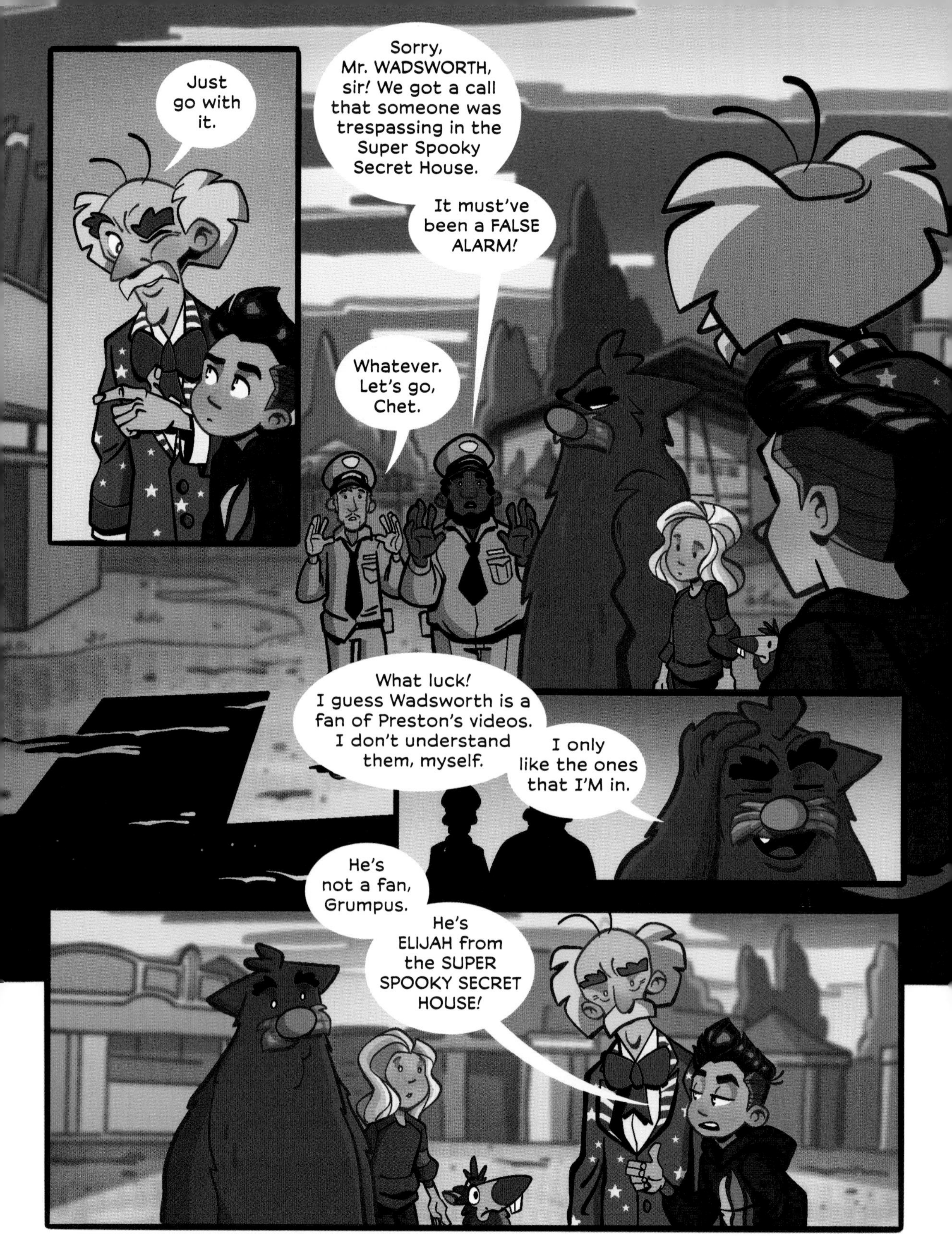
Just go with it.
Sorry, Mr. WADSWORTH, sir! We got a call that someone was trespassing in the Super Spooky Secret House.
It must've been a FALSE ALARM!
Whatever. Let's go, Chet.
What luck! I guess Wadsworth is a fan of Preston's videos. I don't understand them, myself.
I only like the ones that I'M in.
He's not a fan, Grumpus.
He's ELIJAH from the SUPER SPOOKY SECRET HOUSE!

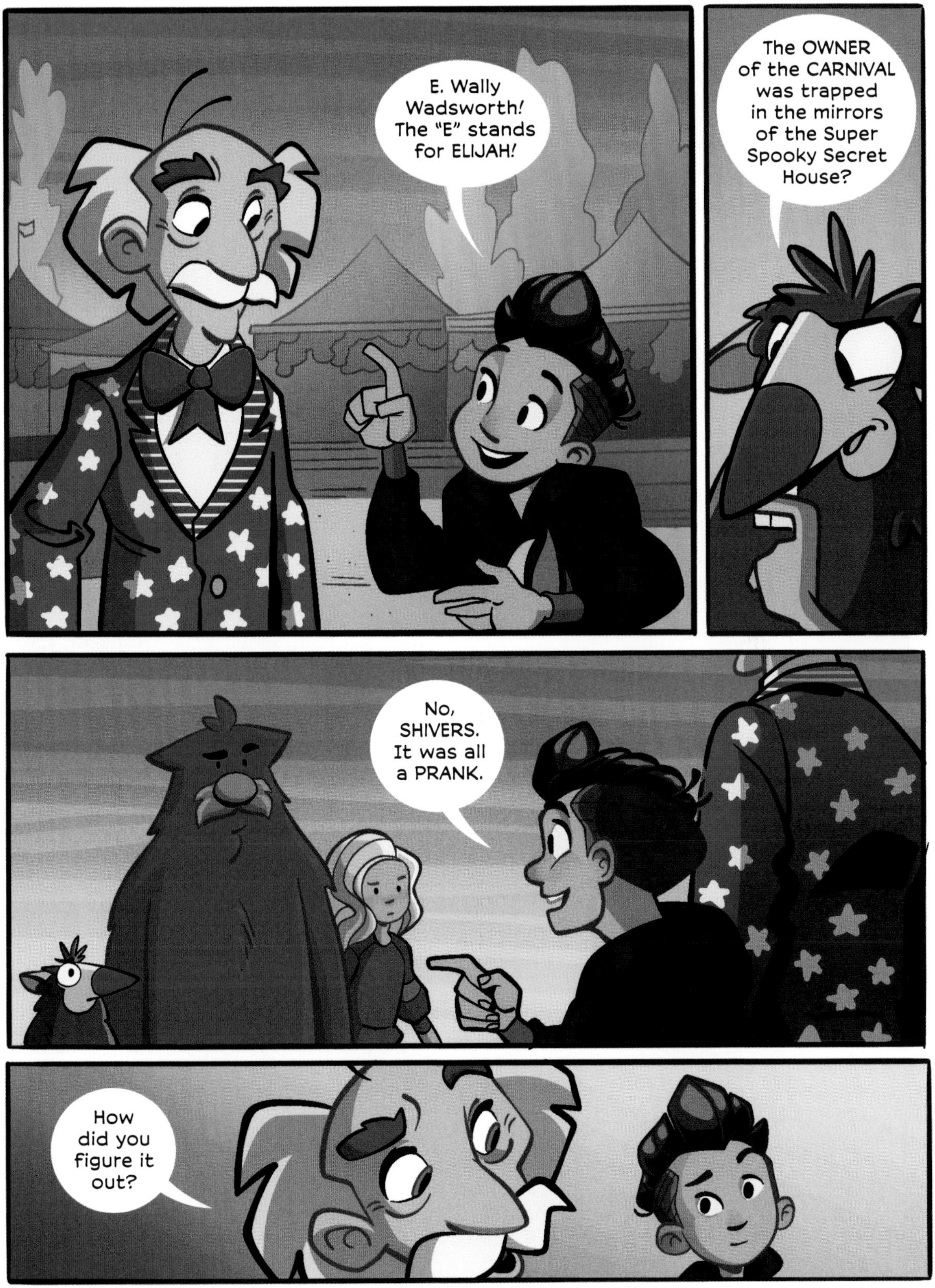
E. Wally Wadsworth! The "E" stands for ELIJAH!
The OWNER of the CARNIVAL was trapped in the mirrors of the Super Spooky Secret House?
No, SHIVERS. It was all a PRANK.
How did you figure it out?

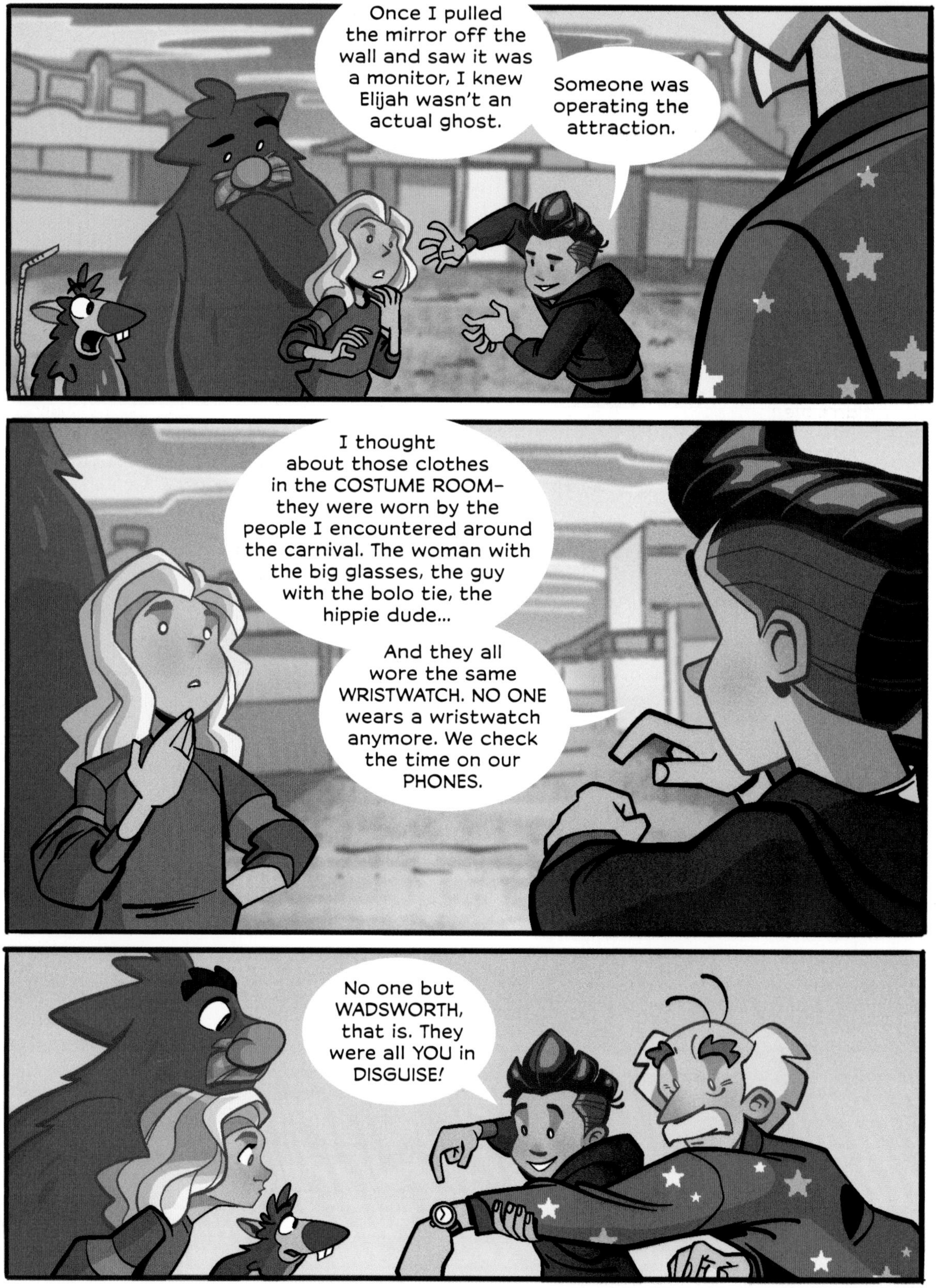

Once I pulled the mirror off the wall and saw it was a monitor, I knew Elijah wasn't an actual ghost.
Someone was operating the attraction.
I thought about those clothes in the COSTUME ROOM– they were worn by the people I encountered around the carnival. The woman with the big glasses, the guy with the bolo tie, the hippie dude...
And they all wore the same WRISTWATCH. NO ONE wears a wristwatch anymore. We check the time on our PHONES.
No one but WADSWORTH, that is. They were all YOU in DISGUISE!

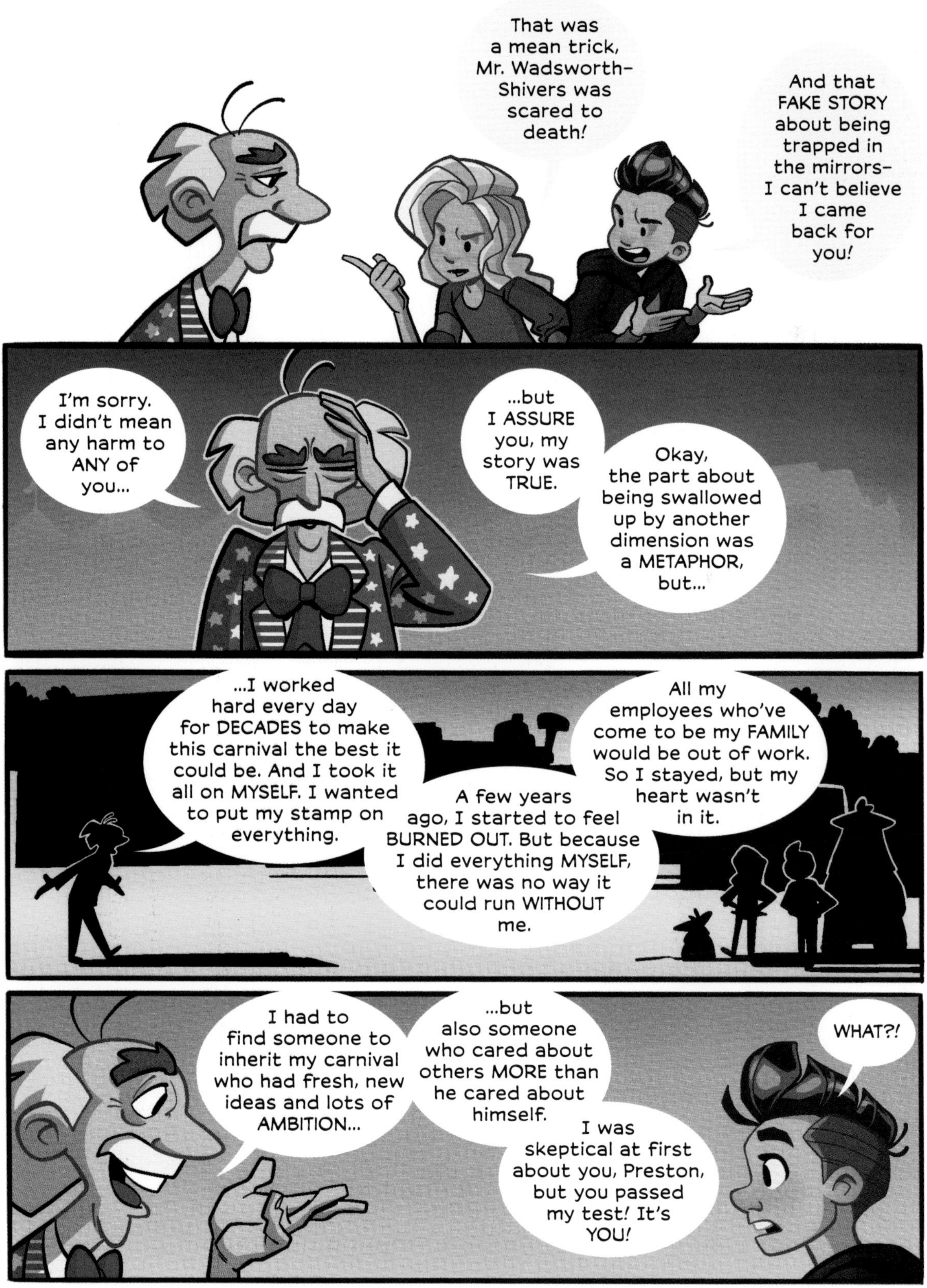
That was a mean trick, Mr. Wadsworth-Shivers was scared to death!
And that FAKE STORY about being trapped in the mirrors– I can't believe I came back for you!
I'm sorry. I didn't mean any harm to ANY of you...
...but I ASSURE you, my story was TRUE.
Okay, the part about being swallowed up by another dimension was a METAPHOR, but...
...I worked hard every day for DECADES to make this carnival the best it could be. And I took it all on MYSELF. I wanted to put my stamp on everything.
A few years ago, I started to feel BURNED OUT. But because I did everything MYSELF, there was no way it could run WITHOUT me.
All my employees who've come to be my FAMILY would be out of work. So I stayed, but my heart wasn't in it.
I had to find someone to inherit my carnival who had fresh, new ideas and lots of AMBITION...
...but also someone who cared about others MORE than he cared about himself.
I was skeptical at first about you, Preston, but you passed my test! It's YOU!
WHAT?!

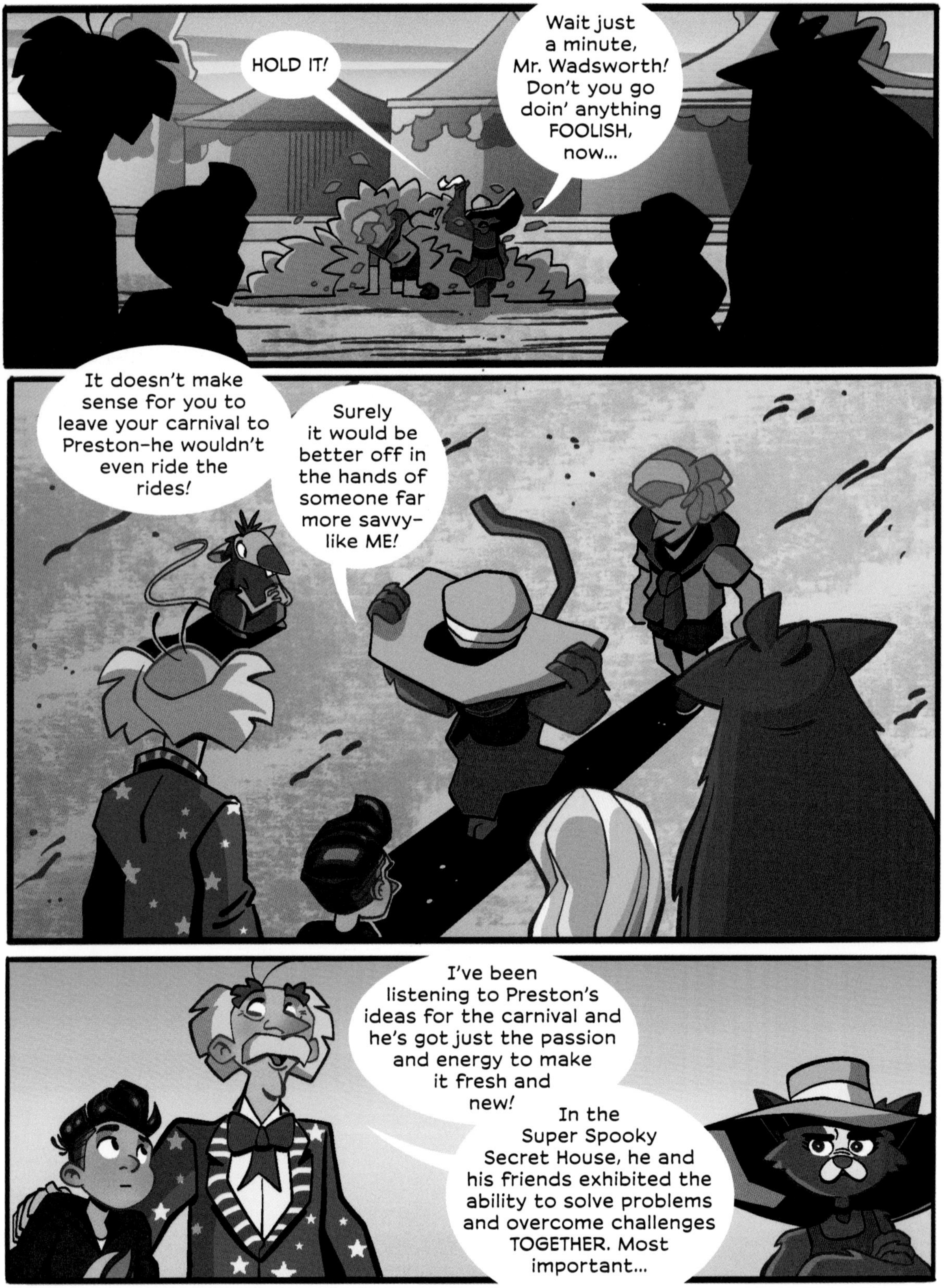
HOLD IT!
Wait just a minute, Mr. Wadsworth! Don't you go doin' anything FOOLISH, now...
It doesn't make sense for you to leave your carnival to Preston–he wouldn't even ride the rides!
Surely it would be better off in the hands of someone far more savvy–like ME!
I've been listening to Preston's ideas for the carnival and he's got just the passion and energy to make it fresh and new!
In the Super Spooky Secret House, he and his friends exhibited the ability to solve problems and overcome challenges TOGETHER. Most important...

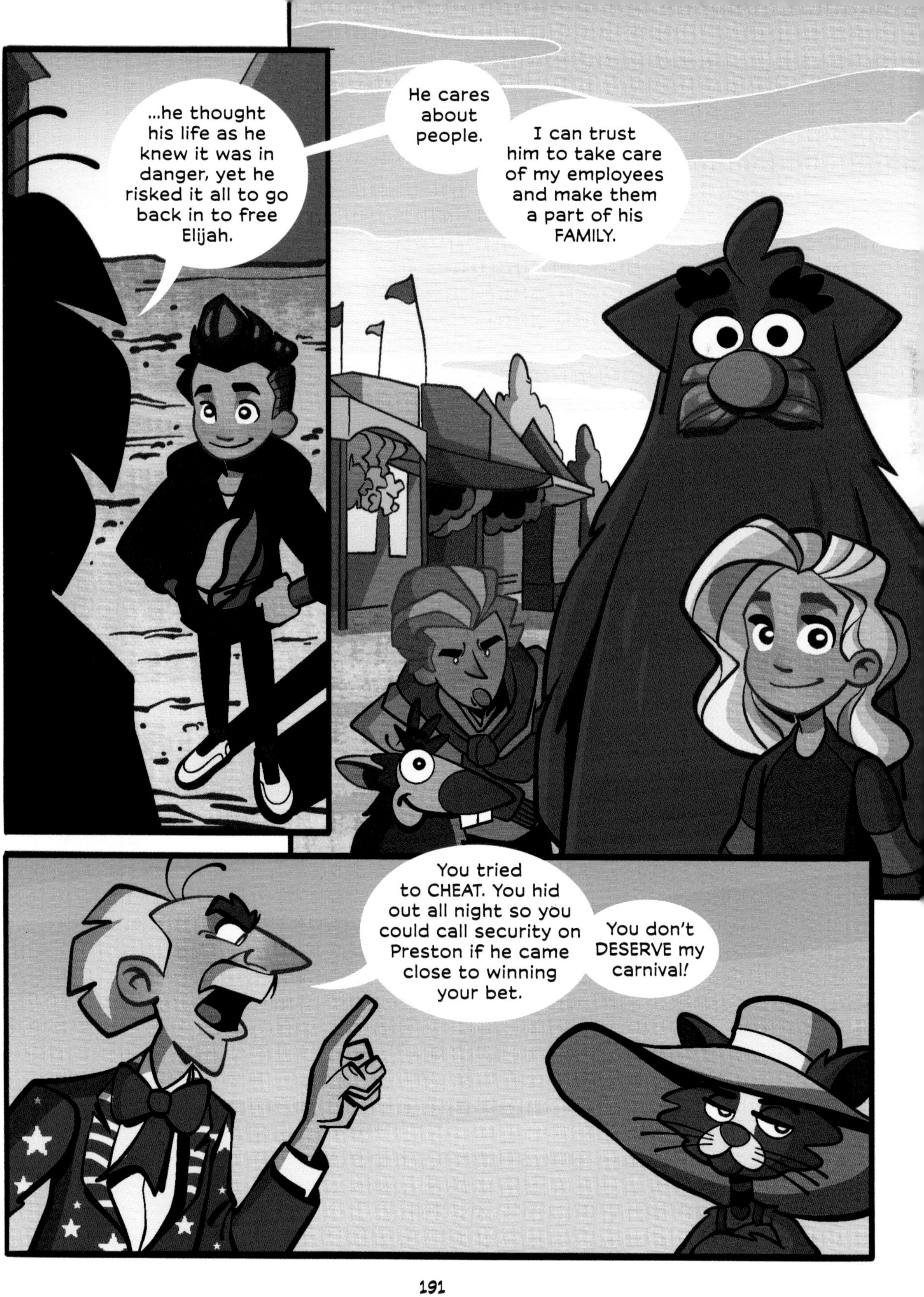
...he thought his life as he knew it was in danger, yet he risked it all to go back in to free Elijah.
He cares about people.
I can trust him to take care of my employees and make them a part of his FAMILY.
You tried to CHEAT. You hid out all night so you could call security on Preston if he came close to winning your bet.
You don't DESERVE my carnival!

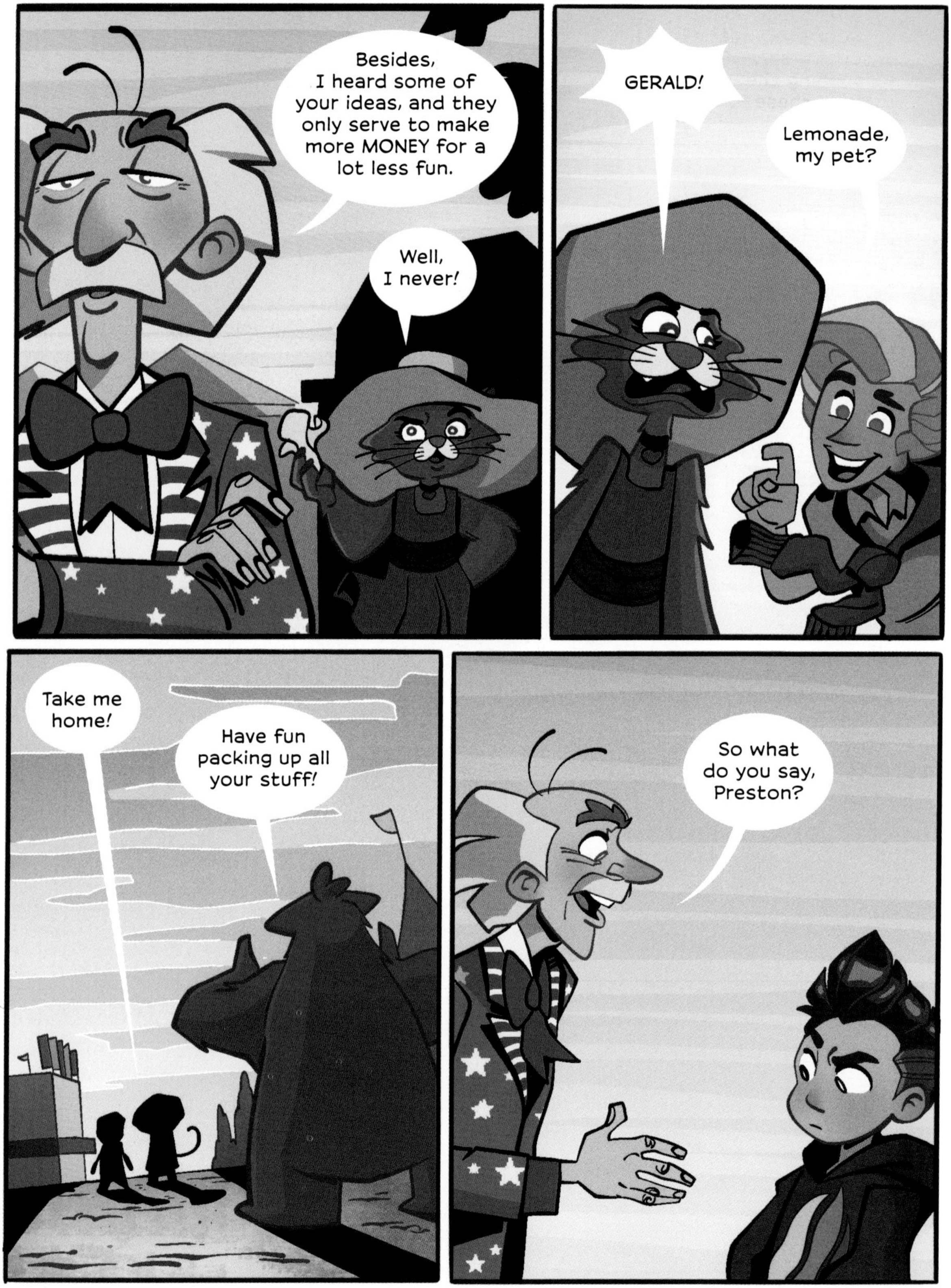
Besides, I heard some of your ideas, and they only serve to make more MONEY for a lot less fun.
Well, I never!
GERALD!
Lemonade, my pet?
Take me home!
Have fun packing up all your stuff!
So what do you say, Preston?

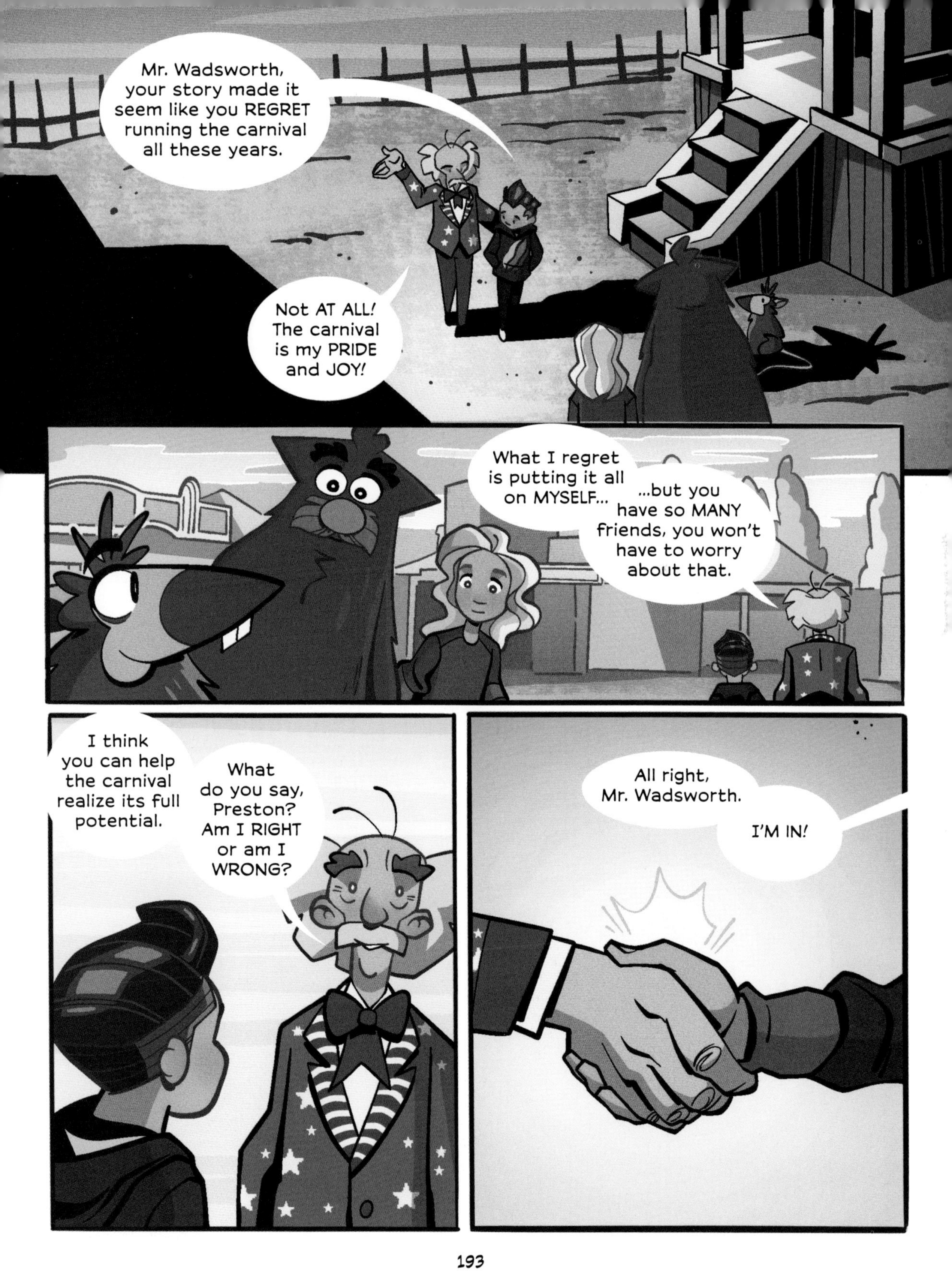
Mr. Wadsworth, your story made it seem like you REGRET running the carnival all these years.
Not AT ALL! The carnival is my PRIDE and JOY!
What I regret is putting it all on MYSELF...
...but you have so MANY friends, you won't have to worry about that.
I think you can help the carnival realize its full potential.
What do you say, Preston? Am I RIGHT or am I WRONG?
All right, Mr. Wadsworth.
I'M IN!

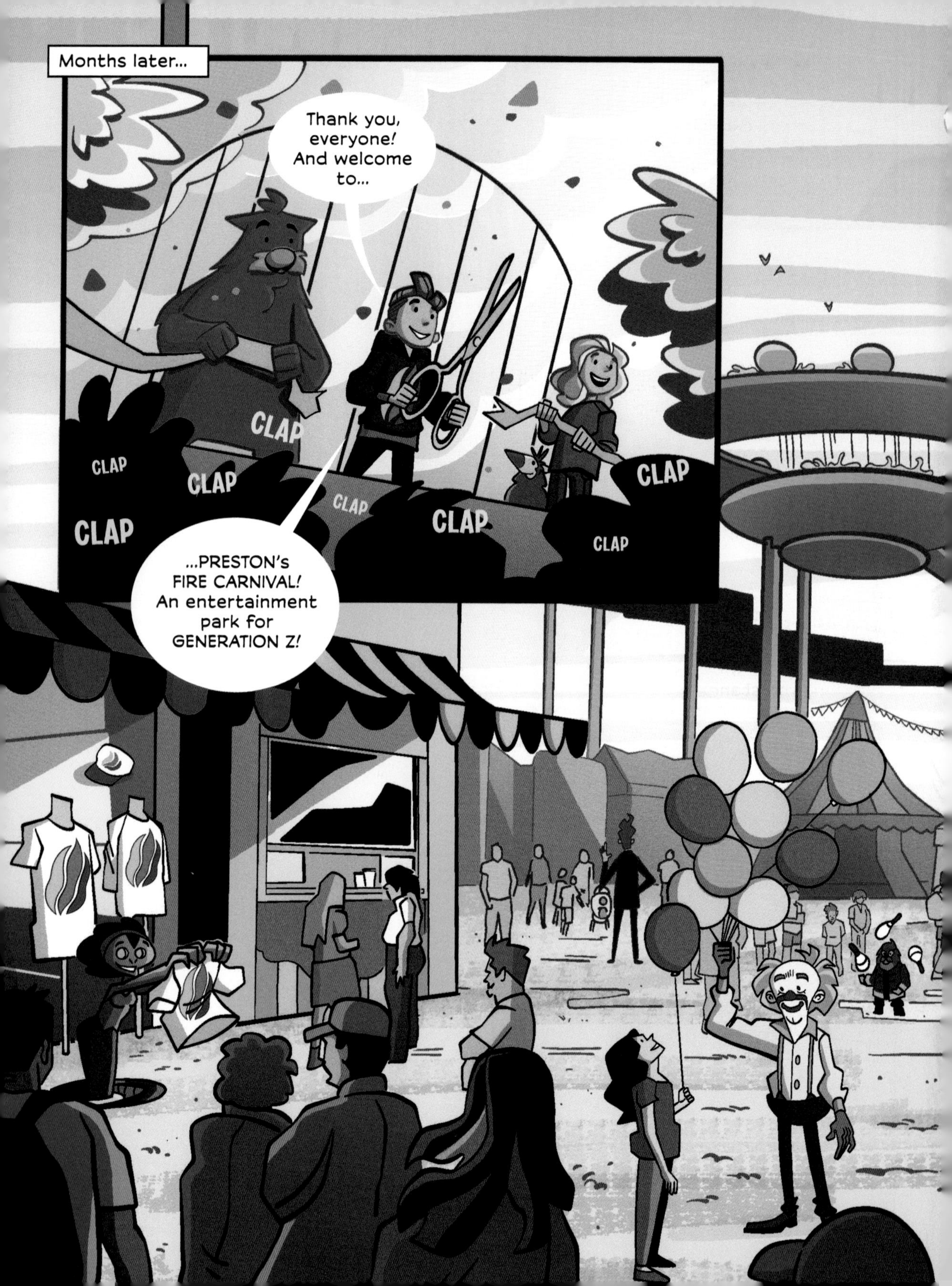
Months later...
Thank you, everyone! And welcome to...
CLAP
CLAP
CLAP
CLAP
CLAP
CLAP
CLAP
CLAP
...PRESTON's FIRE CARNIVAL! An entertainment park for GENERATION Z!

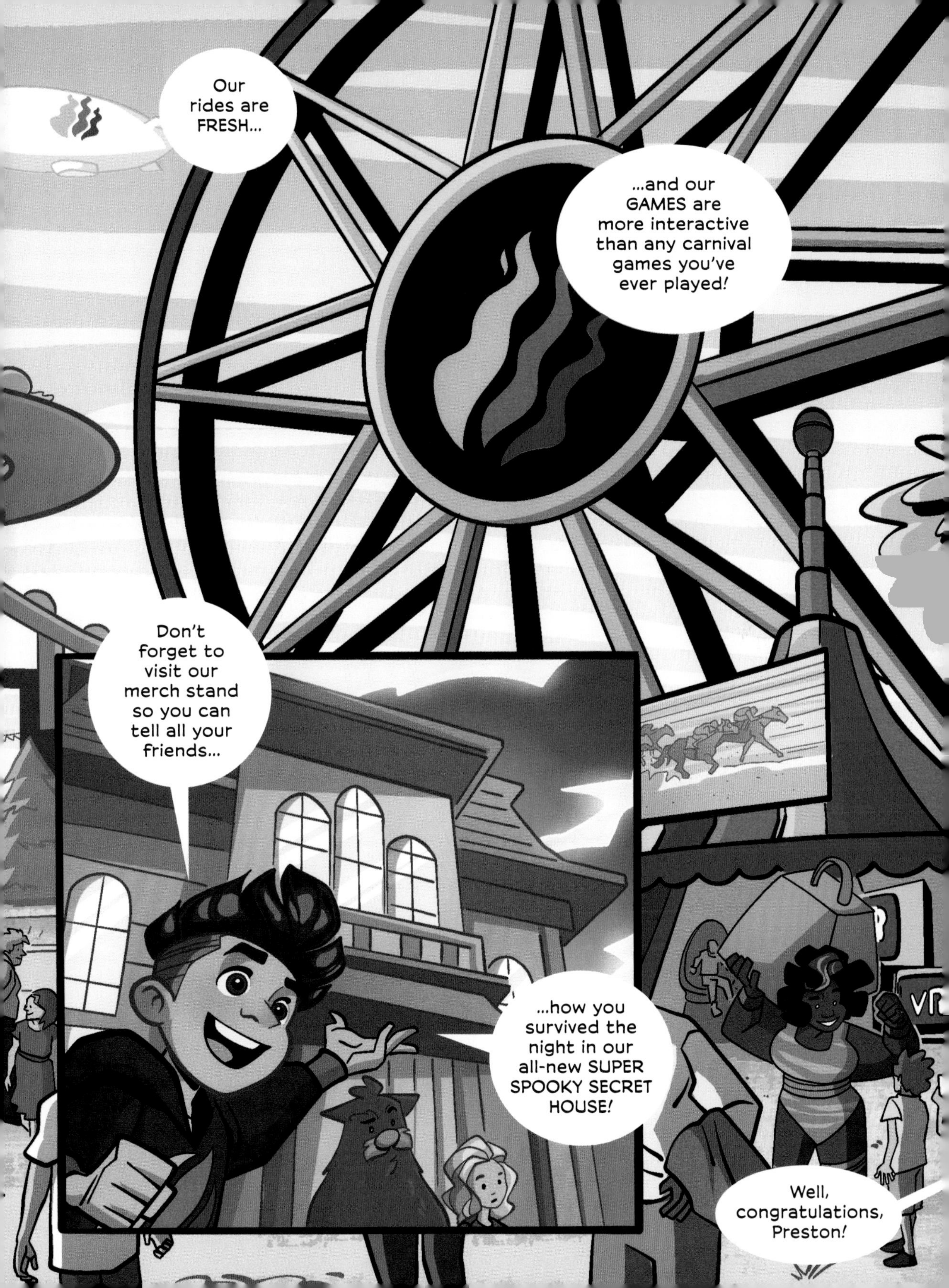
Our rides are FRESH...
...and our GAMES are more interactive than any carnival games you've ever played!
Don't forget to visit our merch stand so you can tell all your friends...
...how you survived the night in our all-new SUPER SPOOKY SECRET HOUSE!
Well, congratulations, Preston!

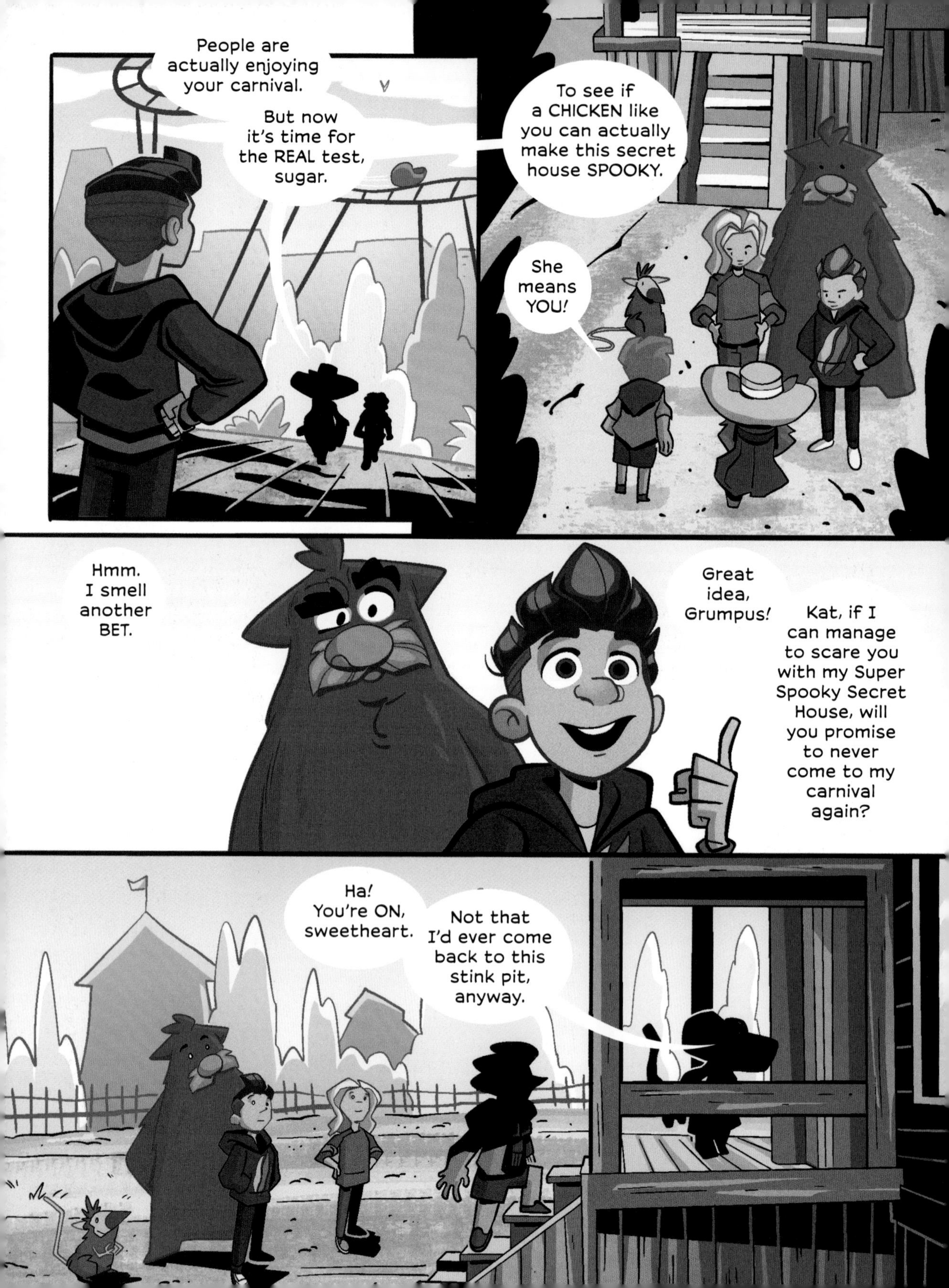

People are actually enjoying your carnival.
But now it's time for the REAL test, sugar.
To see if a CHICKEN like you can actually make this secret house SPOOKY.
She means YOU!
Hmm. I smell another BET.
Great idea, Grumpus!
Kat, if I can manage to scare you with my Super Spooky Secret House, will you promise to never come to my carnival again?
Ha! You're ON, sweetheart.
Not that I'd ever come back to this stink pit, anyway.

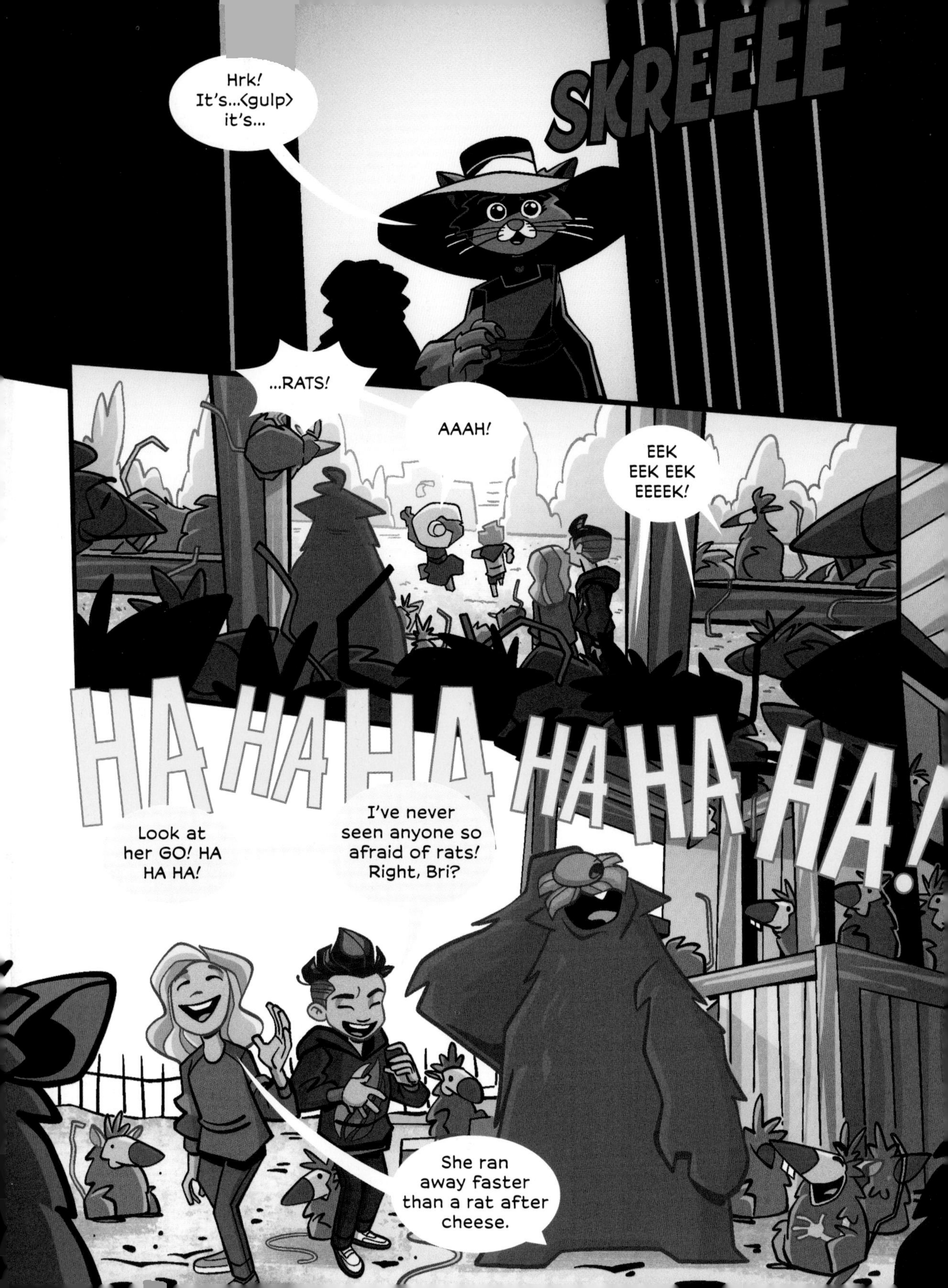
Hrk!
It's...<gulp> it's...
SKREEEE
...RATS!
AAAH!
EEK EEK EEK EEEEK!
HA HA HA HA HA HA!
Look at her GO! HA HA HA!
I've never seen anyone so afraid of rats! Right, Bri?
She ran away faster than a rat after cheese.

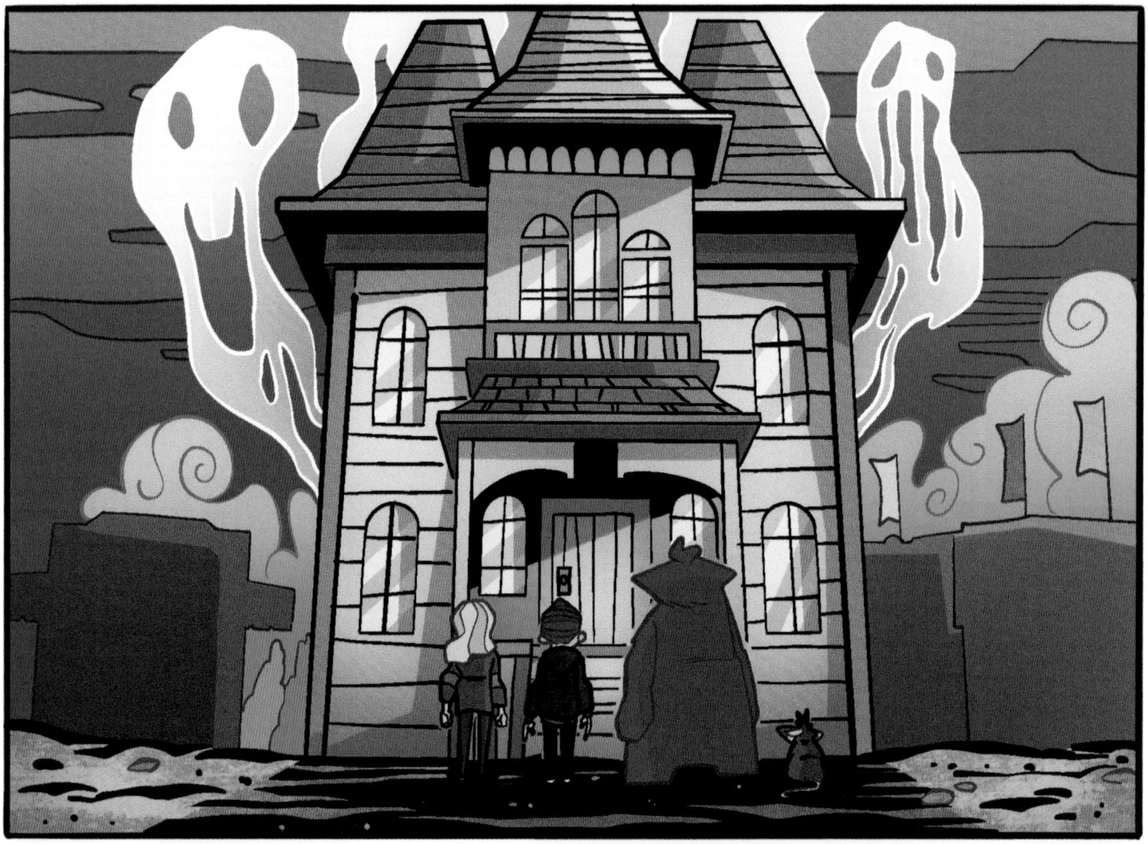

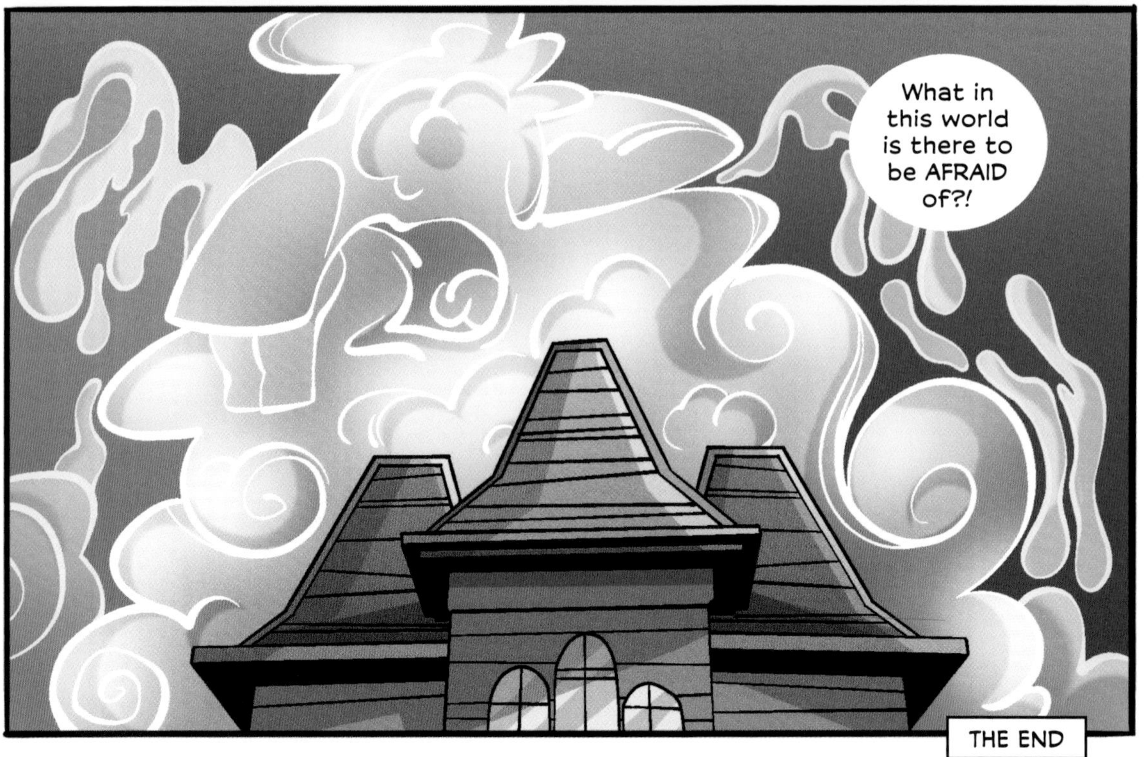
What in this world is there to be AFRAID of?!
THE END